The Callaway
readers swoon!
hands these hard
mem   te to vivid life.

Praise for Annette Broadrick

"I can think of a dozen adjectives that would
apply equally to Annette Broadrick's books,
such as exciting, passionate and irresistible. But I
can wrap it all up by saying simply that her
books make you feel good when you read them.
She's one terrific writer."
—Bestselling author Diana Palmer

LOVE TEXAS STYLE!
"Ms. Broadrick engage(s) your empathy for this
appealing pair of lovers…"
—*Romantic Times*

COURTSHIP TEXAS STYLE!
"This gentle, but powerful love story will warm
the cockles of every reader's heart."
—*Romantic Times*

ANNETTE BROADRICK

is a native of Texas, currently residing in the hill country of central Texas. Fascinated by the complexities found in all relationships, she continues to write about life and love, joy and fulfillment, and the bountiful gifts that are bestowed upon us as we travel along life's path.

SONS OF TEXAS

LOVE AND COURTSHIP!

ANNETTE BROADRICK

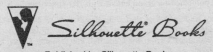

Silhouette Books

Published by Silhouette Books

America's Publisher of Contemporary Romance

If you purchased this book without a cover you should be aware that this book is stolen property. It was reported as "unsold and destroyed" to the publisher, and neither the author nor the publisher has received any payment for this "stripped book."

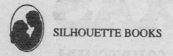

SILHOUETTE BOOKS

ISBN 0-373-20148-6

by Request

SONS OF TEXAS: LOVE AND COURTSHIP!

Copyright © 1998 by Harlequin Books S.A.

The publisher acknowledges the copyright holders of the individual works as follows:

LOVE TEXAS STYLE!
Copyright: © 1992 by Annette Broadrick

COURTSHIP TEXAS STYLE!
Copyright: © 1992 by Annette Broadrick

All rights reserved. Except for use in any review, the reproduction or utilization of this work in whole or in part in any form by any electronic, mechanical or other means, now known or hereafter invented, including xerography, photocopying and recording, or in any information storage or retrieval system, is forbidden without the written permission of the editorial office, Silhouette Books, 300 East 42nd Street, New York, NY 10017 U.S.A.

All characters in this book have no existence outside the imagination of the author and have no relation whatsoever to anyone bearing the same name or names. They are not even distantly inspired by any individual known or unknown to the author, and all incidents are pure invention.

This edition published by arrangement with Harlequin Books S.A.

® and TM are trademarks of Harlequin Books S.A., used under license. Trademarks indicated with ® are registered in the United States Patent and Trademark Office, the Canadian Trade Marks Office and in other countries.

Printed in U.S.A.

CONTENTS

LOVE TEXAS STYLE! 9

COURTSHIP TEXAS STYLE! 237

Dear Reader,

There's just something about a tall, broad-shouldered, lean-hipped man wearing snug-fitting, worn jeans and battered cowboy boots that makes my toes curl. Know what I mean? He usually has a slow loose-limbed walk that I find totally distracting.

The cowboy mystique has always fascinated me. These men became my knights, my heroes and my ideal. This type of man was the inspiration for my *Sons of Texas* series.

The Callaway family began to visit me while I was writing other novels. The original three brothers—Cole, Cameron and Cody—would pop up at inopportune moments, tantalizing me with glimpses of their personalities and their stories.

Tough and determined, Cole Callaway is the head of the powerful Callaway clan of Texas. He's devoted most of his life to his family and holdings—and lost the only woman he ever loved. But now Allison Alvarez has returned with a secret. She teaches him about *LOVE TEXAS STYLE!*

Cameron Callaway, the second brother, has also buried his grief in work. But his little daughter—and her delightful teacher, Janine Talbot—won't leave him alone. They teach him about embracing life and all that it offers. *COURTSHIP TEXAS STYLE!* is a story of hope and laughter and of tears.

These men know that family is everything, and I hope that the Callaways become as real to you as they are to me. If so, I have a hunch you'll find yourself falling for them as I did. And keep your eyes out for Cody and Tony—*Sons of Texas: Cowboys and Wedding Bells* features their stories.

Enjoy.

Annette Broadrick

LOVE TEXAS STYLE!

CALLAWAY FAMILY TREE

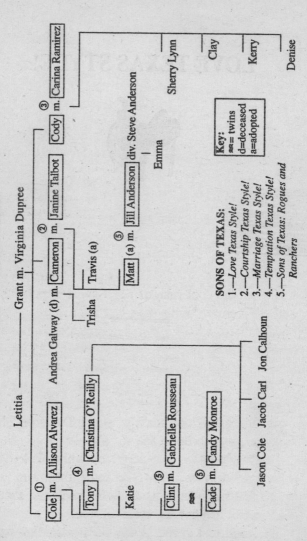

Letitia —— Grant m. Virginia Dupree

Andrea Galway (d) m.

② Cameron m. Janine Talbot

③ Cody m. Carina Ramirez

① Cole m. Allison Alvarez

④ Tony m. Christina O'Reilly

⑤ Clint m. Gabrielle Rousseau

⑤ Cade m. Candy Monroe

Trisha

Travis (a)

⑤ Matt (a) m. Jill Anderson div. Steve Anderson

Emma

Sherry Lynn

Clay

Kerry

Denise

Katie

Jason Cole   Jacob Carl   Jon Calhoun

SONS OF TEXAS:
1.—*Love Texas Style!*
2.—*Courtship Texas Style!*
3.—*Marriage Texas Style!*
4.—*Temptation Texas Style!*
5.—*Sons of Texas: Rogues and Ranchers*

Key:
≈= twins
d=deceased
a=adopted

One

Cole felt the cool rush of water swirl over his feet and eddy around his ankles before the wave ebbed and left him standing on the firmly packed sand once more. Brilliant rays of color shot up into the sky across the wide expanse of the Gulf of Mexico.

Dawn was Cole's favorite time of day, and watching the sun come up from the southern tip of Padre Island off the coast of south Texas was his favorite place to be in the world.

For the first time in a very long while, Cole Callaway felt a sense of peace settle over him. He could feel the tight muscles in his neck and shoulders uncoil and release their tension.

He stood and gazed at the silent, dazzling panoply of brilliant hues splashing the sky with color, changing moment by moment as each ray touched first one cloud lying near the horizon, then another. They appeared to catch fire until the sky turned into a blaze of peach and orange and yellow and gold.

The water continued to soothe his feet and ankles with its soft massage, occasionally splashing as high as the knees of his dress pants. All of his focus remained on the magical splendor displayed around him.

The sun's actual appearance became almost anticlimactic as its fiery brilliance quickly washed the colors until they faded away into muted hues. The waves became more distinct, reflecting the sun's sparkle as they eased into their own colorful display of greens and blues.

Cole released a deep sigh and filled his lungs with the fresh breeze dancing across the water to cool the inhabitants of the island at this early hour. He could feel the new energy swirl into his body…regenerating, cleansing, renewing.

He luxuriated in the moment, knowing that it had been worth the five-hundred-mile drive from Dallas through the night in order to be a witness to this daily ritual of renewal.

Being there, seeing the infinitely varied marvels of nature, helped him view his life from a new perspective, helped him in his search for inner peace.

Somehow no problem appeared insurmountable,

no task seemed overwhelming to him whenever he stood beside the sea. Regardless of the number of beaches he'd visited throughout the world, this particular island in this particular part of the world would always represent home to him. His restless spirit found peace on these shores.

Cole had known the night before that he had to get away for a few hours. The pressure had been building within him for weeks with back-to-back meetings and late-night telephone conversations with overseas offices. No matter how much he attempted to delegate, there always seemed to be decisions that only he could make.

He was so tired. He couldn't remember the last full night's sleep he'd had or the last time he'd been able to enjoy an uninterrupted meal.

Most of his meals were business meetings, in order to fit them all into his schedule. He couldn't remember the last time he'd taken a day off. Hell, he couldn't remember the last time he'd taken a few *hours* off. He felt like a caged animal running inside a spinning wheel. No matter how fast he ran, there seemed to be no end as he circled round and round, faster and faster.

The meeting last night had epitomized the futility of his work as he watched the lack of cohesion among the officers and directors of that particular company. He'd sat there listening to the debates, the accusations, the jockeying for position and power and wondered what he was doing there.

With a sense of shock, he suddenly discovered that he had absolutely no interest in the outcome of the heated discussion going on around him.

So he had walked out. He'd gotten into his late-model foreign sports car and headed south on Highway 35E, back to his high-rise condo in Austin. By the time he reached the outskirts—and his turnoff five hours later—he'd already decided to continue south. At first he'd thought about going to the ranch southwest of San Antonio, but when he reached that exit, he ignored it and continued south, on and on into the night, feeling the powerful engine of the car sweep him along.

He had known he was running, escaping, and he didn't care. Somewhere inside of him something had broken loose and had guided him down through the small towns of Kingsville, Raymondville, Harlingen, San Benito, until he slowed, finally for Port Isabel.

Once he reached that small town, whose wide streets were empty at four in the morning, he'd taken the two-mile causeway across to the island and pulled into the parking lot of his condo. The large high rise had been built on the island by one of his companies ten years ago, when the real estate boom had been at its peak.

He'd left his suit coat and tie in the car, taken off his socks and shoes, and headed toward the water. He had no idea how far he'd walked down the beach, but he'd gone far enough to outdistance the line of cars, trucks and campers that were parked along its shore.

He was alone now, except for the water, the sand, the dunes with the smattering of sea grass behind him, and the sun, gilding each thing it touched with its magic as it continued its daily climb into the sky.

The breeze teased at his dark hair, blowing it into his eyes and reminding him that he needed a haircut. He ran his hand through it, tousling it even more. He needed more than a haircut! He needed respite from his life-style.

Most of the time he accepted the role he'd been assigned in life. He never questioned the sometimes gargantuan responsibilities he was expected to deal with on a daily basis. But last night, when he'd gotten up and walked out of the meeting, he'd felt as though he'd walked out on everything- the businesses, the ranch, his two brothers, his maiden aunt—everything he'd carried since he was twenty years old.

He'd been head of the family, head of Callaway Enterprises, for over fifteen years. It seemed like a lifetime...a lifetime alone.

An image appeared for a brief moment in his mind to remind him of all that he had lost. Black eyes stared at him...wide and slightly slanted like a doe's eyes. He could see them in different moods...sparkling with mischief, soft with love and compassion, spitting fire. He could see a pair of lips...pouting, smiling with delight, trembling with despair.

Allison.

Just thinking her name provoked a familiar pain in his heart. After all these years he still compared every woman he met with his ideal of what a woman should be.

Once he had almost decided to marry someone else until he realized that he'd been looking for a substitute for Allison, which wasn't fair to either him or the woman he was seeing at the time. Even now, whenever he saw a small black-haired woman with fair skin his heart would leap into his throat for that brief instant when he thought she might possibly be Allison Alvarez.

But she never was.

Allison had disappeared out of his life at a time when he'd needed her the most. How could he forget that? How could he ever forgive her for that? There were times, however, such as now—as he turned to begin the long trek back to the condo— when he admitted to himself that he would have forgiven her anything during these past fifteen years if she had shown up in his life once again.

He reached into his shirt pocket and absently retrieved a cigarette. Placing it in his mouth, he cupped his hand around the end and turned his back to the breeze in order to light it. He filled his lungs with its smoke and immediately began to cough.

Damn! He shook his head with irritation at himself and tossed the offending cylinder into the water. His throat was already raw from too many of them. He had to quit, that was all there was to it. His system was rebelling against several things at the moment, including his lack of rest and his irregular meals.

He stayed at the edge of the water on his return walk, his mind drifting back over the past few days. He wished that his brother, Cameron, had been at the meeting last night. Cameron helped him to keep his perspective. He trusted his brother's judgment and his advice.

Without Cam's strong support, Cole would have walked away years ago...like Cody, their youngest brother, who had refused to have anything to do with the corporation. Cody went his own way without explanation. Perhaps that was why Cole found Cody so irritating at times. If he were to face the truth, he was probably more than a little envious of his baby brother's freedom. He wondered if Cody knew that, or whether he felt that he could never measure up to Cole's expectations.

He shook his head. Cody had only been ten years old when their parents had been killed, much too young to have lost both of them. Cole had tried to make up the loss to both Cam and Cody, but he knew that he'd failed them miserably.

At least Cameron had found contentment in his personal life. At thirty he already had a wife and baby daughter. His degrees in law and accounting

made him an invaluable asset to the family holdings.

Cole noticed that a few people were now stirring
as he made his way back down the beach. Ahead
of him three teenage boys played in the shallows,
tossing a Frisbee to each other.

He recalled that this was the week for spring
break for many schools. He wished he had the
boys' boisterousness, their excessive energy, their
sheer enjoyment of being alive. What would it feel
like to be without any responsibility except to have
fun? Had he ever had such a time in his life?

Once again a face flashed into his memory. Was
that why he continued to hold such a special place
in his memories for Allison? Was it because she
represented the best part of his life, those years
when he was growing up, when his parents had
been alive, when his life had been truly golden?

He continued walking toward the boys, idly
watching their game. The Frisbee flew toward the
boy who was directly in front of Cole and he
paused, in case the boy started running backward
to catch it. The capricious wind caught the airborne
missile and lifted it clear of the boy's outstretched
hand, carrying it another twenty feet so that Cole
only had to reach out a hand to grab it. With an
unfamiliar sense of playfulness, he did.

The other two boys began to laugh and dance
around in the water, yelling congratulatory remarks, while the third boy, wearing a grin, turned

and began to jog toward him. Cole knew he must look ridiculous walking the beach in a dress shirt and slacks soaked to the knees, but somehow it didn't seem to matter. Their enjoyment of the morning was enough to create a bond between him and the boys.

"Say, I'm really sorry," the boy said somewhat out of breath as he came splashing up to Cole. "I missed that one by a mile. I really appreciate…"

His words faded into the sounds of the waves as Cole stared at the young boy in front of him. His hair was the color of wheat, with threads of red and deep gold. Black eyes filled with sparkling glints of humor looked at Cole.

Except for the eye color, he felt as though he were seeing Cody all over again…a teenaged Cody with the same-shaped face, the same expression in his eyes, the same infectious grin, the same hair color…Cody at that gawky adolescent stage where a boy is all knees, elbows and gangly arms and legs.

No. There was no way. Even if Cody had been careless enough to have gotten some girl pregnant, he wasn't old enough to have sired this boy.

Cole became aware he had handed the Frisbee to the boy without saying anything. The boy flashed him another one of those eerily familiar grins and turned away, sailing the Frisbee across the waves to his friends. As though from a distance, Cole heard himself ask, "What's your name, son?"

He heard the authoritarian tone in his voice too late to alter it, and winced. He was so accustomed to demanding answers that he'd almost lost touch with common courtesy. He wanted to apologize, to explain, but didn't know how to begin. He wasn't surprised to see the boy stiffen at his brusque tone of voice.

The boy stopped and slowly turned around. "Tony," the boy replied shortly.

Before Tony had time to leave, Cole stuck out his hand and smiled in an effort to counteract his earlier curtness. "I'm glad to meet you, Tony. I'm Cole Callaway."

Tony had already backed up several steps when he heard Cole's name. He stopped dead and stared at the man before him. Slowly he took the necessary steps to reach Cole's hand. He shook it slowly and said, "You mean you're *the* Cole Callaway?"

Cole could hear equal parts of awe and curiosity in the boy's voice and felt an unreasoning sense of elation because he recognized his name. "As far as I know, I'm the only one around."

"The one who's planning to run for governor? The guy with all the—" He stopped, as though embarrassed at what he'd almost said.

Tony had a firm grip, a man's grip. Cole glanced down at the hand that seemed too large and strong for the boy's body. With a vague sense of reluctance he let go of the boy's hand and said, "There's nothing official about my political plans as yet, Tony. But that never stops the media from speculating."

"Wow! It's great to meet you, Mr. Callaway."

"Same here, Tony." As casually as possible he asked, "Your last name is?"

"Alvarez, sir. Tony Alvarez."

The words hit Cole like a massive blow to the midsection. For a brief moment Cole felt as though he were reeling. He felt like doubling over in an effort to protect his midriff from another assault.

Tony Alvarez. A name from the past…belonging to a boy who wore the stamp of the Callaways all over him.

He closed his eyes for a moment in an effort to get his bearings while his mind screamed out denials— No! *No!* It couldn't be! It wasn't possible, it couldn't be possible!—while all the time Cole knew with an inner certainty that of course it was true.

"Is something wrong, Mr. Callaway?" Tony sounded puzzled.

Cole shook his head, trying to clear it of the buzzing sound that seemed to ring in his ears.

"Um, no, son. Nothing's wrong. I guess you caught me by surprise. I once knew a Tony Alvarez, a long time ago."

The boy's grin grew wider. "No kidding? Wouldn't that be something if it was my grandfather? Mom named me after him. He died before I was born, and she said she wanted to keep his name alive.''

One last question. ''How old are you? I would guess you're around sixteen or so.''

Tony laughed. ''Yeah, that's what everybody thinks. I guess I'm just big for my age. I'm fourteen; I'll be fifteen in July. I've always looked older.''

So it was true. The implications of all that Cole was hearing seemed to beat at him from every direction. ''You live around here, Tony?'' Cole managed to ask, his voice sounding hoarse in his ears. He began to walk toward the other boys who were obviously puzzled by Tony's prolonged conversation with a stranger.

''Uh, no, sir. We just came down here for a few days. My mom and I live in a little town called Mason in central Texas. She owns an art gallery there.'' With obvious pride he continued, ''She's an artist and sculptor. She's won lots of awards. Several of her sculptures are on display at the Cowboy Artists of America Museum in Kerrville.''

A sudden vision of a sculpture he'd recently purchased for his office flashed into Cole's mind. Wild horses raced down a rocky incline, their manes and hooves flying. He'd been mesmerized by the freedom, the life, and the artistic splendor of the piece. The sculpture had been signed ''A. Alvarez.''

''Allison.'' He heard his voice as if it were independent of him, speaking her name out loud for the first time in years. She'd been here in Texas all along, no more than a hundred miles from his place in Austin.

"That's right. That's my mom's name. Do you know her?"

"I recently bought one of her sculptures," he responded, sidestepping the question.

"No kidding? Wow, that's neat! I'll have to tell her." Tony saw his buddies standing there waiting for him. He glanced back at Cole and added, "And I'll have to tell her about meeting you."

Cole could think of a dozen rejoinders to that remark, none of them suitable for this boy to hear.

My God! How could he possibly deal with this shock without giving himself away? He had to be alone for a while, a few hours at least, to try to come to grips with the information he'd just been given. "Are you going to be around awhile?" he asked casually.

"Yeah. We just got here yesterday. We'll be here until the end of the week."

"Then I'll probably see you again," he offered quietly, thankful that he'd been granted a reprieve.

Cole found his way back to the high rise by force of habit. He needed a drink. As soon as he let himself into the hallway of the large penthouse suite, he headed for the bar.

Cole had never been one to drink much because he preferred to keep a clear head. However, he knew he needed help in dealing with the shock he'd just received.

The phone rang.

He knew the caller had to be family. The phone number to the condo was a closely guarded secret. Only an emergency would have prompted someone to call him, particularly since he hadn't told anyone where he would be. How could he? He hadn't known himself.

He picked up the phone and growled, "Yes?"

"Cole! Thank God I found you! I've been looking everywhere. The last anyone knew you walked out in the middle of a meeting in Dallas and somehow managed to disappear. I'd about given up when I remembered the beach place."

"Okay, Cody, you found me. What's wrong?"

"Cole, I'm afraid I've got some really bad news. Man, I hate to break it to you like this, but—"

"Something's happened to Aunt Letty?" She was only in her mid-fifties, and Cole would have thought she was too ornery to die this young, but as shaken as Cody sounded, Cole knew the news was bad.

"Aunt Letty's fine, Cole. I'm afraid it's Cameron and Andrea."

Stark terror swept over him. "What! What are you talking about? What happened?"

"They were on their way out to the ranch last night to pick up Trisha from Aunt Letty's. There was a car accident, Cole. Nobody seems to know exactly what happened. Maybe a deer was in the road. The car was discovered around midnight last night."

"How bad is it, Cody? Tell me!"

"Uh, Andrea's dead, Cole. Cameron's been in surgery since they brought him in. He's in critical condition."

"Where are you now?"

"At Methodist Hospital in San Antonio."

"Call Pete and have him pick me up in the helicopter."

"Right away, Cole."

They hung up. Cole slowly sank to the edge of the couch and stared across the room at the fully stocked bar. He'd been going to have a drink because...because he didn't know how to handle the shock he'd just had. And now...he discovered his brother was in critical condition in San Antonio, his sister-in-law dead. A drink wasn't going to help him deal with any of this.

He strode into the master bedroom and stripped out of his clothes. He couldn't remember the last time he'd been to bed. None of that mattered now. He had to get to Cameron. He needed to be there for his brother, regardless of what else was happening in his life.

And the baby. He'd forgotten to ask Cody if Letty was at the hospital or whether she was still at the ranch with Trisha.

Dear God. Trisha was less than a year old. She'd

just lost her mother and possibly her father in the same kind of accident that had taken her grandparents' lives fifteen years before.

What was happening? Were the Callaways cursed? Was history repeating itself?

Cole stepped off the elevator onto the surgical floor and started toward the nurses' station. After less than a half-dozen steps he spotted Cody pacing in a small waiting room. He veered to join him.

"Any word?"

"None."

"Damn."

"I know."

"When did you get here?"

"As soon as I got the call last night. The Highway Patrol had been alerted by a passing motorist who saw the car and stopped to render assistance. According to the police report, Andrea was killed on impact."

Cole rubbed the bridge of his nose with his thumb and forefinger. "Damn, that's tough. How about Cam?"

"He'd been knocked unconscious, which was probably a blessing. He has a broken arm and leg, concussion, busted ribs and possible internal injuries. With surgery taking this long, I would say that was a safe bet."

"Has he regained consciousness enough to explain what happened?"

"No. According to the report, from the skid marks it looked as though Cameron had tried to stop, tried to swerve or attempted to maneuver past something in the road and lost control of the car. The deer are so plentiful in that area, it could easily have been one of them."

"Was there any sign of a deer having been hit?"

"Not that the Highway Patrol spotted."

Cole began to pace while Cody watched him. "We've got to do something," Cole muttered after a long silence.

"I know what you're feeling, Cole. I've already worn a path in the tile since I got here. I tried to think of where you would be, then I'd stop and call. I guess I must have left messages all over the state of Texas."

Cole stopped pacing and glanced at his younger brother. He looked like hell. "When's the last time you got some sleep?"

Cody shrugged.

"Why don't you stretch out over there on that couch? I'll wake you when there's any word."

Cody shook his head. "I can't. Every time I shut my eyes I see the remains of Cameron's car. The wrecker was just getting there when I drove past the accident site on my way into town. That damned little foreign car looked like a giant had stomped on it!" He shook his head in despair. "I always told Cam he needed to get something safer on the road, but he never listened to me. What did

I know, a snot-nosed kid who'd pestered him all his life—''

"He's going to be all right," Cole said in a soothing voice. He went over and sat beside Cody. "He's tough, our brother. Don't you know that by now? Nobody's going to stop us. We're the Three Musketeers, remember?"

Cody slowly nodded. "Yeah. You used to tell me that story when I was a kid."

"All for one and one for all. That's the Callaway motto. Cameron's going to make it. We're going to be right there, on either side of him, making sure he does."

Cole met Cody's anguished expression with a calmness he was far from feeling. He deliberately sat back in his chair. There was nothing he could do for Cameron. The best doctors around were working on him at the moment.

Now he had to look after Cody. He had to distract him in some way. Although he hadn't had much time to think about what he'd just learned about his own past—in fact, he was still reeling from the shock—he knew he could discuss anything with Cody because he was family.

"I got hit with some news this morning, just before you called," Cole began slowly, feeling his way into the labyrinth of painful and confused emotions. "It has certainly given me a brand-new perspective on my life."

Cody had been studying his hands and popping

his knuckles when Cole spoke. He gave Cole a look that revealed his sudden awareness of Cole's peculiar tone. "Yeah? What's that?"

"I just found out that I have a fourteen-year-old son who I never knew existed."

Two

"Allison? Can you keep a secret?" Cole felt so grown-up now that he had started the first grade and was away from the ranch each day. The thing was, he missed his four-year-old companion, who had gamely followed him around the ranch as far back as he could remember. She had met him as soon as he'd gotten home that afternoon. He could hardly wait to show her what he'd found that morning before going off to school.

She was dressed identically to him in shirt, jeans and scuffed boots. She wore her hair in braids that bounced on her shoulders as she skipped to keep up with his longer stride. Her black eyes registered her curiosity as she stared up at him from beneath a thick fringe of hair.

"'Course I can keep a secret," she replied with the proper amount of disgust that he might think otherwise. "What is it?"

He continued to the barn where he'd followed the cat early this morning. "You'll see," he said with a grin, enjoying the mystery. Once inside the barn he led the way toward the storage side of the big building. He paused at the bottom of the ladder that led up into the hayloft and pressed his finger to his lips.

She silently nodded her head in understanding. Cole gingerly climbed the rungs until he could peer into the loft. As soon as he saw that the coast was clear, he crawled onto the wooden flooring and turned, waiting.

Allison didn't disappoint him. She was determinedly climbing the steep rungs, her bottom lip caught between her teeth in concentration, her eyes huge in her white face. By the time she reached his side she was trembling, but she hadn't made a single protest at the height or the scary climb.

Still on his hands and knees, he crawled to the corner of the loft. Allison followed. When he stopped and pointed, she leaned over his shoulder fearfully. Her look of surprise and pleasure had been worth his sharing his secret with her. He sat back with a grin on his face.

"How many is there?" she whispered.

He held up three fingers.

"Where's the momma?"

"I dunno, but she wouldn't like it if she knew we found her hidin' place. She'd prob'ly move 'em."

They inched away as silently as they had come. When they reached the ladder Cole went first to make sure the coast was clear. Both of them had strict instructions *not* to attempt to climb up into the loft. Once down, he waited impatiently for Allison to feel her way, rung by rung, to the bottom.

As soon as her feet touched the ground she spun around, her expressive eyes mirroring her delight. "We've got kittens!"

He nodded, feeling very important to have found them on his own.

"Can we keep them?"

"I dunno. Maybe so."

"Have you touched them?"

He shook his head. "The momma would smell me on her babies and wouldn't like it. I think they just got bornded."

"Oh, Cole, I want one for my very own."

"Maybe your mom and dad will let you have one for your birthday."

She clapped her hands. "Do you really think so?"

"I'll ask."

Later he had asked his dad if he could give one of the barn kittens to Allison for her fifth birthday. After reprimanding him for climbing up into the loft, his dad had insisted he check with Tony and

Kathleen, her parents. Tony was the boss around the ranch. His dad called him the foreman. Cole had always been in awe of Tony. He was dark and never said much, but Cole knew that he was just about the greatest cowboy who ever lived, and he ran the Circle C ranch. Kathleen was easier to talk to. She and his mother could have been sisters, with their fair skin and reddish-blond hair. She was always laughing and talking and hugging people. She had laughingly agreed that what Allison needed more than anything for her birthday was a kitten.

She had picked the tiger-striped one who would grow into a big old tomcat.

Allison named him Crybaby.

By the time he was ten, Cole had more important things to do than to hang around with a girl, even Allison. He'd been sneaking away from the house one hot afternoon when he discovered that Allison was following him.

Disgusted, he turned and confronted her. "How come you have to follow me everywhere I go?"

"'Cause I want to," Allison replied nonchalantly. "'Sides, I figger you're goin' out to where my daddy is." She stuck her hands in her jeans pockets. "I was just goin' to go find him."

"Well, you're not goin' to find him following me around," he pointed out with ill-concealed irritation. "He and Dad left in the pickup to go check on part of the ranch."

Allison stared at him without saying anything more, the expression in her black eyes silently eloquent.

He couldn't stand it when she looked at him like that. She always made him feel so mean. The problem was that there was nobody else on the ranch besides him for her to play with. Cameron was barely five. He knew she got bored, just as he did. Her mother spent a lot of her time resting. His mom was busy taking care of Cameron and getting ready for the new baby's arrival as well as running the Big House. His Aunt Letty was never any fun, always scolding him for making too much noise or for asking so many questions. He'd left the house to stay out of trouble and he'd made up his mind about what he planned to do with the rest of his day. Now here was Allison wanting to tag along.

"Oh, all right," he said disgustedly. "Come on. But you gotta promise not to tell anybody where we're going, because it's my secret place and nobody knows about it."

"Couldn't we go ridin'?"

"No. Remember my dad said we can't ride unless your dad's here to supervise."

She grinned. "That's 'cause my dad's the best rider in the whole wide world. He's got lots of trophies and medals and things to prove it."

Cole was much more comfortable with Antonio Alvarez now that he was older, but he still admired him tremendously. He'd seen all the rodeo medals

Tony had won before Cole's dad had coaxed him into taking over the running of the ranch. That was several years before Cole was born.

His mom had told him how his dad and Tony had become close friends when they'd been in the army in Korea. Now she and Tony's wife were good friends, too.

He just wished that Allison had been a boy so he would have had someone fun to play with. Of course she really wasn't all that bad—for a girl. She could run and could draw her toy pistol almost as fast as he could. She wasn't afraid of nothing. The only time he'd seen her cry was once when he told her he didn't want to play with her because she was a girl and that she had to go home and leave him alone.

Boy, her tears had really upset him. He hadn't meant what he'd said anyway. He'd just been in a bad mood because Aunt Letty had sent him out of the house.

After that one time when he'd made Allison cry, Cole had been more careful about taking his bad feelings out on her.

"So, are you comin' or not?"

"Where you goin'?"

"Swimming."

Her eyes lighted up. "Really? Where?" She glanced around the ranch buildings.

"It's a secret place. Only me and my dad know

about it. He takes me there whenever he can spare the time. You still want to go?'' he asked.

She nodded emphatically.

''It's a long walk. Usually my dad takes me by horseback.'' He pointed in the direction he'd been going when he heard her behind him. ''See those trees back up in the hills over there?'' he pointed.

''Uh-huh.''

''There's a creek along there. My dad says that it must have gotten dammed up one winter when it flooded and some dead trees got washed downstream. They got caught at a bend in the creek bed and just stayed there. Now, there's this neat place to swim.'' He looked at her with a slight frown on his face. ''You do know how to swim, don't you?''

She nodded her head vigorously but wouldn't meet his eyes.

He sighed. ''C'mon, Allison, tell me the truth.''

She hung her head, staring at her toes. Uh-oh. She didn't get that hunch-shouldered look very often, but when she did, he knew she was upset. What if she started to cloud up on him and cry again?

''I could teach ya, if ya want,'' he offered in a gentle voice.

Her head jerked up and she stared at him, the beginning of joy dawning on her face. ''Will ya? Really?''

''Sure. My dad showed me. It's not all that hard.''

She wrapped her arms around her waist and gave a quick twirl. "That'd be fun!"

The more he thought about it, the better he liked the idea. They could make a day of it and stay out of everybody's way. "I tell you what," he said, already planning their adventure. "I'm going to go into the kitchen without Aunt Letty catching me and ask Conchita to pack us a picnic. A man gets real hungry after swimming." He mimicked his dad's tone of voice as well as his words. "Girls prob'ly get hungry, too. You stay here. I'll be back as soon as I can."

By the time they reached the creek, both of them were hot, tired and hungry. "My dad says you can't go in swimming right after you eat. You might get a cramp," Cole explained as soon as they sat in the shade of a large oak tree.

"What's a cramp?"

"Well, it could be one of those things that live in the water that pinch you."

"Like a crab?"

He nodded. "Something like that."

She peered into the water. "But how does it know if you ate or not?"

"Who knows? But that's what dad says."

"Oh." She looked terribly disappointed.

"But we could maybe drink something," he offered.

"That sounds good."

He unpacked two small cans of fruit juice that

Conchita had placed in his knapsack, along with sandwiches, potato chips and cookies. "Here. We'll drink these and rest for a minute, okay?"

When they'd finished their drinks, Allison looked at him. "Now what do we do?"

"Well, first we take off our clothes."

She glanced down at her shirt, jeans and boots. "All of them?" she asked dubiously.

"Well, of course all of them. You wouldn't take a bath in your clothes, would you?" She shook her head. "Well, swimming's the same thing...except it's lots more fun." He immediately sat and pulled off his boots.

She did the same.

He unsnapped his jeans, slid them off his hips, then off his legs.

Slowly Allison did the same.

He stood and took off his shirt.

So did she.

They stood there in their underwear and socks and looked at each other.

He shrugged and turned away. Sliding his briefs off, then tugging his socks off as well, he tossed them onto his pile of clothes and determinedly marched bare-bottomed toward the water.

Allison giggled.

He glanced around. "What's wrong with you?"

She covered her mouth but another giggle escaped. "You look so funny."

"No funnier 'n you."

"You're all brown except your bottom."

Girls were so silly. "That's because I'm out in the sun a lot. Are you comin', or not?"

Hastily Allison slid out of her undies and socks and gingerly walked over to join him. He took her hand and carefully led her into the stream.

"It's cold!" she exclaimed as soon as her feet touched the water.

"It's supposed to be," he said with irritation. "That's why it feels so good on a hot day, my dad always says." He continued to lead her into the water until it was up to her waist. "Okay, Allison. Now, I want you to lean back in the water like it's a bed."

"But Cole, I'll drown!"

"No, you won't, you silly! I'm going to have my arms under you." He held his arms straight out in the water where he knelt beside her. "I won't let you drown."

"Promise."

He looked her straight in the eye. "I promise."

Gingerly she lowered herself in the water, her eyes growing bigger and bigger. He continued to hold her. It was easy in the water. Finally she allowed her legs to drift up until she was floating.

"See how easy that is?"

She smiled. "It's easy because you're holding me."

"Not anymore. My arms are underneath you in case you go down, but they're not touching you."

"You won't let me go under?"

"No way." He waited until she began to relax before he said, "Now you gotta turn over and put your face in the water."

"No!" She came to her feet, spluttering and splashing.

He put his hands on his hips. "All right, Allison Alvarez. Do you want me to teach you to swim or not?"

She nodded.

"Then you're going to have to trust me."

"I do trust you," she insisted.

"Then do what I say. I won't ever hurt you. You know that."

She smiled at him, a smile so sweet that he remembered it for years. "I know, Cole."

"Whoopee!" cried Cole a few weeks later. "Allison! My dad just called from the hospital. I have another brother. They're going to call him Cody."

He'd come racing out of the house, yelling his news.

Her smile was wistful. "You got what you wanted. Another brother."

"Well, I don't guess a sister would have been all that bad," he admitted.

"What did Cameron have to say when you told him?"

Cole grinned. "He was disappointed. He was hoping she would have a puppy!"

They both laughed.

"You're really lucky, Cole. I'd give anything to have a sister or a brother. I wouldn't even care which one."

Cole touched her shoulder gently. "Maybe one of these days you'll get your wish."

She shook her head. "I don't think so. I asked Mom once. She said she'd had some problems when I was born. They told her she wouldn't have any more kids."

"Gee, I'm sorry, Allison."

"Me, too."

She looked so downcast that he immediately searched for a way to cheer her up. He knew just the thing. "Would you like to go swimming?"

She glanced up toward the hills. "You mean now?"

"Why not? Dad won't be home until later, and Aunt Letty doesn't care where I am so long as I'm not underfoot."

She nodded. "All right. I'll go get my suit on and meet you out back." She had insisted on having a bathing suit before going swimming again, which he thought was funny, since he'd already seen her without one. She made him wear one, as well. Who could figure girls out, anyway?

Cole was pleased with his student. They had spent the summer going to the creek as often as they could. Allison was no longer afraid of the water, although she still didn't like sticking her face in it.

Later, while they sat on the side of the bank tossing small pebbles into the water, Allison said, "You know, Cole, I'm really lucky to have you in my life. You're like the brother I never had."

"And you're like the sister I never had."

"I'll always think of you as my brother."

"Whenever you need me, I'll be there for you. Don't ever forget that."

Cole had been fourteen the night his father said to him, immediately after dinner, "Son, I need to speak with you. Let's go into my office."

Cole looked at his mother, then at the rest of the family seated around the table. No one seemed to think his dad's request was unusual.

"What's wrong, Dad?" he asked, looking at his father. His dad shook his head and got up from the table.

His mother began to clear the table without saying anything. With a shrug, Cole followed his father out of the room. When they entered the office, his dad nodded toward the fireplace chairs.

"You know, son," he began when they were both seated, "sometimes it's hard to explain why some things happen in life."

Alarmed, Cole said, "What's the matter, Dad? What's happened?"

"Tony and Kathleen got some bad news today

from the doctor. It seems that Kathleen has inoperable cancer. They only give her a few weeks to live.''

Cole stared at his dad in horror. "You mean Allison's mother is dying?''

"Yes, son. I'm afraid so. I know that you and Allison are close. They intend to tell her tonight and suggested that I explain to you, so that you will understand what she's going through.''

Cole could feel a knot forming in his throat. He was having trouble swallowing. "Isn't there anything the doctors can do?''

"They said it's too far gone...pretty much throughout her system. She hasn't been feeling well for some time. Perhaps if she'd gone in for an earlier checkup, something might have been done. But no one can possibly know for sure.''

Cole hurt. He really liked Mrs. Alvarez. She'd always been friendly to him. She never yelled at him. Tears began to well up in his eyes.

"These things are tough to take, but you needed to know. Allison is going to need a friend.''

"I'll always be her friend, Dad. *Always.*''

"What in the world do you see in Rodney Snyder?'' Cole demanded as Allison's date drove away. He'd been sitting beneath one of the trees near the driveway, waiting for her to come home. He'd gotten up as soon as she started down the lane toward the house she and her father still shared.

He didn't know what her dad was thinking of, letting her date a senior in high school when she was only a sophomore. Why, Rodney was *his* age, much too old for her.

Allison had jumped when he first spoke, and he realized that she hadn't seen him until then.

"Why shouldn't I? At least he notices me and invites me out."

"What's that supposed to mean? I notice you, don't I?"

She turned away and continued down the lane.

"Well, don't I?" he demanded, following her.

She glanced over her shoulder. "How could you possibly have time for me with all the other girls you're seeing? If your mother had any idea you were out with some of those girls, she'd have a fit."

"We're not talking about me. I want to talk about you."

She continued walking. "Well, I don't want to talk to you!"

"That's been obvious for the past six months, and I don't understand why. What have I done that makes you treat me like poison? I thought we were friends!"

He'd stopped walking so that she had taken several steps ahead of him. The bright moonlight gave enough light so that they were able to see each other. Allison turned and looked at Cole standing there, his hands resting at his sides, his legs slightly apart.

Slowly she walked back to him. "You don't have a clue, do you?" she finally said.

He shook his head.

"I've known you all my life and I feel that I know everything about you, but you don't know me at all," she finally said.

"That's not true. I know more about you than anyone else does." He paused, then drawled, "Unless, of course, you're in the habit of going skinny-dipping with every guy you meet."

"Oh, for Pete's sake, Cole. I was eight years old at the time. Aren't you ever going to let me live that down?"

He grinned. "I doubt it. It's a surefire way to get you riled, and it's powerfully hard to resist the temptation."

Allison clasped her elbows and began walking over to the corral beside the barn. She leaned against the wooden fence. "You don't know anything about my feelings, about my thoughts. All you know about is the tomboy who used to follow you around this place—" she waved her hand to encompass the multitude of buildings that constituted the ranch headquarters "—like I was some kind of pet dog."

"Is that what this is all about? You feel that I've been taking you for granted?"

"Yes! No! Oh, I don't know. It's everything.

I'm just tired of all the girls at school trying to be my friend in hopes I'll invite them out here. You're such a big man on campus—class president, football captain, honor student. Not only are you Cole Callaway of *the* Callaways, but you have to make sure you're the best at everything you do!''

''Is that so wrong?''

''Of course not! That's what a Callaway's supposed to do.''

''Then I don't see the problem.''

''You wouldn't, of course.''

''So explain it in simple enough terms so that I can understand.''

She turned away and looked out into the pasture. ''What were you doing waiting up for me tonight?''

''I was worried about you.''

Without looking at him, she said, ''Why?''

''Because Snyder's got a well-deserved reputation where girls are concerned. I didn't want him taking advantage of you.''

She turned so that she was facing him. ''That's a laugh, coming from you.''

''What does that mean?''

''You think Rodney's got a reputation? Why, *you're* the one everybody's talking about. I get to hear all the whisperings among the older girls, and the younger ones all want to know what it's like to kiss you.''

''What! What kind of question is that?''

"Along the same line as the one Rodney asked tonight when I finally had to tell him to keep his hands to himself. 'If you put out for Callaway, why not me?'" She angled her chin so that the moonlight fell full on her face and for the first time Cole saw the silver streaks down her cheeks where the tears had made their paths.

"Oh, Allison, don't cry," he said, pulling her into his arms and holding her against his shoulder. She felt so good pressed to him like that. "I'll find that son of a— I'll find him tomorrow and beat him to a pulp. How dare he treat you like that? He had no right!"

Her voice sounded muffled in his shirt when she said, "Everybody thinks we're sleeping together, didn't you know? They figure I'm part of the hired help out here. My dad's the foreman, you're the owner's son. What could be more convenient?"

"Who's saying that about you? I want to know who. I'll talk to each one of them. I'll tell them —"

"Nobody's going to believe you, Cole. Don't you understand? Nobody's going to believe a word you say because they know—they *know*—how I feel about you. Everybody knows...but you."

Cole stiffened, then stared down at the top of her head. Her face was still burrowed into his chest. Her voice was muffled. Surely she hadn't said what he thought he heard. Surely she—

"Allison?"

She didn't answer him.

"Look at me. Please."

Slowly she raised her head and looked at him. The tears still slipped silently down her cheeks.

The sudden rush of feeling that hit him almost brought him to his knees. This was Allison—the little girl in pigtails, jeans and boots who had dogged his footsteps for years. Allison—his friend. Allison—his love.

"Oh, baby, I didn't know," he whispered, his voice choked with emotion.

She looked away. "It doesn't matter."

He chuckled. "Doesn't it?"

"Of course not."

"Listen, Miss Haughty Allison Alvarez, it makes a very big difference to me how you feel. So why haven't you told me before?"

"Because you were too busy with all those other girls."

"Do I detect jealousy in that statement?"

"No!"

"So what if I told you that none of those other girls ever made a difference to me? What if I told you that there's only been one girl who matters to me, only one girl I've ever wanted to have as a permanent part of my life?"

She looked back up at him, her gaze intense. "Don't tease me, Cole. Please. If our friendship ever meant anything to you, don't use it against me now."

He leaned down and placed his lips delicately

against hers, the first kiss they had ever shared. For a brief moment he felt her grow still. Then she stiffened and pulled away from him.

"What's the matter? Don't you like me to kiss you?"

"You don't have to humor me like a child, Cole. I'm well aware that you think of me like a sister."

He grinned. "Oh, so *that's* it. You don't appreciate my brotherly kiss. In that case, how about this one?"

Cole put every ounce of seductive expertise he'd gained during the past two years into that kiss. At first he wanted to hold back because he didn't want to frighten her, but as soon as he opened his mouth over hers she melted against him. By the time the kiss ended, they were both shaking.

"You'd better go inside now. Tony will be worrying about you."

"But, Cole—"

"I mean it. Get inside. We've got to be careful or things will get out of hand before we're ready. I've still got four years of school back East. You've got to finish high school and plan for college, and then—"

"Cole. What are you talking about?"

"I'm talking about the fact that you're now my girl, from this moment on. I just put my brand on you. I don't want another man to touch you, but I'm not going to take advantage of your lack of experience, either. You hear me? You're too young. Besides, we've got plenty of time. We've got the rest of our lives.''

''You mean we're going steady now?''

''That's exactly what I mean.''

''So you aren't going to see Darlene or Peggy Sue or Jennifer again?''

He grinned. ''I didn't know you knew I was seeing them.''

''I know everything you do.''

''Everything?''

''That's right.''

''Somehow I doubt it, but we'll let it go for now. So do you want to go with me to the senior prom?''

''I'd be honored, Cole.''

''Good. Now go inside.'' He planted a quick kiss on her lips, spun around and loped back to the Big House. She was a temptation few men could resist. But like his dad said, she deserved his love and his respect. He could wait until they were married to make love to her. He'd waited for her this long. What was a few more years?

It was the blackest day of his life.

Cole left the Big House through one of the rear entrances. He didn't want to see anybody. He sure as hell didn't want to talk to anybody. He'd changed out of his suit as soon as the remaining members of the immediate family had returned from the cemetery.

Now he wore his faded jeans, one of his old

chambray shirts and his scuffed boots. He made his way to the barn to the four-year-old gelding his dad had given to him two years ago for graduation. With an ease of long practice he placed the blanket, saddle and bridle on him, stepped into the stirrup and left the main headquarters of the ranch.

He couldn't face any more people saying the same things over and over. He couldn't watch the pain and bewilderment in Cameron's and little Cody's faces. He couldn't bear to listen to his Aunt Letty's voice telling yet another person how she had warned her brother over and over that he drove too fast and how he never listened to her.

He had to get away from them all.

He rode for hours. Had anyone asked him later where he'd been, he couldn't have explained. He had taken one last ride with his father.

"Dad, how could you do this to me?" he said at one point. "I need you so much. You've always been here for me, no matter what problems I had. Remember when we used to ride out like this, just the two of us? You answered all my questions, no matter how trivial. You made me proud of my heritage, proud of my land, proud to be a part of the Callaway dynasty."

He hadn't cried when his Aunt Letty had called him at college in the East, where he was in his second year of school, and told him what had happened. He hadn't cried when he arrived home and saw the devastation of his family and the Circle C

employees. His aunt told him that as head of the
family he was expected to help with the arrangements, which he did. He greeted hundreds of people who had come to pay their last respects to one
of the legendary figures of Texas. He stood beside
the double graves and stoically watched his mother
and father being put to rest.

Despite the crowd of people, despite the fact that
he had a brother standing close on either side of
him and his aunt immediately behind him, Cole felt
alone.

He wasn't ready for this. His dad was supposed
to have lived for years and years. He'd been in his
prime. He didn't deserve to die. Not now. Cole
didn't want to be the head of the family. He still
had two more years of school and then on to grad-
uate school. He and his dad had carefully mapped
out his education and career. He was his father's
son. He would follow in his father's footsteps. But
not now, dear God! Not yet.

Eventually the horse paused and drank from a
stream in the hills. Cole looked around and realized
that he was at his old swimming place, his secret
place—the place where his dad had first brought
him as a young boy, teaching him to swim, teaching him, through example, how to be a man.

Whether or not Cole liked it, the lessons were
concluded. From now on, he was on his own.

On impulse, Cole climbed down. Although it
was October, the day was hot. He sat on the bank

of the stream and pulled off his boots and socks. He intended to cool off by dipping his feet in the water. Once he was barefoot, he decided to go into the water. He jerked off his shirt and shucked his jeans and briefs. In minutes he was completely submerged in the water.

Over the years he and his dad had enlarged the pond, making it deeper, turning it into a reservoir where the cattle sometimes came. Now Cole allowed himself to remember the many happy times he'd spent here with his dad...and with Allison.

He'd seen Allison at the funeral, sitting beside her father. They hadn't talked much this time. When Cole had left for school in August he'd had a tough time leaving her, which irritated him. He didn't want anyone to have that sort of control of him. Not even Allison.

So he had avoided her on this trip, feeling too vulnerable, his emotions too raw to be controlled.

He swam until his muscles quivered with exhaustion, until he could think of nothing but his aching body. When he knew that he could not lift his arms for another stroke he allowed his feet to sink to the bottom of the pond and began to walk to the bank.

That was when he saw Allison sitting quietly beside his pile of clothes, watching him.

"I thought I might find you here," she said as he paused at the sight of her.

"What are you doing here?"

"I was worried about you."

"Don't be. I can take care of myself." He stood where he was, in waist-deep water.

"I never said you couldn't, Cole." She made no effort to leave.

He pushed his hair out of his face with both hands, slicking it back over his head. "Look, Allison, I'm not dressed for conversation at the moment. Why don't I meet you back at the house later?"

"You can't show me anything I haven't already seen," she pointed out with a half smile.

He wasn't in the mood for games. "Fine." He stalked out of the water, directly toward her.

He knew exactly what he looked like. His body had begun to fill out during the past two years. Since he hadn't been working around the ranch, he'd started working out in the gym at school, keeping his body toned. He didn't need her suddenly widened eyes to remind him that there was a considerable difference between a child of ten and a man of twenty.

She hastily averted her gaze, staring up at the trees that surrounded them. He took his time drying off with his shirt, pulling on his briefs and jeans, then sprawling beside her on the grassy slope. He folded his arms behind his head and lay back, closing his eyes.

He must have fallen asleep because the next time he opened his eyes, shadows had begun to form around them and a breeze whispered among the leaves of the trees.

Allison had stretched out beside him and was fast asleep.

He could count on the fingers of one hand the number of times he'd seen her asleep. Most of the times had been when she and Cole had gone camping with their fathers. The men enjoyed getting away and the children loved to tag along.

They hadn't camped in several years. Now the eighteen-year-old beauty beside him bore little resemblance to the dirty-faced little girl with the long black pigtails who had gone camping with him.

He stared at her, enjoying the chance to study her. Her skin was creamy, like the soft-textured petal of a magnolia. Her black brows made a startling contrast, tilted at each end, giving her the look of a startled doe. Long black lashes brushed against her flushed cheeks. He had an almost irresistible desire to trace the bridge of her nose, following it to the slight tilt at the end.

Her lips were the color of raspberries and looked ripe and succulent. He knew their taste by heart. In the two years since he'd first kissed her, they had spent hours exploring each other, kissing and touching, but he never took advantage of his knowledge and experience. He knew when to stop, knew when he had to clamp down on his own emotions so as not to complete what they had started.

He recognized that he was suddenly famished for

the taste of her lips and, yielding to temptation, he leaned over her supine body and kissed her tenderly on the mouth.

She stirred, arching her back slightly so that her full luscious breasts shifted, drawing his attention. She was a gorgeous woman, from the top of her glossy black hair all the way down to her tiny waist, curving hips and thighs, slender ankles and finely arched feet.

He wanted her so much.

When he kissed her a second time, he was having trouble with his breathing.

She shifted so that she was facing him and, still without opening her eyes, drew him into her arms. He pulled her to him, holding her fiercely against him. She sighed and he deepened the kiss. Eventually he had to ease his grip so that they could both breathe.

She opened her eyes and gazed at him from those black depths that seemed to harbor her soul. "Oh, Cole, I've missed you," she whispered, running her hand down his chest. His skin retracted everywhere she touched.

"You're cold," she said.

"I'm burning up," he replied.

She smiled. "Show me."

They both knew that today was different. They had left childhood behind. He pulled the snaps apart on her shirt, then reached inside and unfastened her bra. He nuzzled her breasts, feeling her heartbeat thunder against his cheek, feeling her lungs straining for air.

When she reached for the zipper of his jeans, he froze. "Allison? Are you sure?"

She held his head to her chest. "I've never been more sure, Cole. Never."

There were no more words. Within moments they were out of their clothes. She seemed determined to touch him everywhere with her mouth, her hands, her body. She was like quicksilver in his arms, lightly caressing then darting away, boldly exploring then shyly retreating.

When he shifted so that he knelt between her knees, she looked up at him, her face glowing with expectancy as she pulled him down to her, holding him against her, wrapping her legs around him.

He felt her flinch when he first attempted entry. He started to retreat but she locked her arms and legs around him and lifted her hips, forcing his body past the barrier to sink deep within her.

Cole felt the wonder of being a part of this most precious person for the very first time. She was his own sweet love, and now she was truly his in every way.

She moved with him, imitating his movements, anticipating his wants and needs, loving him until at long last he seemed to burst in a frenzy of pleasure and pain, jubilation and regret, completion and desolation.

For a few moments he'd scaled to the very top

of the joys of pleasure. He'd escaped the pain, but only for a moment.

When he came back to reality, his mind was flooded with all that he had momentarily forgotten.

Cole rolled to his side, dragging her clutched to him. The tears flowed, despite everything he could do. He had no more control to draw from.

His deep, racking sobs shook them both as they lay there beside the peaceful creek. She held him tightly, as though sharing his grief in the only way she knew how.

It was almost dusk when Cole felt as though he could finally regain some sort of sanity. He looked at Allison lying in his arms and whispered, "I'm so sorry, baby. I'm so sorry. I never should have—"

She placed her fingers across his lips. "Shh. Don't say it. Don't even think it. We both needed this. We needed today. It's all right."

"But I made a promise that we would wait and now—"

"I know. But things have changed. Everything has changed."

The horrible pain that had been riding in his chest since Aunt Letty's phone call had somehow eased. He could breathe around it now. He could go on.

"Oh, Allison, I love you so much."

"I love you, too."

"You're the best friend I've ever had. I don't think I could have made it without you."

"You never have to make it without me, Cole. I'll always be right here, whenever you come home."

They helped each other to dress, taking their time, pausing to kiss and touch and explore.

"You know, maybe we should plan to get married before I get out of school. I mean, there are lots of married people going to school. You'll be out of high school in May. There's no reason to wait."

She smiled at him. "Let's talk about it during Christmas vacation, okay? Now isn't the time to be making plans."

"But I want you with me, Allison. I need you."

She went up on tiptoe and kissed him lingeringly on his lips. "We'll talk about it at Christmastime."

They rode the gelding back to the house with Allison seated in front of him in the saddle. Nothing had changed, but somehow Cole knew that he had changed. He knew what he intended to do. He and Allison would be married next summer. Nothing was going to change that.

It never occurred to him when he returned to school after burying his parents that he would never see her again.

Three

Cole's mind was caught up in memories of the past while he waited at the hospital for any change in Cameron's condition.

He sat in the shadowed corner of Cameron's room in the intensive-care unit where he could watch Cameron and see all the machines that were monitoring him.

He'd sent Cody home to get some sleep. He doubted that his stubborn brother had followed his instructions. If anything, he would check into a motel close by for some rest. Cole had promised Cody that he would rest as well, but his mind was racing with too many thoughts, too many memories.

Cameron had successfully come out of surgery.

Both his left arm and left leg were in casts, and his left leg was in traction. Although the seat belt may have saved his life, there had been internal damage where the strap had held him. The exploratory surgery had taken hours while they checked for intestinal tearing. They'd had to remove his spleen as well. There were various tubes in and out of his body. He lay there totally still. At times Cole couldn't tell if Cameron's chest was moving at all, his breathing was so shallow.

"Don't die, Cameron," he whispered. "Hang in there, buddy. I can't lose you, too. Everyone else in my life seems to go. Don't you leave me."

He leaned his head against the back of the padded chair. He wanted someone in the family to be there when Cameron first regained consciousness. If he was in Cameron's place, he would have plenty of questions when he surfaced from the drugged oblivion Cameron was presently in.

He closed his eyes in an effort to ease their stinging. Mason, Texas. Allison lived in Mason. She and his son lived within a hundred miles from his Austin home and he'd never known it.

The boy mentioned something about his grandfather having died before he was born. How could that be? He remembered Tony as an active, virile man. Cole had been furious when Aunt Letty had told him that Tony had resigned as soon as he discovered he'd been named in the will. He'd told her that he didn't need to work anymore, that he was clearing out, buying a place in Colorado.

By the time Cole returned home for Christmas that year, both Tony and Allison were gone.

Had the Callaways meant so little to them that they no longer cared about the remaining family? How could Tony have walked away when he knew how much Cole's dad had always relied on him?

Cole could still feel pain at the thought of their desertion. Was that why Allison wouldn't talk to him about a wedding that last day they were together? Had she already known that they would be leaving? Had she decided to dismiss the first eighteen years of her life and never look back?

Her leaving was one more loss that Cole had had to deal with. Now, fifteen years later, he knew that her abandonment had hidden an even worse betrayal...she had been pregnant and hadn't told him.

A slight sound from across the room caused Cole to open his eyes, then spring from his chair. He was at Cameron's side in a couple of steps.

Cameron made a soft moaning sound deep in his throat. His lashes fluttered. Cole took his hand. "I'm here, Cam. You're going to be all right, do you hear me?" His voice was hoarse with emotion. "You're going to make it. I'll be right here with you."

Cameron's eyes slowly opened and he stared at his brother. "Cole?"

"Yes, Cam. It's me."

Cameron closed his eyes once again and didn't stir. After a few moments Cole went out to the nurses' desk. When one of the nurses glanced up, he said, "My brother just spoke my name. He recognized me."

She smiled and stood. "Sounds like great news. Let me go check on him." Cole followed her back into the room. After checking all of Cameron's vital signs, readjusting the drip and the oxygen, she said, "He seems to be resting now. No doubt it helped for him to find you here."

"God, I hope so!"

"Why don't you go get some rest now, Mr. Callaway? You look in worse shape than he does."

He turned away, too choked up to say anything. Cameron was going to be all right. He had spoken to Cole, recognized him. Cam wasn't going to die.

Cole walked down the hallway, unsure about what to do. His answer came when the elevator doors opened and Cody stepped out. "How is he?" were his first words.

Cole grinned. "He came to for just a moment, but he recognized me. He said my name."

"That's great." He reached into his pocket and pulled out a motel key. "Here, we're booked in there for the duration. It's only a few blocks away. Go get something to eat and sleep, for God's sake. You look near death yourself."

"Thanks for the testimonial."

"You know what I mean. You've had two sizable shocks, fella. How about cutting yourself a little slack, okay?''

''Have you spoken with Andrea's parents?''

''Yes. They've made the arrangements for the funeral. It's scheduled for tomorrow. They saw no reason to postpone it.''

''That's true. Cameron's not going to be in any shape to attend anything for some time.''

Cody rested his hand on Cole's sleeve. ''I know the two of you have always been close. It's understandable because you're so much closer in age. But don't forget that I'm here for you. I'll do whatever I can.''

Cole nodded. ''Thanks, Cody. I appreciate that, more than you know.''

''Now get outta here.''

''I'm on my way.''

The first thing Cole did when he woke up the next morning was to call the hospital and ask for Cody. When his brother came to the phone, Cole asked, ''How is he?''

''He's roused a couple of times. He seemed to recognize me the first time, but didn't say anything. The second time he asked for Andrea.''

''Yeah, that's going to be a tough one. He needs to be stronger before we tell him.''

''That's what the doctor suggested. Guess we'll play it by ear.''

''Are you coming back to the motel?''

"Not anytime soon. Why don't you bring me something to eat and some decent coffee?"

"Will do. Have you talked to Aunt Letty?"

"Earlier this morning. The baby is doing fine, of course."

"Poor little one. She's too young to realize what's happened."

"Maybe it's better this way."

"Better or not, this is the way it is. I'll see you in about half an hour."

While Cole showered, shaved and dressed, his thoughts continually returned to Allison. He knew he was going to have to face her again, and he wasn't certain he was in the best frame of mind at the moment.

He wanted to stay by Cameron's side until his brother was able to handle everything on his own.

Cole knew he needed to call the ranch. Dozens of people were no doubt looking for him by now, although he knew that Letty would have told them about Cam.

He was only one person. He couldn't divide himself into enough people to take care of everything that was going on. Business would either keep or it wouldn't. At the moment he didn't care.

Cameron came first.

After he was sure Cameron would be okay he would go find Allison Alvarez. They had some unfinished business that had waited fifteen years too long.

* * *

Allison Alvarez heard the bell that signaled someone had come into her gallery from the street on the square. She sighed, knowing that she would have to see who it was since her assistant, Suzanne, had gone a few doors down to the bakery for the best hamburgers ever made. She'd promised to bring Allison one, which was why Allison had relented and let her go.

She was trying to finish the small clay model she'd been working on all week so that it would be ready to be cast in bronze by Monday. She'd faithfully promised the client she'd have it to him on time and she was already running late.

It couldn't be helped. She would—

"Mom? Mom, are you here? Where is everybody? Sue?"

"Tony!" She grabbed a towel and dashed through the beads that served as a divider between the working area of the shop and the gallery itself. "You're home!" she cried, rushing to him and hugging him. "I didn't expect you back until late tonight."

"Yeah, but we decided to get up early this morning and head back."

She looked at her son, still marveling that he was that tiny, red-faced infant that had been placed in her arms what seemed to be such a short time ago. Now he was shooting up so fast she could almost see him grow out of his pants and shoes. He was already several inches taller than she was.

"You're really dark. You must have spent the entire time in the sun."

"Just about."

His black eyes in his tanned face made her think of her father. The difference was the hair. In the summer Tony's hair lightened to an almost honey blond, with streaks of red. Her mother had been a redhead. And, of course, his father had red highlights—but she wouldn't allow her thoughts to go any further.

"Where's Sue?"

"Picking up some hamburgers. Knowing you, you're hungry, right?"

"Starved."

"So go ask her to get some for you, too. Meanwhile, I have to get back to work." She turned away and headed toward the back of the gallery.

She was already pushing the beads aside when Tony said, "Oh, Mom. I almost forgot. You won't believe who I met at the beach. Man, oh man! The guys sure were envious. They saw him but *I* got to *talk* to him."

Her mind already back on her work, she absently smiled at his enthusiasm and asked, "Who?"

"Cole Callaway. He was just walking along the beach…"

His voice faded away to nothing, although she could still see him talking, his arms miming the meeting over the Frisbee, but all Allison heard was a loud buzzing in her ears, a ringing that drowned

out all sounds around her. She had to sit. Otherwise
she was going to faint. Allison groped her way to
her chair and sank into it, burying her head in her
lap in an effort to get some blood back into her
head.

How in the whole wide state of Texas had Tony
managed to run into Cole Callaway?

Nothing in her life had prepared Allison for the
shock of Tony's news. They had been in Mason all
of Tony's life. They did not move in the same circles as the Callaways. Tony could have gone his
entire life and never laid eyes on Cole.

Why? Dear God, why?

Tony's voice began to seep into her consciousness once again. He was still explaining. "So then
we got to talking, you know, like what's your name
and where are you from and things like that—"

No! You didn't tell him your name or that we
were here in Mason! No! Please say you didn't!

"I told him about the gallery and all the awards
you won and things. He never did say if the Tony
Alvarez he used to know could have been my
grandpa, but it was neat meetin' him. Really awesome."

So there it was. Cole had discovered exactly
what he had ignored all those years ago. The only
question now was whether he intended to do anything about the information Tony had given him?
Tony looked too much like the Callaways for Cole
not to have immediately recognized him. Over the

years Allison had sometimes wondered if Cole would grow curious and decide to seek out the child she had carried, but as the years moved on, she'd given the matter less and less thought. Tony's news could not have been more unexpected.

Tony pushed the beads aside in a jangle of soft clicking sounds. "Do you think "

"Tony, I thought you said you were hungry?" she said, hoping the interruption would distract him.

"Oh, yeah. See ya," he said with a wave of his hand. In a moment she heard the bell jingle at the front door.

Quiet. Blessed peace and quiet for a few moments while she attempted to gather her thoughts together. She looked down at the piece she'd been so meticulously working on and realized that if she didn't stop right now, she was going to irreparably ruin it.

She got up and walked through to the gallery once again, ending up looking out the large plate-glass window to the courthouse in the middle of the square. Most of the businesses in Mason were directly on the square where the traffic passed through on its way to west Texas or toward Austin in central Texas.

She had stayed in Mason after her dad died because she could think of no other place to go. The people were very similar to the ones she'd grown up with...ranchers, mostly, and she had felt more comfortable there than in San Antonio. A mother at nineteen, her first concern had been for Tony.

Her father had told everybody that her husband had been killed a couple of weeks after their wedding. Poor Dad. Her pregnancy had been the final heartbreak in a series of major catastrophes, all less than a year apart.

The lie about his father was probably the best thing that could have happened for Tony. He'd been raised without the stigma of having an unwed mother. The townspeople had gathered around her when her dad died so suddenly within weeks of her due date. Looking back, she wondered if she could have made it without their emotional support.

Now she wondered if the life she had carefully built here would soon come to an end. If Cole decided to come looking for her, he would have no trouble finding her. Everyone in town knew where she lived, where she worked and what she did in her spare time.

Cole wouldn't even consider the damage he might do to her or to Tony. Now that he had actually met Tony, there was good reason to believe that Cole Callaway would claim what was his. He always had. No doubt he always would.

By the time Tony and Suzanne returned, Tony had already been distracted by food and talk about the rodeo planned for the weekend. He was a natural athlete and he loved to ride. He'd kept every one of his grandfather's trophies and belt buckles from his years of following the rodeo circuit. They were displayed on a bookcase he'd built in his first year of woodworking.

By the time Allison closed the gallery for the day she had a splitting headache and an uncomfortable phone call to make. She was going to have to call one of her customers and explain that she would be delayed in getting his finished sculpture to him.

Tony was already over at a friend's home about ten miles out of town, practicing his riding and his roping. She didn't see much of him these days, with all of his activities, but she refused to hang on to him now that he was growing so rapidly into manhood. Her childhood had been so wonderful...with so much freedom and so much to do...and Cole Callaway always stood in the center of her memories.

Tony deserved to have a similar carefree time to grow up and learn about life.

She gave up on her headache and went to bed early, praying that the last dose of aspirin would take some of the edge off. She needed to sleep. She needed to forget. Instead, all she could do was remember.

Her name was Allison Alvarez. She lived on the Circle C Ranch with her mommy and daddy. Her daddy was an important man on the ranch. He was the foreman. He was the boss over lots of people.

He was the boss over most everybody, 'cept the Callaways. That was the name of the people who lived in the Big House. That's what the C stood for on the brand they put on the cattle and the horses. They put a big C that had a circle around it.

Her best friend was Cole Callaway. He already went to school. Next year she would go, too. She would ride the yellow bus that stopped at the end of the lane up by the highway. Someone always drove Cole up to the highway. Next year, they would drive her, too.

Cole had a little brother. His name was Cameron. He was almost two years old. Allison liked to visit the Big House and play with the baby when Cole's Aunt Letty wasn't there. Aunt Letty didn't like Allison. She didn't know why, but she always got angry when she saw Allison in the house. When his Aunt Letty was gone, Cole's mother would invite her and Cole to come in and play with the baby. He was so much fun. But better than anything else, Allison liked to be with Cole.

He was strong because he worked around the ranch, doing things the other guys didn't have time to do. Sometimes she helped him. Most of the time she tagged along after him. That was what he called it. Once in a while he'd tell her to leave him alone, or he'd pull one of her pigtails, or make faces at her. That hurt so much. She tried not to cry. She didn't ever want him to see her cry, but sometimes she couldn't help it.

He taught her everything she knew. He taught her to throw a ball and to catch it. He taught her to swing a bat. He taught her how to race him to the barn and back without stopping.

Cole Callaway was her very best friend.

"Mom, Cole's mother had her baby today. It was another boy."

"Oh, honey. How wonderful! Is Cole excited?"

"Yeah."

"I know you wish you had a little brother or sister, don't you, darling?"

"Not really. Cole's my brother, or the same as."

"Well, not exactly. He's a Callaway."

"That doesn't matter."

"Maybe not now. But eventually it will make a big difference."

"I don't understand."

"Well, Cole's daddy is a very important man in Texas politics. He's got a great deal of power. Whatever he says goes."

"Does that make him a bad man?"

"Not necessarily. But power can be a very tricky thing, sweetheart. When you're born with it, sometimes you don't even realize when you're using it."

"I don't know what you mean, Mama."

"I know you don't. It doesn't matter. I'm just

saying that the Callaways are very rich, very important people. Your dad just works for them."

"But he and Cole's dad are best friends. I've heard them say so."

"So have I. They are very close. That's one of the reasons why your dad decided to stay here and help to run the ranch, so that Cole's dad would have more time to spend in the city. He trusts your dad."

"Like I trust Cole?"

"Like you trust Cole."

"I can trust him like a brother, can't I?"

"Oh, honey, I hope so. I really hope so."

"Oh, Cole, what am I going to do? They told me last night that Mom is really sick and the doctors can't do anything to make her better."

They were sitting on the bank of the stream near their swimming hole. Allison had stayed home from school but could no longer stay in the house and see her mother's pain, knowing there was nothing she could do. She had run to their secret place to be alone. She didn't know how Cole knew where to look for her. She wasn't sure why he'd bothered.

Now he lay on his side with his head propped up on his hand, tossing a small pebble in his other hand.

"I know," he said quietly. "My dad told me about it last night, too."

"What am I going to do? I need my mother. I

thought she'd be with me until she got really old. Why does she have to die so soon?"

"I don't know, Allison. I really don't. I can't imagine what life would be like without my parents."

"Me, either," she whispered. "Me, either."

"You've got me, though. Always remember that."

She turned and looked at him, really studied him, so that his fourteen-year-old face was forever etched on her mind: the scattered freckles across the bridge of his nose, the deep blue-green of his eyes, the shock of light brown hair bleached by the sun into variegated colors of gold and honey and silver.

His eyes carried the message in his heart. They were filled with compassion and empathy and understanding. It was that look that caused the tears to flow. He sat up and put his arm awkwardly around her shoulder and laid her head on his bony, narrow chest. He held her and held her and held her until all the tears had been shed and the pain had been acknowledged.

He continued to be right there by her side through the following weeks when her mother's condition quickly worsened. Cole was there when her father came to school to pick her up and to tell her that her mother was gone. It was Cole who stood on the other side of her and her father at the grave site, each one holding her hand. Each one giving her strength.

She would certainly be glad when Cole Callaway graduated from high school and was finally out of her life.

Good riddance!

She was sick to death of hearing about Cole from every girl in senior high school. There wasn't one of them who didn't have a crush on him. They were always trying to make friends with her so she would invite them out to the ranch. But she saw through their silly games. None of them had ever paid attention to her before.

He was too busy these days to know she was alive. He no longer rode the bus. His dad had given him one of the old pickup trucks to drive to school when he was sixteen. He always had to stay after school for ball practice or some meeting.

He got home in time to eat, then he was off every night giving as many of the girls he could see a real thrill. He definitely played the field. Some of the girls didn't have the greatest reputations, either. His parents didn't say much to him. He'd done chores around the place for years. Now Cameron and Cody were doing them. He made good grades so he wasn't wasting his time in school.

He'd forgotten her. Oh, if he passed her in the hall he gave her a cocky grin and waved. Big deal. He was usually walking somebody to class.

What did she care? She'd outgrown him as well. Since she'd started her sophomore year, the boys that had ignored her all her life were now beginning to stop at her locker to talk with her. A few had asked her out, but it was a problem since they couldn't drive and she lived so far out of town.

But it was nice that they asked.

Sometimes her dad let her stay with a girlfriend in town on Friday nights. She always had somebody to ask her to go to the movies with him on those nights. She had a social life. But she was no longer a part of the Callaway life-style.

Her mother had warned her. She just hadn't understood. She was the foreman's daughter, that's all, a childhood friend whom Cole had long since outgrown.

When Rodney asked her out she was delighted. He was the same age as Cole, played football and was a real tease. She couldn't believe her luck. He had a car and everything.

The problem was that she didn't really enjoy the evening with him. She couldn't quite put her finger on what bothered her, but it was something in his attitude toward her. Like, he was possessive for no reason. They went for sodas at the regular hangout after the movie and he kept his arm around her shoulders. She kept moving away from him, but he would just laugh and pull her against his side.

His buddies were all making suggestive remarks. One of them had the gall to say, "Better watch it,

Rod. You're handling some of Callaway's private stock there." Then they'd all laughed as though she were a big joke. So what if her dad *did* work for the Callaways...that didn't mean they were slaves. She didn't belong to anybody!

When Rodney brought her home, Allison hopped out of the car before he had completely stopped it. "Thanks, Rodney. I had a lovely time." She'd hated every minute of it, but she knew the polite thing to say.

"Say, babe, what's your hurry? Why don't you—"

"I've got to go in. My dad will be worrying."

That's when he'd made his disgusting remark about her and Cole. She'd turned away without saying a word, refusing to let him see how much he'd hurt her. She didn't care what he thought. She didn't care what *any* of them thought!

Rodney left, and from the sound of his tires, he wasn't happy with the ending of the evening. Too bad.

She had deliberately told him to stop by the barn, not wanting to wake up her dad by driving down the lane to her house. She started the long walk to the house when something moved in the shadows.

"Who is it? Who's there?" she demanded.

"It's me."

Cole stepped out of the shadows into the bright moonlight. She couldn't help being startled. She hadn't seen him in weeks, except for occasionally passing in the hallways at school or the lanes at home.

"What are you doing out here?"

"Waiting to talk to you."

"It's late. I've gotta go inside." She began to walk down the lane away from him.

"Allison?"

"What?" she asked while she continued to march away from him.

"I don't want you going with Rod Snyder."

She stopped in her tracks, then slowly turned around. "It is none of your business who I go out with," she said, enunciating each word.

"I'm making it my business."

She turned her back and continued toward the house. The next thing she knew he had grabbed her arm and spun her around to face him. "Don't you ever walk away from me again when I'm talking to you. Do you hear me?"

"Oh, that's right. Mr. Callaway has given his orders. The peons around here are supposed to tug on their forelocks and bow, isn't that the way it goes?"

"What the hell are you talking about?"

"Don't you cuss at me, Cole Callaway!"

"I'm not. I mean, I just want to know what's wrong with you lately. Every time I see you at school you stick your nose up and go sailing past as though there were a bad smell in the air."

"Well, maybe there is."

"What's wrong? What have I done? We used to be friends and now you treat me like dirt."

"*I* treat *you* like dirt? Oh, that's really funny, Cole. You've been so busy with every good-looking girl in school that you never know I'm around."

He began to laugh. She tried to pull away from him but he still had her arm in a firm grip. "You're jealous," he said, obviously delighted with himself.

"I am not!"

"Of course you are, which is funnier than you know." She tried to twist away from him, but he began to pull her inexorably closer until both of his arms were clamped firmly around her.

She hadn't been this close to Cole in a long time. He'd grown considerably during the past few months. Her head barely came to the top of his shoulder, and his chest had broadened. She had to tilt her face up to see him. When she did he leaned down and kissed her.

This kiss was nothing like she had ever experienced before. It wasn't a slobbery wet kiss like the one Rodney tried to give her, nor was it the shy, tentative kisses offered by her classmates. An experienced male was showing her exactly what kissing was all about. By the time he finally raised his head, Allison's knees were wobbly.

"Allison, honey. I want you to be my girl."

"You do?"

"Yes."

"You mean, like go steady?"

He grinned. "That's exactly what I mean."

She thought her heart was going to burst, it was beating so fast. Cole Callaway wanted her to be his girl. He hadn't forgotten her; he hadn't seen her just as the foreman's daughter. "Oh, Cole." She threw her arms around his neck, effectively pulling him down so that she could kiss him again.

"Whoa, honey. Enough of that for now. I'm only human. We've got a long time ahead of us."

"What do you mean?"

"I've got years of schooling, so do you. We've got plenty of time. I just wanted you to know how I feel about you and how much it's hurt me to have you ignore me for months."

"Oh, Cole, it's hurt me, too. So much."

"So you'll go to the prom with me?"

"The senior prom?" The dream of every sophomore girl, to go to the senior prom.

"Yep."

"Oh, Cole, I'd love to go with you."

"Good. Now go on, get in the house before I do something we'll both live to regret."

Years later, Allison lay in bed, staring up at the ceiling, lost in her memories. His words had been prophetic, after all. They had dated through the summers and during the holidays when he was home from school, but Cole had kept a tight rein on his passion.

He'd taught her a great deal, and she'd learned some heavy-petting techniques. But he had refused to go all the way, insisting that he wanted to wait until they were married.

Only they ended up not waiting. And he had regretted it enough to allow her to get out of his life. He'd made no effort to stay in touch, even after she wrote and told him that she was pregnant. Those months had been even blacker than the time right after her mother had died. Never before had she felt so much shame. She had let her dad down, she'd let herself down.

She had made a vow not to let her unborn child down.

For over fourteen years she had been the very best parent she knew how to be. She had raised Tony with firm values, the same ones her parents had instilled in her. The same values, unfortunately, she had ignored in an effort to comfort Cole when he'd needed someone to love and hold him.

She had to second-guess what the man he was now might decide to do now that he'd come face-to-face with his son for the first time.

She knew from magazines and newspapers that Cole had been involved with many beautiful, socially well-connected women. But he had never married. She often wondered about that. Maybe the thought of marriage had so frightened him at twenty that he had never recovered.

She didn't care what he did. But if he decided

that he might like to befriend the child he'd ignored for years, then she would set him straight really fast. He'd made his decision years ago. He would have to continue to live with it.

Four

Cody stopped Cole as soon as he stepped off the elevator. "We need to talk," he said quietly.

"What's wrong? I thought Cameron was doing much better."

"Yeah. They're talking about letting him get out of here soon."

"Then what's the problem?"

"I finally brought up the accident and asked him if he remembered anything about that night."

"And?"

"He said there had been little traffic, but all at once lights flashed directly in his eyes from the middle of the road. He swerved and then felt the impact of something hitting the side of the car, which put it into a spin."

"My God! Is it possible someone actually forced them off the road, causing them to crash?"

"I don't know, but I'd sure like to find out." Cody was quiet for a moment. "There's something else that's been bothering me about Cam's accident."

"What's that?" Cole asked, hardly believing this could be true.

"I know I was just a kid at the time, but I remember when our folks were killed that there was never an explanation for the crash, just speculation. There were no witnesses. If Cam hadn't pulled through, there would have been no witnesses this time, either."

Cole stared at Cody. "Are you saying there could be some connection between the two crashes?"

"I don't know what I'm saying exactly. I just know I have this funny feeling about the similarities. Think about it. No deer were found, there was no traffic and no witnesses. Nobody questioned the accident fifteen years ago. Suppose someone did get away with murder at that time? Whoever it was might feel confident enough to recreate the crime, particularly if he hated the Callaway family enough."

Cole thought about Cody's suggestions and theories. After a few minutes, he mused, "We've never been short of enemies. We've lived with that knowledge all of our lives."

"I know. That's one of the reasons this whole thing has been eating at me. I don't want to sit around waiting for the next so-called accident to take another family member."

"What can we do about it?"

"I've got friends who've got access to records. I want to take a look at the reports filed on the old accident and find out what actually happened the night our folks were killed. I'll be looking for similarities between what happened then and what happened now. Maybe I won't find any connection, but if I do, we need to be warned."

"Cody, if you're right about this, you could be endangering yourself by asking questions and stirring up more trouble. So be careful."

"I hear you. If there really is a connection, then whoever's responsible has been incredibly patient to have waited all these years to strike again. We all need to be alerted to the possible danger."

"Have you said anything to Cam about this?"

"Not yet."

"Good. He's got enough to deal with at the moment. When you find out anything, let me know."

"Will do." Cody doubled his fist and lightly tapped Cole on the shoulder. "I'll see you later."

Cole stood there and watched Cody step onto the elevator and waited while the doors quietly closed between them.

He would call their corporate headquarters and get the security staff to do some research on any other trouble that might have occurred through the years, the origin of which had never been resolved. The more he considered the matter, the more he agreed with Cody. The similarity between the accidents bothered him. He had never believed in coincidences.

Cole walked down the hall with a brisk stride and pushed open the door to the private room that Cameron had been transferred to from ICU a few days before. "How's it goin'?" he asked, walking into the hospital room and pausing beside the bed.

"They're talking about letting me out of this place."

Cole smiled. "Somehow that doesn't surprise me. They'll probably be thrilled to get rid of you."

"So that battle-ax of a night nurse informed me. If she thought she was hurting my feelings, she was wrong."

There was an unspoken agreement that no one mentioned Andrea's death. The doctor had broken the news to Cameron when he thought he was strong enough to hear it. Even so, it had set his recovery back. Now, Cole and Cody waited for him to pick the subject for conversation when they visited him. Cole knew that Cam would talk when he was ready, not before. The main thing was that Cameron knew his brothers were there for him, no matter what.

Whatever demons Cameron wrestled with, he fought them alone.

Cole pulled up a chair and sat beside the bed. "How would you like to come back to the ranch to live?"

He'd been dreading having to ask the question, knowing it was going to stir up a great deal of emotion.

"I suppose it makes sense," Cameron responded slowly, "at least at first."

"I was hoping that you'd feel that way. Letty's grown quite attached to Trisha. She'd miss her."

"That really surprises me. I never thought the witch ever cared about anybody."

"Cam! That doesn't sound like you."

"Well, maybe you don't know me, or maybe I've been keeping my thoughts and opinions to myself for too long. There's nothing like almost dying to make you take another look at the way you live."

"What have you got against poor Aunt Letty?"

"Poor Aunt Letty, my rear end. The woman terrorizes everybody around her."

"Where would we be without her, Cameron? You and Cody wouldn't have had anybody if she hadn't been there for you."

"You don't know how lucky you were that you never had to live with her rules and regulations. I swear the woman took pleasure in punishing us whenever we didn't live up to her expectations."

"I had no idea you felt that way."

"I know. I've never told you before. I didn't

want to leave Trisha with her at all, but Andrea thought I was being silly. Her parents are definitely not the parenting type. They scarcely knew Andrea was around when she was growing up.''

"They asked Letty if they could keep the baby for a while, but she wouldn't let them.''

Cameron shifted, as though he were trying to find a more comfortable position. Cole stood and paced over to the window, not sure how to deal with this newly belligerent brother.

"It's just as well,'' Cameron finally muttered. "They would have turned her over to one of the maids.''

Cole turned back to look at his brother. "What did Letty do that was so bad?''

"It wasn't what she did. It was her whole attitude toward everybody. Especially the Alvarezes. God, she was brutal to them, even more so after our folks died.''

"Well, Tony's leaving like that left everybody stunned.''

"That's what I'm talking about. I don't care what Letty said about their leaving, I don't believe either Tony or Allison wanted to go.''

Cole walked over and sat beside the bed once again. "What do you mean?''

"I was there, Cole. You weren't. I saw Tony's face when he came out of dad's old study after talking with Letty. He was devastated, utterly wiped out. He walked right past me like he didn't even see me. Later, when I heard they were leaving, I went over to talk to Allison and Tony. She was crying something fierce. I've never heard worse sobbing.''

Cole felt something clutch at his chest, constricting his breathing. ''Are you saying that Letty said something to make them leave?''

''I've always suspected it, but I could never prove it. After Tony was gone, she ruled the place like some petty tyrant, ordering all of us about.''

''How come I've never seen that side of her?''

''Because you've never paid that much attention to her. She always waited until you had left to pull her shenanigans. Remember, you've spent most of your time in Austin these past few years. You just let the ranch run as it always had.''

He was right, Cole knew. There had been so much to learn about all the businesses that he'd bought a place in Austin where he could more easily travel over to Houston or up to Dallas, or down to Corpus Christi. He'd been thrown into the business world like a nonswimmer into the deep end, with very few people there to help keep him afloat.

''Uh, Cameron. There's something that I need to talk to you about, something that's been eating at me. Almost losing you made me face how important you are to me. I don't have very many people in my life I can trust. You're not only my brother, but you're my business consultant, my tax attorney, my friend.''

Cameron narrowed his eyes slightly. "Glad to know I'm appreciated. What's up?"

"I recently discovered that more was going on with the Alvarezes than either of us were made aware of at the time."

"What are you talking about?"

"Allison was pregnant when they left."

Cameron sat up in the bed, let out a groan because of the pain his sudden move had caused him and subsided back on his pillow. "She what?"

"The morning after your accident, before Cody found me, I was down at the beach, walking, when I saw a kid that could have been Cody at fourteen. All except for his eyes. They were black, that deep glittery black that always gave Tony and Allison their exotic looks. I stopped and asked him his name. He told me he was Tony Alvarez, and lived with his mother, Allison Alvarez, in Mason, about a hundred miles northwest of here. He said he was named after his grandfather who died before he was born."

"And you think that—"

"I *know* he's my son. There isn't a doubt in my mind."

"God, Cole, what are you going to do?"

"I haven't decided, yet. I've been trying to cope with that knowledge all the time I've been worrying whether I was going to lose you. Now you're telling me that there are some discrepancies in the story about the reasons why the Alvarezes left the Circle C.''

"Do you think Letty knew that Allison was pregnant?''

"There's only one way to find out.''

"You think she'd tell you the truth?''

That stopped him. Cole stared at his brother. "Are you suggesting that she might lie about it?''

Cameron shrugged. "It wouldn't be the first time she's lied. She always manages to cover up one lie with a bigger one.''

"My God, Cam. Surely you're exaggerating. We can't be talking about the same woman.''

"The trouble with you, Cole, is that you've always seen what you wanted to see, not necessarily what was happening around you. You've got this thing about family loyalty and family heritage and all that bunk. Since Letty is a Callaway you automatically assume she's an upright, outstanding example of loyalty and compassion.''

Cole had gotten sidetracked. "What do you mean, all of that bunk? We *are* a family. We *do* have a heritage. A damn fine one. When Granddad Caleb first came to Texas—''

"Oh, hell, Cole, don't get started on Granddad Caleb. You and Dad always treated him as some saint, of all things. He was nothing but a gunfighter too bored after the First World War to stay home in Ohio. So he came to Texas looking for some action, and he found it. He managed to amass a fortune down here, acquired the ranch in ways that have always been glossed over—"

"He *bought* the ranch, dammit. He didn't steal it. He bought it!"

"Of course he did. For less than a quarter of what it was worth. The owner was glad to get away with his life!"

"Where the hell did you get such stuff?"

"I read, Cole. I've always enjoyed history and, I'll admit, I've especially enjoyed Callaway history. It never ceases to amaze me how respectable we are now considering how all of this got started."

"What did you read?" Cole demanded to know.

"A bunch of letters and journals stored in the attic. While you were busy trailing after Dad all over the ranch I was curled up with some of the juiciest scandals that ever got jotted down by a series of observers—our feminine ancestors."

"And you never told me?"

"Hell, no. I doubt that Dad ever knew it, either. He took *his* dad's word for everything, just like you always did. If Dad said it, you took it for gospel."

"And what's wrong with that?"

"Nothing, except that Dad wasn't a hundred percent right all of the time. He was a human being. He had his faults. But you never saw them. To you, he was your dad and he was perfect. Aunt Letty is the sister of a perfect man and that makes her perfect too. Cody and I are your brothers, making us perfect also.''

''I wouldn't go so far as to say that,'' Cole responded with a grin.

''Then there's hope for you, yet, thank God. I realized while I was telling you about Letty that I felt just like some kind of pervert telling little kids that there's no Santa, no tooth fairy, and that the Easter bunny is a fake.''

''I'm not some unsophisticated kid, Cameron.''

''You are where your family is concerned. Now you tell me that you have a son, that you've known for—how long?—where he lives but you haven't gone to talk with Allison. Who are you protecting now, Cole? Have you ever, just once in your life, done something that was for you alone, or have you always put the family's needs, desires and reputation before your own?''

Cole discovered that he couldn't answer him. He sat there and stared at his brother, his mind racing. He'd always done what he was supposed to do, what was expected of him. And now, Cameron was saying that was wrong? He was wrong?

''Cole?''

''Yeah.''

''Do me a favor.''

''Sure. What do you need?''

Cameron smiled. ''See what I mean? It wouldn't matter to you what I would have wanted, you would have busted your butt getting it for me.''

"Well, sure. I mean, you're my brother and—"

"I know, I know. Well, this request is going to be a tough one for you."

"That's doesn't matter. I can—"

"I want you to leave the hospital and I don't want you to come back."

"What?"

"Let Cody handle getting me home. I'll be able to leave by tomorrow probably, no later than the day after. I want you to forget about me for a few days, okay?"

"But, Cameron—"

"I want you to ask yourself what you would like to do most in the world right now? This is going to be the toughest question you've ever had to face, I'm sure, because you don't have a clue. Not one clue. So take your time. Go home, or wherever you've been staying that allows you to be at the hospital sixteen hours every day. Somehow you've managed to put business concerns aside, so let them stay there for a few more days.

"Decide what you want to do most in the world, Cole. Then go do it. I mean it. That's what I want, and you said you'd do anything. I want you to go do it."

"You don't have any idea what I might do."

Cameron grinned. "Oh, yes I do. But you don't and it's you we're talking about here."

"Well, if you're so all-fired smart, why don't

you just tell me and save me all that soul-searching?''

''It's the soul-searching that's so important, bro. That's the part that is crucial, because when you finally face what you truly want, then you'll be ready to go after it.''

Two days later, Cole was on his way to Mason, Texas. After following Cameron's advice and allowing Cody to look after Cameron, he had felt at loose ends.

Cameron's remarks had unnerved him, particularly the ones about Letty. Actually, everything he'd said had shaken him...about Granddad Caleb, about how he'd worshipped his father, about his being blind to what went on around him in the family. How could that be? He'd managed to improve the businesses he'd inherited over the years. He'd doubled, sometimes tripled, the income produced by Callaway Enterprises. He was no dummy. He knew that. But he obviously had a blind spot.

His family.

Tony was part of his family, whether he had known about him or not. When he finally allowed himself to feel all of the feelings that went with the thought of having a son, he was almost brought to his knees. The pain was intense. How could he have had a son all of these years and not known? Shouldn't he have felt something?

As for Allison, he was more confused than ever.

He wanted some answers. Most important, he wanted to know why she hadn't bothered to tell him she was pregnant.

Had she told her father? Had he told Letty?

He had considered talking to Letty first, but then Cameron's words had come back to him. Would she tell him the truth?

He knew that Allison would not lie to him. She had never lied about anything in all the years he'd known her...until she chose to live the biggest lie of them all.

Allison was in the gallery visiting with possible customers who had seen her shop on the way through town when she saw the large luxury car turn the corner of the square.

Large, late-model luxury cars drove through Mason on a regular basis, but this one was different, and she knew it with the instincts of a cornered animal.

She watched with a sense of inevitability as it pulled into the angle parking space in front of the gallery.

So he had come.

She turned back to her visitors. "Yes, the work we carry here is done by local artists and craftsmen. Those photographs, the Indian medicine wheels and Kachina dolls, and the oils are the product of various people who live in and around Mason."

The front door gave its distinctive tinkle and she turned.

The years had made a considerable difference in the man. He seemed taller, and considerably broader. He was dressed informally, in a Western shirt, boots and well-worn jeans that clung to his muscular legs. She would have known him anywhere and yet he looked different—harder, somehow. The smile lines were gone from his face. In their place was an austerity in his expression that made him look more somber. His eyes were narrowed and they glittered in the darkness of his face.

"Hello, Cole. It's been a long time."

He hadn't known what to expect, but the woman who stood before him with so much poise and confidence was a far cry from the teenage girl he'd last seen.

She still wore her hair long. Now she had it in a single braid, draped over her shoulder. She was in a multitiered full skirt, a matching blouse, doeskin moccasins, and she wore a matching beaded headband. Her skin was still as fair as ever, which made a startling contrast to her black eyes and hair.

"Pocohantas, I presume?" he drawled, slowly scanning her from her toes to the top of her head.

One of the men among the two couples in the gallery laughed.

"May I help you?" she asked Cole, meeting his eyes with a deliberately steady glance.

"Good question. I'll think on it," he replied and

began to study the many paintings, photographs and artifacts in the store. She turned away from him and went over to the others.

One of the women said, "Now, honey, don't let us keep you from your work. We're just lookin' at everything."

Allison smiled. "That's what you're supposed to do. Enjoy yourselves. If I can answer any questions, just let me know. I'll be in back."

She turned away, leaving Cole and the other people staring at the contents of the gallery. She walked through the beads and sat at the desk. All right. He was here. The world had not come to an end. She knew that he would follow her, but for now she was determined to keep her head. She was no longer a child. She was a thirty-two-year-old woman who'd managed to raise a fourteen-year-old son on her own. She had a successful career; she was independent. No man was going to intimidate her, not even a Callaway.

She heard the front door and got up to see if she had more visitors.

"Don't bother," she heard Cole say as he pushed the beads aside and stepped into the back room. "It's just your visitors leaving. Do you get many browsers here?"

"Quite a few."

"Doesn't help business much if they don't buy."

"You might be surprised. They'll see something

that captures their imagination. Maybe they won't buy it today, but it will nag at them until the next time they happen to be driving through town. Then they come in and buy it.''

''What if it's already sold?''

''That's the chance they take, of course. Things change.''

''Yes. It's good to see you again, Allison. I tried to picture what you might look like, but it was difficult after all this time.''

''You weren't expecting Pocohantas?''

He grinned. ''No.''

''I dress this way because it's comfortable, because it's colorful and because artists are expected to be a tiny bit eccentric.''

''Ah. Your marketing technique.''

''Exactly.''

''Where's Tony?''

She had been leaning back in her chair during their exchange without offering him a chair. He didn't seem to be bothered and had leaned his shoulder against the door frame and crossed his arms in a negligent pose.

She slowly straightened in her chair at his abrupt change of subject. ''Why do you ask?''

''Just wondered.''

''He's staying with friends at the moment.''

''The same ones he was with on Padre Island?''

''Yes.''

''They live around here?''

"Yes."

He sighed and slowly straightened. "So when do you close this place?"

She glanced at her watch. "In about fifteen minutes."

"Good. Is there someplace we could go to talk?"

"There are all kinds of places to talk in Mason," she said with a whimsical smile. "You only have to say it once and by the end of the week everyone knows about it. That's the beauty of a small town. We're a friendly bunch."

"Then let me rephrase my question. Is there someplace we can talk privately?"

She stared at him thoughtfully. If she thought that he would go away if she said no, she'd immediately give him a negative answer. However, she had a hunch that although Cole looked different from the young man she'd known, he was probably as stubborn as he ever was. He'd driven to Mason to talk to her. He wouldn't leave until he'd said his piece.

"My place is private enough," she admitted.

"When will Tony be home?"

That was none of his business. "We'll have time to talk," was all she said.

At five-thirty she flipped the Open sign on the front door to read Closed, pulled the shade on the display window, then looked around at him. "I'm parked in back. I'll drive around in a few minutes."

She opened the door and held it for him. He eyed her suspiciously and she smiled. What did he think she was going to do? Make a run for it?

He had no choice but to go through the door. She locked it behind him and walked back through the gallery, turning off the special lighting as she went. When she got to her office area she reached in the drawer for her purse, then let herself out the back door.

She hopped into her Bronco, drove down the alley to the street and turned right. He was sitting in his car, watching for her when she drove past. She tooted her horn. He immediately pulled out and fell in behind her.

She made a left at the corner and headed up the hill. She had a home overlooking the town, near historic Fort Mason. By the time she pulled into the driveway of her modern, brick, ranch-style home, Allison had given herself a stern lecture on not allowing her emotions to sway her tonight.

Cole Callaway may have been the most important person in her life for years, but he was nothing to her now. In fact, he was less than nothing. He had come for his own reasons and would no doubt let her in on them shortly. Until then, she would treat him politely, as she would any visitor. She would treat him like the stranger he now was.

She stopped outside the two-car garage, choosing to leave the truck outside for the moment. She had to get some groceries a little later, anyway. By the time she hopped out of the Bronco, he had gotten out of his car.

"Quite a place you have here," he said, looking around at the quiet residential area and the view of the town in the valley below.

"You can see the clock tower on the courthouse from here."

"Lived up here long?"

"About ten years."

He made no other comment.

She led the way to the front door, which she and Tony seldom used, unlocked the door and pushed it open. She started to step to one side and he waved her through. Rather than argue she walked into the hallway that ran between the front room on one side and the dining room on the other, back to the family room. A sliding glass door opened onto a patio. The view of the west Texas hills was impressive.

"What can I get you to drink? I thought we could sit out on the patio."

"Do you have any beer?"

"I may have." The kitchen was divided from the family room by a kitchen bar, so that Cole watched her walk into that room and open the refrigerator. "You're in luck. There are two in here."

She grabbed a long-necked bottle and set it on the cabinet, then reached for a pitcher and poured what looked like lemonade into a tall glass.

"Do you want a glass for your beer?" she asked.

He grinned. "'Fraid not. Nobody's managed to civilize me quite that much."

The look she gave him was challenging. "I doubt that anyone would even try." She handed him the beer, picked up the glass and walked to the sliding glass door.

The sun was setting, casting the patio area in shade. They sat in comfortable lounge chairs with a small table between them.

"Is this private enough for you?" she asked cheerfully.

"You act as though you've been expecting my visit."

"Why shouldn't I? Tony told me that you and he met. I knew you'd probably show up, out of curiosity, if for no other reason."

He frowned. "You think that's why I'm here? Because I'm curious?"

"I can't think of another reason, offhand. If you have one, I'll be glad to listen."

Cole took a drink in an effort to get his thoughts in order. Whatever attitude he'd expected to run into...anger, rebelliousness, defensiveness, hatred...he'd been certain he could handle it.

But this? He couldn't understand her, not at all.

Finally he said, "I guess I came because I was hoping to get some answers."

She looked at him, puzzled. "Answers about what?"

"Everything. About why you and your dad left

the ranch, about why you never told me you were leaving, never told me anything, most especially why you never told me you were pregnant. Can you imagine what a shock it was for me to see Tony, to suddenly discover that I was a father? I need to understand, and I can't. I've lain in bed night after night trying to figure it out. I should never have made love to you that day. I knew that. I never gave a thought to the possible consequences. Not once. But when I left, you knew I was coming back for Christmas. You had my address. Were you so angry at me for taking advantage of you that you didn't think I deserved to know you were pregnant?''

All the time he was speaking Allison stared at him, her puzzlement becoming a frown. When he stopped speaking she was silent for a long moment before she asked, "Are you trying to pretend that you don't know why we left, that you didn't know I was pregnant? Because if you are, I'm really concerned about you, Cole. I mean, that was a traumatic time in your life, the worst possible time, I'm sure. But I can't believe that you just erased everything that happened back then in an effort to forget your pain.''

She spoke in a calm, soothing voice that Cole found irritating as hell, as though he'd just escaped from the funny farm and she was trying to mollify him.

He consciously refrained from grinding his teeth,

but he could feel a muscle in his jaw jump as a result.

"I haven't forgotten a thing, Allison. Not a damned thing!"

"I disagree with you. But to refresh your memory—my dad and I left within a week after your parents' funeral for the simple reason that your aunt fired him without notice and gave us forty-eight hours to pack up everything we owned and get out."

He stared at her in horror. "You can't mean that."

"I mean it."

"But why? Did she find out—no, of course not. You couldn't have known yourself about—"

"The baby? Oh, wouldn't she have loved to have known that as well! No, there was no way to know then."

"She told me that when your dad inherited the money from my dad's estate, that your dad resigned, saying he was moving to Colorado."

She shook her head. "Your aunt couldn't wait to get us out of there. At the time she fired Dad, we didn't know about the inheritance. Dad had our mail forwarded, otherwise we might never have been notified. The attorneys sent a letter that finally caught up with us."

"In Colorado?"

She stared at him. "No, of course not. We didn't know where to go at first, so we moved to San

Antonio. The shock of your dad's death was really rough on my father. I don't think he took in any of it right away—the death, having to leave the ranch. He seemed to be in a daze for several weeks.

"He happened to run into a guy he'd known on the rodeo circuit who furnished the bulls for the bull-riding events. He'd bought a place near here and invited us to visit. We came out for a weekend and Dad ended up accepting a job working on the ranch."

"But according to the will, your dad wouldn't have had to work. He had enough to retire," Cole insisted.

"The letter hadn't caught up with us by then."

She stared off at the hills that lay in deep shadows for a long time before saying, "It was my pregnancy that killed him, though. He'd just about come to terms with losing his job on the ranch. In a way, I think he was relieved not to be reminded of your dad on a daily basis, and neither one of us missed being around your aunt. He'd begun to settle in, he'd even found a small place he was thinking about buying when I had to tell him I was pregnant. He became real quiet after that. Wouldn't talk to anybody. When I started showing and it became obvious that I was pregnant he told folks that I'd only been married a few weeks when my husband was killed and that I had reverted back to my maiden name, not knowing I was pregnant at the time."

She continued to look at the hills, her face averted from Cole. "He used to sit there at night just staring at me with this sorrowful look that cut right through me. I was all he had left and I'd disappointed him. One night he went to bed and just never woke up. I don't think he wanted to live." Her voice had grown softer and softer as she spoke.

"Allison, why didn't you tell me you were pregnant?"

She glanced at him as if surprised to find him there, she had been so lost in her memories.

"Is that the way you choose to remember it, Cole? Is it easier to live with that way? I've always wondered how you justified your behavior to yourself."

"What are you talking about?"

"Look, Cole. It's just you and me here tonight. No one else. You don't have to lie, or defend, or justify a thing. It all happened a long time ago. But don't pretend that you didn't ignore all the letters I wrote to you. I wrote daily at first. Then when you didn't respond, I began to write once a week. Then I told you about the baby. You never bothered to answer a single letter, Cole, which was an answer all of its own."

Five

"What are you talking about, Allison? I never got any letters from you. Don't you remember—you used to hate writing letters. That first year I was away at college, and homesick as hell, I used to plead with you to write me and you sent me a Valentine's card. Period."

Of course he was right that she hadn't liked to write letters. Plus she'd been so busy with school and related activities. It had only been after she'd left the ranch and had been so homesick that she had felt the need to communicate her thoughts and feelings. No wonder he had begged her to write him when he had first gone off to school. It had never occurred to her, until now, how he must have felt that first year away from everything and everyone familiar. She hadn't understood.

"I'm talking about after we left the ranch, Cole. I wrote to you to give you our San Antonio address, then later the post office box number at Mason."

Cole leaned forward, bringing him closer to her. "I never got a single letter from you, do you hear me? Not one. I didn't even know you'd left the ranch until I got home for Christmas vacation. I assumed you had moved to Colorado by then."

She could feel her frustration mount. "We never *lived* in Colorado, I don't care what your crazy aunt said!"

Cole came to his feet. "She isn't crazy!"

She came to her feet as well. "Oh, that's right. She's a Callaway, so that makes her perfect!"

"I never said that."

"You don't have to, Cole. I know how you are about your family. Maybe she isn't certifiable, but she's certainly twisted in her thinking. She hates the world and everybody in it and she always took a particular dislike to my family. Don't pretend you don't remember that, either!"

"I'm not pretending anything, dammit."

She turned away and walked to the edge of the patio, her back to him. "Fine. You're not pretending. You're saying you never heard from me. I'm saying I wrote you at least a dozen letters…the last one telling you that you were going to be a father."

He moved up behind her and placed his hands

on her shoulders. "Allison, honey, don't you know that if I had ever, ever gotten a letter with that kind of information in it that I would have been here on the next plane?"

"No," she stated baldly.

"Why not?" He truly sounded bewildered.

"Because I wrote you and wrote you and wrote you and you didn't come."

He turned her around. "Do you think I'm lying to you?"

She stared up at his angry face. His eyes snapped with irritation, but there was no mistaking his sincerity. For the first time, for the very first time, Allison wondered if he could be telling the truth.

What would it mean to the way she viewed the events of her life, particularly during that traumatic time when both of them had lost their parents, if Cole had never gotten her letters?

A sudden rush of feeling swept over her. She recognized it as grief.

She moved her trembling fingers up to her mouth in an unconscious gesture, to suppress the sound of the pain she was beginning to feel. "But how could that be?" she finally whispered.

"How the hell should I know? I don't understand any of this, but I'm going to get to the bottom of it if it's the last thing I do. As far as I knew, when I left you in October, we were going to plan our wedding when I came back during the Christmas holidays. I came home with all kinds of ideas for a wedding and a honeymoon only to find that you and your father had moved, leaving my aunt and my two little brothers alone with a ranch to run. Half of the crew had left by then. Everything was in an uproar. I was going to stay there and manage the ranch but Letty insisted I go back to school, that my education was more important than anything else at that time.''

She looked at him with a feeling of horror because his words made so much sense.

"How did you mail those letters?''

She stared at him in confusion. "What?''

"I said,'' he enunciated slowly, "how did you mail those letters?''

Was he demented? What kind of question was that? "I mailed them the way anyone uses the mail. I put them in the box at the post office.''

"You did? You personally put them in the mailbox?''

She thought back for several moments before she said, "Well, I think so. I mean, I would give them to Dad to mail whenever he went to town…'' Her voice faded away and there was a long silence between them.

Cole didn't know what to say. How could he accuse her dad of not mailing her letters? What reasons would he have? He and Tony had always been close, hadn't they? Hadn't Tony known how he and Allison felt about each other? I mean, he had never actually sat and discussed his feelings with Tony, or with his own dad, either, for that matter, but both men knew they were seeing each other exclusively. They had been kids back then, with their entire lives stretching ahead of them as though into infinity. They'd had all the time in the world...until the day their world had ended.

Allison feverishly searched her memories. Surely she had personally mailed at least a few of the letters, hadn't she? But that was during the time when her dad had been so upset, when he hadn't known what to do with himself and would take off on long walks in the city.

Had she suggested he mail her letters as a reason to get out? And what about after they moved to Mason? Hadn't he gone into town each morning to meet the other ranchers for coffee? Hadn't it been logical that he take her letters in with him?

"I can't believe this," she finally whispered, her voice sounding ragged.

"Neither can I. None of it makes any sense to me." After another long silence, he asked, "Did your dad leave you a letter or anything, some papers, something?"

She shook her head. "He'd banked the money he received, allowing it to build up interest while he decided whether to buy a place. When he died so suddenly I didn't know what to do. Tony was born less than a month after Dad died."

"How did you manage?"

"I'd moved into town by that time and had

rented a small house near the post office. The
townspeople were wonderful to me. After Tony
was old enough to stay with a sitter I started helping a local artist make sculptures. I worked with
her for several years until I was able to buy the
gallery. I'd won some awards by that time, gotten
some recognition and my work began to sell.
That's how I was able to buy this place.''

''Then you've made a success of your life here.''

''Yes.'' She'd done it on her own. She'd done
it to prove to the Callaways that she could do it.
That she hadn't needed them or anyone. She and
Tony had managed just fine.

''Allison?''

''Yes.''

''Does Tony know who I am?''

That brought her out of her thoughts in a hurry.
She moved away from him. ''No. He knows nothing about the Callaways. He knows I was brought
up on a ranch in south Texas, and that we moved
to Mason shortly before he was born.''

''But surely he's asked questions about his father.''

''Not for a long time. I told him that his father
had been an orphan so there was no family left.
He's found several surrogate fathers here who've
worked with him and taught him about ranching
and rodeos.''

''Rodeos? You mean he's already leaning in that
direction?''

"Falling is a better description, but yes. He loves the life."

"Are you going to let me get to know him?"

"That would be a little difficult under the circumstances."

"Dammit, Allison, would you give me a break here? I'm beginning to see that this situation isn't as cut-and-dried as I first thought. We both had some misconceptions about what was really going on, but we're looking at a new perspective here and—"

"I don't care what sort of perspective you're looking at, Cole, I don't want you in my life or in Tony's life. All you'll do is hurt us, and I for one have had all the hurt I want from the Callaways."

"Hurt you! Hell, woman, I loved you! I would *never* have hurt you, you *know* that."

She could no longer see his face and she realized that night had settled on them while they had been talking. She could turn on the patio light, or they could go inside. Even better, she could ask Cole to leave. She could ask, but she had a strong hunch it would do her no good.

The problem was that she didn't think she could take much more of this. Cole was acting like he was the wronged person through all this, which was absolutely outrageous considering what she— Considering that she had been—

Allison sank onto the edge of her chair. "I don't know what to do," she finally admitted out loud.

He followed her and sat beside her. "Well, I suggest that we eat something. I don't know about you, but I haven't eaten since early this morning and I've never been able to think very well on an empty stomach."

"Oh, you're always hungry, Cole. I swear you must be a bottomless pit—" She paused abruptly, suddenly aware that she had fallen back into their old habit of teasing each other, just as though the past fifteen years had never happened. After a moment, she started again. "Come on inside. I'm bound to have something in there to eat."

He followed her into the house and sat at the counter when she walked over to the refrigerator. "Shouldn't Tony be getting home soon?" he asked.

She pulled out part of a ham, some leftover vegetables and a fruit salad. "He won't be home tonight."

"Why?"

She wanted so badly to point out that he had no right to be concerning himself with his son's whereabouts, but she couldn't. How would she feel if she were in his situation? What would she do if she had only recently discovered that she had a child she'd never known existed?

Cole was handling the situation much more calmly than she would have, she was certain. In fact, he was handling it more calmly than the Cole she had known so many years ago.

"The friend he's staying with lives on a ranch where they keep riding stock. They've been prac- ticing every afternoon after school. Since this is Friday, I told Tony he could stay the weekend."

"Oh."

So now he knew.

"What about your plans for the evening?" he asked in a tentative voice.

"What plans?"

"I mean, don't you usually go out on the week- ends or something? Have I interfered with some- thing?"

"No, as a matter of fact you haven't. The man I'm seeing is out of town."

"Oh."

They were both silent. Cole wondered what he could say that wouldn't sound as though he were prying.

Finally he cleared his throat and said, "I know this is going to sound strange, but I'd really like us to become friends again."

Allison kept her back turned while she gathered plates, silverware and glasses, then set two places at the bar. She answered without looking at him. "I don't think that would be a good idea."

"Why, for God's sake?"

"Because it wouldn't work, that's why. I would feel that you were watching and judging everything I did and said, trying to decide if I was raising Tony the way you think I should, or—"

"Hey, wait a minute. If I haven't already said it, then you need to know that I think you've done one hell of a job with that boy. He's a delightful kid—warm and friendly and polite. He's not bashful or overly forward. I was very impressed with him. You don't think I'd come in at this late date and try to cause trouble, do you? Hey, Allison, this is me, Cole. You've known me all my life. When did I turn into such an ogre?"

She didn't reply; her expression said it all.

He sighed and ran his hand through his hair. "Oh, I get it. When I didn't answer the mythical letters."

"They weren't mythical. They were very real."

"I know that. I just meant that—oh, hell, I don't know what I meant. I'm just trying to find some basis on which we can establish a new relationship."

"I don't want a new relationship."

"Well, I do, dammit. This is important to me. Family is important to me."

She finished placing the food on the bar, then sat across from him. "Do you think I don't know that?" she asked. "Family is everything to you. But I'm not family. Remember. And Tony is my son."

"Tony is a Callaway."

"Try and prove it."

"All you have to do is to look at him and—"

"That's not legal proof."

He stared at her in shock. "Are you talking about going to court?"

"Aren't you?"

"Of course not. I don't want to create a problem for you."

"Well, you are. Just your coming to Mason creates a problem for me. If Tony finds out you're here he'll have all kinds of questions, like why I've never mentioned you before, like how well do I know you, like why haven't we ever seen you before, like—"

"Okay, okay. But can't we work all of that out? I just want to get to know him. What is wrong with that?"

She didn't want to see the anguish in his eyes, or hear the pain in his voice. She especially didn't want to get caught up in the magic once again of being with Cole. Already she'd made one slip tonight, falling back into their old repartee. What would repeated exposure to him bring to her? Heartbreak, pure and simple. Not to mention what it would do to Tony.

"What do you suggest?" she finally asked him, toying with her food.

"Well." He obviously was taken aback by the question. "School's out in a few weeks. Why don't the two of you come and stay at the ranch for a—"

"Absolutely not."

"Why not?"

"I don't intend to go anywhere near Letty Callaway."

"Oh, Allison, don't be that way."

"I mean it."

"All right. So what if I send her off on a trip somewhere? Would you come, then?"

"I don't know."

"Both Cameron and Cody are living there. I didn't tell you, but Cameron and his wife were in a bad accident about the same time I saw Tony. Cameron's wife was killed and he was severely injured."

"Oh, Cole, no! How horrible."

"He has a little girl, Trisha. She's around a year old."

Allison's eyes filled with tears, tears she couldn't shed for her own situation but were permissible for someone else's pain.

"It would give Cameron something to look forward to, if I told him you two were coming."

"I'd have to think about it."

"Do that. You've got some time. I also wish you'd talk to Tony and tell him about me."

Her eyes widened in alarm. "That you're his father?"

"Well, at least tell him that we grew up together. Let him know how important you've always been to me." His steady gaze caused shivers to run up and down her spine.

"If I come, it would be to give you a chance to

get to know Tony. It wouldn't have anything to do with me."

"If that's the way you want it."

"That's the way it's got to be."

"How will your boyfriend feel about it?"

She shrugged. "It isn't any of his business. I am my own woman. I don't belong to anyone. I never will."

She made them coffee and afterward, Cole took his leave. She walked him to the door.

"I'd have you tell Tony hello for me, but under the circumstances, that probably isn't a good idea."

"You're right."

"I can't tell you how glad I am to have found you after all these years. I feel that I've been given back my youth."

She looked at the self-assured man standing before her, the kingpin who was being touted as the next governor of the state and shook her head.

What a complex man he was. He acted as though finding her and Tony was the most important thing that had happened to him.

"Cole?"

"Yes?"

"Why haven't you ever married?"

"Because there's only one woman I ever wanted to marry, Allison." He touched his forefinger lightly to her cheek. "I'll call you about your visit."

"Don't make definite plans. I haven't really thought it all through."

"I can hope, though, and believe me, there will be plenty of that going on." Before she had a chance to react he leaned down and kissed her full on the mouth. The kiss spoke volumes...of his frustration, of his nervousness, of his desire. When he eventually lifted his head he stared into her eyes for the longest time without saying a word.

Then he turned and walked away.

Six

By the time Cole reached San Antonio he felt weak with exhaustion. The tight self-control he'd kept over his emotions had taken its toll. He had another two hours of driving ahead of him before he reached the ranch. He decided to get a room in one of the hotels along the river downtown.

He awoke early the next morning, before the sun had been given an opportunity to do more than brush the city with its golden light. He should reach the ranch in time for breakfast.

His thoughts kept returning to Allison. She'd been a striking young girl. Now she was stunning, her looks even more exotic than he had remembered. She could have made a fortune modeling. Instead she was the one who used models.

He'd been steeled against feeling much of anything when he drove into Mason, but it had taken only one look at her to know he'd been kidding himself.

He had loved this woman with an intensity he'd felt for few people in his life. Being near her again had stirred up all of those reactions within him.

The kiss had been a mistake. Even though he hadn't touched her with anything other than his lips, he'd felt the searing heat spring up between them. It had always been there without their understanding it. Even though he now understood it, he sure as hell didn't have to like it.

His life was complicated enough.

The adobe pillars that marked the ranch's entrance came into view and he began to slow down. They'd had the lane blacktopped a few years ago, which kept the dust under better control. He drove beneath the high wrought-iron arch with the giant *C* circled in its center.

He loved every inch of this place. The mesquite trees, the live oaks, the cacti, the tumbleweeds, the deer, lizards and snakes, the armadillos...the heat, the fleas and the flies. He loved the rolling hills with their outcroppings of limestone and granite. This was his country. He'd been born here. He would die here.

He was home.

The ranch buildings were almost six miles from the main highway. The blacktopped road wound among the hills with an occasional barbed-wire fence running parallel to it. He slowed down when he topped the last rise and surveyed the scene spread out in the bowl-shaped valley below.

The house had been built in the late 1800s by a Mexican don. It was two stories high in front, three stories along the back, with an interior patio filled with a fountain and masses of greenery. The white adobe walls sparkled in the morning sun.

From the distance he could trace the remains of the original exterior wall that had been built to protect against the Indians and outlaws. The arch across the driveway was still there and most of the wall on the entrance side. However, as the ranch had grown and more buildings had been needed, the wall had been removed on both sides and only half of it remained in the rear.

The bunkhouses for the single men were at some distance from the neat row of housing for the married men and their families. He could see a corner of the rooftop of the foreman's house from where he sat.

He accelerated and headed toward the Big House. He had a great deal to take care of today.

When he pulled up in front of the massive front door with its intricate carvings, Cole got out of the car and stretched. The circular driveway directly in front of the Big House was protected from the sun by large shade trees. A breeze rustled the cottonwood leaves, a familiar sound that meant home to him.

He crossed to the front door and went inside. The Spanish tiled floor of the two-storied foyer gleamed, reflecting the light from the end of the hallway that opened directly onto the patio.

He strode down the hallway, glancing into the various empty rooms he passed. He came to an abrupt halt in front of one of the rooms, a sharp pain seeming to hit him in the chest.

Trisha was in her playpen, gleefully throwing out her toys while Rosie, one of the women who worked for his family, laughed and teased her by scooping them up and tossing them back inside.

Here was a stage of Tony's life that he had missed. This domestic scene brought home to him—more than anything else that had happened— how much he had been deprived.

He paused in the doorway, then slowly walked into the room. "Hello, little girl. Do you have a hug for your Uncle Cole?"

Trisha glanced around and when she saw him she started bouncing on her bottom, holding her arms up.

"Uh-huh, just as I thought." He leaned over and picked her up. She began to finger his collar and play with one of the buttons. He nuzzled her neck, smelling her powder-scented skin, feeling its softness, and for a brief moment he wanted to cry out at the injustice.

Trisha babbled to him in her special language, pulling his nose with one hand and patting his cheek with the other.

"You're a beauty, did you know that, sugar?" he said with a wistful smile. "You're going to be a real heartbreaker someday."

Reluctantly he put her back into the playpen where she immediately picked up a rubber giraffe and threw it at him. "You're also going to be a hell of a pitcher, with an arm like that," he added, chuckling.

He turned and went back out into the hallway. He decided to look upstairs to see if Cameron was settled in. He passed three doors in the upper hallway before pausing in front of the fourth and quietly opening it. Cameron was on the bed, staring out the window.

"Care for some company?" Cole asked softly.

His brother looked around. "Why not? There's not much else to do. I called the office this morning and was told you'd left orders not to send me any of my files."

Cole smiled. "You didn't think I'd know what your first request would be?"

Cameron shifted restlessly. "It would at least give me something else to think about. I feel so helpless at the moment."

"I understand the doctor intends to put on a walking cast in another ten days or so. That will give you some freedom."

"Did you talk to Allison?"

Cole wandered over to the window and looked out. "Yeah, I talked to her."

"Did you get any answers?"

"None that I liked."

"You didn't expect any of those, did you?"

Cole shrugged. "Guess not."

"Tell me."

He turned away and walked over to the easy chair that sat near the immense four-poster bed. "You've got enough on your mind without adding my problems."

"Which explains exactly why I ask. I'd rather think about yours for a change."

Cole gave his brother a half smile. "I can see your point." He sank into the chair and leaned back, propping his feet on the side of the bed. "Allison told me her dad was fired and given forty-eight hours to get off the premises."

"Good God, Cole! I was right."

"Seems that way. Plus, she said that she wrote me several letters, at least a dozen. When I never responded she gave up."

"Letters you never got, I presume?"

"Right. This was the first time it ever occurred to me that she might have written. She was a lousy correspondent."

"What happened to the letters?"

"We'll probably never know for certain. She recalls giving them to her dad to mail."

"But that makes no sense! Why would he not mail them?"

"Who knows? He was upset over losing his job and having to move. He died a few months afterwards. Who knows what was going through his mind?"

"Are you going to talk to Letty?"

"You're damned right I am. I've asked Allison to come to the ranch for a visit when school's out."

"And she said?"

"Not if Letty's around."

"And you said?"

"I'll take care of Letty."

Cameron laughed. "The hell you did! Good for you, old man."

"Have you talked to Cody?"

"About?"

"He was going to check to see if he could find out anything more about your accident."

"No, we haven't discussed it. No doubt it was some drunk who probably doesn't even remember that night. The sooner we all put it behind us, the better off we'll be."

"I suppose you're right," Cole conceded slowly, not wanting to bring up his suspicions at the moment. "Do you know where Cody is?"

Cameron rolled his eyes. "Cody is a law unto himself and you know it. He keeps his own hours. He does his own thing."

Cole sighed, silently agreeing with Cameron's

assessment. "I feel that I'm letting him down. He's always been something of a loner and I didn't attempt to get closer to him. I buried myself in my work."

"We both did."

"But if Letty treated him the same way she treated you—"

"You have to hand it to her in one respect, Cole. The woman's consistent."

"I need to talk to Cody about it."

"Good luck. Maybe you'll be more successful than I've been in the past. He's always kept his own counsel with me. But then you've always been his hero, so maybe he'll open up to you."

"What's this hero business?"

Although he smiled, Cameron's eyes were bleak. "You're an easy man to idolize—every fibre of your being is heroic material."

"That's bull—"

"And modest besides. How can any woman resist you?"

Cole straightened in his chair. "Man, you're getting more ornery with each day. I'll be glad when they let you up."

"I'll be glad when you let me get back to some of my work."

"All right, you win. I'll call and tell them to let you have anything you want. The worst that can happen is that you'll end up in bed again." He came to his feet and stood beside the bed. "Hang in there, buddy. You've almost got this thing licked.''

"Sure I do.''

"Have you seen Trisha this morning?''

The flash of pain that suddenly appeared on Cameron's face at his words caught Cole off guard.

"I, uh, no, I haven't. I'm not ready to face her just yet. She's such a reminder of...'' His voice trailed off.

"I can't tell you what to do, Cam, but I think you're making a mistake. Just be thankful you have her and that you've been given the opportunity to be with her every day of her life.''

Cameron's eyes registered his understanding of Cole's meaning. "I know what you're saying and I know you're right, but every time I see Trisha, all I can think about is Andrea.'' His voice roughened during the last few words.

"Do what you have to do,'' Cole said softly. "I understand.''

He left Cameron's room, and went looking for Letty. When he found her she was out in her vegetable garden, criticizing one of the hired hands for some dereliction of her instructions.

Letitia Callaway was of average height and in the past few years had added some weight to her gaunt frame. She wore her hair, a heavy mixture of gray and brown, pulled tightly back from her face into a bun. Her face might have been pretty at one time, but years of frowning and irritableness had made their indelible mark.

"When you're through there, Letty," he said, pitching his voice so that she would hear it from where he stood at one of the rear entrances, "I'd like to have a word with you."

"What is it now, Cole? Can't you see I'm busy?"

"I can see that you're keeping that man from doing his job. Why don't you let him do it without your help?"

She spun on her heel and marched toward him. She wore her usual jeans and shirt and boots, as though she were ready to go horseback riding at any time. Cole couldn't remember ever having seen her on a horse.

"He's not doing what he was told," she exclaimed as she came up to stand beside Cole.

"Alfredo has managed to keep us with fresh vegetables for more years than I can remember, Letty. I doubt that he needs your advice."

"But I told him that—"

"Come in and have a glass of iced tea. I want to talk to you."

"So you said. I don't know what's so all-fired important that it can't wait. What are you doing here, anyway? Cody said you probably wouldn't be here for another week or more. What's going on in Austin? Have those idiots made up their minds yet what they want? I can't believe—"

"Letty?"

"What?"

"Let's allow the politicians to run the government without our help for a moment, all right?"

She sniffed, then turned away and started for the kitchen, her back stiff.

Cole shook his head. What made a woman turn out to be so filled with resentment, so bitter about so much? He wished he knew. She'd been this way for as long as he could remember. Not that he'd ever let her disposition bother him. He'd adopted his dad's attitude toward her, tuning her out most of the time, tolerating her the rest.

He followed her into the kitchen. She had two large glasses filled with ice and was pouring their tea while Angie, the family cook, worked across the room chopping up vegetables.

"How's it going, Angie?" Cole said.

She glanced around and when she saw who it was, she gave him a brilliant smile. "Why, I didn't know you were here, Cole! Are you looking for some of my fresh baked cookies?" Before he could answer, she reached over and pulled out a handful from the cookie jar and put them on a small plate.

"Thank you most kindly, Angie. You sure do know how to treat a man."

He heard Letty snort in the background. Angie handed him a tray. He reached around Letty and picked up the two glasses, added the plate of cookies to the tray and started out of the kitchen.

"Where do you think you're going with that?" Letty demanded.

Without breaking his stride, Cole called back over his shoulder. "I know where I'm going with it, Letty. Into the study."

By the time she caught up with him he'd sprawled himself in the big chair behind the desk and put his boots on its shining surface.

"Cole! Get your feet off the furniture. That's no way to sit. My gosh—"

"Enough, Letty," he said, reaching for a cookie. "Sit down. We need to talk."

She marched over and sat on the edge of the chair in front of the desk, her spine rigid. "All right, then talk."

"I want to know about Tony Alvarez."

She froze, staring at him as though he'd used a particularly obscene phrase. "I beg your pardon?"

"You heard me."

"What in the world is this all about?"

"I want you to tell me about Tony Alvarez." He said it clearly and with precision.

"I have nothing to say on the subject."

"Letty, you have run this place for the past fifteen years with an iron fist in an iron glove. Unfortunately I've allowed it. I can make excuses for my behavior—I was young, grief-stricken, overwhelmed by new responsibilities, attempting to get an education, trying not to fail in my duties...you name it. What I want to hear from you is how do you explain your behavior during this time?''

She started to get up and he gave her a level stare that seemed to freeze her in place, halfway out of the chair. Slowly she lowered herself. In a voice that he hadn't heard in years, she asked, ''What's wrong, Cole? What's upset you? Tell me about it.''

He heard the traces of the warm, compassionate woman she must once have been, but only traces. Her face showed almost no expression.

''We're not talking about me, Letty,'' he said, ignoring her gambit. ''I want to know about you.''

She held his gaze for several minutes in silence before she finally dropped her eyes to her lap.

''Why, Letty? Why did you fire Tony Alvarez?''

Her head jerked upward. ''I never—''

He held his hand up as though halting traffic. It had the same effect on Letty. ''I want to know the truth, Letty. I've listened to your lies for years. It's time for the truth.''

''I don't know what you're—''

''Letty...'' The warning in his voice stopped her exhortations of innocence. ''The day after the funerals—'' neither one of them needed to be reminded of the funerals he referred to ''—you called Tony Alvarez into this office and you fired him. You told him he had forty-eight hours to leave the ranch. I want to know why.''

She lifted her chin slightly. "What difference does it make? All of that happened years ago."

"I want to know why, Letty. We will sit here until I get the information I want from you. So it's your choice how long we sit here and play this out."

"Tony Alvarez was trash. He was never any good. I could never understand what Grant saw in him in the first place."

Cole reached for a cigarette and carefully lighted it before he said, "For your information, Tony Alvarez was the only reason that Dad made it back from Korea. He'd been wounded and left for dead. Tony went back and got him. He managed to carry Dad to safety."

"Ha! Is that what Tony told you?"

"No. That's what Dad told me. Tony was given a Medal of Honor for his heroic act, but nobody ever heard about it around here. He made Dad promise not to mention it."

"So why did he?"

"Because I was asking about Tony one day and Dad told me that if it hadn't been for Tony, none of us—me, Cameron or Cody—would have been here. That we would never have been born."

"That sounds like Grant. He was always so dramatic."

"He wasn't the only one with a flair for drama, Letty. You've certainly provided enough scenes over the years to have won several awards."

She stared at Cole in astonishment. "Cole! I've never seen you like this before. You've always treated me with love and respect. What is the matter with you? Has this affair with Cameron been too much for you? I don't—"

"So you decided to get rid of Tony and Allison as soon as Dad was gone. What was it, a chance to flex your newfound power over three young boys?"

"We didn't need him around."

"On the contrary. By the time I got home for Christmas, the place was in total chaos."

"We survived, didn't we?"

"This isn't about survival, Letty. I want to know what you had against Tony that you couldn't wait to get rid of him."

"I told you. He was trash...an opportunist. He always played his cards for the main chance...flirting and smiling, flashing those black eyes as though he were God's gift to all woman-kind."

"What rot! Tony was totally devoted to Kathleen and Allison. I've never known a more devoted family man."

"Oh, sure, by the time you came along, he'd settled down. You don't know what he was like before he married. He was wild. He was—"

"You were in love with him, weren't you?" Cole said quietly, with sudden insight and, at long last, understanding.

"Don't be ridiculous! He might have saved Grant's life but he was a nothing, a nobody. How he could even think that a Callaway would look twice at him, would actually be interested in his advances, would be willing to forget her upbringing! Why, it was out of the question, completely absurd. And so I told him."

He could see that his remark had hit home. Red blotches appeared on her face and neck as she talked, showing more and more agitation.

"When did you tell him that?"

"The afternoon we went out riding, of course. He'd suggested we stop and rest awhile, cool off at the stream. Well, I *was* warm. It had been a beastly hot day. Perhaps I should have made it clear to him that I was not with him for any reason other than wanting to get away from the house for a few hours. I had no idea he'd see my going with him as encouragement. I was young. Too young. Ignorant about men. Nobody had ever paid any attention to me before. I knew I wasn't attractive. It didn't matter. When he kissed me I didn't know what to do. I was flustered. Then he kept on kissing me and kissing me. It was horrible!"

"Horrible?"

"The way he made me feel, like some wanton who cared nothing about herself or her reputation. Who only wanted a man to—to—" Her words began to slow down and she realized what she was saying. She stared at Cole in horror at her loss of control.

"So he seduced you?"

"No! But he told me a bunch of nonsense about loving me and wanting to marry me. Lies. They were all lies and I knew it. I laughed at him. Told him he was a fool to even consider that a Callaway would marry him. He was nothing—less than nothing. I remounted my horse and rode home. I learned my lesson well that day. I've never been on a horse since. I'll not be tempted by the earthiness of riding a sweating horse. I hated it. Just as I hated Tony Alvarez!"

Cole studied the woman across from him, seeing her as though for the first time. Letty Callaway— a person so filled with ridiculous pride that she had forbidden herself the most simple of pleasures— the joys that can be shared between a man and a woman. Instead she had become a twisted carica- ture of an old maid, taking out her anger and re- sentment on all those around her.

How could he not have seen her for who she really was? How could he have allowed this woman to care for his brothers at the impression- able ages of ten and fifteen?

She had fired Tony Alvarez because he was a constant reminder of her own sensual nature. He knew now that she would never tell him what she told Tony that day. Perhaps she had only told him to get out, without giving a reason. So he had left, grief-stricken, mourning not only the loss of his best friend but of the life he'd established there on the ranch.

What must he have felt when Allison had told him she was pregnant? It wasn't the pregnancy he must have been ashamed of, but the fact that his grandchild would be a Callaway. Of course he hadn't wanted Allison to have any contact with Cole. He probably thought that Cole was enough like Letty to merely laugh at the idea of marrying an Alvarez.

Dear God! What a mess.

Letty sat watching him with a hint of uncertainty. When she saw that he was aware of her once again, she said, "Don't you see, Cole? It doesn't matter anymore. All of that happened so long ago. None of it matters."

"You think not? Then let me disabuse you of your misconception, Letty. When Allison Alvarez left the Circle C, she and I were unaware of the fact that she was carrying my baby."

Letty gasped. All color left her face. She sat there staring at him, her horror almost tangible.

"Because of your hatred, because of your stupid, silly pride, because of your ridiculous belief that being a Callaway meant anything at all, you deprived me of my son for the past fourteen years."

"Oh, no, Cole," she whispered, her hands clenched together and pressed against her mouth.

"I only found out a few weeks ago that I had a

son and that he lives within a few hours of me.
Yesterday I went to see Allison and we talked
about what had happened and why. The day you
told him to leave, you succeeded in killing Tony
Alvarez as surely as if you had shot him. It took
him less than a year to die after that.''

She let out an anguished cry, but he ignored her.

"The irony is that my son is also named Tony
Alvarez—the son who should have been brought
up on this ranch, the son who will someday inherit
all that I have, carries the name of the man you
scorned and turned away from here.''

Tears streamed down her face. "Oh, Cole, I
didn't know. How could I have known? I would
never have— You know I couldn't have possibly
sent them away if I'd known!''

"Letty, after what I have learned these past few
days, there isn't anything that you could do that
would surprise me." He studied her for a moment
in silence. She looked as though she'd aged ten
years. Her rigid spine was now bowed, her head,
which she had always held like royalty, was bent.

She had to live with what she had done, just as
he did. The difference was, he had never been
given a choice.

Cole stood and walked over to the door. Just
before he opened it, he said, "I've invited Allison
and Tony to visit the ranch as soon as school is
out. I would prefer that you take a nice long trip
somewhere, preferably out of the state or even the

country. I don't care where you go, I'll pay for it. I just want you away from here for the summer. Come September we'll talk about this, when we've both had more time to think about the situation. I want my son. I don't know if Allison will ever be able to forgive me for allowing you the freedom to send them away. I'm not sure I'll ever be able to forgive myself. You see, I've trusted you because you were family. As a result, you deprived me of the family I've always wanted.''

Cole opened the door and walked into the hallway, quietly closing the door behind him. Then he went out to the barn and saddled one of the horses. If there was any peace to be found, he knew he would find it in the hills.

Seven

"Mom?"

"Yes, sweetheart."

"Is something wrong?"

Allison looked up at Tony seated across the kitchen bar from her. "No, of course not, why?"

"I dunno. You just haven't said much since I got home. Are things all right at the shop?"

"Everything's fine. Sorry I've been distracted."

"Guess you miss Ed, huh?" he offered tentatively.

"Who?"

His eyes widened. "Ed, Mom. You've been seeing him for over a year now! Whadaya mean, who?"

Allison could feel the heat fill her face and knew that the color had betrayed her. She knew she was going to have to explain, but she wasn't sure how much to say, or what to say, for that matter. She wasn't surprised that Tony noticed her preoccupation. They were both highly tuned to each other's moods.

"Guess who came into the shop Friday afternoon?" she asked brightly.

He eyed her with suspicion. Apparently her cheerful tone hadn't fooled him, either. "Who?"

"Cole Callaway."

He dropped his fork into his spaghetti and stared at her in shock. "You mean *the* Cole Callaway? The one I met on Padre? The one—"

"Yes, Tony. That Cole Callaway."

"Wow! He actually came to Mason! Why didn't you call me? We could have come into town and seen him. Maybe we could have gone to dinner or something. Or maybe—"

"He couldn't stay long," she told him. "He was just passing through, but when he saw the gallery on the square he remembered running in to you, so he stopped in to say hello."

"You mean you know him?"

"Yes, I know him."

"And you never told me?"

"It never occurred to me to mention it to you, Tony. I wasn't aware you knew who he was."

"I didn't until last fall," he said matter-of-factly.

"We studied him in current events when he was in all the papers about trying to get a legislative bill passed regarding offshore drilling rights. I had to do a bunch of research and give a report on him."

It was Allison's turn to stare at him in astonishment, struck by the irony of the situation. "Why didn't you tell me?"

He gave her a superior smirk and repeated, "It never occurred to me to mention it to you," he said in a sweetly falsetto voice. "I wasn't aware you knew who he was."

"Touché," she murmured, as the shaft went home.

"So how do you know him?" he asked after another bite of food.

She gave a quick prayer requesting immediate assistance and said, "Well, actually, we grew up together."

"You did?"

"Uh-huh. Your grandfather was foreman of his father's ranch."

"Then it *was* Granddad—the Tony Alvarez he knew."

"Yes."

"Wow. That's totally awesome."

She tried to sound as casual as possible when she said, "He asked if we'd like to come to visit him at his ranch as soon as school is out."

"Are you serious?" he asked, skeptically.

"As a heart attack," she responded gravely.

"Mom!" he shouted, leaping from his chair. "You really mean it! He wants us to go see him? He wants us to actually visit his home? He wants—" He stopped in mid-hop and stared at her. "Why?" he suspiciously demanded to know.

She took a deep breath, exhaled and smiled at her son. "Well, because we managed to lose contact with each other over the years. He thought it providential that he ran into you like that, and found out where we lived. He thought it would give us a chance to catch up on what's been happening with each other and give you a chance to see where I grew up."

"I thought you grew up in San Antonio."

"Well, we lived there for a while."

"How come you've never told me about growing up on a ranch before?"

She shrugged. "Because I was trying to put the past behind me. There were many very painful things that happened to me back then. I didn't need the reminder by discussing my childhood."

He sank back into his chair and nodded. "Oh, yeah. First your mom died, then my dad died, then my granddad died. I guess that was pretty rough on you, wasn't it?"

She looked down at her plate, where she had wound spaghetti around the tines of her fork as well as around the handle of her fork. "Yes...yes, it was."

"So are we going to go?"

"If you'd like."

"You bet I would. When do we leave?"

"We haven't made any of the final arrangements. He said he would call in a few days and we'd discuss them."

"Well, when he calls, can I talk to him?"

"If you're here, of course you can."

As it turned out, though, Cole called the gallery the following Friday, while Tony was still at school. As soon as she heard his deep voice she knew who it was.

"Sorry I haven't been able to get back with you sooner," he said, once he'd unnecessarily identified himself, "I had several things to take care of that took more time than I thought."

"No problem. We never specified a time."

"True, but I was eager to get back with you to see if you'd given the matter any more consideration."

"I've more than considered it...I mentioned the invitation to Tony. Now the whole idea is out of my hands. He's been packed, ready to go, since five minutes after I told him you'd come to visit."

There was a silence that made her wonder if he was taken aback by her remarks. When he spoke, she realized that she was right. He hadn't expected her to be so open to the idea of returning to the ranch, even for a visit.

"How, uh, did he take it? I mean, about my visit...the reason for it."

"I didn't tell him. I haven't decided what to do about that aspect of the situation. He thinks his father is dead. For the time being, I see no reason to upset him with another explanation."

"I see."

There was another long pause.

"Look, Cole. I know this is hard for you. It isn't easy for me, either. Learning that you never got my letters has been quite a shock for me. It's taken time for me to adjust to the idea that you've never known. I mean, for years I assumed that you didn't care, and now to find out that—well, it's just hard to readjust years of thinking something happened a certain way, then discovering it didn't."

"I'm in the same place, Allison, believe me. I've lain awake nights thinking about the things I could have done. I could have hired somebody to find you. I could have insisted Letty tell me where you'd gone. I guess what I've discovered is that regrets are the most useless waste of energy known to man."

"I know."

"The thing is, I'd like to put all of that behind us, if you think you can. I'd like to begin again. I just met this very attractive widow with a fourteen-year-old boy. I'd like to get to know them both a great deal better."

Allison's heart leaped in her chest and began to race in reaction to his remark. "Uh, Cole, I, uh, don't think that's a good idea." She rushed into an explanation. "I mean, I can understand that you want to get to know Tony. That's only natural. And I know he's going to want to get to know you. Would you believe that he did a report on you last fall for his current-events class? That's positively eerie when you think about it. But as for me, well, that's behind us now and besides, I'm seeing Ed and it wouldn't be right if—"

"Ed? Who's Ed?"

She smiled at the irritation in his voice. "He's the fellow I've been seeing for the past year. You remember, I mentioned that he was out of town last week."

"You mean you and this Ed are serious?"

No, she wanted to say. But Ed was safe. She was comfortable with him. He was undemanding, appreciating her companionship when he was in town, which was usually only once a month or so. But did she want Cole to know that?

"All I'm saying is that you and I were friends a long time ago. Let's see if we can continue that friendship without any complications, okay?"

Cole clinched his teeth in an effort not to say what immediately came to mind. No, it wasn't okay. Of course he wanted a friendship with her, but he wanted a hell of a lot more than that. He'd been cheated the first time around, but this time he intended to fight for what he wanted.

"Sure, Allison," he said instead. "Whatever you say."

He heard her sigh of relief. "Thanks for being so understanding, Cole. I really appreciate it."

"No problem. Oh, by the way, I drove Letty to Austin today. She and a friend decided to tour Europe this summer. They plan to take a couple of cruises through the Scottish Isles and along the Riviera. So you'll be visiting the Callaway brothers as we 'bach' it here on the ranch."

"How is Cameron?"

"Improving. Cross as a bear. I think seeing you would really cheer him up."

"You think so?" she asked, intrigued.

"I know so." But don't even think of volunteering to nurse him through this bad time in his life!

Eventually they got around to discussing when school let out and when they could get away. Allison had already arranged with Suzanne to run the gallery while she was gone. By the time they hung up, Allison had agreed to allow Cole to come to Mason to pick them up.

Cole smiled with satisfaction as he moved away from the phone. Though he knew that he would have to work eighteen-hour days for the next few weeks in order to spend some time at the ranch the first part of June, he didn't care. He'd do whatever he had to do in order to have Allison back at the Circle C.

She'd always been stubborn. It was part of her charm. He had a definite advantage over this Ed character. He knew her so well. He knew what made her tick. He knew what could set her off.

He could only hope that somewhere, deeply buried within her, she still loved him. That hope would fuel his resolve during the next hectic weeks.

Allison elected to sit in the back seat of the luxury car so that Tony and Cole could visit. Cole had carefully hidden his smile when she first suggested the seating arrangements, blandly agreeing to whatever the two of them wished to do.

They hadn't been on the road half an hour before Cole realized that he might have been a little too smug. Tony Alvarez had a sharp mind that he continued to hone with a startling array of insightful questions.

"How long have you known my mom?" he asked, starting off innocuously enough.

Cole glanced through his aviator shades into the rearview mirror. Allison was turning the pages of a magazine, seemingly oblivious to the conversation in the front seat. Fine with him. He would be delighted to give his son as many details as requested.

"Since she was born, although I don't remember that particular time in our relationship," he said, eyeing the back seat in hopes of a reaction. "I was only two and a half at the time. The first memory I have of your mother was her following me everywhere I went, like an eager puppy."

Tony laughed. "I would've liked to've seen that!"

"She was a good sport, though, I'll have to admit. From the time I could dress myself I always had chores to do around the place. Allison would be right there helping me."

Tony glanced over his shoulder. "No wonder she's so big on my doing chores. She probably thinks they build character or something." Only a hint of disgust betrayed his attitude on the subject.

"Probably," Cole agreed without giving way to a smile.

"So how come the two of you lost touch with each other, if you're such good friends?"

Ouch. The kid had unerringly gone to the touchiest button and leaned on it with nonchalant skill.

Once again Cole looked into the rearview mirror. This time Allison was looking at him, waiting to see what he would say. It would serve her right if Cole told him the truth, but he knew that now wasn't the time to hit Tony with a full view of the past. He wouldn't do that to him, no matter how much he ached to get beneath Allison's guard.

"Several things happened at about the same time that were traumatic for both of us. You have to remember that we weren't much older than you are now." He heard the words and felt the emotional impact of them at the same time. My God! Allison had only been a little more than three years older than Tony when she got pregnant! She'd been a mere baby! "I was going to college back East when my folks were in an automobile accident. They were both killed."

"Gee, that's too bad. I'm really sorry."

"Thanks. Nobody's ready to lose their folks, but especially not in such a sudden, brutal fashion." He was quiet for a moment, remembering. "I was really wrapped up in my own grief at the time. It was only later that I discovered your mom and grandfather had moved away from the ranch. I never heard from them again."

"Did you know my dad?"

"Your dad?" he croaked, then cleared his throat.

"Yeah. Mom never talks about him much. I guess it must be really painful for her, even after all this time. Sometimes I wonder if I remind her of him or something. She'll look at me once in a while and get this really funny expression on her face, like she's remembering something...or somebody. I used to ask her about him a lot when I was younger but I could tell it upset her whenever I brought him up, so I just stopped asking."

"Well, uh, I don't remember him," he finally said. "She must have met him after they moved away."

"Oh. I guess it really doesn't matter. I mean, I'm sorry he died and all, but I'm just glad he was around then. Otherwise I wouldn't be here!"

"That's true."

"The way I figure it, it isn't as important where you came from if you know where you're headed."

"Sounds like a sound philosophy to me. I take it you know where you're going?"

"I hope so. Mom insists I go to college and I guess she's right, but what I really intend to do is work the rodeo circuit for a few years, like my granddad. Boy! You should see the trophies and things he won. I figure with the prize money I'll make I'll save enough to buy a ranch."

"Is that what you want to be, a rancher?"

Tony grinned. "I know, you're going to tell me that you can't make any money being a rancher. I've heard all those stories all my life. But I notice that everybody who tells me that is real content to remain a rancher!"

"The thing to do is to diversify."

Tony looked at him, puzzled. "What's that mean?"

"That means that you do a little ranching, invest in some real estate, maybe get into the oil business, or find a little business somewhere, or—"

"Oh! You mean like you did. But then, you already had a lot of that stuff in your family, didn't you? I mean, you didn't have to go out and do it all on your own."

Nothing like a fourteen-year-old to cut you off at the knees! "That's true. But I've made our businesses even more profitable, improved our strain of cattle—"

"Got laws passed to help your oil business," Tony added helpfully.

Cole's eyes cut to the boy sitting beside him watching the scenery roll by. What the hell did the kid breakfast on, anyway, the *Wall Street Journal?* He glanced into the mirror. All he saw was the top of Allison's head as she continued reading the magazine.

"Are you hungry?" he asked in a desperate attempt to change the subject.

Tony grinned. "I'm always hungry. Mom calls me the bottomless pit."

"We can stop up here for something to eat, if that's all right with you. They make the best smoked ribs I've ever eaten. Their barbecue sauce is a highly guarded secret."

"Sounds great." Tony turned his sparkling black eyes toward Cole in anticipation. It was at that exact moment that Cole truly lost his heart to his son.

Eight

"Of course I remember you, Allison," Cameron said, standing in the hallway on his crutches, grinning. He'd had the walking cast for a couple of weeks. The cast had come off his arm the week before. "I had the biggest crush on you when I was growing up. You were my idea of the perfect woman."

Cole and Tony had their bags still in their arms when Allison had opened the door and held it for them. What he didn't need at the moment was for his brother to be gushing over their houseguest. He glanced at Allison. She had a delightful confusion about her, which gave her an even more attractive glow. She didn't need to look any more attractive than she already did.

"Why, thank you, Cam," she managed to say with a husky laugh.

Cameron sighed. "There's just something about you older women that can really get to a guy." He pretended to dodge her expected retaliation and turned to Tony. "Hi! You must be Tony. I'm Cameron, Cole's brother. His much younger brother."

"All right, all right. You made your point." Cole turned to the others. "He's really become incorrigible since he's been home. Too much free time. I can hardly wait to ship him back to the office."

Tony turned and looked at Cameron. "I'm very pleased to meet you, sir."

"Ah, now here's someone who knows how to show some respect."

Cole drawled, "Oh, Cameron, why don't you have Tony share with you his views on real estate versus oil investments over the profit margins of raising cattle?" Cole's smile couldn't be more innocent. "Meanwhile I'll show Allison where they'll be staying." He motioned to Allison to follow him up the stairs, wishing he'd had a camera to capture the look on Cam's face when Tony accepted the choice of subject and started to talk.

Cole chuckled to himself all the way up the stairs.

"Cameron seems to be adjusting well to everything that happened, hasn't he?"

"Don't kid yourself. He's keeping it all bottled up inside. One of these days he's going to blow."

"Oh. I remember him as very quiet. Really shy."

Cole gave her a wolfish grin. "I'm sure he was, around you."

She shook her head in a gesture signifying the futility of having a serious conversation at the moment.

He stopped in front of one of the doors, put the luggage down, then opened the door. "I thought I'd put you in here. It will be a little more convenient for you, as this room has a bathroom attached." He set her bag just inside the door, then continued down the hallway. "I thought I'd put Tony in here. This was Cody's old room. Rather than take down all the posters and things, he just moved to a bigger bedroom." He turned to her. "Do you realize that Tony is the same age difference with Cody as I am with Cody? They could easily be brothers."

"Except they aren't."

He didn't look at her, but set the suitcase at the end of the bed. When he turned to look at her, he could see the pain in her eyes. Forgetting his own apprehension, Cole walked over to Allison and slipped his arms around her waist. "It's going to work out all right. You'll see. I'm just glad to have you both here."

She slipped her arms around his waist, hanging

on to his belt loops in the back. "All of this seems so strange."

He leaned back so that he could see her face. "How do you mean?"

"I don't feel that I should be upstairs. In all the years I lived on the ranch, I was never upstairs. I could visit in certain designated rooms downstairs, but not up here. I don't feel like I belong here."

"Oh, honey, that isn't true. Who told you that you couldn't come up here?"

"It was never said out loud. It was just something that I understood from a very early age."

"Then it's time to get rid of those ideas, okay? Come on. Let's show Tony around the place. I'd like you to see some of the changes we've made, as well."

By the time Allison retired to her room that night, her head ached with confusion and anxiety. She felt as though she were in some kind of a time warp, as though the past fifteen years had never happened, as though she'd never left the ranch, her father had never died, everything had continued on. And then she would glance around and see Tony eagerly asking questions...touching, patting, stroking, looking at everything around him, absorbing it all like a tall, gangly sponge.

She ached for him. All of this should have been a part of his growing up. How could she possibly let him know the truth? How could she explain all of the circumstances? He'd never heard of Letitia Callaway, and she sincerely hoped he never did.

Even now, standing in the spacious bedroom that Cole had given to her, she felt guilty—as though Letty might burst in at any moment and tell her to get out!

What a bunch of nonsense. She was just tired, that's all. She hadn't been able to sleep last night except for short intervals. All she could think about was the fact that she was returning to the past she'd tried so hard to forget. As soon as they had turned off the highway onto the ranch road, she had known that this homecoming was going to be even more painful than she could have guessed.

She had immediately spotted the changes that had updated and modernized the place. The new Spanish tile roof sparkled in the sunlight, a brilliant contrast to the dazzling-white freshly painted adobe.

This time they didn't take the lane down to the married quarters, but pulled up in front of the ten-foot-high door. She was a guest, now—a guest of the Callaways.

Looking around the bedroom, she reminded herself of that fact. Well, then, she would enjoy her new status to the fullest.

She walked over to the door of the bathroom and peered inside. This one displayed all the latest innovations a luxurious bathroom could possibly have. A square Jacuzzi tub took up almost one whole wall. There were steps leading up to it. A double-size shower stall with glass panels on three sides was on another wall. The long countertop had two sinks. The mirrors reflected each other—one above the counter, the other an entire wall of mirrors.

She'd never seen anything quite so decadent or more inviting. With a giggle she hadn't heard out of herself since she was a child, Allison began to run her bathwater.

The shelves along the side of the tub had an array of bath oils, soaps and other toiletries. She hurried back into the bedroom only to discover that someone had been in earlier and unpacked her things. She found her sleep shirt in the second drawer she opened.

By the time she returned, the tub was full. She noted a large pillar candle on the shelf with a small package of matches. On impulse, she lighted the candle, then turned out the overhead light. Immediately the mirrors caught and reflected the soft glow of the candlelight, softening the edges of her world. She slipped out of her clothes and stepped into the tub.

The water felt heavenly to her tired body. She touched a switch that started the jets on all sides of her. Slowly she dropped her head back on the padded side of the tub and closed her eyes. She felt like the pampered darling of the rich and famous.

The slight click she heard sounded like a door

opening, which couldn't be possible, she thought, opening her eyes. They continued to widen. Cole walked into the bathroom from a door on the opposite side of the one she'd entered from. He wore a short, bright green terry robe.

The water's continual churning had created a concealing froth of foam; nevertheless Allison sank into the water up to her chin.

"What are you doing here?" she tried to say, but ended up choking on some bubbles that popped into her mouth as soon as she opened it, so that the end of the sentence came out in a sputter. He seemed to understand her well enough, however.

He raised his brows. "Oh, didn't I tell you?" he asked in an innocent voice. "Our rooms share the same bath."

"No," she managed to say in a strangled tone, "you neglected to mention that *insignificant* little fact."

"Oh." He glanced around the room, then back at her. "This is my favorite part of the day, when I can come in here after a hard day and relax. I see you found the candle. The light's much better like that, isn't it?"

He reached for the sash of his robe.

"What do you think you're doing?"

He looked a little puzzled. "You don't mind if I share the tub with you, do you? I mean, there's plenty of room for two without crowding."

While she was trying to spit out her objection,

Yes, I certainly do mind, the words soon lost their purpose because he'd discarded his robe and stepped into the tub.

The sight of his massive, nude body took her breath away, effectively demolishing her communicating abilities.

She hadn't seen a grown man nude before, she realized now. The changes that she had only guessed at when she saw Cole again were now vividly and advantageously displayed. His broad chest was liberally covered with hair. His arms and shoulders were immense. His hips and thighs were—she closed her eyes with fierce determination while she felt the turbulent action of the water shift to accommodate his bulk.

He'd been right. There was room for two, as long as they didn't mind their legs intertwining. With a nonchalance that she could only marvel at, Cole lightly lifted her ankles and placed them on each side of his hips. His calves, ankles and feet were meanwhile insidiously enfolding her thighs and hips.

She heard his sigh of pleasure. "Isn't this great? I just had this bathroom redone last winter, but it was well worth the inconvenience and expense. Guaranteed to make all those aches and pains go away."

He didn't mention the aches that it suddenly created.

"Cole, you have no business coming in here and

you know it. How do you think Tony would react if he knew you were in here with me?''

"Is there any reason for him to find out?''

"Of course not, it's just—''

"It's no one's business what you do in the privacy of your own bathroom, is it?''

"The point is—''

"The point is that you're supposed to be relaxing and now you're getting all tensed up.'' He ran his hands along her legs, from thighs to calves, kneading the muscles.

"Cole! Stop that!''

"Relax, honey. I'm not going to take advantage of you.''

"What do you think you've just done? You placed me in a room where you knew we would be sharing a bath, but you didn't bother to tell me. You wait until I'm in a very vulnerable position, then walk in on me. You...'' She seemed to run out of words.

"Yes?'' he asked helpfully, lifting a brow.

"Would you please get out until I'm through with my bath?''

"No. Anything else?'' he asked with a smile.

"Fine. Then I'll get out and you can have your bath and your fancy—'' She had been matching actions with words until it suddenly occurred to her that if she were to crawl out of the tub at this particular moment, she would be even more exposed.

Allison slid back into the water up to her chin and glared at him.

"Come on, relax and enjoy yourself, honey. I promise I won't bite." His grin suddenly flashed. "Of course I might consider doing a little nibblin' here and there, if I was coaxed." Cole picked up the hand soap and began to smooth it across his broad and brawny chest.

Determined to ignore his provocative comment, Allison focused on his movements and slowly found herself mesmerized by his sensual actions. The thick hair on his chest swirled as the soap and water coaxed them into patterns.

Once again she became aware of how good the water felt swirling around her. There was no reason for her to get into such an uproar. She was certainly in no danger.

Aren't you? a nagging little voice asked. When was the last time you reacted to a man like you're reacting now?

How was she supposed to act, for heaven's sake? She'd never been in a bath with a man before.

"Cole, why are you doing this?"

His eyes met hers. "All I've been able to think about for the past several weeks was this visit. I went over and over what it would be like to have you back here on the ranch. What it came down to was that I wanted to get close to you again. I wanted to reestablish the line of communication we had all our lives. I know we can't just forget about what happened or dismiss the past fifteen years, but I want to overcome the pain we both went through.'' He shrugged. ''I don't want the visit to be a polite gesture. We scarcely talked today because of the people around us. I need more than that. I think we both do.'' He spread his soapy hands, ''So, here we are, getting reacquainted.''

''I won't make love to you,'' she stated firmly.

''Thanks for the information, honey, but I haven't asked.''

She could feel her face heating up. ''Just so we understand each other,'' she muttered.

''Now that we have that out of the way, come here and let me scrub your back.'' Saying that he reached for her and pulled her toward him, turning her as she came closer so that her back was to him.

He began to knead the muscles at the back of her skull, whispering in a low voice, ''Relax,'' as he continued to work down each vertebra of her spine. The combination of knowledgeable touch and soothing tone soon took effect and she began to relax against him. Eventually she realized he was no longer stroking her back. Now she lay against his chest while his arms encircled her waist.

In this position she had no trouble recognizing that he was aroused. His hands lightly stroked her midriff, occasionally brushing the underside of her breasts, which felt full and tingling.

Allison knew that she should be protesting the intimacy of the situation, but a sense of lethargy had taken over...her limbs felt heavy, as did her eyelids. Her neck no longer felt strong enough to support her head, and she allowed it to droop against Cole's shoulder. She closed her eyes and sighed in contentment.

"Allison?"

"Hmm."

"I want you to think about something for me during the next couple of weeks, and give me your answer then, not now."

"What is it?" she murmured drowsily.

"I want you to marry me so that you and Tony and I can be together all the time, not just a few days here and there."

An alarm began jangling within her head. She began to stir.

"No, don't start trying to find something negative to say about that statement. I just want you to think about what I've said. I wanted you to know what I want, what I'm planning to work for. You don't have to remind me that I wasn't there when you needed me. I know that. What I'm saying to you is that I want to be there now and for the rest of our lives, not just because you might need me, but because I know in the very depths of my being how very much I need you to make my life whole. I've spent the past fifteen years without you and I've managed. I'd prefer not to continue my life without you." He nudged her head aside slightly and placed a row of fleeting kisses along the side of her neck. "So you think about it, honey, all right? We'll talk about it before you leave."

He eased away from her, then stood, water cascading off him so that she held up her hands in a protective gesture and gasped. He stepped out of the tub and walked down the steps. After toweling himself briskly he pulled the terry robe around him. "Don't drown in there now, you hear?" His smile was wistful as he silently closed the door behind him, leaving her to the solitude of flickering candlelight and the soft sounds of bubbling water.

Allison blinked her eyes a couple of times in an effort to make sure she was awake. She hadn't dreamed the past half hour, had she? Cole had actually walked in on her, hadn't he?

And done what? Caused her to become more aware of him than she had thought possible. She'd known as soon as she made the decision to come to the ranch that she would have to guard herself against his charismatic presence, but she had thought herself safe in the haven of her room and bath.

So what should she do now? Demand another room? Keep the door locked when she was in there? Or wait to see what developed in the coming weeks?

She smiled to herself.

What would be wrong with enjoying her time on the ranch, facing and releasing old memories and hurts, and collecting new, more joyful memories to take back home with her?

She reluctantly pushed the button that stopped the jets, and the water slowly swirled to a few ripples as she got out, feeling a complete lassitude that was belied by the inner excitement that raced through every atom of her being.

The feel of the towel against her sensitive skin made her excruciatingly aware of her body as it brushed across her shoulders and down her back, over her buttocks and the back of her thighs, knees and calves. She returned her attention to her throat and down across her breasts and their rigid tips, down her stomach and abdomen, the gentle brush of cloth causing a tingling that made her shiver with—

"I almost forgot," a low voice said behind her. She looked into the mirror and saw Cole's reflection standing in the doorway as though he'd been watching her for some time. Allison's heart bounded in her chest, more from excitement than fear. Her back was bare, as was her upper torso. Their eyes met in the mirror and he slowly advanced, sliding his arms around her and palming her breasts. "Allison, you are so beautiful." He kissed her on the nape of her neck, his hair brushing against her jaw. As though she were no more than a windup mechanical toy, Allison slowly turned in his arms until she was facing him, her neck arched so that her lips were only a hairbreadth away from his. She came up on her toes until her mouth pressed against his, feeling their firmness gentle and warm at her touch. Audaciously she flicked her tongue across them. He made a growling sound in the back of his throat and scooped her up into his arms without lessening the pressure of his mouth.

Allison's head spun from the sudden movement. The only solid, dependable point in her universe at the moment was Cole, and she clung to him, her arms around his neck, her mouth yielding to his.

The next sensations she became aware of were the softness of finely woven sheets at her back and his weight on top of her. When he raised his head for a moment they both took in great gasps of air before he sought her breast with his tongue, stroking, flicking and rolling the pink tip in energetic play. She arched her back, holding his head against her.

He ran his callused palms along her sides and down her thighs, smoothing, then inciting a response. Each stroke brought his hands closer to her inner thighs until he paused at the top of her inner thigh and touched her inquiringly.

Any doubt as to her readiness for him was immediately dispelled. She undulated her hips, moving as close to him as she could with his weight pinning her down. He shifted, so that she could ease her legs wider apart, giving her the freedom she needed to arch up into him.

This time his groan was mixed with a muttering of, "I'm sorry, honey, but I can't—" before he plunged deeply inside.

Allison no longer cared what it was he couldn't. She was all too aware of just what he could—and was—doing to give her pleasure.

The years had faded her memories of the only other time this man had made love to her. There was no comparison she could make at the moment. All she could do was to feel and respond to his touch and masculine scent, to the sound of his harsh breathing and the taste of him on her lips.

The fast fury of their coming together was too intense to be prolonged. She felt herself suddenly contract, then begin a series of spasmodic movements deep inside that caused him to lose what little remaining control he had.

He cried out as he made a convulsive movement, burying himself deep within her. He wrapped his arms around her and held her tightly, almost sobbing with the intensity of the moment.

A longing never to let go of him swept over her, and she squeezed him to her, her legs wrapped fiercely around his thighs. He sighed and rolled so that they lay side by side, locked into each other's arms, his eyes closed. His face was flushed and damp. She smiled, touching her finger to his cheek. He opened his eyes and stared into hers a short distance away.

"That wasn't part of the plan," he murmured ruefully.

"Oh?"

"No. What I intended to do was to make you aware of me on a more physical basis."

"You certainly managed to do that."

"What I mean is, I wanted you to want me. I hoped to get past that barrier you've had around you ever since my first visit to Mason."

"Well, you succeeded there."

"I thought I would have more self-control. I thought I could see you and touch you without taking it any further."

"Ah. You planned to get me all stirred up and then walk away?"

He gave her a tentative, half smile. "Something like that."

"How ungentlemanly of you."

"Perhaps."

"Tonight doesn't prove anything, Cole."

"It proves that we're both very compatible in bed."

"But it isn't a reason to base a decision on."

"It's a hell of a start."

"Cole, we were a couple of kids before who knew nothing about what we wanted in life."

"Speak for yourself. I always knew what I wanted. Nothing's changed."

"*I've* changed, Cole. I'm no longer the little pig-tailed girl that used to follow you everywhere."

He ran his hand down her side, tracing her curves. "I'll admit to some changes, but I see nothing wrong with them."

"I've been on my own for a long time, Cole. I've learned to appreciate my freedom and my independence."

"Do you think that I'm asking you to give those up?"

"Aren't you?"

"Hell, no. I'm proud as punch you've made a name for yourself, that you found your talents and developed them. All I'm saying is that I want you in my life."

"You want me...or Tony?"

He leaned up on his elbow and stared down at her. "What are you saying?"

She stared at him for several moments before she admitted, "I'm not certain. All I know is that I've never made any effort to hide from you in all these years, yet you showed no interest in looking me up...until you met Tony. I can understand your desire to get to know your son, Cole. Just don't think that you have to include me in your plans. It doesn't have to be a package deal."

His eyes narrowed and he pulled away from her. Rolling over he flipped on the bedside lamp and reached for his cigarettes. He took his time lighting one, drawing in the smoke for a long moment before exhaling. Finally he glanced around at her. "I don't think this is a good time to discuss Tony, or you, for that matter. If you can think that I would make love to you the way I did just now as part of a plot to have Tony in my life, then you're right, I don't know you very well. And just as important, you sure as hell don't know me.''

The tender lover was gone. For a brief moment Allison felt a wave of despair wash over her as a memory of her grief years before resurfaced. Why had she thought that they could talk about all that had happened without touching some nerves that were still raw?

She reached for his crumpled bathrobe and slipped it around her, then left the bed. ''You see, Cole? Sex never solved a thing.'' She turned away from him and started to the door.

''Is that what it was for you, Allison? A little romp in the hay? No wonder you've stayed single all these years, if it's just a temporary moment of pleasure to you. Afterward you can forget it and walk away.''

She paused, then turned and looked at him as he sat there on the side of the bed, nude, smoking his cigarette.

''Don't start throwing accusations at me, Cole. I haven't heard about you running to the altar in the past fifteen years.''

''You're damn right. I learned at an early age that women can't be trusted to mean what they say.''

Her smile was wry. ''Funny, but I learned the

same lesson about men. I guess we're more alike than I first thought. Good night, Cole.''

She turned and walked out of the room, leaving him to stare at the closed door that symbolized all that stood between them.

Nine

"**H**ow can you stand to live anywhere else, Cole?" Tony asked the next day while they were out riding.

Cole had spent a sleepless night wrestling with ghosts of the past. The early-morning ride he'd planned had been his reason for going back into the bathroom the night before. He'd waited until morning to tap on Allison's bedroom door and ask if she wanted to go with him and Tony.

When she'd joined them downstairs at the breakfast table she didn't look as though she had slept any better than he had. Dark circles lay beneath her heavy-lidded eyes. Although they had been out riding for some time now, she had yet to say a word to either of them, seemingly content to ride over old haunts and renew her memories of the place.

Tony was doing what he could to keep the conversation going.

"It's difficult, I'll admit," Cole finally said. "But I have other businesses to run besides the ranch. That's why I leave the running of this place to the others."

"Like Cameron and Cody?"

"Well, Cameron works fairly closely with me. And Cody, well, I'm not sure that Cody's decided what he wants to do when he settles down. He's in and out of here, but pretty much goes his own way."

"Then who looks after the place?"

"We have a main foreman, and several others who take care of specific areas, and of course my aunt—" Oh, hell, now he'd done it.

"Your aunt?"

"Uh, yeah. She usually oversees the running of the Big House and the domestic duties...that kind of thing."

"How come I haven't seen her?"

"Oh, she's away right now," he said, looking off into the hills to avoid both Allison and Tony.

"Will she be back before we have to leave?"

"I don't think so."

"Oh."

Letty was another problem he'd have to deal with if he was to convince Allison to take a chance on him again. Damn, but he was tired of juggling all of the pieces of his life so that everyone was treated fairly. No matter what she had done, Letty was family. She'd held the family together for years after his folks had died. Somehow, someway, he needed to bring things together in such a way that Allison would accept all of his family as well as him.

After last night, he felt that his battle was definitely uphill. She was probably more apt to accept Letty at the moment than she was him. He'd let his foolish emotions overwhelm him the night before. It was such a stupid mistake to lose control like that. He must have thought he was above succumbing to temptation. Well, he'd sure as hell learned differently.

"Cole?"

Tony's voice broke through Cole's preoccupation with his thoughts, and he realized that Tony had repeated his name a couple of times with no response.

"Sorry, I guess my mind drifted away for a moment," he said with a smile to the teenager riding alongside of him.

"No problem. Mom does that a lot, too," he explained with a grin. "So I'm used to it. I was just wondering where your property lines are. It seems like we've ridden for a few hours and haven't seen anything but occasional cattle and windmills pumping water in reservoirs."

Cole paused and looked around. They had come a fair distance from the ranch buildings. Once he got his bearings, he pointed to a line of rolling hills in the distance. "Those hills mark the northern boundary. The western boundary is near the Mexican border at the Rio Grande."

Tony's eyes widened. "But that's miles and miles."

"That's right."

"Wow!" He glanced around at his mother. "Did you know the Circle C was that big, Mom? It's as big as the King Ranch in south Texas."

"Not quite," Cole admitted, "but close."

Allison wore dark sunshades today as well as a Stetson pulled low over her forehead, so that her eyes were completely hidden and her face was in shadows. "I hate to call a halt to all this fun, fellas," she finally said in a rueful voice, "but it's been awhile since I've been on a horse. If we don't turn back soon, I'll be sitting on a pillow for the next few days."

Tony laughed and glanced at Cole. "Guess we should have left her at home, huh?"

Not on your life, Cole thought to himself. Not with Cameron waiting to entertain her. His thoughts moved to Cody. And where was his younger brother? Surely he'd found out something about the accidents by now.

"Actually, I do need to get back soon. I've got a conference call coming in at eleven."

Even while he spoke, Cole felt a helpless sense of frustration. There was so much he wanted to say to Allison that couldn't be said in front of Tony, and so much he wanted to say to Tony but couldn't. At least, not until he could tell him the truth. He felt as though he'd had his ankles and wrists tied and was expected to function normally.

For the first time in a long while he was faced with a situation over which he had no control. He didn't like it. Hell, he wasn't used to it. He glanced over at Allison who had yet to look at him directly since she'd come downstairs that morning.

What more could he say? He'd been a class-A jerk the night before. What good would an apology do now?

By the time he got off the conference call it was almost one o'clock. When he went looking for the others he found Tony and Cameron in a hot game of poker.

"Where's your mother?" he asked with what he hoped was a casual tone.

Tony glanced around. "Oh, she went upstairs after lunch. Said she was already getting sore from the ride." He flashed the grin that reminded Cole of his Callaway blood. "Guess she's having a tough time keeping up with us, huh?"

Cameron was stretched out on his side on the couch, playing cards off the coffee table, while Tony sat cross-legged on the floor. Cameron glanced up at Cole. "You look a little weary, old

man. Why don't you get yourself a nap? I'll entertain the young 'un here.''

Rosie came in, carrying a tray of lemonade and
cookies. "Did you save me any lunch?" Cole
asked.

"Of course. Do you want me to bring it to
you?"

"No. Just tell me where it is."

"It's on a covered tray in the refrigerator."

He went looking for it, pausing to glance into
the garden room. Originally part of the interior
patio, they had glassed a portion of the area in so
that it could be air-conditioned. Trisha lay sound
asleep in her playpen, her stuffed animals all
around her.

Cole had such a yearning for a daughter just like
her, one that he and Allison could raise together,
one that— A sudden thought struck him, one that
should have surfaced long before now. Oh, no. Oh,
hell! He strode into the kitchen and opened the refrigerator. A salad and several sandwiches awaited
him. He ate them at the breakfast bar, perched on
the edge of the stool, needing to eat but regretting
the time it took. He needed to talk with Allison.
He needed to find out if— What an unthinking idiot
he was. He'd never once thought...

He placed his dishes in the sink, finished off his
second glass of milk and bounded up the stairs.
Allison's door was closed. She could be asleep. If
so, he wouldn't waken her. He went into his bed-

room and began to strip out of his clothes. He needed a shower after that long ride this morning. He stepped into their shared bathroom and instantly caught the scent of her perfume. Her brush and comb lay on the shelf above one of the sinks. He smiled, enjoying the sight of their things sharing the same space.

After finishing his shower, he dried off and went back into his room to dress. He was just about finished buttoning his shirt when he thought he heard a noise from the other room. Still barefoot, he padded into the connecting room and pushed slightly against her door. It swung open noiselessly, revealing Allison in her robe lying on the bed on her stomach, her eyes closed, a frown etched across her forehead.

"What's wrong?" he whispered, in case she was still asleep.

She opened her eyes and saw him. "Don't you ever knock?" she demanded without moving.

"I didn't want to wake you in case you were asleep."

"I hurt too much to sleep."

"Why didn't you say something earlier?"

"And spoil the fun? I haven't seen Tony that animated since his favorite country-western singer appeared in concert in Austin."

"Hold on." He went back into the bathroom and opened the medicine cabinet. Grabbing a bottle, he returned to Allison's room, strode across to the bed and sank onto the side.

"What are you doing?"

"I'm going to give you some relief," he said with a grin.

"I just bet you are!"

"No, I mean it," he reassured her. He began to slide her satin robe up her legs. She pushed up on her elbows with a groan and said, "Cole, you are taking unfair advantage of a crippled person. Now please go away."

He began to laugh. "Honey, I promise that what I intend to do will only give you pleasure, not to mention easing the pain." By the time he'd finished his reassuring speech he'd slid the material to her waist, exposing a delectable backside that he determinedly refused to admire. Detachment was the key.

He warmed the liniment in the palms of his hands, then gently laid his palms on each bared cheek. She flinched. "There now, honey, you're okay," he said in a soothing tone.

"Don't talk to me like—ouch—I'm some kind of—oohh—filly you're trying to calm."

"Wouldn't think of it," he agreed, hiding his grin by looking away.

He ran his hands down the back of her thighs to her knees, then slowly moved them upward, rubbing in a circular motion, until he reached her buttocks once more. He continued the movements until he felt her muscles beginning to relax beneath his experienced fingers. He moved along her legs, sliding his thumbs to her inner thighs and moving them in a circular motion, moving upward by infinitesimal degrees.

Her sighs and moans became more muted and less based on pain. By the time he paused at the top of her inner thighs she was breathing softly and regularly, her eyes closed.

Silently he moved off the bed, capped the liniment bottle and returned to the bathroom. After putting away the medication, he looked ruefully at the shower and contemplated the soothing relief of cold water hitting his overheated body.

Stoically he reminded himself that he'd just showered and he could get his thoughts on other things. He returned to his bedroom and finished dressing, then headed down the stairs. By the time he reached the bottom he could hear Cameron and Tony talking.

"What I don't understand," Tony was saying, "was how come Mom never told me that she knew you guys? I mean, the Callaways are famous. There's always some news about one of you doing something, or winning something or buying something. She sat and watched all of that without saying a word. Don't you find that strange?"

Cole waited to see what Cameron replied, glad that for once *he* wasn't the recipient of Tony's pointed questions.

"Guess you'll have to ask your mom about that. Nobody knows what's going on in another person's head, Tony. It's sheer arrogance to think we can guess."

"Well, I'm beginning to think there's something fishy going on."

"What do you mean?"

"I think Mom and Cole had a fight...like maybe a lovers' quarrel or something."

Cole realized that he was standing just outside the study blatantly eavesdropping. He also recognized that he wasn't about to let his presence be known at this point. He waited for Cameron to respond.

"What makes you think that?"

"It's the way they look at each other, you know? The way they look when they don't think the other is looking. A guy could get scorched if he got caught in the middle of one of those looks." Cameron started laughing and Tony reluctantly chuckled. "It's kinda weird, thinking about my mom interested in somebody."

"I thought you said she was seeing someone."

"Oh, yeah, but that's different. I mean, Ed happens to be in town once or twice a month. They're more friends than anything. Mom doesn't tense up or get all flustered and bothered around Ed like she does Cole."

"Is that right? Interesting."

"Do you think they had a fight?"

"If they did, no one ever mentioned it to me. Of course, I was your age when your mom and grandfather moved away."

"Did you know my dad?"

A pregnant pause followed that one and Cole smiled to himself, wondering if it wasn't time to rescue Cameron.

"Don't believe I did."

"See? That's another thing. How come nobody remembers him? It seems to me—"

"So who's winning?" Cole asked, strolling into the room with his hands in his pockets. Cameron looked at him like a drowning man suddenly tossed a life preserver.

Tony glanced around. "Cameron is."

The three men looked down at the poker chips scattered across the table.

"You can take my place," Cameron said, reaching for his crutches. "I think I'm going to take a nap. It's been a busy day." He glanced at Tony, then gave Cole a meaningful look.

Cole sat on the couch after Cameron left. "Did Cameron tell you why he's on crutches?"

"Yeah, he mentioned it. That's too bad, losing his wife and all."

"Have you seen his daughter?"

Tony's face lit up. "Oh, yeah, Rosie brought her in awhile ago after her nap. She's a real cutie."

"I think so."

"Cole, how come you never married? I mean,

here you are the head of the family and all, don't you want to have children to leave all of this to someday?''

Why couldn't this kid talk about cars and girls and the latest rock group like every other teenager Cole had met?

"Have you ever thought about a career in journalism?" Cole asked, reaching for a cigarette.

Tony looked puzzled. "No, why?"

"Because you have a hell of an interviewing technique."

"Does that mean I'm being too nosy?"

"Well, I have to admit I never know what's going to come out of your mouth."

"But how do you learn about things unless you ask?"

"There is that, of course. Well, as to any marriage plans I might have, I—"

The front door slammed and the rapid tattoo of boot heels on the tiled floor in the hallway preceded a voice, calling, "Where is everybody?"

Cole grinned and winked at Tony. "In here, Cody." Then he came to his feet. Cody rounded the corner and came to an abrupt halt when he saw Tony getting up from his position on the floor. He stared at first one, then the other, his face a marvel of mixed expressions.

"Come on in, Cody, and meet Tony Alvarez. Tony, this is my youngest brother, Cody."

Tony held out his hand awkwardly. "Pleased to meet you, Cody," he said diffidently.

Cody took in the boy standing there before him, his eyes widening at the Callaway likeness. Then he took his hand and shook it. "Glad to meet you, Tony. Didn't know you were going to be visiting us."

"Uh, yeah. Me and my mom arrived yesterday."

"Allison's here?" he asked, looking at Cole in surprise.

"I would have told you if you'd ever bother checking in once in a while."

Cody grinned at his brother's peeved tone. "Sorry. I'm not used to having to report to someone."

Cole raised his brow. "Letty didn't have as much influence over you as I would have guessed."

Cody laughed. "You got that right. She considers me incorrigible. So!" He glanced back at Tony. "How long are you staying?"

"A couple of weeks."

"Great. We'll have to get together and do something, get acquainted."

"How did you know my mom was Allison Alvarez?"

"Because only Allison would have named her son Tony Alvarez," he replied immediately.

Cole knew that Tony wasn't going to be put off

by half answers for long. He needed to talk to Allison about the situation and soon.

He waited until after she left the bathroom that night before tapping on her door. He even waited until she said "Come in," before opening it. He found her at the vanity brushing out her hair.

"We need to talk."

"Go ahead," she said noncommittally.

"About Tony."

She stopped running the brush through her hair and stared at him in the mirror. "What about Tony?"

Cole began to pace. "Look. This is one brilliant kid we've got here. He's quick to put things together and he's already asking questions. I don't want to lie to him."

"What sort of questions?"

"About his father, for one thing. Remember he was asking me, then today I overheard him questioning Cameron." He turned and looked at Allison. "He's got to be told the truth, Allison."

She looked down at her hands. "Is this the first step in turning him into a Callaway?"

He moved over to where she sat and knelt beside her. "Honey, you know better than that. Whether you want to hear it or not, I love you. I have always loved you. I will always love you. I told you last night that I want to marry you. I mean that. Can't you see that we need to sit with Tony—together—and explain to him what happened?"

"Putting the blame on my father and your aunt?"

"Forget blaming. Just tell him the truth. We made a mistake, okay? We're human. Tony is going to have to accept that." He slid his arms around her waist and hugged her to him, his head resting on her breast.

Slowly she ran her fingers through his hair, loving the silkiness of it, reminded of the number of times she'd held Tony in her lap and done the same thing. She loved both of them so much. She felt torn between wanting to protect her son from hurt and wanting him to understand his heritage.

"You're right, of course," she finally said, sighing. "I can't continue to protect him indefinitely from the truth, particularly now that he's met you."

"Will you let me tell him that we're going to get married?"

"No!" She straightened, dropping her arms. "It's too soon to consider."

"Not necessarily. Unless you're on some form of birth control, we could easily have begun another child last night, or haven't you thought about that?"

She stared at him in horror.

"From that look I would say that there's a distinct possibility," he said, when she didn't say anything.

"Oh, Cole," she finally whispered. "I never thought about it. Not once. I can't believe I was so irresponsible…after what I went through with Tony."

"Neither one of us was thinking very clearly last night, and that was my fault, I'm afraid."

Tears began to roll down her cheeks. "I never wanted you to marry me because you *had* to."

"Honey, I would never feel that I had to, can't you understand that? What do I have to say to convince you I love you?"

She wiped her hands across her eyes, not answering.

Cole felt the familiar gnawing of frustration at not being able to control the outcome. "Why don't we talk to him tomorrow? We'll take a picnic lunch out near one of the creeks."

"No more riding for me for a few days," Allison warned him.

"We can go in one of the trucks. We'll get away, just the three of us, and I'll explain. What do you think?"

"At this point, we don't have much of a choice."

He rose, then took her hand and lifted her from the vanity seat, slowly drawing her into his arms. "He's your son, darlin'…filled with courage and full of compassion. He'll understand, I'm sure of it."

She tried to smile, but it wobbled on her lips. "He's also your son, impetuous and hot-tempered.

He's not going to like knowing he's been lied to, Cole. Don't ever think he will.''

"Granted. But he'll listen to our explanations, won't he?''

"I hope so. I can only hope he'll linger long enough to listen to what we have to say before he bolts.''

Ten

"You're making this up, right?" Tony said, staring at Allison and Cole.

They had just finished off the contents of a large picnic basket and were resting in the shade of a cottonwood tree near a small creek not too far from the Big House.

Before Cole could respond, Tony added hoarsely, "It's because you don't want me to know about my real father." He turned to Allison, his eyes filled with pain. "You've always been afraid of telling me about him, haven't you? He was somebody bad, someone you were ashamed of. So you and Cole have decided to make up some lie to tell me."

Her eyes met Cole's for a moment before she looked at Tony. "I've never been ashamed of your father, Tony. Your grandfather was the one who made up the story about my brief marriage. Whether it was the wrong thing or the right thing to do, I never corrected it, even after he died. I suppose I found the established situation easier to go along with as you grew up. I could see no reason to drag up the past because I thought it was all behind me. I never expected to see or hear from Cole again, so it didn't seem to matter who your father was."

Tony stared at her in despair. "Not matter! How could it not matter? All these years I thought my father was dead, that I had no one but you. And now..." He looked at Cole, his eyes accusing. "If you're really my father, how come I'm just hearing about it *now?*"

"Because I never knew you existed until that day we met on the beach, Tony. Believe me, I would never have allowed you or your mother out of my life if I had known about you."

Tony's accusing gaze met Allison's. "Why didn't he know? Why didn't you tell him about me? Why did you have to keep me a secret?"

She took a deep breath and said, "I thought he did know, Tony. It's only been since we've seen each other again that I discovered he never received any of the letters I wrote, so of course he didn't know about my pregnancy. All he knew was that we'd moved away suddenly. He didn't know where we were or how to contact me. It was a series of happenings that neither of us could have anticipated."

"You're always harping about my being responsible and how everyone needs to practice safe sex and all, and here you're telling me that you and—" He paused and gulped. "I don't believe this. It's just too weird. I mean, I run into some guy on the beach and now you're telling me that—" He shook his head in bewilderment, then sprang to his feet. "You've been lying to me my whole life! You've pretended that my dad died when all the time he was somebody I could have gotten to know. You lied to me!"

He spun away and raced up the incline and over the hill toward the road back to the Big House.

Allison sprang to her feet. "Tony! Wait! We—"

"Let him go," Cole said in a low voice behind her. "Give him a chance to get used to the idea. It's all so new to him."

"He's going to hate me," she said in a choked voice.

"Why do you say that?"

"Because I lied to him about you. He's going to remember how much I talked about the need to be honest and to tell the truth, regardless of how much he might get into trouble." She moved her hands restlessly. "Now he'll see how I didn't follow my own beliefs."

She hurt inside, so much so that she felt as though she were in a vise that continued to squeeze her harder and harder. "I didn't want him hurt. He's so young! I wanted him to see that I love him, and that I was only trying to protect him."

Cole stood and pulled her into his arms. "He knows you love him, Allison. I promise you, he knows. But he has to work through this on his own, don't you understand? It's time to stop trying to protect him. He deserves to know the truth and to act on it in any way he chooses. What we have to do is to give him the space to feel all of those conflicting emotions that are tearing through him at the moment. He's got to be able to cry if he feels like it, curse if it helps, scream and shout." He glanced around them. "This is where he can do that, don't you see?"

She, too, glanced around. "But what if he gets lost?"

"He won't—we're too close to the house. But what he needs is time to get some perspective on all of this. Remember when he told me in the car that it wasn't as important to him where he came from as much as where he was going?"

She nodded, wiping the silent tears streaming down her cheeks. Cole continued in a gentle voice. "Now is his chance to see how deeply he carries his belief. He is still the same person. Nothing has really changed except how he sees himself. He needs time to adjust, but he'll do it. I know he will.''

She pulled away and knelt, placing the picnic remains in the basket. "He feels so betrayed."

"Yes. He *was* betrayed. So were you. So was I. From a more mature perspective I can see where we might have done things differently. You could have telephoned me when I didn't answer your first letters...I could have insisted on finding out where the two of you had moved. But what each of us needs to see is that at that time in our lives we were doing the very best we could. Regrets over past actions are the most futile waste of energy there is. What I hoped to do today was to give Tony the heritage that he didn't know he had. It was as painful for me to tell him as it was for you to listen to and for him to hear. But it had to be done."

He picked up the blanket and repacked basket and placed them in the truck. "Give him some time, okay? I have a hunch he'll come around eventually. At least he now knows the truth."

As they drove back to the Big House, Allison spoke in a low voice. "I thought I'd come to terms with my past," she said slowly, "until we arrived here. Being here again has brought back so many memories."

"Not all bad, I hope."

"No, but painful, nonetheless. I emotionally buried the young girl who lived here...and now, all at once, she's alive and feeling everything all over again." She turned her head so that she was looking at Cole's profile. "I'm not at all certain I want this much feeling in my life. I was content before. I had Tony and my work. I had peace of mind. All of that is so important to me."

"I don't want to take any of that away from you. I just want to be a part of your life. Whatever part you're willing to share."

She glanced down at her hands, surprised to see them clenched in her lap. She forced herself to unclench them. "We'll see," she finally whispered, knowing that she couldn't run from what had happened today. The life she had known with Tony would never be the same, now that he knew the truth.

Cole sat in his study late that evening. He'd stayed there for two reasons. One, to give Allison plenty of time and privacy should she want to use their shared tub. And, two, to be there when Tony returned. As large as the ranch was, there was a possibility that the boy had lost his bearings and headed off in the wrong direction. He'd give him another hour. If he wasn't home by then, he'd go looking for him.

Allison had been upset when Tony hadn't shown up by dinnertime. Cole had reassured her that he couldn't have gotten too lost, since the road they had taken to the creek was one of the main ranch roads and easily followed. Cole figured that Tony would be home when he was ready to face people again.

He'd been waiting almost half an hour when Cole heard the front door ease open and quietly close. He tossed down the pen he'd been making notes with and admitted to himself how relieved he was to know he'd guessed correctly. He walked with a silent tread to the hallway door and looked out. Because of the hall light he had no difficulty seeing Tony as he tiptoed across the tiled floor toward the stairway.

"I thought you might be hungry," Cole said in a low voice that froze Tony in his tracks, "so I had Angie make up a plate of food for you. Why don't we go warm it up?"

Slowly Tony turned to face Cole. His eyes were red and swollen, his face dirty. Exhaustion was etched in every line of his body, but his gaze was steady and clear. Tony had met his ghosts during the past few hours and had faced them.

In that moment, the man he would become was there in the boy's face.

Cole headed toward the kitchen and prayed that Tony would follow. He found the heavily laden plate in the refrigerator and placed it in the microwave. Without looking around he said, "What would you like to drink?" in a casual voice. He hid his relief when he heard Tony answer.

"Milk, if you have it."

After he poured the milk and placed the warmed food in front of Tony, Cole rummaged through the pantry and found the cake he knew was there. He cut two big chunks off and placed them on cake plates. By the time he came out, Tony was busy eating. Cole poured himself a glass of milk and found a fork, then seated himself across the small kitchen table from Tony.

He silently ate his cake and waited. Tony methodically ate every bite of food on his plate, then devoured the cake with no sign of diminished appetite. Cole hid his smile. He remembered the appetite he'd had at that age.

"I guess I owe you an apology for running off like that," Tony finally said in a gruff voice.

"Well, I'll admit your mother was quite worried when you didn't show up for dinner. She said you're not one to miss a meal."

Tony's mouth quirked into a half smile and he finally raised his gaze to meet Cole's. "Yeah. She's right."

"It's not surprising, really. Your body is changing and growing at a rapid rate. You're almost grown."

"I bet it was a shock for you to find out that you had a son, wasn't it?"

So he'd had time to think about other people's feelings as well as his own. A good sign. "Yes, it was."

"I remember how you acted that day at the beach. How did you know?"

Cole smiled, remembering his shocked reaction. "You looked just like Cody did at your age. It was like seeing him all over again."

Tony nodded, looking down at his plate. "My mom used to tell me that I looked like my dad. But I don't think I look much like you."

"Don't you? Well, maybe it's more of a family resemblance."

"Is that why you invited us to come visit, because I'm your son?"

"Partly," Cole admitted. "I wanted to get to know you better, there's no doubt about that. I also wanted to spend some time with your mother."

Tony nodded, his eyes meeting Cole's, then glancing away. "Yeah, I kinda figured that."

"Your mother's had a rough time of it, through no fault of her own."

"I guess so."

"You probably won't be surprised to hear that I love your mother very much. I always have. Losing her was a devastating blow to me. It came at a time when I'd already been knocked to my knees by other equally devastating blows. I suppose that's why I did nothing about looking for her. I thought she had chosen to leave, that she didn't want to be with me anymore, so I made myself accept her absence in my life." He took a sip of his milk. "Now that I know the truth, I want to make up for what she's gone through, if she'll let me. I'd like to make things a little easier for her.''

Tony nodded, as though understanding Cole's need to make amends, then offered his comment. ''My mom's pretty independent, you know.''

Cole recognized the man-to-man tone of voice and respected it. ''Yes, I know.''

''I guess she felt she had to make it on her own.''

''I guess so.''

Tony straightened his shoulders. ''The thing is, I've always felt guilty because she had to work so hard to take care of me.''

''There's no reason for that, you know. Allison loves you very much. She told me today that she didn't know how she would have survived without you all these years. Without you, she would have been totally alone.''

Tony was quiet for several moments, then slowly smiled. ''I've been company for her, huh?''

''You've been family for her. Family is very important to Allison. Just as it is to me.''

Tony studied him for quite a spell before he asked, ''Do you intend to marry her?''

''There's nothing I'd like more.''

''Have you asked her?''

''Yes. But she isn't ready to give me an answer.''

''If you two got married, would we live here on the ranch?''

"We'd probably divide our time between here and Austin, where my headquarters is."

Tony glanced around the kitchen. "This place has been in the family for a long time, hasn't it?"

"Yes, it has."

"I'd like to learn more about it."

"Your Uncle Cameron can tell you just about anything you want to know about the place."

"Do your brothers know about me?"

"Yes."

"And they don't care?"

Cole grinned. "They're delighted."

Tony smiled. "You know something? I think I'm gonna like being a part of a family."

A lump suddenly formed in Cole's throat so that he had to clear it before he answered. "I'm glad, son. Really glad."

Allison stood looking out the bedroom window, watching the activity near the barn. Although the sun had been up less than an hour, Cole and Tony were ready to ride out.

In the two weeks she and Tony had been at the ranch, he and Cole had become inseparable. Tony had unconsciously picked up Cole's mannerisms, his walk, even the way he rode a horse.

The pain in her chest was intense. Her son was rapidly becoming a full-fledged Callaway who no longer needed her. Had he always yearned to have a man in his life? If so, he'd carefully kept it from her, accepting their situation with a minimum of comment.

Cole had kept his agreement. Not once had he come to her room again, nor entered the shared bathroom when she was there. He was friendly enough when she saw him, but that was seldom, since he and Tony spent most of their days away from the Big House. Each evening over dinner Allison listened with a smile as Tony regaled her with tales of his day. Most of his sentences began with ''Cole says,'' or ''Cole thinks,'' or ''Cole suggests'' and Allison found herself biting her lip to keep from saying something to them.

After all, what could she say? She'd been aware that Cole had wanted to get to know his son and she'd told Cole to leave her alone.

Well, now she knew what her life would be like if she were to accept Cole's proposal of marriage. He would have his son. She would fade into the background of their lives.

Allison turned away from the window. She couldn't do that. Not now. Perhaps if she had married Cole fifteen years ago, as soon as she'd graduated from high school, she would have been willing to stay at home.

Those fifteen years had made her into another woman…an independent woman who was used to looking after herself. She didn't want to lose her identity by becoming one of the Callaway women.

She was Allison Alvarez. She owned a gallery in Mason, Texas. She was ready to return home.

Allison was in the family room when she heard Tony and Cole come into the house from the back. Glancing at her watch, she realized they had decided to come home for lunch. She tossed down the magazine she'd been thumbing through and walked into the hallway.

"Hi," she said, leaning against the open doorway.

"Oh, hi, Mom. You should have come with us. We found some baby armadillos."

Cole paused beside her and said, "I peeked in this morning to see if you might want to go but you were sleeping so peacefully I didn't have the heart to wake you."

When he stood so close to her, she had trouble thinking clearly. Flashes of memory inundated her of Cole in the tub with her, of Cole leaning over her, of Cole— She straightened, edging away from him and spoke to Tony. "I called Suzanne this morning and told her we'd be home this evening."

"But, Mom—"

"I thought—"

Both Cole and Tony stopped speaking and looked at each other, then at her. Cole said, "I'm sorry. I forgot about your shop. You've been missing it, haven't you?"

"Yes."

"But, Mom, Cole said that—"

"I know what I said, Tony. I guess I lost track of the days. If your mom needs to get back to work, then we'll have to postpone our plans."

She lifted her head and looked at him. "I'm sure you have work that needs attention as well."

Cole nodded. "That's true, although I've been able to handle a great deal over the phone."

Tony dropped his head. "I guess I've been selfish, expecting you to spend all your time with me."

The unhappiness in his voice tore at Allison. It was at that moment that she knew what she had to do. "If Cole agrees, I see no reason why you can't spend the summer with him. Both of you have a great deal of catching up to do."

Both pairs of eyes met hers with equal intensity. Tony's dark ones shone with happiness. "Oh, wow! Could I really?"

"If Cole agrees."

Cole's blue-green gaze glittered. "Is that what you want?" he finally asked.

"It's not a matter of what I want, necessarily. I just know that Tony isn't ready to go home, and I need to get back. I was offering an alternative."

"I'd like to stay if you'll let me," Tony said to his father, his eagerness apparent.

Cole never took his eyes off Allison. "Let me think about it, Tony. I want to discuss it more fully with your mother."

Tony glanced at the two adults who were staring at each other, suddenly becoming aware of the tension between them. "Sure. No problem," he said in an offhand voice, then went up the stairs to his room, leaving them alone.

"What is it?" Cole asked. "What's wrong?" He reached out as though to touch her face, then dropped his hand.

"There's nothing wrong. I can't ask Suzanne to continue to work without relieving her of some of the responsibility."

"Are you sure you want to leave Tony with me?"

She lifted her chin. "He's your son. He's a Callaway. He needs to understand what that means."

"Are you angry with me?"

"Why should I be?"

"Because I've spent so much time with him these past two weeks."

"Wasn't that the purpose of this visit?"

"I wanted to be with you, too, but you've made excuses every time we invited you to come along. Then I finally stopped asking."

"I thought it better for the two of you to talk without my being there."

"Allison—"

His low tone caused a shiver to race up her spine and she knew she was going to have to get away from him before she betrayed herself.

"If it won't be too much trouble, I'd appreciate

it if you'd take me back to Mason this afternoon,'' she said, turning toward the stairs.

"Allison, we need to talk."

She turned back and looked at him. "About what?"

"About us."

"There is no us, Cole. Whatever we had ended fifteen years ago. We're two different people now with our own lives. I'm glad that Tony is going to have the summer with you. I know it's important for you both."

"I was hoping that you and I could—"

She interrupted him before he could finish. "No. I can't go back to being that young girl, Cole. I'm happy with the way my life is now."

"I'm not asking you to give up your work, you know. Since I spend so much time in Austin, we could buy you a gallery there. I thought we might look around for a larger place to live than my condo, one with room for a studio. I want you to be happy, Allison."

"Then take me home."

What could he say to that?

Cole forced himself to nod and turn away while she continued up the stairs. He loved her so much that he ached with it. He walked into his study and sat down, staring at the top of his desk without seeing it. He hadn't allowed himself to consider the possibility that Allison wouldn't be willing to marry him and make a home together.

He closed his eyes and leaned back in his chair. He knew that she was running because she was afraid—afraid of being hurt, afraid of losing her newly found identity, afraid of making a mistake.

Didn't she know that he understood her fears? Didn't she know that he could appreciate her uncertainties for the simple reason that he shared them?

He knew that he had to let her go, but it was the hardest task he'd ever had to face.

Eleven

The deer hunters were everywhere she looked in Mason that particular November morning when Allison opened the gallery for the day. Business had been brisk this season. Several of the hunters had stopped in and purchased either photographs of the area or some of her smaller sculptures these past few weeks. She had kept busy filling commissioned orders. However, she intended to take the weekend off to rest.

The high school football team had a game in Mason that night. Tony would be playing, at least for part of the game.

She smiled when she thought of her son. He was growing up so fast. Cole had called her in July and suggested that she meet them in San Antonio to celebrate Tony's birthday. Coward that she was, she couldn't face Cole again so soon.

She'd talked to Tony and explained that she couldn't get away, but that she would plan a special outing in the fall when he returned. He had accepted her explanations without comment. She had no idea how Cole had reacted.

She knew that she would have to get used to seeing him now that they were going to share Tony. The problem was that she wasn't certain how she would manage. Just the sound of his voice on the phone set her pulse pounding and caused a distinct shortness of breath in her lungs. Cole called the house with alarming regularity to talk to Tony. She'd gotten to the point that she wouldn't answer the phone. Since most of the calls were for Tony, anyway, he'd never commented on her behavior.

She didn't want to react to Cole that way! He was part of her past, that's all. She'd made her decision last summer and it had been the right one for her. It was just taking her emotions a little longer to accept her choice.

During the call he'd made in July he point-blank asked if she was pregnant and had not disguised his disappointment when she'd told him that she wasn't.

Thank God she wasn't pregnant.

She couldn't have handled the idea of marrying Cole because she was pregnant, not after spending fifteen years of her life thinking he hadn't wanted her when she was pregnant the first time.

Everything had worked out for all of them. She had her life, her work, her gallery. Tony had come back to Mason in September and announced to his friends that he had spent the summer with Cole Callaway and that they were friends. She wondered how the townspeople would react if they knew the truth?

She stepped inside the shop. There was a real nip in the air this morning and she was glad to get inside. As soon as she warmed up her office, she began working on a new sculpture—a wild horse standing on a bluff looking off into the distance. The only peace Allison found anymore was when she was working with her clay. She spent her day working quietly in the backroom while Suzanne handled any customers who came in. By the time she got home that evening, she was feeling more relaxed than she had in weeks. Her sculpture was coming along very well. She had scarcely thought of Cole all day.

Tony had already eaten by the time she got home, since he wasn't supposed to eat too close to game time. He was excited about the upcoming game. Tonight they were playing their archrivals from a neighboring town.

"I've gotta go, Mom," Tony said, giving her a quick kiss on the cheek. "See ya at the game."

She smiled. "You're not supposed to be looking

into the stands, you know. You're supposed to be paying attention to what's going on with the ball.''

"Hey, no problem. I can do both," he said with a grin. He took off, slamming the front door. She shook her head, wondering if he would ever slow down.

She heated the remains of dinner from the night before, ate them, then headed toward the bedroom to change into warmer clothes. By the time she had her turtleneck sweater, vest, wool skirt and knee boots on, she figured she'd be warm enough when she added her coat. Trying to decide what to do with her hair, she had finally parted it in preparation for a braid when she heard the front doorbell.

She hadn't a clue who would be visiting at this hour. Everyone in Mason knew about the game. All other activities were put on hold during football season. She let go of her hair, allowing it to drape around her shoulders like a shawl and went to the door.

When she opened the door, she froze.

"Hello, Allison. May I come in?"

It was Cole. Stunned, she stepped back so that he could enter. She watched as he walked down the hall and into the family room, then hastily closed the door and followed him. When she entered the room he turned away from the sliding glass door and said, "You're looking good. How've you been?"

"All right." She couldn't say the same about

him. He looked as though he'd lost twenty pounds. His face was drawn and there were definite traces of gray over his ears.

"I know you're wondering what I'm doing here after you asked me not to come," he began, only to be distracted. He walked over and picked up Tony's latest school picture, which she'd framed and set on a bookshelf. "When was this taken?"

"About three weeks ago. He just brought that one home Monday. He saved you one."

He smiled. "Good. I'd love to have it."

His smile almost undid her, it seemed so familiar. He was so much a part of her. How could she expect herself to push him out of her mind?

"I'll be right back," she said, grateful for a few moments by herself. When she returned with the picture set aside for him, Cole took it carefully in his hands, as though she'd given him a priceless object that needed fragile handling. He stared at Tony's likeness for several minutes before he finally said, "Thank you," without looking up.

"Why did you come, Cole?" she asked.

When he raised his head, his eyes glittered with moisture. "I need to talk to you about something and I thought it would be better to discuss it in person. But I guess the real truth is, I couldn't stay away any longer." He turned his back to her and walked over to the sliding door once more. "I had to see you, to see if this is really what you want for us. I can't imagine not being in your life somewhere. I've picked up the phone a hundred times to let you know I was thinking of you, and realized that if I called you whenever I thought of you, I'd be on the phone all the time."

"Don't, Cole," she pleaded softly.

"Don't what?" he asked, turning to look at her. "Don't think? Don't feel? Don't ache to hold you again? Do you have any idea how many nights I lay awake wishing you were there to touch, to hold, to talk to, to love?" He looked away again. "I even subscribed to your local newspaper, so I could see your weekly ad, read every item of news just in case you or Tony are mentioned. When I read that there was a game tonight I decided to accept Tony's invitation to see him play. I've been turning him down, thinking it would be too painful to see you. I decided that nothing is as painful as not seeing you at all. So I'm here."

She bit her bottom lip in an effort not to respond. He was hurting. She could see it in his face, hear it in his voice.

"I thought that having Tony in your life would be enough," she said, finally.

"Enough?"

She turned away. "He's your son and—"

"And you're my love, and I want you both, can't you understand that? What is it you think I'm going to do that you can't accept?"

She sighed. "I'm not sure. I've thought about it

over the past few months and I guess what I'm afraid of is losing my identity.''

"I can't take that away from you, you know."

"Perhaps not," she admitted.

He nodded, seemingly content that she was at least looking at their situation.

"One of the reasons I wanted to see you in person was to let you know that I want both of you to come to the ranch for Christmas. Cameron is doing better now. He's working again, dividing his time between his office and the ranch. Letty's home and, Allison, she's different. She really is. She had no idea about your pregnancy. She knows what she did was wrong. I think you'll see the changes."

"I don't know, Cole. I'll have to think about it."

"That's something I guess. In the meantime, I'd like to go to the game with you tonight. I want to sit there with you and the rest of the parents and cheer our son on."

She almost smiled at the determination in his voice. "All right."

"You aren't going to argue?"

She shrugged. "Cole, I learned a long time ago not to argue with you when your mind's made up."

"Well, that's a relief," he replied with a grin.

"I need to finish braiding my hair. Then we need to go if we're going to be there for the kickoff."

He helped her with her coat when she returned, and tugged her beret so that it sat saucily over one eye. "You look about sixteen, yourself."

"Thank God I'm not," she said, allowing him to take her hand and lead her out to his car.

"The idea of going back and doing it again doesn't appeal to you?" he asked, tucking her into the car before walking around to the driver's side.

"Living through all of that once was more than enough."

"But maybe we could change things the second time around."

"I doubt it. Given the same set of circumstances, I don't see things changing all that much. Human nature being what it is, we would probably all act out our roles in a similar way."

"A rather dismal thought. Surely we've learned something from the first time."

"Ah, but we wouldn't be given the advantage of remembering. It would all be new to us."

He reached over and took her hand, placing it on his thigh and dropping his hand over it. They rode down the hill toward the football field in that position.

"There is something else I need to discuss with you while I'm here."

"All right."

"I've been approached to run for governor in the upcoming election."

"You'd make a good governor."

"Actually, I'm seriously thinking of disqualifying myself."

She looked around at him in surprise. "Why?"

"Because of Tony."

"I don't understand."

"A politician's past is open to scrutiny once he announces his candidacy. The other side would like nothing better than to get hold of a juicy piece of news such as Tony's birth."

"But, Cole, they couldn't prove a thing. There's no way to tie you with Tony, or to me, for that matter."

"You're missing my point, honey. I want to tie myself to both of you. I don't intend to deny that he's my son. I'm damned proud of it."

"That's political suicide. You just said—"

"I know what I just said. That's why I want to talk to you about it. I don't want you and Tony hurt by something that might come out of the campaign. So I wanted to talk to you and get your views about it. I'm not that fired up about running for a public office, anyway. I can do just as much in other ways. The guy sittin' out there on top is the one who gets all the potshots aimed at him. I just needed to talk to you about it. Your opinion is important to me."

"Oh, Cole. I don't know what to say. You'll have to decide what to do."

"Would it make a difference to you, Allison? Being with you is more important to me than anything. I've been trying to give you space over the past few months, but I'm not sure I can keep this up much longer."

She looked away from him. So he hadn't accepted her decision as final. Was she relieved to know that, to know that he still wanted her as much as ever? Why was she so afraid to accept what he was offering to her?

"I don't know," she whispered out loud.

"You don't know what? Whether you love me? Whether you're willing to marry me? What?"

"I'm afraid," she finally admitted.

"So am I. But more than anything else, I'm afraid of having to spend the rest of my life without you."

"Here's the parking area," she pointed out, grateful that there was a timely interruption to the conversation.

By the time they found some seats the team had run out on the field and was warming up. The night was cool but pleasant. Everyone was excited about the upcoming contest, and the stadium was noisy.

Cole seemed to fit right in with the others. She introduced him to more than a dozen people between the time they bought their tickets and the time they found their seats. Some people recognized him and spoke. He looked relaxed and friendly. If he hadn't been gripping her hand like a drowning man she would have had no idea he was nervous.

"If you don't ease up on my hand, gangrene is going to set in," she whispered. "Circulation was cut off some time ago."

"There he is!" he said suddenly. "Over there."
He pointed with his other hand without releasing
his death grip. She started prying his fingers from
her hand and he looked down in surprise. "Oh! I'm
sorry. Was I hurting you?"

She flexed her cramped fingers and smiled.
"Tools of the trade, you know. I've gotta be careful." Cole took her hand, and ignoring the fact that
they were the object of many an interested ob-
server, brought her fingers to his lips and kissed
them, one by one.

"Is that better?"

"Cole!" she whispered through a smile.
"You're embarrassing me." She tugged on her
hand, but he held on to it, tucking it firmly between
his elbow and his side. She turned away in time to
see Tony, while doing warm-ups, look toward the
stands. She waved with her other hand and he saw
her. His smile lit up his face and then froze with
astonishment when he saw Cole. After a pause, he
clasped his hands and raised them above his head.
Cole laughed.

"What's that all about?"

"I think he's glad I came to see him. I'm glad,
too, but I have to admit I've been a little nervous
about seeing you again."

"Does Tony know that?"

"I may have mentioned it to him a time or two,"
he said in a casual voice.

"Something tells me I've been set up here," she

murmured, watching her son speculatively. Once again he glanced up in the stands, this time giving her a thumbs-up signal. She glanced around and discovered that Cole was wearing an identical grin to his son's. She shook her head and said, "You two are just alike."

"Really?" Cole asked, obviously pleased.

"I wouldn't be so proud, if I were you."

"You really think he's like me?"

"Who are we kidding here? Of course he's like you. The older he gets the more he looks like you. He has to know the truth every time he looks into a mirror."

Allison had never seen Cole with quite that expression on his face before. He glowed with pride. She knew then that she had never loved this man who clutched her hand to his side as much as she did right at that moment. For a brief minute the knowledge was almost overwhelming. Now that he was here, she didn't see how she could let him walk away again. Ready or not, she was going to have to accept that this man would always be a part of her. No one had been fooled by her denials, least of all her heart.

The game was in the third quarter and Mason was a touchdown behind when a whistle ended a play where several players were in a pile. Cole came to his feet. "Tony was the one with the ball. Is he all right?" he muttered.

This was the part that Allison hated. She tried

not to worry about injuries, but the game was rough enough without the extra adrenaline flowing tonight, as they fought against their archrivals. Most of the people in the stands were on their feet.

When the field cleared one player still lay on the field. It was Tony. Allison gave a gasp and frantically started to climb over people, absently excusing herself. Cole was right behind her. They were on the sidelines by the time he was carried off on a stretcher. The volunteer ambulance squad took him to the ambulance where they began to check him over.

"Is he all right?" she asked, following them.

"He's unconscious, Allison," one of the men said. "I think we'd better take him into Fredericksburg to the hospital, to be safe."

That was over forty miles away. Cole took over. "You ride with them in the ambulance, honey. I'll be right behind you in the car."

Never had Allison felt so frightened. As an energetic little boy, Tony had gotten several scrapes and bumps in his life, but nothing like this. She wanted him safe. She wanted him to open his eyes and give her that special grin of his, reassuring her that he was all right.

Never had she felt more alone.

Riding in the back of the ambulance through the night, she reminded herself that for the first time in a very long while she was not alone...Cole was there.

She didn't have to go through this alone. Not now. Not ever. She took a deep breath and let go...let go of her fears, her indecisions, her apprehension about the future.

She didn't have to do anything alone, not anymore.

By the time the ambulance reached the hospital, Tony had regained consciousness, but he remained groggy. They took him into emergency for tests and X rays.

Allison was giving the admissions clerk information on him when Cole walked in. In the most natural gesture of her life, Allison held out her hand to him. "He's with the doctor now but they don't think it's too serious. Perhaps a minor concussion. He was awake in the ambulance and didn't have any problem answering their questions."

Cole closed his eyes for a moment. She could feel the surge of relief that flowed through him. "Thank God."

Yes. Thank God. For so many things, she realized.

"Will he have to stay overnight?" he asked, looking around.

"We don't know yet."

By the time the doctor got through with him, Tony had been pronounced well enough to go home that night, provided he took it easy over the weekend. Allison didn't think she was going to have any trouble keeping him down.

When she and Tony came out of the examining room Cole was waiting. With no hesitation Tony walked into Cole's arms and clung. Allison saw Cole's eyes fill with tears before he dropped his head and hugged his son.

When Tony finally raised his head, his grin was crooked. "When I invited you to come see me play, I didn't mean to knock myself out showing off."

Cole laughed and Allison could feel herself relaxing.

"I bet you have the granddaddy of all headaches about now," Cole responded.

"Just about."

"I'll take you home," Cole said, still with his arm around him. He glanced at Allison. "Ready?"

She looked at the two of them, standing there together. What had she been so afraid of?

"Yes...I believe I am."

By the time they reached Mason, Tony was asleep in the back seat. He offered little resistance when Cole helped him out of the car. Following the two of them up to the front door, Allison suddenly realized that Tony was almost as tall as Cole. Somehow the thought that her son was no longer a child swept through her and she almost wept. Where had all the years gone?

"Do you need any help getting ready for bed, Tony?" she asked once they were inside.

"Uh-uh. I'll see you later," he mumbled, and started down the hall. He paused halfway and looked back. "Thanks for coming to see me, Cole," he said. "Even though I didn't finish the game," he added wryly.

"I'm glad I was there. I'm just sorry you were hurt."

Tony shrugged. "It comes with the territory, you know?"

Cole nodded. "Yep. I know."

"Night, Mom," he mumbled, then went on into his room.

Cole and Allison were left by the front door. "Would you like some coffee before you head back?"

He stretched and yawned. "You mean you're going to insist on my leaving tonight?"

She thought about that for a moment. She did have some things she needed to say before he left. "I suppose you could sleep in the guest room, if you'd like."

He grinned. "I'd like."

She turned away to make them some coffee. Cole's grins were next to impossible to resist, and she needed to keep her wits about her. While she measured the coffee and water, she said, "I can't tell you how much it meant to me tonight, having you there." She turned and came toward him. "I can't remember ever having been so afraid for someone in quite that way. I felt so helpless...and alone.''

''I know what you mean.''

They stood there looking at each other for a moment before Allison stepped forward, walking into his arms as though there was no place she would rather be.

Cole could feel his heart thundering in his chest. The sweet scent of her wrapped around him, soothing him. He hugged her to him.

''I love you, sweetheart,'' he whispered. ''So much that I sometimes wonder if I can live with the ache it causes.''

She sighed, her contentment obvious as she laid her head on his shoulder. ''I'm tired of fighting this thing, Cole. I love you. How could I not love you? I'm raising another Callaway just like you. It continues to amaze me how much he reminds me of you.''

He only intended to comfort her with a light kiss, but the moment his lips touched hers, he felt as though he'd gone up in flames. He drew her ever closer to him, loving the feel of her body pressed so intimately against him, wanting her so desperately that he wasn't at all certain he could survive without her.

When he finally lifted his head and looked down at her, her face glowed with a loving radiance that humbled him.

"Does this mean that you'll marry me?" he finally whispered.

She nodded her head, unable to speak.

His next kiss was even more eloquent. He wasn't sure he could let go of her, now that he knew she had agreed to marry him. When he finally paused for air, he decided to risk the next question.

"Would you consider having more children?"

Her eyes opened in a lazy and extremely seductive way. "As a matter of fact, I'd insist on it. I never wanted to raise an only child, but it couldn't be helped. We'd need to have at least a couple more, don't you think?"

With a muffled shout of joy, he picked her up in his arms and carried her over to the sofa. "Oh, I think we can manage." He sat with her on his lap. "When?"

"Well, it takes at least nine months, as you know, and—"

"Not that! I'm asking about marriage. How soon?"

She shook her head. "I have no idea."

"I have several. How about Christmas?"

"So soon?"

"Soon! That's over six weeks away!"

"But there's so much I need to do."

"Why don't we have a quiet family wedding at the ranch? I don't think Cam's going to be in the mood for many festivities this year."

She leaned her forehead against his. "You're

right, of course. Maybe we should wait a few months.''

''Honey, I've waited fifteen years. Cam will understand.'' He slid his hand across her breasts, feeling her suddenly catch her breath.

''We can't, Cole. Not tonight. Not here.''

He sighed. ''You're right. I know you are. It's just that I need you so much.''

She smiled. ''Just look at what we have to look forward to, though.''

''If I can survive the cold showers,'' he growled and kissed her again, determined to leave no doubt in her mind regarding his desire for her.

Epilogue

The Big House glowed inside and out with Christmas decorations. Inside, the fireplaces burned mesquite wood, scenting the air. Trisha's giggles and delighted squeals echoed along with the Christmas carols playing on the stereo system and the conversations from the many adults standing around in the foyer greeting the new arrivals.

Allison and Tony had just arrived. Cole had gone to get them and was just now setting the last of their luggage inside the door.

The first person's eyes Allison caught were Letitia Callaway's. The woman had aged considerably. Her hair was completely gray. She looked old and tired. Her gaze was almost shy as she looked at Allison.

Allison walked over to the older woman, bringing Tony with her. "Letty, I want you to meet Tony."

The older woman flinched at the familiar name, but she didn't look away. "My, you are a big one, aren't you?" she said, her voice shaking slightly. "You look just like the pictures of your dad at that age. Except for your eyes, of course." She faltered a little on the last words. "You got those beautiful eyes from your grandfather."

Cameron and Cody were both there, Cameron holding Trisha, Cody teasing Rosie who was passing a tray around. But everyone stopped talking and looked at the tableau before them.

Tony took the offered hand and shook it. "I never knew my grandfather," he said in his baritone voice that on occasion slid up an octave.

She nodded slowly. "He was a fine man. A man to be proud of. Wear his name well."

Tony grinned. "I'll try."

Cole walked in at the beginning of their remarks and he held his breath, having no idea what either the crotchety old woman or the outspoken teenager might say to each other.

He breathed a sigh of relief when general greetings were started up once again. "I'll take the luggage upstairs," Cole said to no one in particular.

He placed Tony's in the room he'd had on their previous visit. He placed Allison's belongings in his room. They would discuss the proprieties later.

They would be married in less than a week, and he didn't intend to wait another night for her.

Dinner went well. Everyone was excited to see each other. Cody had been gone for almost two months without telling anyone where or why he'd disappeared. He smiled his familiar cocky smile when asked and had a smart-aleck come-back that told them absolutely nothing.

Although Cameron now spent several days a week in San Antonio, he continued to have Trisha stay at the ranch. She was settled there and comfortable. Everyone doted on her. Cole knew that the child received a great deal of love and attention, but he worried about Cam. He couldn't help it, even though he knew he had to accept Cam's way of dealing with his grief.

"What did you tell them today, Cole?" Cameron asked over dessert and coffee.

"To find somebody else. I had other plans." He took a sip of coffee.

"Good for you," Cameron said with a toasting gesture of his cup. "I'm glad you didn't let them push you around."

"They tried."

"I'm sure they did."

"What are you talking about?" Letty demanded to know.

Cameron explained. "Oh, just some of the guys pushing Cole to run for governor."

Cole's glance met Allison's and he smiled.

Tony's eyes got round. "So you're going to run for governor?"

"No. I don't intend to run."

"Why not?" Tony asked, shocked.

Once again Cole's eyes met Allison's. "I've got more important things to do with my time."

Cody jumped in with a hilarious anecdote that soon had them all laughing.

The subject was not brought up again. Instead the family spent the evening in front of the fireplace, chatting and getting better acquainted with Tony.

When Allison finally decided to go upstairs for the night, she opened the door to her room and was surprised not to see any of her things laid out, or at least her luggage waiting to be unpacked. Puzzled, she walked into the bathroom where she found her toiletries neatly set out. Curious, she peeked into Cole's bedroom.

Her gown was draped at the foot of the bed, with her robe and slippers nearby. She could feel her face grow hot. What did he think he was doing? He wasn't even making a pretense of anything. He was—

The door from the hallway opened and Cole walked in. He glanced around and saw her and a very wicked grin appeared on his face.

"Now, Cole..."

He stalked over to her and grabbed her up in his arms. "Now, Allison," he mimicked.

"You know I can't stay in here with you. What will—"

"Don't give me any of this 'what will people think' routine. In the first place, it's none of their business. In the second place, there's no reason for anyone to know. I put your things away so no one else knows you're here, but even if they did, so what? We'll be married in a few days, so what difference does it make?"

"It isn't that, I just feel that Tony's not going to understand and—"

"On the contrary, Tony is quite understanding. Tony and I had a nice man-to-man talk last night after you went to bed."

"Oh?"

"Yes. I explained how long I'd waited for you and how eager I was for the three of us to become a family. He didn't have a problem with any of it, except to ask why it had taken me so long to convince you!"

"Oh, Cole," she said, recognizing his teasing. "I love you so much."

"Glad to hear it," he growled, hauling her up tight against his body. "What's the possibility of getting you to mention that little tidbit of information more often?"

She touched her lips to his jawline and whispered, "I'm just afraid, that's all."

"Afraid? Of what, for God's sake?"

"All of this is so new to me. I know all about

being independent. Now I need to learn how to be a wife.''

He brushed his fingertips across her cheek. "You don't have to worry about any of that, you know. I love you, no matter what you do or how you behave.''

He reached around to the back of her dress and tugged at the zipper. "I don't want to wait another night for you, love. I've been extraordinarily patient these past few weeks. There's no way I could sleep knowing that you're in the next room.''

She began to unbutton his shirt with trembling fingers. She knew exactly what he meant. She'd had a difficult time falling asleep the night before, knowing he was there in her home. Tonight, they didn't have to pretend.

Allison tilted her head back so that she could see his eyes. "Whatever you say, dear," she replied demurely. His shirt fell to the floor and she brushed her palms across his broad chest.

He began to laugh. "I've never heard you so meek. I think I'm going to like your new attitude.''

"Enjoy it while you can," she said with a smile, leading him to the bed. "I have some very definite ideas about what I want to do with you.''

"Honey, I'm all yours. I always have been.''

She gave him a gentle push so that he sat on the bed, then stretched out across it. She reached for his belt buckle. "Cole?''

"Hmm?''

"Do you have an idea when you want to start expanding our family?"

His heated gaze met hers. "The sooner, the better, as far as I'm concerned."

"How about the number?"

"I'd have a dozen more, if that's what you want, honey."

She smiled, her black eyes dancing. "Even for a Texan, that's really bragging."

He grabbed her arm and pulled her down beside him. He turned, holding her to him with his arm and leg over her. "I want whatever you want, darlin', for now and ever more."

She kissed him—a short, hard kiss. Then a second time she softened the kiss to include all the love and tenderness she felt for this man.

"Then I may have to keep you in bed for a while over the next few weeks," she said when she raised her head.

His eyes were as bright as the Christmas lights that surrounded the house.

"Whatever you say, dear," he mimicked, his pleased expression effectively wiping out all the years they had spent apart. The present was much more important.

*   *   *   *   *

COURTSHIP TEXAS STYLE!

One

Without warning, bright lights leaped in front of the car, blinding him. Cameron swerved in a desperate attempt to miss the idiot who had suddenly appeared in the roadway ahead. His wife's scream echoed around him as the lights loomed ever larger, filling the windshield of the car with brilliance. He broke out in a cold sweat, his clammy hands clutching the steering wheel. He could feel his chest pounding, his body shaking. The metallic taste of fear filled his mouth.

He fought for control in a herculean effort to avoid a collision, feverishly regretting that he'd driven the small foreign sports car rather than their sedan.

Despite everything he could do, the larger car slammed into them and he knew with a sickening certainty that he had lost what little control he had.

They began to spin, faster and faster, rolling over and over until—

"Aaaugh!"

Cameron jerked into a sitting position and groaned, burying his head in his hands. He was drenched with sweat and was shaking. His heart pounded in his chest like an overworked piston. He ran a trembling hand through his hair, shoving it off his forehead, forcing himself awake.

My God! Was he never going to stop dreaming about the wreck? Almost four years had passed since the night of the accident that had killed his wife, yet it continued to haunt him.

He shoved the twisted sheets away from his legs and stumbled out of bed. He felt for his cigarettes and lighter on the bedside table without turning on a lamp, knowing they were never more than a hand's reach away. After lighting one, he made his way over to the window and stared out at the turbulence of a south Texas spring storm.

Perhaps the bright flashes of lightning followed by crashing thunder had triggered his recurring dream. He hadn't dreamed about the horror of that night in several months, and he'd begun to believe the nightmares were buried at long last.

Obviously he had been wrong.

He took a long drag from the cigarette, feeling

the smoke curl its way into his lungs, knowing he was slowly killing himself with his habit and not giving a damn.

Hard-driving rain slashed the window glass. He shook his head in resignation. Much more of this spring rain and the whole ranch would be washed away.

During the midnight drive from San Antonio, he had listened to agitated announcers on the radio warn of flooding in low areas. For the past week the papers had been full of reports about flash flooding, damaging winds and destructive rainfall. He had witnessed the results firsthand when he turned off the highway and followed the six miles of private road to the main buildings of his family's ranch. Both bridges along the road were flooded with racing water. He had barely managed to inch his way across the last one.

Because he hadn't left his office until after midnight, he had considered sleeping at his condo in San Antonio, but he had felt too wired to sleep and had headed south toward the ranch, instead. The hour-and-a-half drive sometimes soothed him, gave him a chance to unwind. He hadn't counted on the weather continuing to be so wild.

He hadn't visited the ranch in almost three weeks. The guilt that constantly lived with him stirred at the thought. Three weeks had passed since he'd seen his daughter, Trisha. Three weeks without seeing her father was asking a great deal of a motherless five-year-old child.

He stubbed out the cigarette, then scrubbed his hand across his face. He reminded himself that Trisha was far from being neglected. Between his aunt Letty doting on her and the constant entertainment provided by Angie and Rosie, two of the family's employees, his daughter was far from being a waif. Still, he knew they weren't enough. His daily telephone conversations with Trisha made him very much aware of her feelings on the subject. She was always asking when he was going to come see her. He had promised that, no matter what, he would be there this weekend.

He was a man who never broke his promises. No matter how tired he was, nor how much work had stacked up at the office, he would be there.

He loved Trisha dearly. How could he not? She was his last link to Andrea, the woman he had loved so much. Trisha looked so much like Andrea that he was forever reminded of her.

He and Andrea had been on their way to the ranch to pick up Trisha that fateful night four years ago. Andrea had been so happy. They had spent the evening with some of his business associates. Letty had suggested they leave the baby for the whole weekend, but Andrea thought the teething infant would be too fretful without her mother there to hold her. They had left the gathering early, ex-

PLAY TIC-TAC-TOE

FOR FREE BOOKS AND A GREAT FREE GIFT!

Use this sticker to **PLAY TIC-TAC-TOE.** See instructions inside!

THERE'S NO COST • NO OBLIGATION!

Get **2** books and a fabulous mystery gift! **ABSOLUTELY FREE!**

Turn the page to play!

Play TIC-TAC-TOE and get FREE GIFTS!

HOW TO PLAY:

1. Play the tic-tac-toe scratch-off game at the right for your FREE BOOKS and FREE GIFT!

2. Send back this card and you'll receive TWO brand-new Harlequin Superromance® novels. These books have a cover price of $4.25 each, but they are yours to keep absolutely free.

3. There's no catch. You're under no obligation to buy anything. We charge nothing — ZERO — for your first shipment. And you don't have to make any minimum number of purchases — not even one!

4. The fact is, thousands of readers enjoy receiving books by mail from the Harlequin Reader Service® months before they're available in stores. They like the convenience of home delivery, and they love our discount prices!

5. We hope that after receiving your free books you'll want to remain a subscriber. But the choice is yours — to continue or cancel, any time at all! So why not take us up on our invitation, with no risk of any kind. You'll be glad you did!

YOURS **FREE** A FABULOUS **MYSTERY GIFT!**

We can't tell you what it is…
but we're sure you'll like it!

A FREE GIFT –
just for playing

TIC-TAC-TOE!

NO COST! NO OBLIGATION TO BUY!
NO PURCHASE NECESSARY!

DETACH AND MAIL CARD TODAY!

First, scratch the gold boxes on the tic-tac-toe board. Then remove the "X" sticker from the front and affix it so that you get three X's in a row. This means you can get TWO FREE Harlequin Superromance® novels and a **FREE MYSTERY GIFT!**

PLAY TIC-TAC-TOE

YES! Please send me all the gifts for which I qualify. I understand that I am under no obligation to purchase any books, as explained on the back of this card.

(II-H-BR-08/98)   **134 HDL CH59**

Name _____

(PLEASE PRINT CLEARLY)

Address _____ Apt.# _____

City _____ State _____ Zip _____

Offer limited to one per household and not valid to current Harlequin Superromance® subscribers. All orders subject to approval.
© 1997 HARLEQUIN ENTERPRISES LTD.
® and TM are trademarks owned by Harlequin Enterprises Limited.

PRINTED IN U.S.A.

The Harlequin Reader Service® — Here's how it works:

Accepting free books places you under no obligation to buy anything. You may keep the books and gift and return the shipping statement marked "cancel." If you do not cancel, about a month later we'll send you 4 additional novels and bill you just $3.57 each, plus 25¢ delivery per book and applicable sales tax, if any.* That's the complete price — and compared to cover prices of $4.25 each — quite a bargain! You may cancel at any time, but if you choose to continue, every month we'll send you 4 more books, which you may either purchase at the discount price...or return to us and cancel your subscription.

*Terms and prices subject to change without notice. Sales tax applicable in N.Y.

If offer card is missing write to: Harlequin Reader Service, 3010 Walden Ave., P.O. Box 1867, Buffalo NY 14240-1867

BUSINESS REPLY MAIL
FIRST-CLASS MAIL   PERMIT NO. 717   BUFFALO, NY

POSTAGE WILL BE PAID BY ADDRESSEE

HARLEQUIN READER SERVICE
3010 WALDEN AVE
PO BOX 1867
BUFFALO NY 14240-9952

NO POSTAGE
NECESSARY
IF MAILED
IN THE
UNITED STATES

plaining that they had to pick up their daughter after her two-day visit with his family.

How many times had he gone over the circumstances in his mind? If only they had waited until the next day. If only he had seen the other car in time. If only he could have done something different! Then Andrea would be alive and here with him now.

His younger brother, Cody, couldn't let go of the fact that a hit-and-run driver had caused yet another fatal accident in the Callaway family. Fifteen years before Cameron and Andrea's accident, his mother and father had also been killed by one.

Cody was convinced that the two events were somehow linked. Cameron hadn't cared enough at the time to try to find out. Nothing could bring Andrea back to him. Nothing.

In the ensuing years, he had buried himself in his work. There was certainly enough to keep him busy. His older brother, Cole, was the head of Callaway Enterprises, which was a combination of real estate, oil and mineral interests, as well as various cattle businesses. Cameron was more than willing to let Cole run the show. He preferred to stay in the background, putting his degrees in accounting and law to work, being there whenever Cole needed him.

He walked through the familiar darkness of the bedroom that had been his since he was a child to the adjoining bathroom, where he flipped on the light. Its brilliance caused him to flinch. His sudden movement drew his eyes to the mirror and he caught a glimpse of himself. He shook his head in disgust. His blue eyes were swollen and rimmed with red. He rubbed his hand across his darkly stubbled jaw and chin. He looked ten years older than his thirty-four years. He felt more like sixty. His brown shaggy hair reminded him once again that he needed a haircut.

Reaching for the glass sitting beside the sink, he rinsed and filled it with water. After draining the contents, he flipped off the light and made his way back to bed.

He'd gone to bed around two in the morning. It was almost five now. His body ached with fatigue, but his mind continued to whir with too many thoughts to shut down.

He kept thinking about the trial he was in the middle of. All the evidence had been presented by Friday afternoon, and Cameron had hoped to go to summation on Monday morning, possibly turning the case over to the jurors by the afternoon. Unfortunately the judge had called a one-week recess because of previous commitments. Cameron felt caught in a state of frustrated limbo at the delay. He wanted to finish the case and get on with other pressing matters. But he had no choice now. Trial would resume when the judge said so. He might as well accept the situation.

Presentation had taken three weeks. He'd spent

more than six months preparing for this one. He was determined to win. He was tired of Callaway Enterprises being made to look like a hungry conglomerate devouring smaller businesses. He and Cole had decided to plant their feet and fight back this time.

The battle was almost over, even though he had a week of enforced pause before beginning the next step in due process.

The Callaways were named in a number of lawsuits, either personally or as officers of various corporations. He supposed being the target of other people's ire came with the territory.

He and his brothers had inherited the family wealth when their parents were killed twenty years before. For more than seventy years the Callaway name had grown in prestige and power in Texas. With each succeeding generation, their companies had prospered and new companies had been formed.

He gave Cole the credit for most of the recent expansion. His brother had an uncanny knack for spotting trends of the future. He kept his businesses up-to-date, with state-of-the-art equipment in each one. He hired men who were brilliant strategists, willing to take responsibility, ready to stay at the forefront of the shifting and treacherous world of business.

Cole's business acumen was legendary.

Cameron, on the other hand, enjoyed the role of

counselor and consultant to Cole. He couldn't have handled Cole's position. He didn't even want to try.

He sighed, consciously forcing his body to relax in a technique he had learned to reduce stress. He knew the stress of his heavy schedule wasn't making his life any easier. However, he preferred staying busy to having time—such as now, in the small hours of the night—to think, to remember, to grieve.

Slowly his body responded to his mental commands and Cameron managed to drift off to sleep once more.

He heard faint sounds in the distance and knew he needed to respond to them. They were persistent, no matter how much he tried to ignore them. He hated to move, though. He wanted to continue to drift in this netherworld, allowing himself to float away without thought or feeling. But the sounds wouldn't leave. They continued to call to him...

"Daddy? Are you asleep? Daddy? Wake up, Daddy. There's a big lake out in front of the barn. You wanna see it, Daddy?"

Reluctantly, Cameron drifted upward, still longing for the oblivion of sleep. He could feel small hands patting both of his cheeks.

"Daddy? Wake up, Daddy," Trisha sang in a small soft voice.

His eyes felt swollen and glued shut. He forced

them open, blinking. The first thing he saw was a pair of wide sherry-colored eyes staring back at him from a pixie-shaped face. As soon as his gaze met hers, she laughed in delight. "I knew you was awake! You was just playing possum, wasn't you, Daddy?"

He groaned. She was draped across his chest, her head bobbing in front of him.

"Trisha, sugar," he managed to say, "Daddy can't breathe very well when you lie on his chest like that."

Obligingly she began to slide down his body. Suddenly realizing what a five-year-old's weight would do to a full bladder, he woke up with a vengeance. Before she could continue moving, he lifted her off him and rolled so that they were side by side on the bed, facing each other.

"You know what, Daddy?" she asked, not missing a beat despite the sudden move.

"What, angel?"

"You missed breakfast."

He widened his eyes in simulated shock. "Really?"

She nodded vigorously. "An' you know what?"

He sighed. "What, baby?"

"Aunt Letty said it's 'bout time you showed up around here. She said—"

"You know something, sugar?" he interrupted, hugging her to him. "Your aunt Letty is a hundred percent right, as usual." He placed a kiss on her nose and she giggled.

"It stopped raining," Trisha said.

"Glad to hear it," he replied with heartfelt sincerity.

"Are you hungry?"

He couldn't remember the last time he'd eaten. He skipped more meals than he thought about eating. "You bet," he said, more to be agreeable than honest.

Trisha gave him a heart-stopping smile. "Good, 'cause I helped Angie bake cookies this morning, and she says we gotta save you some."

"So why don't you run downstairs, darlin', while I shower, okay?"

"Okay." She slid away from him on her stomach, wriggling backward until she landed on her feet with a light bounce. "Hurry, Daddy." She dashed out of the room, slamming the door behind her.

He checked the time and discovered that it was almost eleven. When he had finally gotten to sleep he had been dead to the world. Yawning widely, he scratched his chest and rolled out of bed. Cookies, hmm. Angie knew he was particularly susceptible to her chocolate-chip cookies. He smiled to himself. It felt good to be home.

If Janine Talbot hadn't been determined to speak to Mr. Cameron Callaway today, she knew she never would have attempted this trip. Ever since she had left the highway, she had inched her car along a narrow blacktopped surface surrounded by water. At times the water ran across the road, causing her to stop. This was truly a case of come hell or high water, she intended to speak her mind to Mr. Callaway. She considered high water the better of the two choices.

She knew she was on the Circle C ranch. She had headed south from the town of Cielo, where she lived, knowing that the Callaway ranch was in that general direction. When she saw adobe pillars supporting an arching wrought-iron sign with a giant C in a circle, she knew she had found the ranch. Unfortunately, after she had driven under the sign, there was no indication that anyone or anything lived in these godforsaken hills. Other than water, she hadn't seen anything moving for what seemed like miles.

At least the rain had finally stopped. The weather forecast on the radio had been filled with warnings of flooding in outlying low areas. Surely the Callaway ranch was protected. From everything she had heard in the year since she had moved to Texas, the Callaways were a force to be reckoned with. No doubt they controlled wind, rain, fire and flooding with nonchalant ease.

A small elfin face flashed into her mind, and she found herself smiling, despite her unease about her unknown destination. Trisha Callaway. What a darling she was. Trisha had captured Janine's heart the first time Janine had seen the little girl and learned that she had lost her mother when she was barely a year old.

Trisha had been placed in Janine's preschool class a few weeks earlier. She had been shy with the other children at first, preferring to stay with the adults, Janine in particular. Janine had done everything she could think of to coax the little girl into playing with the others. After more than two weeks, she could see Trisha finally beginning to warm toward the other children.

Not that she was shy! Janine thought. Heavens, no. Trisha Callaway was a scamp. Janine knew that the little girl's family would be horrified if they had any idea of some of the things Trisha had told Janine. A recent conversation with Trisha came to mind, typical of their exchanges.

"My aunt Allison is going to have another baby, and she says the doctor told her there's going to be two at once! Won't that be neat? They already have a boy that's big and a girl that's littler 'n me, and Aunt Letty says she wonders if they ever get anything else done the way they're always huggin' and stuff. Do you know my aunt Allison?"

Janine bit her lip in an effort to hide her smile and shook her head.

"She's pretty. She's got long black hair that comes down to here." Trisha turned around and pointed to her buttocks. "She can sit on it!" she added with a giggle.

"Does she live with you?"

Trisha looked somber. "Not really. She and Uncle Cole come to visit when they can. They live in Austin. Tony goes to school there."

"Tony?"

"My cousin. He's big, even bigger than you."

"Really?" Janine responded. "Does your aunt Letty live with you?"

Trisha nodded solemnly. "Yes. Aunt Letty's always lived at the ranch, and she'll live there forever, Uncle Cody says, 'cause she's older 'n God!"

"I see," Janine said, nearly choking in an effort to stifle her laughter. "Does your uncle Cody live there, too?"

Trisha cocked her head for a moment, obviously giving the matter careful thought. "Sometimes he does, but most times he's gone off somewhere and nobody can find him. Aunt Letty says he's wild and up to no good, but I like him. He plays with me when he's home and answers all my questions and stuff like that."

"Does your daddy play with you?"

Trisha's face clouded. "When he's there. Most of the time he lives in San Antonio."

"San Antonio! That's more than an hour's drive from here."

Trisha nodded sagely. "Uh-huh. That's why he sleeps in town mostly. He comes to see me when he can.'' She looked down at her hands. "I miss him." She glanced back at Janine and said stoutly, "My daddy loves me and misses me a bunch."

"I'm sure he does, punkin. How could he not love someone as sweet as you?" She patted the little girl's shoulder with affection.

Maybe the man did love his daughter, Janine thought now as she carefully followed the wet winding road back through sagebrush, cactus and mesquite, but he wasn't paying much attention to her—otherwise, he would see that she was not happy and know that she was having difficulty in adjusting to preschool.

The child was too well mannered to cry when she was brought to the school each morning by one of the ranch employees, but her woebegone face was a clear indicator of how she felt.

For the past week she had barely touched the midmorning snack the school supplied. True, she was a small-boned child. However, Janine couldn't help but wonder if Trisha was eating enough. The child was obviously unhappy about something, and when Janine had asked her the morning before if something was wrong, tears came to the child's eyes and slowly rolled down her cheeks. "I want my daddy," she whispered.

"Oh, honey, I know you do. Have you talked to him?"

She nodded her head. "He promised he'd come to see me this weekend, and he never breaks a

promise, but Aunt Letty said she didn't care if he
promised to come or not, even a idiot would know
better than to drive out here in this weather.''

"Maybe he'll make it, anyway,'' Janine had said
in an effort to console her small charge.

"You think so?''

Janine had closed her eyes in a brief prayer. She
had wished she knew the man better. Did he understand the importance of keeping a promise to a
child? She had known then that she was going to
have to do something about Trisha. No matter how
many times she had reminded herself not to get
emotionally involved with her students, she knew
that this particular child had slipped past all the
barriers around her heart.

When she had awakened that morning, she knew
she was going to drive to the ranch. If Trisha's
father hadn't come, at least *she* would be there to
cheer up the little girl. If he *was* there, well, then
she would talk to him.

Now that she was within a few miles of him,
Janine began to feel butterflies fluttering in her
stomach. She wasn't exactly sure what she was going to say to him. Of course she knew what she
wanted to say, but she would have to word her
comments very carefully. Not that she was afraid
of him or even intimidated by the fact that he was
a Callaway, but she didn't want to make him angry
if she could prevent it.

Let's face it, she told herself. *You're meddling*

and you know it. She'd spent hours trying to talk herself out of coming, but in the end, she knew she had to do everything she could to help remove that terrible look of longing and sadness from Trisha's face.

"Oh my God!" She pressed down hard on the brakes, jerked back to the present by the swollen creek racing through a gully. A wooden bridge spanned it, but the water was slithering over its sides and swirling across the top. Maybe she should turn around and come back some other time.

She looked up at the heavy clouds, which seemed so low they appeared to be touching some of the taller trees in the area. Surely she was almost there! Chastising herself for being a coward, Janine eased her car down the hill and onto the bridge, creeping forward until she reached the other side.

She hadn't been aware she was holding her breath until she finally let it go with a *whoosh*. She still hadn't adjusted to Texas. Everything was bigger and better and higher and deeper in Texas than anywhere else, to hear the natives tell it. Colorado could have some rough storms, particularly in the mountains, but she would have to give Texas its due. When it decided to rain and storm here, the results were tumultuous.

She reached the top of the incline and released another sigh of relief. There, in the hollow of the hills below her, was one of the most beautiful sights she had seen in south Texas.

A rambling multistoried house made of adobe and whitewashed a gleaming white with a Spanish-tile roof sat in the middle of a group of buildings; the place looked like a small village. A high wall encircled the compound, with an arched opening for the road she was on.

There were barns and paddocks, some with horses, others with cattle. There wasn't much sign of activity, only a few men around one of the barns.

Well! She had made it. Janine started down the winding road. She still had a distance to go, but at least she could see her destination.

By the time she drew up in front of a massive wooden door and turned off the car, she was trembling with exhaustion. She hadn't realized how tense she had been on that drive until now, when she knew she was safe. She sat for a moment, drawing deep breaths and reminding herself that she was there for Trisha's sake.

She checked in the mirror to make sure her reddish-brown hair was still tucked in a coil on the nape of her neck. Her green eyes reflected her apprehension. Darn! She wished her face didn't instantly signal her every emotion. She had long since learned not to play any games where a stoic expression counted.

"Come on," she muttered to herself, opening the car door. "You can do it. Just think of Trisha."

She stepped out and brushed the skirt of her yellow suit. She had deliberately chosen something bright on this gloomy day—to give herself courage, if nothing else. Had she mentioned her intentions to any of the other staff members, they would have been shocked that she would consider confronting one of the Callaways—which was exactly why she hadn't told anyone of her plans. Perhaps she could mention to them that she had happened to be passing by. She glanced around and realized that nobody could be just passing by this place. It had taken her almost half an hour to drive the private road from the highway.

So! She would go back to her original plan. If Cameron Callaway had decided to show up this weekend, she would meet him. She would explain who she was, and depending on his response, she would decide how to broach the purpose of her visit.

There. She felt better, now that she had mentally prepared herself for the next few moments. After gripping her purse, Janine walked to the front door and knocked.

A moment later, the door was opened by a young Hispanic woman with a pleasant face. "Hello. May I help you?"

From somewhere in the looming foyer behind the woman, Janine heard a gruff male voice say, "Who is it, Rosie?"

Janine cleared her throat before stating, "I came to see Mr. Cameron Callaway."

Rosie opened the door wider and motioned for

Janine to come inside. With a wave of her arm Rosie indicated the man on the stairway.

Janine caught her breath. *Please, God. Please don't let this be the man I came to see.*

The first thing she noticed was his height. He was tall and broad-shouldered, with a lean waist and hips and long muscular legs. Then she noticed that he was only half-dressed. He wore a pair of faded jeans that looked as though they had been sewn on him. They hung low on his hips, the fly button left undone. Other than a pair of dilapidated moccasins on his feet, that was all the man wore.

As he moved down the stairs, she stared at the crisp curls that covered his chest. She barely noticed the blue chambray shirt clutched in one fist. When her gaze finally lifted she saw a pair of blazing blue eyes staring at her with a mixture of irritation and curiosity.

He needed a shave. The dark stubble on his jaw and chin made him look like some desperado from an earlier era. All he needed was a six-gun on his hip. His hair looked damp, as though he had just come from the shower. Although he had obviously combed it back from his face, a stray lock had fallen across his forehead.

"I'm Cameron Callaway. What can I do for you?"

Put on some clothes, was her first thought. Then she tried to get a grip on herself. "I, uh, was wondering if I could speak with you," she managed to say with a tongue that felt foreign to her mouth.

He moved on down the stairs and paused beside her. She had to tilt her head to continue to meet his eyes. He seemed to be taking inventory of her. That knowledge caused her to stiffen her spine. "I know I should have called first, but I thought I'd take a chance on catching you at home."

He studied her for a moment in silence before saying, "You were lucky to find me here. This is the first time I've been home in three weeks."

This was worse than she had thought. "Three weeks! But that's awful!" she blurted out, thinking of Trisha. No wonder the little girl had missed him.

He raised a brow slightly, looking puzzled. "Awful? That isn't the word that first comes to mind, but if you say so, I suppose it will do."

Janine could feel herself blushing. How she hated her fair skin and her annoying inclination to turn colors with the least amount of provocation.

He shook out his shirt and slid his arms into it, rolling the sleeves while he left his chest bare. Determined not to stare, Janine glanced around. They stood in a large foyer. The ceiling was more than two stories high. The red Spanish tile of the floor gleamed. Toward the back she could see a glass door that framed an inner courtyard filled with a profusion of flowers and a fountain.

When she glanced back at the man beside her, his shirt was buttoned about midway down his chest, but the tails hung out. He motioned her through one of the arched doorways. "I just got up and I really need a cup of coffee. I'm afraid I use coffee to help me become civilized," he said with a slight smile. "Care to join me?"

She tried to hide her disapproval. It was almost noon, for heaven's sake. But at least he appeared amiable enough. For some reason she felt as though she had approached a lion in his lair. At the moment he was groggy and not particularly aware of her, but she had a hunch he could focus his attention rapidly with a laserlike gaze.

"Rosie, set another place for..." He glanced at her and said, "I'm sorry. I forgot to ask your name."

"Oh!" She had neglected to introduce herself. "I'm, uh, Janine Talbot. I live in Cielo. I came to talk to you about Trisha."

"Oh? Well, have a seat."

Janine found the massive table with its long row of chairs almost intimidating. Place settings were at one end of the table. After pouring their coffee, Rosie smiled at her and disappeared into what Janine supposed was the kitchen.

Cameron sat down, picked up his cup and took a sip. He gave a sigh of pleasure before taking another sip.

Janine wasn't certain why he seemed so much more male to her than the other men she knew, but he did. He also made her very aware of herself as a female.

"How do you know my daughter?" he asked after he finished his first cup and poured himself another one. He reached over to refill her cup, then paused, when he noted that she still had most of a cup left.

"She's one of my students," she said, wondering how to begin the conversation now that she was face-to-face with the man.

He stared at her. "One of your what?"

"My students."

"What do you teach to a five-year-old?"

She stared at him in astonishment. "We have a schedule of various activities, which I could go over with you, if you'd like. The preschool is quite—"

"Preschool! Are you telling me that Trisha is attending a preschool in Cielo?"

"Well, yes. I thought you knew."

He closed his eyes and massaged the bridge of his nose with his fingers. "Letty's at it again," he muttered.

She wasn't certain that she heard him correctly. "I beg your pardon?"

He dropped his hand wearily and sighed. "Nothing. Go on. So you have Trisha in your class." The last thing he needed right after getting out of bed in the morning was a parent-teacher conference about his daughter.

She clasped her hands in her lap. "Yes. And she doesn't seem to be very happy."

"I'm not surprised. I could have told that to you or Letty or whoever thought Trisha should be carted off to school. She hates to be penned up...and she's not scheduled to start school until the fall. She should be out running and playing like the rest of the five-year-olds."

Janine warned herself not to become defensive. If he hadn't been in contact with his daughter for three weeks, it was no wonder the child was so lonely. Her heart ached for the neglected little girl. Choosing her words carefully and attempting a neutral tone, she replied, "Well, actually, we do have plenty of recreational time for the children. The problem is, Trisha refuses to join them."

He took a sip of his coffee before saying, "That's Trisha for you. She's definitely got a mind of her own."

"It's obvious that she's not used to being around children her own age. She's not at all happy there. She prefers staying inside and talking with me. That's why we felt she should spend this semester at the school."

"Then the obvious solution is for her not to go. I don't understand what Letty was thinking about in the first place. I'll have to talk to her." As far as Cameron was concerned, the discussion had come to an end. If Trisha didn't like preschool, then she didn't have to go.

"We keep hoping she will adapt to being around children her own age," Janine said. "By going to school now, she will have an easier time of adjustment when she begins kindergarten in the fall."

He didn't respond to her comment. Instead, he shoved his fingers through his hair in a frustrated movement, rumpling the combed appearance into unruly waves, and frowned.

She placed her clasped hands on the table and leaned forward. "Mr. Callaway, I think she's upset about more than going to school, which is why I decided to come to see you today."

He lifted his gaze to hers, and she felt pinned to her chair by its intensity.

"I'm glad we're getting to the point of all of this. What do you think is the problem?"

This discussion was much tougher than she had anticipated. Cameron Callaway was nothing like the man she had pictured while listening to Trisha's stories over the past few weeks. He was much harder, for one thing. The longer she was in his company, the more nervous she became. She cleared her throat. "Are you aware of how much your daughter misses you? She talks about you all the time."

He sat back in his chair and grinned at her. She hadn't been prepared for the sudden glimpse of the charming and very attractive side of the man. She found him quite disconcerting.

"Well, I miss her, too. We don't seem to have

much time togeth—'' He stopped and stared at her. ''Is this what your visit is all about? You drove all the way out here just to tell me that my daughter misses me?''

She could feel her cheeks turning red again. ''Well, you see, I—''

''Or did you come out here to tell me that I'm neglecting my daughter, that I don't spend enough time with her, that I...'' He shoved back his chair and stood. So did she. ''Look, Ms. Talbot, I don't need some prim and proper schoolmarm to tell me how to raise my own child.'' The look he gave her would have melted steel at ten paces. ''If Trisha isn't happy at school, then let her stay home. If she misses me, then I'll take care of it. I don't want someone like you, who doesn't know a damn thing about raising kids, to give me advice!'' He seldom lost control of his temper but the combination of overwork, lack of sleep and lack of proper meals had pushed him beyond his normal self-control.

He placed his hands on the table and leaned on them, glaring at her. In a low voice shaking with intensity, he said, ''The problem with you, lady, is that you obviously have too damn much time on your hands. I would guess that teaching school is your life. Well, you drove all the way out here to give me the benefit of your advice. I wouldn't want you to go away empty-handed, so I've got some advice for you. Why don't you get married and have your *own* family and quit worrying so much about mine!''

By the time he finished speaking Janine was already at the door to the hallway. She was shaking with indignation and anger, but she refused to allow the man to have the last word. She turned and looked at him, standing there glaring at her from the end of the table as though he was at a board of directors' meeting. Perhaps his manner quelled his opposition in the business world, but she was not going to let it quell her!

She braced her shoulders and with her chin high, responded, "At least now I better understand why your daughter is the way she is. I feel sorry for you, Mr. Callaway, I really do. With all your wealth and power, you haven't recognized what you have. You have been given a priceless jewel and you don't even understand her value. I feel even sorrier for Trisha, however. Unfortunately she can't move to another family who might have more time for her, a family that would nurture her and make her feel secure. She has no choice but to stay here and emotionally wither away!'' She spun on her heel and marched out of his sight.

Cameron sat back down in his chair with a thump and stared at the empty doorway where the young woman with the flaming temper had been standing just a moment ago. He heard the front door slam with a resounding crash. A few seconds later, he heard an engine rev and the sound of tires peeling out.

Trisha chose that moment to come tearing into the dining room. "Daddy, Daddy! You're up, you're up!" She threw herself into his lap and he absently hugged her to him. His daughter? Emotionally withering?

"Angie said I could ask you what you want to eat."

"Anything. I don't care."

"You want breakfast or lunch?"

"Breakfast."

She threw herself out of his arms and raced to the kitchen door. "I'll tell her."

Withering? Any more energy and the house wouldn't contain her.

He sat there in the large room by himself, feeling ashamed. He usually kept a tight rein on his temper. He had been provoked by much more scathing critics before and hadn't allowed himself to be affected. But somehow this was different. She had attacked him in the most vulnerable area of his life.

She had immediately zeroed in on his weakest point, recognizing his lack of parenting skills. He was aware of his shortcomings. He just didn't know what to do about them. His intentions had been good. He had never intended to go so long without being with Trisha, and had hoped the daily telephone calls had made a difference.

Who was he kidding? He hadn't even known

something as important as his daughter, his only child, being enrolled in school.

Why hadn't Trisha mentioned it to him when they talked? She went to great lengths describing a frog or a television cartoon, but hadn't mentioned how she had been spending her weekday mornings.

The mystery of what went on in a child's mind continued to elude him.

Who was this Janine Talbot? He thought he knew most of the people in Cielo. He had grown up in this neck of the woods. He had attended the local schools, but he sure as hell didn't know her. He would have remembered. How could anyone forget those green eyes, filled with accusations? Beneath the chandelier her dark brown hair had glowed with red highlights. She had definitely brightened the day in her saucy yellow suit, which set off a great pair of legs. The rest of her figure was nothing to sneeze at, either. He cringed when he remembered some of the things he had said to her and knew that he would have to look her up and offer her an apology. That was the least he could do.

He reached over and poured himself another cup of coffee.

So why *wasn't* she married with a house full of kids? He had noticed that she wasn't wearing any rings. Not that it mattered to him.

He wasn't interested in anyone and didn't intend to be. He would never go through the pain of falling in love and possibly losing that love again. Not ever. At least he had Trisha. Despite Ms. Talbot's accusations, he did love his daughter, very much. He wanted the very best for her.

Rosie brought him his breakfast. He thoroughly enjoyed every bite, feeling almost mellow by the time she came in to remove the dirty dishes.

He decided to go find Letty and talk to her. Since the solarium was his aunt's favorite room, rain or shine, he would start there. He had just stepped into the hallway when he heard a pounding at the front door.

"I'll get it, Rosie," he said, and opened the door. His mouth fell open in shock.

The rain coming down in buckets must have started since he had come downstairs. This was the rainy season, so there was nothing shocking in that discovery. The shock was seeing Janine Talbot on his front doorstep once again, soaking wet. She was trembling.

Already ashamed of his earlier outburst he took her arm wordlessly and gently pulled her inside, where she stood, dripping. Tiny rivers of water began to snake across the floor. Her once immaculate suit was now mud-spattered and clung to her body, confirming his earlier assessment of her figure. There were certainly no flaws there.

Her hair hung in several long ropes around her shoulders, each one dripping. She shoved some wisps off her forehead and stared at him helplessly.

"What happened? Did you wreck your car? Are you all right?"

She shivered, then wrapped her arms around herself. "I... Your bridge... When I got to the first bridge I couldn't believe it. It's gone!"

"What? The bridge is gone?"

She nodded. "I got out of the car and walked down to the water. There was just nothing there. I didn't know what to do." She glanced up at him, then quickly away. "I didn't want to come back here. I was just standing there, staring at all the water, when suddenly the rain started again without warning. I felt as though I was standing beneath a rushing waterfall." She glanced down at herself and moaned. "I couldn't think of anything else to do, so I came back."

Obviously the drenching had cooled her off a bit, but he didn't consider it polite to point that out just then.

"Look, you need to get out of those wet clothes. And we need to talk. I owe you an apology for blowing up at you like that. What I said was really unforgivable, I know. It's just been a bear of a week all the way around. I shouldn't have taken it out on you, though."

He placed his hand on her back. If anything, the shivering increased. "Let's get you upstairs and dried off, okay?"

Janine closed her eyes, trying to think. The whole morning had been an unmitigated disaster.

When she had left this man earlier she had vowed never to see him again. Now she was in a position where she had little choice, but to accept his help.

How demoralizing.

Nothing so embarrassing, so potentially humiliating, had happened to her in her thirty-two years. For the first time since she had moved to Texas, she wondered if she had made a mistake. Perhaps she should have stayed in Colorado, after all.

Two

Once again Cameron urged her forward. Janine realized there was nothing for her to do but go with him. She couldn't continue to stand there in the hallway and watch the rivulets of water form liquid patterns on the highly glossed tiles.

He removed his hand from her back once he saw she was willing to follow him up the stairs. Janine stayed a couple of steps behind, looking around at her surroundings.

She had never had a particular curiosity about the Callaways, and that had made her a definite minority at the private school where she had been teaching for a little more than a year. She still remembered the flurry of excitement when a member of the new generation of the Callaway family had begun attending the school. She had been amazed at her fellow workers' eagerness to learn anything they could about Trisha and her family.

She could well imagine the questions she would receive when she told them of this latest mishap of hers. She was known for her mishaps. If anyone had a problem with any of the school equipment, it invariably was her.

Once she had inadvertently locked herself in her classroom, something no one had thought about when a particular style of locks had been placed on the doors. She had left the building for the day when she suddenly remembered some papers she needed. Leaving her purse in the car, she'd dashed back into the school and unlocked her door, leaving her keys in the lock. It never occurred to her to brace the door. When some other door was opened in the building, the ensuing draft sucked her classroom door shut and there she was, locked in.

Thank God someone had heard her banging on the door. The louvered windows would have been next to impossible to crawl out of. Nobody since had ever allowed her to forget the incident!

Now she told herself to try to remember everything she saw. Perhaps a detailed description of the place would satisfy their curiosity when she was questioned about her visit. Maybe no one would have to know that she had ended up being trapped at the Callaway ranch.

There were three hallways leading off the balcony overlooking the foyer below. Cameron started down the center one. She hurried behind him, aware of the squishing noise her shoes made with each step. Her beautiful, almost new shoes were totally ruined. At the moment they were the least of her worries.

Cameron paused in front of a door. "Excuse the mess. I'm going to let you get out of those sodden clothes. You can shower here in my room. Meantime, I'll look to see what Allison has here that you can wear."

"Allison?"

"My brother Cole's wife. They live in Austin, but they spend as much of their time as possible here at the ranch. They keep clothes here for when they come down." He held the door open and waved her through, then closed it behind him, leaving her alone.

Janine stood in front of the closed door and gazed around at the masculine bedroom. The twisted bedclothes gave mute evidence that he had spent a restless night. A suit jacket and pants were tossed over the back of a comfortable-looking chair positioned in front of a fireplace.

Remembering that she was now leaving soggy tracks in the plush carpeting, Janine hurried over to the open doorway of the bathroom. Wisps of steam seemed to linger in the room. She shivered, feeling the coldness of her damp clothes seep through to her bones. With shaking fingers, she peeled off her jacket and gazed at it with sorrow. This suit was one of her very favorites, and the children loved it. She sighed. Perhaps the cleaners would be able to salvage it. She carefully draped it across the clothes hamper, then slipped out of her blouse and skirt. Even her slip and underclothes were damp.

As soon as the hot water from the shower hit her chilled body, she groaned with relief. She couldn't remember when anything had felt so good. She stuck her head under the water and massaged her scalp. Heaven. Absolute heaven.

By the time Janine stepped out of the shower, she felt like a new person. She found an oversize thick towel that enveloped her from her shoulders to her knees and began to dry off, leaving her skin looking rosy.

A soft tap on the bathroom door startled her so much she almost dropped the towel. "Yes?" she asked, grabbing the slipping cloth.

"I found one of Allison's lounging robes for you. It's on the bed," she heard Cameron say.

"Fine," she managed to reply in a calm tone, which covered the quavering feelings this man managed to evoke. She wasn't certain exactly why. Of course he was a Callaway, and that was intimidating enough, right there. But it was more than that. He caused a reaction in her that she couldn't understand. She was embarrassed by the fact that she had lost her temper with him. She couldn't have been more unprofessional if she had tried. His comments had upset her because he had been right. The school and her job *were* her life. Most of her friends were coworkers there.

He had called her prim and proper. Was that how she appeared to him?

Janine glanced into the mirror, which was slowly clearing from the steam of her shower. The towel left her shoulders bare. Her freshly shampooed hair was already beginning to dry and to bounce into waves and curls. The only way she could keep it straight and tidy was to blow-dry her hair immediately after shampooing.

Searching around for a hand-held drier seemed a little too nosy, so she would have to allow her hair to dry naturally.

She leaned toward the mirror. Prim and proper. Did it show so plainly? Her wide green eyes gazed back at her. Was it the way she dressed or wore her hair or her makeup? Maybe it was her clothes. What gave her away?

She felt that she had made the very best life she could make in her circumstances. She loved children and therefore had decided to devote her life to them, even if they weren't hers. Did the children see her as prim?

Her mind flashed back to a time earlier in the week when she had been down on the floor with her class, taking her turn at pretending to be a chicken—flapping her wings, shaking her neck, pecking at grain on the floor.

Or the time she had brought in a life-size papier-mâché turtle's shell and proceeded to climb under it to demonstrate the difficulties in carrying your home around on your back. The children had loved it. She wondered what Trisha's father would have thought of her lying on her back attempting to flip herself over.

She gave her hair a final toweling, then peeked around the bathroom door to make certain he had left. The room was empty. She tiptoed out and then laughed at herself. Why was she trying to be quiet? In a house this size a party could be going on in one wing and few would hear it in the other, she was certain.

The lounging robe on the bed was absolutely gorgeous. Never had she felt material so soft. The colors were a swirl of blue and green with brief touches of gold. Obviously Allison Callaway had a marvelous eye for color, texture and style. She found a note beside the robe that read, "I wasn't sure of your shoe size. Here's a pair of my socks for now." A big "C" was scrawled at the bottom. His handwriting was bold, slashing across the page.

He was being very genial, considering the way they had parted earlier. She couldn't believe how she had behaved, which was totally out of character. There was just something about that man that made her feel—and act—in a way she couldn't understand.

After she slipped on the robe and socks, she returned to the bathroom and draped her clothes over the various rods, in the vague hope they would dry sometime soon. Then she returned to the bedroom and peeked out the window.

Rain continued to fall, setting up a syncopated rhythm as it hit the panes of glass. She smiled. If her students were there she would have them listen very carefully to see if they could recognize a tune.

By the time she had brushed her hair a few times with the small brush she carried in her purse, she knew she was as ready as she would ever be to find Cameron Callaway. He had been gracious with his apology. She could be no less.

She realized as soon as she stepped into the hallway that she wasn't sure how to find her way back downstairs. Which direction had they come from? She looked both ways and saw nothing that seemed familiar, despite her earlier efforts to remember details.

Hesitantly she turned left and started down the hallway. When it ended, she was standing on the balcony overlooking the foyer, and she allowed herself a quick sigh of relief.

So far, so good.

She came downstairs and noted that the puddle of water by the front door had already been mopped up. The floor looked as polished as ever, thank goodness. She wandered toward the back, glancing into opened doors and wondering what she was supposed to do now.

"Missy Talbot! You came to see me!"

She spun around in time to catch a human dynamo as Trisha shot out of one of the rooms and grabbed her around the knees, almost toppling her.

"Hi, Trisha!"

"Oh, Missy Talbot. I didn't know you knew where I live. Do you want to see where I play?"

Janine immediately felt more comfortable now that she was with the little girl. "Sure, Trisha. Lead the way."

The room they entered was a child's fairyland. Three sides were glass, as was most of the roof. It jutted into the interior courtyard so that the fountain and flowers seemed to be a part of the room.

Inside, comfortably padded rattan furniture took up part of the space while the rest was devoted to toys and games. A miniature child's kitchen was in one area, complete with tiny dishes, as well as pots and pans.

An old fashioned rocking horse sat in another corner.

Hanging baskets hung from various supports, adding color and greenery to the room.

"This is marvelous, Trisha. I bet you have lots of fun."

"Uh-huh, but it's more fun when Katie comes to visit."

"Is Katie one of your friends?"

"Uh-huh. She's my cousin. That's kinda like a sister, but she lives with her own mommy and daddy. Her mommy's going to have two more babies sometime."

"Ah, I remember now. Katie must be your aunt Allison's little girl."

"She's littler than me. She's only two and a half. She brings her baby dolls and we play like we're mommies."

Janine felt a lump form in her throat at the reminder of how young the urge to have a baby begins. She swallowed painfully. "I see."

"Do you want to see my dolls?"

She sank into one of the chairs, nodding.

Trisha spun away and went over to a line of tiny beds. She first picked up one doll, then another, until her hands were full. She returned to Janine and placed them on her lap. "Aren't they pretty?" she whispered, leaning against Janine's knee.

Each doll showed the results of being well loved, although their gowns were clean and well kept. Janine stared down at the blond-headed little girl and wanted to weep. She had obviously been giving her dolls the love and the nurturing that she, herself, wanted from a mother. Was there anyone in her life who gave that to her?

"Trisha, it's time for your lunch and then nap time." Janine glanced around and saw a tall thin woman with gray hair standing in the doorway. The woman nodded to Janine. "You must be Ms. Talbot. I'm Letitia Callaway, Cameron's aunt. Cameron said you had stopped in to see him this morning. We must apologize for the inconvenience of the bridge. You were very fortunate not to have been on it when it was swept away."

Janine hadn't considered that gruesome thought. She shuddered inwardly.

"Cameron's out with the men now," Letty went on, "checking the damage all this water has done. Would you like to have lunch with Trisha?"

"Oh, yes!" Trisha replied, clapping her hands. "We could have a tea party."

The older woman's face softened for a moment. Janine wondered if she ever smiled. The lines in her face seemed permanent, as though she seldom changed expression. "That might be nice," Letty conceded, glancing at Janine for confirmation.

"Oh, whatever is convenient for you. I'm so sorry to have gotten stranded here like this. I had hoped when I left home this morning that the bad weather was over." She helped Trisha return the dolls to their respective beds and followed the older woman out of the room.

They arrived in a small room that looked like a breakfast nook, nothing as grand as the large dining room where Cameron had taken her earlier. Rosie was placing food on the table when they walked in. She smiled and left the room. Janine noted there were only two places set.

"Aren't you going to join us?" she asked Cameron's aunt.

"No. I don't eat much during the day. None of us keep regular schedules around here until evening, when we make it a point to gather for dinner at seven." She glanced at the robe Janine wore. "You're about the same size as Allison. She won't mind if you borrow more of her clothes."

"Oh, surely I'll be able to get home soon."

The woman just looked at her. "Don't count on it. It won't be the first time we've been marooned here. I'm sure it won't be the last."

"Oh, but—" She stopped talking when she realized the woman wasn't staying to hear anything she might say. The door swung shut behind her.

"I'm so glad you're here to eat with me," Trisha said. "It gets lonesome eating by myself."

"Do you always eat alone?"

"Sometimes I pretend Daddy is here. Sometimes my pretend friend stays to eat."

"Your pretend friend?"

"Ralph. He's a giant who used to live in the hills, but he's scared of the dark so I invited him to stay with me."

"I see. And he agreed?"

"Most of the time. Sometimes he goes and checks on things, like giants have to do."

By the time they finished their meal, Trisha's head was nodding. It took little effort for Janine to convince her to go lie down for her nap, especially after she promised to be there when Trisha woke up.

Janine stayed with her until she fell asleep, more aware than ever of what a lonely existence the child had. Perhaps she had been out of line talking to the girl's father, but she had done it out of love and concern for Trisha. Her heart ached for her, but she knew that she could say no more. She had already done enough damage.

When Cameron returned to the house, he was wet, cold and disgusted. There wasn't a damn thing anyone was going to be able to do until the rain let up and the water slowed down. There was no sense in risking someone's drowning in an attempt to re-establish a connection to the main highway.

He had discussed the matter with Alejandro, the ranch foreman, who assured him that he would keep an eye on the flooding creek. As soon as it was feasible, he would get the men working on something to provide temporary access, until the family could get the bridge rebuilt.

Cameron had come into the house in the back way. On his way upstairs to change clothes, he glanced into the family room and saw Janine sitting curled up at the end of the couch in front of a crackling fire, glancing through a magazine.

He had trouble recognizing the woman as the same one who had arrived that morning. With her hair down and curling around her face, she looked considerably younger. The flickering flames high-lighted the burnished red of her hair. She looked as though she belonged there, waiting for him to come home. Cameron had an almost irresistible urge to walk in, stretch out on the couch and put his head in her lap. He could almost feel her long slender fingers stroking through his hair and along his jaw.

When he realized where his thoughts were lead-ing him, he silently cursed and spun on his heel, heading toward the stairs.

He had been too long without a woman, that was all. He wasn't yearning for a relationship, no matter how his thoughts betrayed him.

He took the stairs two at a time, pulling at the snaps on his shirt. What a mess. There was no way to get rid of her. He supposed he could contact Pete in San Antonio and have him pick her up in the company helicopter, but what reason could he give? The situation wasn't an emergency, by any means. Surely by Monday the water would have gone down enough to rig up something to use tem-porarily to get across the creek. Besides, there was no sense risking a flight in this kind of weather.

He glanced out the window of his room. The rain continued to beat down. Alejandro had told him that he had most of the crew moving cattle from low-lying areas up into the hills. That was more important than the bridge. Hell, this place was like a town. They had enough provisions at the ranch to take care of those who lived there for weeks.

The shower felt good, and Cameron allowed his mind to go blank as he stood beneath the soothing spray. His thoughts drifted back to Janine Talbot.

They were both stranded for the time being. With his case in recess for the next week, he had intended to catch up on correspondence and other work at the office. He supposed he could have his secretary fax him whatever needed to be taken care of immediately.

In the meantime, he and Ms. Talbot would be forced to tolerate each other.

Her sudden outburst of temper had surprised him. She had seemed very calm and quiet when they had first spoken. Obviously he had touched a nerve.

Well, hell. So had she. Who did she think she was, coming in here and telling him he was neglecting his child?

He sighed. Damn. He knew she was right. Even though he spoke to Trisha every day, he had not seen her for weeks.

His biggest problem was that he knew so little about children. He was doing the best he could. So why did the woman's green eyes keep popping into his head, staring at him in silent reproach?

He turned off the water faucet and stepped out of the shower. Grabbing a towel, he rubbed his head and body vigorously, then tossed it onto the clothes hamper and—

How had he missed the fact that her clothes were hanging here in his bathroom? He stared around him. Her jacket, blouse, skirt, slip and the laciest bra and pair of briefs he'd ever seen were draped everywhere.

He felt as though he had received a punch just below the heart. Visions of life with Andrea crowded into his mind. He had been alone for four years. In that time he had forgotten what it was like to have feminine apparel around him. He also had forgotten how much he had enjoyed sharing space with someone he loved.

He closed his eyes, waiting for the sudden rush of pain to subside once again.

Cole and Cody had assured him that he would get over feeling so much anguish. They had pointed to the horrible time in their lives when they lost their parents. They had learned to live with tragedy. What Cameron realized was that a person never stopped feeling the ache of loss; he just grew used to living with it.

Something would trigger a memory and he would travel back in time and be with Andrea before he could control the sudden mental leap. When he was told she was dead, he had wanted to die, too. His brothers had later told him that the doctors had been worried about his recovery once he had learned Andrea was gone.

Didn't anyone understand that he hadn't cared whether he lived or died? He hadn't known how he could go on without Andrea.

But he had. He had made it by dealing with each day as it came and never looking too far ahead. He couldn't bear to think about the future and know that Andrea wasn't going to be there when Trisha grew older. They had talked about what it would feel like to send her off to school for the first time. They had talked about having other children, so Trisha wouldn't grow up alone.

None of that seemed to matter anymore. Trisha was growing up alone, and he hadn't even known when she had started school.

By the time Cameron came downstairs, he had pushed all the memories away, forcing himself once again to concentrate on the present. When he walked into the family room, he was again shaken by the scene he found there. Janine had discarded the magazine she had been reading and had leaned her head against the couch. Her eyes were closed, and Cameron wasn't certain whether she was asleep or just resting.

Moving silently past her, he added a couple of small logs to the fire, rearranging what was left. When he finished he stood and turned. Although she hadn't moved her position, her eyes were open.

"I didn't mean to disturb you," he said.

"You didn't. I was, uh, waiting to see you, to thank you for looking after me so well and to…"

She paused and took a deep breath before continuing, "And to apologize for my behavior earlier. I was totally out of line and I'm sorry. I should never have said those things to you."

He nodded, then looked away as though uncomfortable with her apology. When he looked back at her, they just stared at each other without speaking. Finally Janine asked, "Were you able to do anything about the bridge?"

He shook his head. "I'm afraid we're both stuck here for a while yet."

She raised her head. "Both?"

"Yes. I had planned to return to San Antonio tomorrow. I've been in trial for the past three weeks. Although we have a one-week recess, there are several matters I need to deal with at the office. Now I'll have to deal with them from here the best way I can."

"You're an attorney?"

"Yes. I thought you knew."

She shook her head, and her hair flowed around her shoulders. "No. I don't think Trisha understands exactly what it is you do," she added with a smile.

He didn't return the smile. "I assumed you had other sources than Trisha."

She raised her chin slightly, her gaze never leaving his. "If you're insinuating that I've been prying into your family's affairs, Mr. Callaway, then you're wrong. I know very little about any of you."

He allowed himself a brief smile of acknowledgment. "I wasn't insinuating anything, Ms. Talbot. It has been my experience that for some reason the media finds our family fascinating. Almost everything any one of us does gets mentioned in newspapers, magazines or the television news. It would be difficult not to know anything about us."

"Oh. Then I must appear to be grossly uninformed. I only moved to Texas a year ago. Either the Callaways have been unnewsworthy during that time, or I must have missed catching sight of you on the six-o'clock news reports!"

He grinned at her tart tone and sat down at the other end of the couch. "Where are you from?"

"Colorado."

"Ah. Beautiful country. What caused you to move to Texas?"

"I was offered the position I now hold here. I'd decided to get away from the area where I grew up. I wanted to start over somewhere else once my mother died. I wanted to make new friends and enjoy a new life."

He heard an edge in her voice that didn't seem to fit in with the information she was readily offering him. All of it sounded innocuous enough on the surface, but there were brief hints of some buried emotion. Pain?

"I wouldn't expect Cielo to be the kind of town that would draw a person away from the spectacular beauty of your home state. The last I heard, the population of Cielo was about twenty-five thousand people.''

''I like it.''

''Glad to hear it.''

Once again a silence enfolded them. When he saw that she wasn't going to say anything more, he spoke. ''I want you to know that I really am sorry for what I said to you earlier. The truth is that I'm aware I don't spend enough time with Trisha, and I'm a little sensitive about it. Added to that is the fact that Letty didn't bother to tell me she was putting her in preschool. I didn't expect her to be going to school until next fall.''

''When she came in this spring for testing, we felt that she needed to learn how to be around children her own age. The head of the school discussed the matter with someone in your family. I assumed it was you, Mr. Callaway. It was agreed that she would start attending classes this spring.''

Cameron leaned forward, rested his elbows on his knees and ran one of his hands through his hair, his gaze on the floor. ''No,'' he said wearily, ''it wasn't me.''

''She loves you very much, you know,'' he heard her say softly. Why didn't that make him feel any better?

''And I adore her, but I know that she hasn't seen many signs of that.''

Once again she was silent, and Cameron felt the

silence condemning him. Slowly he straightened, then turned and held her gaze. "Look, since we've been thrown together for the next few days, why don't we dispense with the formality. My name is Cameron. My friends and family call me Cam."

He looked so uncomfortably earnest that she smiled. "I'm Janine."

"Janine. That's very pretty."

"Thank you."

"Does the rest of your family still live in Colorado?"

She shook her head. "The only family I had was my mother. She died two years ago."

"Oh. I'm sorry."

"Don't be. She'd been bedridden for some time. She was in a great deal of pain. She looked forward to the release."

"It must have been difficult for you to go through."

"Yes."

He leaned against the back of the couch. "So you were an only child. I was the middle of three boys. We're each five years apart, so we didn't grow up particularly close. But for all of that, we've managed to get along fairly well through the years."

She didn't say anything, and Cameron again felt himself getting edgy. Damn, didn't the woman make any conversation other than polite brief answers to his questions?

"Would you like something to drink?" he asked. "We have a fully stocked bar, some fairly good wine, whatever you'd like."

"A glass of wine would be nice."

"Great. Give me an idea of the kind you like, and I'll see if I can find something to your taste."

She suggested a dry white wine, and he went off to get some, wondering if he should change his mind and ask Pete to fly in to the rescue. The problem was he wasn't certain who needed rescuing, himself or his very reluctant guest.

Three

"And then she announced to the class that she wouldn't sit next to David because boys had cooties."

Cameron began to laugh and Janine joined in. Dinner was over, and the rest of the household had long since retired. He and Janine had returned to the family room, built up the fire and continued to enjoy their wine and the relaxed conversation that had evolved imperceptibly during dinner.

"Where in the world did she get something like that?" Janine asked when she could draw breath.

"No doubt that's one of Tony's stories. I think it started when he told her that all girls have cooties. She denied it vehemently even though she didn't have the vaguest idea what he was talking about. Obviously she switched the gender to suit her own convenience.''

"Tony?"

"Cole's son. He'll be eighteen this summer, but when he and Trisha get together, I swear he's no more than six!''

"Ah, yes. Trisha has spoken of him.'' They sat side by side on the couch, watching the flames. Never had he felt so aware of another person as he did of Janine at the moment. Letty had spoken to Allison by phone and had reassured Janine that Allison was delighted to share her clothes with her. Janine had found a tailored silk shirt and a pair of deep green slacks. Fortunately she had also been able to wear Allison's shoes, although she was barefoot at the moment. Her feet now rested next to his stockinged feet on the coffee table.

"It's late. I really should get to bed,'' she murmured.

"Why? You've got all day tomorrow to sleep.''

"Well, actually, I promised Trisha I would color with her in the morning.''

"She'll forgive you if you're a little late.''

Janine rolled her head lazily to the side so that she could see him. "I've really enjoyed this evening, Cam. You've made me feel like a welcomed guest instead of a gate crasher.''

"You're not a gate crasher. Not by any means.

I thought I made that clear earlier. I'm touched that you care enough about Trisha to come talk to me.''

"But you were right. It's really none of my business.''

"I'm glad you care, Janine. Believe me.'' He touched his finger to her cheek, verifying what he had already suspected. Her cheek felt like satin. She smiled and her eyelashes fluttered once, then closed. He cupped her cheek with his hand and pressed a soft kiss on her lips.

She made a sound in her throat, a light humming sound of pleasure that caused a flame to shoot through him. He shifted so that he could pull her into his arms and kiss her more deeply.

When he finally lifted his head, she whispered in a drugged voice, ''I don't think this is a very good idea.''

He smiled at her token protest, since she hadn't moved at all, even to open her eyes. "I disagree. I think it's a wonderful idea. I've been wanting to kiss you for hours.''

She opened her eyes, the lids heavy, and peered at him. ''Even when I was so prim and proper?''

He grinned. "Especially when you were so prim and proper. I had a sudden longing to see you hot and bothered.''

"Really?''

"Mmm-hmm.''

"You are a wicked man, Cameron Callaway.''

"So I've been told.''

"You've plied me with gourmet food and excellent liquor. Now all I want to do is curl up like a cat and go to sleep."

"That's *all* you want?"

Even her smile was sleepy. "I guess I'm more prim and proper than you expected, huh?"

"Don't get me wrong. I'm not complaining," he replied, helping her from the couch. After thinking about that for a moment, he said, "Well, to be completely honest, maybe I *am* complaining, but just a little. I know that if I allowed you to have your way with me tonight, you'd have absolutely no respect for me in the morning."

She choked on her laughter. "I'm impressed that you understand the situation so clearly," she said dryly. They were starting up the stairs. She glanced around and asked, "How do you keep from getting lost in here?"

"I suppose because I've lived here all my life and I've explored every inch of the place." He paused at the top of the stairs and waited for her to join him. "Remind me to take you up to explore the attic tomorrow. If you want the real scoop on the Callaways, there are several titillating journals that would scorch your fingertips to read."

She glanced at him. "And you'd let me read them?"

"Are you planning to write an exposé about us?"

"Of course not."

"Then I don't mind your reading them."

He took her hand and smoothed it across his callused palm. She had long narrow fingers that he kept fantasizing about. "May I walk you home, Ms. Talbot, ma'am?"

"Why, I'd be delighted, Mr. Callaway, sir."

She had been given one of the guest bedrooms a couple of doors down the hall from his room. In one respect she felt safe knowing that he was nearby. In another, she didn't feel safe at all.

. They stopped in front of her room and he leaned his hand against the wall beside her head. "Sleep well."

"Oh, I'll do that all right. I'm almost asleep on my feet."

He leaned down and kissed her, meaning to be casual, but the kiss got out of control. He braced his other hand on the wall, effectively caging her between his forearms. She tasted so good to him, and it had been so long since he had enjoyed being with a woman.

An alarm kept ringing in the back of his head, but he ignored it, enjoying the moment. When she slipped her arms around his neck, he allowed his body to press against her so that she knew exactly how she affected him.

When they broke apart this time, they were both obviously shaken. Her eyes glittered in the shadowed hallway as she brushed her fingertips across his lips. "Good night, Cam. I'll see you in the morning."

Before he could think of anything to say, she had slipped inside the room and closed the door. He stood there staring at the door for several moments before he forced himself to walk down the hallway to his room.

Muttering, Cameron strode into the bathroom for his third shower of the day, this time without benefit of hot water. Even after he crawled into bed, he had trouble going to sleep. What the hell was happening to him? His behavior toward his daughter's teacher was incomprehensible. She was nice enough, but he wasn't interested. Not in her, not in anyone.

So why did his pulse pick up every time his thoughts turned to how she had looked leaning against the wall—her hair mussed, her eyes half-closed, her lips softly swollen from his kisses?

What was wrong with him, anyway? He was too old to be behaving like a schoolboy with his first crush.

He punched his pillow vehemently a couple of times, flopped over onto his stomach and buried his head beneath the pillow.

Not more than a few minutes later—or so it seemed to Cameron—he felt a light touch on his shoulder. For an instant he thought it was— No, he knew better. He raised his head and discovered that the small lamp next to his bed was on. He distinctly remembered turning it off when he crawled into the sack. What in the— He rolled to his side and saw Cody standing nearby, grinning, his hands on his hips.

"How did you—? Where have you—? Damn, Cody, but you can be downright exasperating," he said as he got out of bed and grabbed his brother's shoulders. "Man, you're a sight for sore eyes."

Cody chuckled. "It's good to see you, too, Cam." He paused, flicking his gaze over Cameron's nude body and added, "All of you."

Cameron shook his head, still groggy from sleep, and, covering himself with a sheet, sat down on the side of the bed. He reached for a cigarette and said, "You could call once in a while, you know, just to let somebody know you're okay."

"I'm here now, aren't I? Isn't that good enough for you?"

"How the hell did you get here? Nobody's been able to get in or out."

Cody sank into a chair near the bed. "Why not?"

"The bridge nearest the house is out. How could you not know that?"

"Because I didn't come by road."

Cameron straightened and looked at his younger brother. "You came across the Rio Grande?"

"Yep. Borrowed a friend's horse and rode over to check on things."

"What are you doing over there?"

"Minding my own business."

Cameron sighed in disgust and lit a cigarette. Then he took a long drag.

"Tell me about the bridge," Cody asked after a prolonged silence.

"Nothing much to tell. This damned rain has stirred up all kinds of trouble. Alejandro and his men have been building a modern-day ark in the barn for more than a week, convinced we're all going to need it."

"Did you get yourself a new car?" Cody asked.

"No, why?"

"I saw a little white car sitting out there with the other ranch vehicles. At least I think it was white at one time."

"Belongs to Janine."

Cody settled back in his chair with a grin. "Janine, huh? Tell me more."

"There's nothing to tell. She's Trisha's teacher and she—"

"I didn't know Trisha was in school."

"Dammit, Cody, do you want an answer or do you want to interrupt me?"

"You mean I can't do both?"

Cameron finished his cigarette and crawled back under the covers. When he reached for the light, Cody said, "All right, all right. Damn, you're a grouch, Cam. So tell me what Trisha's teacher is doing here."

Cameron plumped up his pillow, then placed his

hands behind his head. "She came out to see me to talk about Trisha, and before she could leave the bridge was washed away."

"So what does she look like?"

"I didn't notice."

"Hmm. Either you're lying to me or you're in even worse shape than I thought." Cody got to his feet. "Either way, maybe I'd better talk to Cole about this latest information I've managed to dig up."

Cameron propped himself up on his elbows. "Cut the clowning, Cody. What have you found out?"

"Just what we suspected. The fire in the cotton warehouse was without doubt arson, the broken drilling equipment on the offshore rig was no accident, the lost shipment to Chicago was claimed with forged papers in St. Louis, the—"

"Swell. Just what I needed to hear."

"I tried to contact you at your office all week. All that sweet talkin' secretary of yours would tell me was that you were in court."

"I was."

"All week?"

"For the past three weeks. As far as I'm concerned I've proved that the series of so-called unrelated incidents in Corpus Christi were part of a plan to have us miss our deadlines, ruin our ability to fulfill orders, and that we are somehow being set up to lose the company."

"And what does your opposition have to say?"

"What they've said all along—prove that it was us."

"And have you?"

"At this point I just don't know. Everything's so damned circumstantial."

"What an interesting time for you to receive a visit from somebody who says she's Trisha's teacher."

"She is. I mean, Trisha recognized her."

"Of course. My point is, how did it come about that Trisha is in school in the first place? She isn't due to start until the fall."

"Yeah, I know. I had a little talk with Letty about that. It seems that when Trisha was tested she showed a lack of certain social skills, and the school felt she needed some extra time with children her own age. Letty said she didn't want me worrying about it, so she went ahead and enrolled Trisha in a semester of preschool, then told her to wait to tell me until I came home as a surprise." He thought about the confrontation between him and Janine. Some surprise. "The biggest surprise was that Trisha could keep a secret that long. She hasn't been very happy with school, from what I can gather."

"Interesting."

"But not surprising. I didn't like school, either, at first."

"No, I mean that Trisha's teacher developed

such an interest in her new student that she came out to discuss her with you, just at this time.''

''You think there's some connection?''

''It isn't paranoia when someone really is out to get you, bro. We've got an overwhelming amount of evidence to show that somebody, somewhere, has a real hatred for the Callaways.''

''I don't think it's Janine,'' he mumbled, thinking about the evening he'd just spent with her.

''Probably not, but I'm far from convinced that she isn't being used by someone to get more information about us. Isn't it convenient that she's now stranded here with you, so that she has full access to the entire house?''

Cameron groaned. ''And I just offered to let her read some of the diaries and journals upstairs that would tell her even more.''

''How did she respond?''

''Well, she didn't say no. She acted a little surprised that I offered.''

''I'm more than a little surprised. I'm flabbergasted. You're the most private one of our whole bunch.''

Cameron grinned. ''And you're the most suspicious.''

''What did you say she looked like?''

''I didn't.''

''Maybe you'd better. I may have seen her, or at least heard about her.''

''I doubt it. She's only lived here a year. She's

from Colorado. I'd guess she's somewhere between her late twenties or possibly early thirties. She's about the same size as Allison, so she's wearing her clothes. She's got long reddish-brown hair, I guess you'd call it auburn, and green eyes. She's slender but well proportioned."

"For somebody who didn't notice what she looks like, you did a damn fine job of describing her. I was planning to leave tonight, but I may stick around tomorrow to get acquainted."

Cameron had a sudden urge to tell his brother to leave her alone, but stopped himself. What difference would it make to him if Cody met Janine? Maybe they would hit it off. Did he care?

For some reason he couldn't fathom, he *did* care. He shut his eyes for a moment, wishing he had a better understanding of some of his actions over the past several hours.

"Sorry I woke you," Cody said, coming to his feet. "I think I'll go on to bed. I'd hoped to get in and out of here without Letty knowing about it, but I suppose I can listen to her scolding with good grace. I should be used to it by now."

"Letty's not so bad. I'm sure it wasn't the greatest moment in her life to have her brother and his wife killed, leaving her three boys to look after."

"Two. Cole was already twenty. So that left all her time to concentrate on you at fifteen and me at ten."

"She never could find you."

Cody flashed the grin that always caused everyone to forgive him, no matter what he had done. "Yeah, but she certainly did everything in her power to keep me hemmed in when she did."

"Is that why you've refused to help Cole and me with the businesses?"

"Partly. My mind doesn't run to figures and strategy."

"Just to disappearing and partying?"

"Something like that."

Cameron shook his head. "Cole and I worry about you, you know."

"What a waste of energy. I can take care of myself." He opened the door and glanced over his shoulder. "Your little schoolteacher isn't sleeping in my bed, is she?" he asked with a wolfish gleam in his eye.

"She's not even in your wing. Go to bed and try to stay out of trouble, if that's possible."

Cody gave him a two-finger salute, a parody of a parade-ground sign of respect, and closed the door behind him.

Cameron shook his head wearily, then leaned over and turned off the lamp beside the bed. He continued to lie there, staring up at the shadowy ceiling.

Could it be possible that Janine was somehow connected to the events of the past few years? The Callaway brothers had finally faced the fact that someone behind the scenes was working hard to discredit them wherever possible, to inflict as much property damage as possible, and was probably responsible for the deaths of their parents and Cameron's wife.

He wasn't certain where Cody found his sources, but they had become invaluable in tracing people and events. Perhaps Cody was using his playboy image to cover the investigative work he had been doing for the family for the past few years. Then again, he might be using the investigation to cover his urge to be free to roam as he pleased, to refuse to have anything to do with the family business, and to pop in and out of their lives at will.

Cameron would be interested to see what Cody thought of Janine. For the first time in a long while, he no longer trusted his own judgment. Sometime during that last kiss they had shared he had lost his objectivity about the woman who showed so much concern for his daughter.

Janine awoke the next morning with a raging headache. She had no one but herself to blame. She knew better than to have more than one glass of wine, but she had ignored her usual good sense. She found Cameron Callaway captivating, and she had wanted to stay in his company for as long as possible the night before. She had spent the evening looking for ways to bring a smile to his face.

She had rejoiced in his laughter, intuitively knowing that he found few things in his life amusing.

She felt his suffering and wished for some knowledge of how to relieve it. Their evening in front of the fireplace, watching the dancing flames, had been magical, as though time had been suspended while they learned more about each other.

She had told him a little more about her childhood, about growing up without a father, about spending her free time after school looking after the younger children who lived in her neighborhood.

He had told her what life had been like for him, growing up on a ranch in south Texas, knowing that he was observed and reported on because he was a Callaway. According to him, he had been the quiet one, the one who entertained himself by reading and studying, the one who hated the spotlight that shone on him.

Cameron had become very real to Janine during those few hours together. Very real, and for the first time since she met him, she had recognized his vulnerability.

Janine forced herself out of bed and into the shower, praying that she had something in her purse to help her aching head. By the time she was ready to go downstairs, the aspirin she had taken had eased her pain somewhat, and she vowed not to make a similar mistake in the near future.

As soon as she walked into the large dining

room, a man she had never seen before came toward her, his hand extended. "You must be Trisha's teacher. I had no idea teachers came in such delectable packages these days."

He was tall, with golden-blond hair and audacious eyes, but it was the outrageous grin that told her his teasing was all in good fun and not to be taken seriously. She took his hand and shook it gravely.

"Janine Talbot," she said in her most prim tone.

He immediately ducked his chin and said in a mock-shy voice, "Cody Callaway, at your service, ma'am." He kept her hand and led her to the place next to him at the table.

"Cody," she repeated. "You're the youngest of the three, aren't you?"

He peered both ways before leaning forward and saying, "Just a nasty rumor the other two started about me, you know. I let them get away with it, of course. Gives them such a sense of superiority."

He really was incorrigible. She began to laugh. He nodded as though pleased with her reaction to his teasing, and poured her a cup of coffee.

"Have you seen Trisha this morning?" she asked.

"Nope. I haven't been downstairs all that long, myself. Had a rather late night."

Janine caught herself rubbing her forehead in an effort to ease the ache. "I know what you mean," she said ruefully. "I'm afraid I don't have much of a head for wine."

"Aha! Everything is coming clear to me now, my pretty. My dastardly brother took advantage of your weakness, did he, and plied you with spirits in order to have his evil way with you." He paused, and she knew he saw the blush that covered her cheeks, blast it. In a nonchalant tone, he added, "Cam's smarter than I gave him credit for," and took a sip of coffee, his eyes filled with amusement.

"Of course he didn't take advantage of me," she said in an attempt to explain her betraying color. "He was very much a gentleman."

"Are we talking about my brother? The guy that's about my height, with brown hair and—"

"Oh, you. Are you ever serious?"

He clasped her hand between his two and peered soulfully into her eyes. "I would be quite willing to show you my serious side," he said, his voice sultry. "If you wish."

"All right, Cody." Janine heard Cam's voice behind her and turned to see him coming toward them, a frown on his face. "Do you have to hit on every female you meet? Give it a rest, will you? At least let her have her first cup of coffee."

Janine tugged her hand away from Cody's grasp, knowing that she was turning every shade of red. Cameron would think that the two of them had been flirting when, in fact, they had been making fun of the idea. Surely he didn't think she was the type of woman who would be sharing kisses with him in the evening and making up to his brother the next morning?

From the aloof stare he gave her as he sat directly across the table from her, that was exactly what he was thinking. Either that, or he didn't care what she did or with whom.

Well, she wasn't about to explain to him. She owed him nothing, regardless of the previous night's events.

"Did you notice the sunshine today, bro?" Cody asked.

"No."

"Didn't think so. Maybe this means there's going to be a change in the weather pattern. I know how you're itching to get back to work. I bet you can hardly wait to—"

"Cody, would you chill out for a while—please? I didn't have the best of nights, and I would really appreciate being able to enjoy my morning coffee in peace and quiet."

"Oh, sure, no problem. You and Janine seem to have suffered similar ailments." He glanced at Janine. "Would you like some aspirin?"

She shook her head. "I've already taken some, thanks. I'll be all right." She kept her eyes on her coffee.

Cameron looked at the two of them seated side by side. "I don't guess I need to introduce the two

of you. You seem to have struck up quite a friendship already.''

Cody beamed. ''So we did. It must have been
kismet, or maybe—''

''Cody,'' Cameron growled warningly.

His brother gave him a sparkling smile and
picked up his cup of coffee.

Janine watched the brothers, wondering whether
or not they got along. There was a strong family
resemblance, but their personalities were very different. Janine had always wanted a brother. Cody
was exactly what she had imagined a brother would
be. She had immediately felt relaxed and at ease
with him.

Her feelings toward Cameron were considerably
different.

Rosie brought platters of eggs, bacon, biscuits
and gravy out and set them all on the table. The
three of them ate in silence except for brief requests
to pass the butter, or salt and pepper, or for more
coffee.

By the time they finished, Janine felt uncomfortable with the silence, but she had no intention of
being the one to break it. All she knew was that
she didn't want Cameron to be angry with her. She
wasn't certain why, exactly. She just knew that was
the way she felt.

The swinging door from the kitchen opened, and
Janine looked up, thankful for the interruption,
thinking that Rosie had come to pick up their

dishes. Instead, a middle-aged man in worn jeans and shirt, wearing boots and carrying a hat, stood there.

"Sorry to bother you at breakfast, Cameron," he began.

"No bother, Alejandro. We're just enjoying last cups of coffee. How about joining us?"

"No, thanks. Thought I'd let you know that me and the boys think we can start on some kind of temporary bridge today, but I wanted to check with you first."

Both Cameron and Cody pushed back their chairs and stood. Cameron looked at Janine. "If you'll excuse us, we'll see what we can do to help you leave as soon as possible."

Cody began to laugh. "Why, Cam, you sound downright inhospitable. Here's your hat and coat, ma'am. Don't let the door hit you on the way out." He winked at Janine. "He just never did get his social graces down pat like he should have." He took her hand and raised it to his lips. "Sorry to have to leave you, pretty lady. We'll be back as soon as we can."

She kept her eyes averted, not wanting to see Cameron's reaction to his brother's clowning.

The three men left the room through the kitchen doorway, which presumably led them to a back exit. Janine felt a great deal of relief at having the chance to be alone for a while. She finished her coffee and stood.

She would go find Trisha in an effort to recreate the comfortable existence with which she was familiar—being around children.

Four

Alejandro headed toward one of the pickup trucks
and Cameron and Cody followed him. Cameron
knew that Alejandro was being polite in seeking
advice. He ran the ranch in its entirety, carrying
full responsibility for what took place on the premises. Letty was in charge of the Big House and the
employees who worked inside, but Alejandro had
the final word on everything else. However, in all
the time Cameron had known him, Alejandro
would always consult whatever brother happened
to be in residence at the time. The fact that, in the
end, each of them went along with his suggestions
never changed his way of handling things.

Alejandro got behind the wheel. The other two

slid into the front seat of the pickup from the other side.

"What the hell was that all about?" Cameron growled once Cody slammed the door behind them and Alejandro drove out of the parking area.

Cody gave him an innocent smile. "What are you talking about?"

"Why were you coming on to Janine?"

Cody lifted his brow. "Was I?"

"Is it some kind of game with you, to flirt with every woman you meet?"

"If it is, what does it matter to you?"

Normally Cameron had no reaction to what other people chose to do. So why was he so upset now?

He had to face his own feelings and stop running from them. He was attracted to the woman, no doubt about that. So what was he going to do about it?

He had been alone for four years now—not that he was considering matrimony. He wanted none of that, no reminders of a past that still carried too much pain for him. But what was wrong with an intimate friendship? They were both adults, weren't they?

"It matters in this case. So how about slacking off with this one and giving me some space," he finally muttered.

Cody gave him a sharp look. "I thought you weren't interested."

Cameron knew he looked as sheepish as he felt. "So did I. Guess I was wrong, huh?"

Cody laughed and Cameron found himself joining in.

"Good for you, Cam. It's just what you need."

"Nothing serious, you understand." He felt it imperative that Cody not read more into this than he intended.

"Sure. Who better than me can understand that kind of relationship?"

For some reason, that didn't make Cameron feel much better about what he was considering. Both he and Cole had always been troubled by Cody's life-style. Was he now actually considering imitating it?

He had never played the adult dating game. He and Andrea had met in college, had dated for three years and had gotten married the month after graduation. Their lives had flowed smoothly. She had become a buyer for one of the stores in San Antonio and had enjoyed traveling until they decided to start their family. He had planned his work in order to travel with her. They had had a wonderful time together. They had enjoyed doing the same kinds of things. Once Andrea was gone, he had buried himself in his work. Any spare time he had was spent with Trisha.

Now he was looking to change all of that by the simple task of asking Janine Talbot for a date. With a sinking feeling in his stomach, he realized that he didn't know how to go about it.

He wasn't at all sure he was ready for this next step. Having met her, he also realized that he didn't want to let her slip out of his life.

"I like butterflies best," Trisha said, a small furrow between her brows as she concentrated on her picture.

Janine looked at the picture and smiled. This was going to be one of the brightest butterflies nature could have possibly created. Trisha had used every color she could find in the shoe box where her crayons were kept.

"What do you like about butterflies?"

"They is so pretty, and they fly around and do things, and...," She paused, thinking, then shrugged. "You know. I bet it would be fun being a butterfly, don't you?"

Janine grinned. "Only if you don't get airsick!"

"What's that?"

"When you're flying around and your stomach acts like it's still on the ground."

Trisha studied her teacher. "Did that ever happen to you?"

Janine nodded. "Once, when I was flying and the plane was trying to get around a storm. My stomach much preferred staying on the ground that day."

Trisha grinned. "Was you scared?"

"Maybe a little."

"What do you like best?" the girl said, gazing down at her butterfly.

Janine thought for a moment. "I think that, of everything I like, rainbows are my favorite. They seem magical to me somehow. I'm always excited whenever I see one."

"Me, too. Maybe we can look for rainbows together some day."

"Maybe."

"What interesting thing have you two been up to?"

Janine whirled around and looked toward the doorway of the family room. Cameron strode in, a grin on his face. His earlier somber mood had obviously left. Either that, or he had recently received some very good news.

"Were they able to make a temporary bridge?" she asked as Trisha scrambled from her chair and went racing to her father.

"Daddy! Come look and see what me and Missy Talbot colored." He leaned down and picked up his bouncing daughter and carried her over to the coffee table, where Janine sat and where their creative efforts were displayed. "See? Hers are panda bears. Aren't they cute? Mine's a butterfly."

"Two artists obviously hard at work," he said solemnly, studying each piece as though considering the purchase of major art. Janine enjoyed watching Trisha puff up with pride as he made first one comment, then another, about the various efforts. He seemed to know exactly what to say without a hint of self-consciousness.

Then he glanced up and caught her watching him. His gaze seemed to pin her where she sat. "I'm afraid there's not much hope of our getting out of here for at least two, possibly three more days. The runoff is still too swift to chance working in the water, and the creek continues to be at flood level."

He sounded remarkably cheerful for a man marooned.

"I don't know what to do," Janine replied, expressing her worry out loud. "I'm expected to be at work at eight in the morning."

"You'll have to call and explain the situation. With the flooding in surrounding areas, there's a good chance there'll be no school."

She eyed him uncertainly. He appeared almost pleased.

"Isn't this going to pose a problem for you?" she asked.

"Not really. As soon as my secretary arrives at work in the morning, I'll give her a call and have her fax the most urgent business to me." He leaned back so that he was sitting next to Janine, their shoulders almost touching. Meanwhile, Trisha had scooted off his lap and was now attacking a brand-new picture with renewed fervor.

Janine had trouble meeting his gaze. He seemed to be amused by something.

"Well," she said uncertainly, "I suppose we'll have to make the best of the situation."

His smile broadened. "My sentiments, exactly. We'll use the time to get better acquainted."

Janine thought of his words later while she dressed for dinner. Cameron had spent the rest of the day with her and Trisha, entertaining them, asking questions. He had continued to draw her out until she realized with something of a start that she had told him almost her whole life story.

At one point she commented on the fact that she hadn't seen Cody since breakfast. She had been startled by his smile, which could have been one of satisfaction, when Cameron casually explained that Cody had left. Cody had chosen an unorthodox way to get there, and she assumed he had left on horseback, as well.

She had liked Cody and was comfortable around him. She felt anything but comfortable around Cameron, who was waiting for her to join him downstairs.

Now she gazed into the mirror, struck by the bold colors of the gown she wore. The shimmering emerald green of the cloth made her hair look redder and her eyes seem greener.

Cameron had told her a little about his artistic sister-in-law. She and his brother Cole had grown up on the ranch together. Janine wondered what it would be like to have had someone in her life besides her mother. She almost envied Cole and Allison their closeness.

She attempted to twist her hair into a coil, but it seemed to have developed a will of its own, defying her every effort to subdue it. Tossing her head in frustration, she grabbed her brush and once again allowed her hair to fall to her shoulders. As a result, the combination of the hairdo and the bright hue of the beautiful gown made her feel, when she stared into the mirror, as though she were looking at a stranger.

With a defiant toss of her head, she decided that for the next few days she would allow herself to play a new role, one that allowed her to flirt gently with a very attractive man. He had made no effort all day to hide his interest in her. She could only conclude that his earlier gruff demeanor at breakfast meant that he didn't happen to be a morning person.

As soon as she started down the stairway, Cameron appeared at the bottom. The look he gave her was so heated it caused her temperature to rise. She stood firm with her new resolve and met his gaze with a smile.

"I have a surprise for you," he said, reaching for her hand and pulling her close when she stood beside him.

"That's nothing new," she said with a grin. "You're full of them."

He looked pleased. "You think so?"

"Without a doubt." She glanced around. "Where's Trisha?"

"That's part of the surprise." He led her toward the back of the house, then through a couple of rooms to the solarium, where she and Trisha had been the day before. If she had thought it a magical room then, it was even more so now in the soft moonlight that came through the glassed ceiling. A table for two was set next to one of the glassed walls, with candles illuminating the surrounding area. A candelabra filled with candles sat among the greenery and the candlelight was reflected in the many panes of glass surrounding them. "Oh, Cam. This is beautiful."

"I sat with Trisha while she had her supper, oversaw her bath, tucked her into bed, read her two stories and left her sound asleep, just so you and I could have some time together."

"But what about your aunt?"

"Actually, I got the idea for this when she told me she was tired and decided to have a small tray in her room. She'll probably watch television until all hours, but at least she'll be resting."

"Is she feeling okay?"

"She insists she's fine. She becomes infuriated if any of us dares to suggest that her age might hold her back some. She made it clear that she was able to rest now that I was home to look after Trisha.'' He seated her at the table and then sat across from her. ''Of course she's right. Between the two of you this weekend, I've definitely been made aware of my shortcomings as a parent.''

Janine suddenly felt very small. She made herself hold eye contact with him. ''It was very presumptuous of me to think I knew what was best for your daughter.''

''The point was well taken, though—once I calmed down and thought about it. I'm thinking about taking Trisha to San Antonio so that she'll be with me there. However, I'm going to have to find a live-in housekeeper, check out the schools and see how she feels about relocating, beforehand. Although we lived in San Antonio her first year, she doesn't remember it. This has always been home for her. I made that my excuse for leaving her here for so long, but what I've come to understand is that home for her will be anywhere I am.''

Janine felt a pang somewhere in the region of her heart. She had grown to love Trisha in the few weeks the girl had been in her class. ''I know she'll want to be with you. There's not a doubt in my mind, after all of my conversations with her.''

''I think that's what really got me to looking at our situation. If she discusses her feelings with someone she barely knows, she must be more disturbed by my absences than I had guessed.''

''If you need to hear it from me, I think you're

doing the right thing, even though I'm going to miss her very much.''

He leaned over and took her hand. ''Well, maybe we can do something to alleviate that somewhat.'' He gave her hand a gentle squeeze and picked up the bottle that had been resting in a small bucket of ice. ''How about a glass of wine?''

Wasn't he going to explain his enigmatic remark? Apparently not, as he waited for her to respond to his question.

''One glass. I'm definitely making that my limit.''

He smiled. ''Never let it be said that I lured you past any of your limits.''

Rosie came in, carrying a tray. She placed salads in front of them and left with a small smile hovering on her lips.

''Thank you for thinking of this. I can't believe how beautiful everything is.'' She looked toward the fountain and discovered that the water was flowing for the first time since she had arrived. Its musical trickle could be heard in a muted subtle way she found captivating.

She was hardly aware of what they had for dinner. All she knew was that Rosie unobtrusively served them while they talked. They seemed to have so much to discover about each other. They talked about the most recent books they had read, their favorite pastimes, their hobbies, and both discovered that they were often content to be alone.

Most of their enjoyment came from solitary entertainment.

"I know this is impertinent of me, but I really want to know," Cameron began when they were having coffee.

She smiled. "Ask away."

"I can't understand why you're single. It has to be through choice. Or am I erroneously presuming that you've never been married?"

Her bubble burst with his words and she came tumbling back into reality. Not that she blamed him for his curiosity. On his own accord he had told her about Andrea—how they had met, their life together and the devastation of her death. She knew that by opening up to her he had assumed that she would be willing to do the same.

She searched for something to say, something that would explain without touching the core of her pain.

"I, uh, never had any desire to marry, I guess. Or met anyone with whom I thought I could be happy. As I said earlier, I'm really a very solitary person and quite content with my own company."

"But you're so wonderful with children. I would expect you to want a houseful of your own."

She dropped her hands to her lap so that he could not see the tension as she gripped them. "That's why I chose my particular vocation. I enjoy children. I just don't want them around all the time. I need my solitude. This way I have the best of both worlds.''

His gaze never left her face. She wished she could tell what he was thinking, but she couldn't. Not that it mattered, of course, what he thought.

''Well—'' she began to push her chair backward ''—I think I'll—''

He came to his feet. ''I hope you aren't too tired for at least a dance or two.''

That stopped her. ''Dance?'' she asked, hearing her voice squeak with surprise.

Cameron walked over to the wall and flipped a switch. Soft music filled the room. When he came toward her, he looked amused. ''I'd intended to turn that on earlier, but I forgot. It's wired to play in every room, but we seldom use it.'' He held out his arms to her. ''Shall we?''

How could she resist? She moved into his arms and felt as though she belonged there. The music was evocative of another era, the smoky sounds of a saxophone nudging something deep inside her to awaken.

She rested her head against his shoulder, allowing him to draw her closer until both of his arms were around her and her arms were around his neck. She could smell the freshly laundered scent of his shirt, mingled with the spicy aftershave he wore. Never before had a man had such an effect on her.

He explored the length of her spine with a light

touch that nevertheless seemed to leave his imprint tingling along her back.

By the time he lifted her chin with his forefinger, she knew she was rapidly losing control of her reactions to him. For that brief moment in time, she didn't care.

He brushed his lips lazily across her mouth in a gentle teasing motion, causing her to want more. She wanted him to kiss her the way he had the night before when they had stood outside her bedroom door. For that fleeting instant she had allowed herself the luxury of feeling everything she was experiencing, without her mind controlling her emotions and shutting them down. Like a potential drug addict with her first rush of pleasure, she was hungry for a similar experience. She tightened her arms and he seemed to understand, for when he claimed her lips, she felt scared with his heat.

Because of the tight rein she had always kept on her emotions, she had had no idea what it would feel like to experience passion—until now. Like a sudden flame, her newly awakened desire swept over her, engulfing her, leaving her trembling in its wake.

Cameron seemed to sense her abandonment to the moment. With a groan that she felt echo deep within her, he picked her up and carried her to the rattan sofa nearby. Sitting with her draped across him, he continued to kiss her.

When he slid his hand over one of her breasts

she tensed. His fingers moved tenderly across the tip, teasing and tantalizing. Instead of drawing away, she surprised herself by pressing closer to him.

When he finally lifted his head, Cameron said, "Lordy, woman, but you go to my head."

Her laugh, when it came, was shaky.

He hugged her, his touch soothing now as he stroked her back. "I owe you an apology. I know you're going to find this hard to believe, but this really isn't a seduction scene."

She leaned back to look at his face. Even with the shadows in the room, she could see he was flushed.

"What is it?" she asked, unable to resist.

He glanced around the room, at the cozy table for two with the tall taper candles still gleaming, then at the other candles placed about the room.

"Would you believe romantic?"

"It's certainly that," she agreed.

He leaned his head against the back of the sofa, shut his eyes and sighed. "I feel like a fool."

"Why?"

He opened his eyes and looked at her with a hint of a smile at the corners of his mouth. "I don't know anything about dating. I guess maybe I've watched too much television. I just thought maybe I'd set a mood and see what happened. I didn't mean to get carried away."

"You weren't alone. As I recall, you had my full cooperation."

He raised his head, his smile growing. "Hey, that's right."

"You certainly didn't force me or take advantage of me."

He slipped his hand, which he'd moved to her waist, back to her breast. "No?" His eyes gleamed with mischief in the candlelight.

She lifted his hand and slid her fingers between his. "No," she replied with a smile. "However, we don't want to start something we have no intention of finishing."

"We don't?"

He looked so crestfallen she almost laughed. She was ninety percent certain he was teasing her, but that ten percent doubt made her careful of hurting his feelings.

"No," she said gently. "We don't."

Once again he closed his eyes and leaned his head back. "Darn."

She began to laugh and he joined her. When the laughter faded she realized that he was staring at her intently. When he kissed her this time, there was a difference, a new tenderness that touched her heart. Each time she felt his lips lessening the pressure against her mouth to draw away, she felt a sense of regret. He must have felt the same way, because he never quite released her lips. Instead, he increased the pressure once more.

Finally she realized that she was losing control again. She hid her head in his shoulder.

"What's wrong? I've kept my hands to myself."

They were still holding hands.

"This is dangerous."

"You think so?"

"I know so."

"But it's fun," he offered hopefully.

"Yes, I'll certainly admit that."

"And I think we're both enjoying it."

She loved this light side of him, a side she hadn't seen before this evening. She wondered how often he allowed himself to unbend and tease in this way.

"Cameron?"

"Hmm?"

"Neither of us is the type to lose our heads and hearts in passion."

"We're not?"

"Uh-uh."

"You're sure?"

"Uh-huh."

"So what do you suggest we do?"

"Go to bed."

"Hell of an idea! Let's—"

"No, no, no," she said with a chuckle. "It's time for each of us to retire to our respective bedrooms where we will then go to bed and get some sleep."

The look he gave her was no longer teasing, but

filled with heat. "Do you honestly believe that last part?"

She sighed. "Perhaps not completely. But it's for the best."

"Why?"

She looked down at their clasped hands. "Because I'm not the kind of person who has casual affairs."

"Neither am I."

This time she had no doubt in her mind that he was serious. The intensity of his look caused her to tremble. She briefly closed her eyes, then forced herself to meet his gaze. "I don't date much, either."

"Neither do I," he repeated, "but I'd like to change that."

"I suppose the point I'm trying to make is that I don't want to change it." After the way she had been behaving, she could understand his skeptical expression. She felt the heat in her cheeks and knew she was blushing. "There's no future in it," she attempted to explain.

"Does there have to be a future?"

"Well, most people expect a relationship to go somewhere."

"Well, I'm not ready for a relationship that's going to 'go somewhere.' But I would like to get to know you better, and I've been encouraged to think you might feel the same way."

She could feel her heart racing. "Is that all?" she finally asked.

He cocked his head and grinned. "Well, I don't have a master plan mapped out just yet to submit for your approval, but give me a few days and maybe I can come up with something."

When she didn't respond he went on. "I'm not talking about something serious here, you know. There are times when I receive invitations where I'm expected to bring a guest. There are times when maybe I'd like to have a little company. There are even times when I'd like to pick up the phone and chat with someone. Do you see anything wrong in our forming a friendship that might include those activities?"

In all honesty she couldn't. She shook her head.

"Good enough," he said, standing up but still holding her as her feet came to the floor. "Then we know where we stand, don't we?"

"I, uh, suppose so."

"I'll try not to monopolize your time, but it would be nice to know I could call you once in a while."

She gazed into his shadowed face. "I'd like that."

"So would I," he murmured, before kissing her good-night.

Five

Cameron came awake with a start, blinking in an attempt to clear his vision. Early-morning sunlight poured through the window. He groaned. How the hell could it be morning when he didn't feel as though he had slept all night?

His dreams had kept him restless and wakeful for the past three nights. He was no longer dreaming about the crash. Now the only subject his subconscious dwelled on was Janine. Janine in bed with him, reaching for him, wanting him… Janine who left him aching and feverish, enticing him even in his sleep….

Damn. He sat up and rested his elbows on his knees. For the past two days he had not touched her. He had learned a valuable lesson after that first night of heated dreams. He had seen no reason to continue torturing himself by kissing her again. Unfortunately his new decision in no way lessened his awareness of her whenever he saw her.

Letty had made herself scarce since Janine had arrived, leaving Cameron and Trisha to entertain her. Trisha had certainly done her part. She made it clear that she was delighted to have Missy Talbot all to herself.

Cameron had worked in the study, going through papers, giving dictation over the phone to his secretary, until the sounds of laughter often impinged on his concentration and he would wander into the other room to see what was so funny.

Later he would become aware that he had ended up playing games with them and leaving his work unattended.

Cameron couldn't remember a time in his life when he had been quite so distracted in such a positive way.

He smiled to himself, thinking about the sound of Trisha's uninhibited laughter. He had never before heard such a spontaneously joyful sound coming from his daughter. He had been touched, even while he felt guilty, realizing how little he had done to add to her enjoyment of life.

Letty had been right. Trisha *had* needed to be around other people. Typically Letty had gone ahead and done what she felt was best without bothering to check with him. What he had to face was that, as long as he left Trisha with Letty, she would be the person in charge.

Was that what he wanted? Was that what Andrea would have wanted?

Andrea. This was the first time she had come into his mind unaccompanied by pain and a sense of loss. How strange. He had grown accustomed to thinking of her in those terms. Now he could see her more clearly. He knew with a certainty that Andrea would not have tolerated her daughter's isolation. She would have done something to prevent it long before now.

Cameron knew he would have to do something about it, too, and soon. He had some ideas but wasn't certain how to go about implementing them. He threw back the covers and strode toward the bathroom and shower. He would discuss the matter with Janine.

Janine was already at the table sipping coffee when he appeared.

"You're up bright and early today," he said with a grin, taking a seat across from her.

"I'm used to getting up early, I suppose. Plus, I'm feeling so guilty not being there to help with classes."

"You're sure they've opened the schools again?"

"Yes. I listened for school announcements this

morning on the radio. Everything's returning to normal. Three days of sunshine has helped tremendously."

Rosie brought in their breakfast and for several moments there was little conversation. Once he was finished, Cameron poured them another cup of coffee and said, "Then there's a good chance we'll be able to cross the creek today."

He watched her eyes light up and recognized his own dismay that she was so eager to get away. "Why, that's wonderful. I'm sure you'll be pleased to be back at work."

Normally he would be, so he nodded without committing perjury by verbally agreeing with her.

"Janine, I need your help."

She picked up her coffee and held the cup with both hands. "Oh?" she asked, and he could not only hear but see her wariness.

"About Trisha."

Her smile of relief was almost comical. "Why, certainly, Cam."

"I've been giving serious consideration to what we discussed about her. I know it will be a major adjustment for her, but I'm definitely considering moving her to San Antonio to be with me."

"I think she'd love that. I really do."

"The thing is, I'll need someone to look after her."

"That goes without saying. I'm certain that if you check with the employment services they'll find someone qualified to stay with her when you're not there.''

''I was wondering if you would consider being the one. I mean, Trisha already knows and trusts you, and I...'' He paused when he saw the shocked look on her face.

''I can't do that,'' she finally said. ''I'm sorry. I would like to help you as much as possible, but that just wouldn't work. I mean, I have a contract at the school, and I can't just walk away from it. They're depending on me. And besides...''

He waited, and when she just shook her head he repeated. ''Besides?''

She dropped her gaze to her coffee. ''I don't think it would be a very good idea for the two of us to live in the same place.''

''Oh?'' He was more than a little interested to hear her elaborate on that one!

''I mean, Trisha is used to having a more mature woman, like your aunt, looking after her. I doubt she would accept me.''

''But she already has.''

''As her teacher, yes. For a few short hours in the day when she sees all the other children obeying me. But I don't think she'd respond in the same way on a daily basis.''

''You've gotten along with her during this visit.''

''Of course. We both understand the rules. I am the guest. She is playing hostess and has been very diligent in entertaining me. Knowing my role, I have been most careful not to correct her in any way, or to suggest how she conduct herself or what schedule to keep. Your aunt has continued to be in charge.''

Cameron felt frustrated. All her arguments were rational and logical, but they had nothing to do with the real issue. ''Andrea was about the same age as you. Trisha would have been raised by a young woman had her mother lived.''

''Yes, I understand that. But the fact is that Andrea isn't here and Trisha's not used to someone my age taking charge of her.''

''So you're saying no?''

''That's correct.''

''Damn.'' He stared at her, wishing he could think of something to say to change her mind.

''However...''

''Yes?''

''I could still come to San Antonio and visit with Trisha so that she won't feel cut off completely. Perhaps my school could recommend a preschool near your home. I'll ask.''

''You'd do that?''

''Certainly.''

''Would you consider coming to visit me, as well?''

She eyed him a little uncertainly.

''I mean, just as a friend, of course. Nothing serious. I've enjoyed getting to know you. I'd miss seeing you."

She smiled. "I'd like that."

He held out his hand across the table and she willingly placed hers in it. "Thank you," he said, feeling as though the jury had just come in with a favorable verdict on a case he hadn't been at all certain he'd had a chance of winning.

The phone rang two days later. Without glancing up from the contract he'd been looking over, he hit the intercom button. "Yes?"

His secretary's voice answered. "A Ms. Janine Talbot on line three."

Cameron felt as though he had just been zapped by a bolt of lightning. His whole body tingled at the mention of her name. "Thanks."

He reached for the phone. "Janine! It's good to hear from you. I take it you made it home all right the other day."

"Yes, thank you." She sounded very prim and proper. "I spoke with the principal of our school and she gave me the names of a few schools in your area of San Antonio. I thought you might want to look them over."

"Great idea. Hold on, let me find something to write on." His desk looked as though a tornado had come through. Piles of paper were everywhere. He pulled out a lined yellow pad from the bottom of one disordered stack, further dislodging other papers. "Ready."

She gave the names to him, along with addresses and telephone numbers. A very thorough lady. When she was finished she added, "Trisha came back to school today. She told me that her aunt had insisted she get out of the house because she was driving them all crazy. Trisha was quite proud of her accomplishment."

Cameron chuckled. "Knowing her, I'm sure she was."

"She misses you."

"Yeah. I talked to her last night. She wanted to know when I was coming back."

"And you said?"

He sighed. "I've got to stay in town over the weekend. I go back to trial on Monday, and I need to go over my summation a few more times to make sure I'm covering everything."

"I see."

"You have to understand that by the time I get there, Trisha is already in bed and I need to leave so early to get back that she's still in bed. She wouldn't even know I was there."

He didn't know why it was so important for him to make her understand. He just knew that it was.

"Cam?"

"Hmm?"

"How would you feel about my bringing her in to see you tomorrow evening for a couple of hours?

We could be there when you take a break, maybe have something to eat. She could always sleep on the way home.''

For a moment he was too choked up to say anything. "You'd do that for us?"

"Yes."

"I'd like that. I'd like it very much."

"Fine. Let me know where to meet you and when. You might want to let your aunt know our plans, so she won't think I'm kidnapping Trisha."

"I'll do that." He gave her the address of his condo and said, "I should be there by six-thirty, no later than seven."

"I'll let you get back to work. We'll see you tomorrow night at seven."

Cameron hung up the phone, smiling to himself. Whether Janine Talbot wanted to admit it or not, she was growing attached to the Callaways. He planned to do everything in his power to become a habit in her life.

The next afternoon, Janine stood in the middle of her bedroom floor turning slowly so that she would view the clothes laid out on the bed, over the chair, hanging on the closet door, and draped over her vanity stool and bentwood rocker.

Practically everything she owned was strewn around the room. She couldn't believe how undecided she was about what to wear on her trip to San Antonio. Glancing at her watch, she groaned.

She had less than twenty minutes before she needed to leave to pick up Trisha.

Why was she being so silly about this? It wasn't as though she hadn't just spent last weekend around him. However, the fact that she wore someone else's clothes may have given him a different impression of her. Now that she looked at her own wardrobe, she realized how drab it was. Her suits were basic tans and browns, light and navy blues and one black one. Her blouses were brighter, but not by much. The pink dress on the rocker was the most colorful thing she owned, and she wasn't at all sure it was appropriate for the occasion.

But then, what was? She was arranging transportation so that a little girl could see her daddy, that was all. Before she could finish the thought, a tiny inner voice whispered, *Oh, yeah?* She couldn't honestly respond with a firm rebuttal.

Okay. She would admit it. She had missed him. Janine had been delighted when Trisha showed up at school once again, full of mischief and vitality. In the past, she had taken special pains not to get too involved with her students and most especially not to have a favorite. However, even before she met Cameron she knew that Trisha had gotten past all her rules and defenses. She made every effort not to show favoritism, nor let Trisha get away with misbehaving.

Interestingly, Trisha was more outgoing with the

children yesterday than she had ever been before. Was she feeling more secure? Janine wondered.

She grabbed the pink dress and slipped it over her head, smoothing it at her waist and hips. The soft color looked brighter with her auburn hair. One of her friends at school had coaxed her into buying it. She had no reason to wear it before, feeling that it was too light-colored for school; it would quickly get soiled there.

For the first time since she had purchased it, she was glad her friend had urged her to buy it. She looked younger somehow, more like the woman she had been at the ranch.

There was no time left to put her hair up, so she brushed it out and allowed it to hang around her shoulders. She stared into the mirror, amazed at the sparkle in her eyes. She couldn't fool herself—she was eager to see Cameron again. Her feelings for him were continuing to grow without encouragement of any kind.

By the time she reached the ranch house, or as Cameron and Cody had called it, the Big House, she was more in command of herself. As soon as she knocked, Rosie opened the door.

"Hello, Ms. Talbot. It's good to see you again."

Janine grinned. "It's good to be back. Is Letty here?"

"No, ma'am. She's visiting with friends, but Trisha is all ready to go."

Trisha had heard their voices and now she came

running out of the solarium. "You're here! You're here!" she shouted, running full tilt toward Janine and throwing her arms around her.

Janine took a quick step backward in an attempt to regain her balance so they wouldn't end up on the floor.

"You di'nt tell me yestiddy we was goin' to see Daddy today!"

"I know. I didn't know we were going to see your dad when you were at school. Even if I had known, we wouldn't have discussed it then."

"How come?"

"Because when we're at school, I'm your teacher. Away from school I'm your friend."

"How come you can't be both all the time?"

"Well, I guess I can. I suppose the difference is what we talk about. At school we only talk about school things."

She could see Trisha mulling that one around in her head, which gave Janine a moment's breathing space. Five-year-olds were notorious for asking questions. Even though she was accustomed to the constant barrage for information, she wasn't always prepared to give comprehensive answers at a moment's notice.

"I take it you're ready to go?"

"Uh-huh. I been ready a lo-o-ong time!"

Janine laughed. "Then let's get on the road, young 'un."

The drive to the city was filled with happy chatter. Janine discovered that Trisha seldom visited her father there. He generally came to the ranch, so she was excited at the prospect of visiting his place again and seeing if he had changed anything since her last visit.

While Janine listened, she mentally prepared herself to stay in the background and not distract either of the Callaways from their visit. She rehearsed brief answers in her head as she followed the directions Cameron had given her to his place on the north side of the city.

As soon as she pulled to a stop in front of the building, all her rehearsed lines swept out of her head. Trisha was already excitedly recognizing various things from her last visit. By the time they were out of the car, the little girl was tugging Janine's hand to get her to hurry.

Cameron answered on the first ring, which was one of her worries answered; she had been afraid he might not be there and then she would have had to figure out what to do to entertain Trisha until he arrived to let them inside.

"Daddy!"

Cameron swooped his daughter into his arms. Trisha wrapped her arms around his neck and gave him quick kisses on his cheek, ear and jaw.

"It's good to see you, too, angel," he said in a gruff voice, hugging her to him. For a moment Janine forgot her self-consciousness and allowed herself to enjoy the scene before her—the tall lean man in jeans, checkered shirt and moccasins holding the little blond girl as though she were fragile glass, his face shining with love.

When he focused on Janine she felt as though a spotlight had been shone on her. She forced herself not to fidget.

"Thank you for bringing her," he said, holding out his hand. In a movement as natural as breathing, she placed her hand in his and allowed him to guide her into his home.

Once inside, she had to catch her breath. The place was nothing like she expected. Perhaps because he was alone, she had assumed that he would have a typical bachelor pad, messy and with minimal decorations. Instead, she could tell that he had put a great deal of thought into the decor to meet his own personal needs. The living area was open to the second story. A balcony hallway ran around three sides of it. The fourth wall was made entirely of glass. The view was of a secluded garden, enclosed for privacy by a stucco wall. She could see a path wandering toward the back, disappearing behind the lush foliage. When he saw where she was looking, he said, "I have a pool out there. I try to spend at least an hour a day in the pool for exercise. I don't always manage it, though."

She turned away and noticed the cream colored walls, and the Southwestern motif, with its touches of peach, turquoise and copper. "I made reservations for dinner." He looked at his daughter, still in his arms. "Are you hungry?" She nodded vigorously and he laughed. "Me, too." Once again his intent gaze focused on Janine. "You're looking very springlike tonight. I like that color on you."

She couldn't stop the silly grin she knew she was wearing. She couldn't believe how wonderful it was to see him again, to have him notice what she wore and comment on it, to be there in his home.

"Thank you."

"I need to run upstairs and change. I dress very casually for work on Saturdays, but if I'm going to be taking my two favorite ladies out to dinner, then I want to look my best." He set the giggling Trisha on her feet, then went up the wrought-iron staircase to the second floor. He glanced down at Janine. "Go ahead and look around if you like."

She peeked through one of the open doors off the living room and found a very comfortable-looking study with a large desk and chair, a computer, fax machine, copier and a wall of bookcases filled to overflowing.

Next she saw a small dining room that connected to a kitchen filled with the latest cooking devices. The counter extended into a bar where he had obviously left some of the work he'd had with him earlier.

"Ya wanna see upstairs?"

Trisha had been following her from room to room. "Would you like to show me?"

"Uh-huh." She took Janine's hand and led her

up the stairs, then turned right where Cameron had turned left. She took her all the way around the balcony to the last door, then opened it dramatically. "This—" she paused impressively "—is my room. Daddy let me help decorate it. I picked out the paper on the wall and the furniture and everything."

The French Provincial furniture made the room look as if it belonged to royalty. The canopy and its ruffled edge was in the same pattern as the border print that encircled the room.

"This is beautiful," Janine said slowly, taking it all in.

Trisha walked to a door and flung it open. "I have my own bathroom and everything." She walked through the bathroom and paused in front of another door. "'Course this door goes into the other room for the person who stays here, see?" She held open the door. "For guests and things."

Janine peered in and saw a room done in quiet good taste. When they were back on the balcony, Trisha pointed and said, "All of that over there is my daddy's room. It's bigger 'n big, my uncle Cody says. Do you wanna see?"

"Uh, no, Trisha, I don't think that would be a good idea. Your dad's getting dressed in there, and I don't think he would appreciate it if he had visitors."

Trisha covered her mouth with both hands, but couldn't disguise her giggles. Finally she burst out with, "Wouldn't it be funny if we walked in and he was nekkid?"

Janine could feel her cheeks heating up and fought to control her voice. "I doubt if he would find it funny at all."

At that moment Cameron came out of his room, buckling his belt. "What wouldn't I find funny?" he asked, meeting them in front of the stairs.

"Nothing, really," Janine hastened to say.

"I said if we was to walk in your room while you was puttin' on your clothes, we'd find you nekkid." Trisha giggled. "Wouldn't that be funny?"

" 'Funny' isn't the word that immediately pops into my head," he said, obviously noting Janine's reddened cheeks. How she hated that betraying trait. She felt even more embarrassed when he winked at her.

Cameron picked up Trisha in one arm and held out his hand to Janine. They walked down the stairs and out through the kitchen to the garage, where his car was parked.

She was able to regain her composure on the way to the restaurant because Trisha kept Cameron occupied answering her numerous questions. It was nice to see someone else dealing with a constant barrage of questions. She smiled to herself, but Cameron caught it.

"Are you going to share what you find so amusing, or just sit over there, keeping your secrets?"

"No secrets, really. I can tell that you're used to

answering her questions. You never have to search for an answer as I do. Sometimes she stumps me, I must admit.''

He grinned. ''Ah, but you see, I'm a trained trial lawyer. Cross-examination is a technique I learned years ago. Being the one cross-examined can get a little uncomfortable, of course, but it all goes with the territory.''

''Well, I must commend you on how well you deal with her.''

''Thank you, kindly, dear lady. I would have thought with your training that you would be used to it, too.''

''Oh, I am. But the questions I get at school are considerably different than some she was throwing my way earlier today.''

''Such as?''

''Well...''

Before she had to think of one, Trisha obligingly asked a new one. ''Daddy, how come Missy Talbot's your dear lady?''

''That's just a figure of speech.''

''What's a figure of speech?''

''Well, it's not to be taken literally.''

''What's lit—''

''Okay, okay. You win. Let me try to explain a little differently. I was teasing Ms. Talbot. She is a lady and she is dear to me, so what I said was the truth, but put in a joking way.''

''Oh.''

Janine looked out the side window, afraid to face Cameron at the moment. Her heart had suddenly gone into double time when he said that she was dear to him. Dear God, what was happening here? She was already drawn to these people more than she cared to be. Somehow all her careful plans and ideas seemed to leave her whenever she was in close proximity to Cameron Callaway.

"Is something wrong?" he asked, and she quickly looked at him and forced herself to smile as casually as possible.

"Not a thing. Just looking forward to dinner."

"Good. I think Trisha might enjoy eating downtown along the river. There's some beautifully decorated outdoor places. We might go for a boat ride later, if you'd like." He glanced at Trisha.

"Oh, yes."

The evening went by in a blur of color, spicy, delicious food and lots of laughter. By the time they arrived home, Trisha was sound asleep.

"I have a suggestion to make," he said when they drove into his garage.

"Yes?"

"Why don't the two of you stay overnight and go back in the morning? There's no reason to rush back tonight, is there?"

"Other than we didn't bring any clothes for an overnight stay."

"Oh, Trisha has plenty of things here for her. I might be able to find you something to sleep in, though I'm afraid nothing of mine would fit you for day wear." His grin was filled with mischief when he added, "Unfortunately I don't know any women who might have left their clothes here."

Their eyes caught and held. Janine read the message in his. His eyes had haunted her every night this week and now here she was looking into them, being captivated by them once again.

"I suppose we could. I know you have a great deal to do tomorrow."

"Yes," he agreed. "But I decided to bring it home so that I can work here. I'll feed you breakfast and send you on your way."

"Won't your aunt be expecting Trisha and me tonight?"

"I'll give her a call once we get inside."

She shrugged. "Then we'll stay. Thank you."

He got out of the car and walked around to her side. Once he had the door open he leaned in to take Trisha from her arms. His fingers brushed against her breast, and both he and Janine froze for an instant before he picked up his daughter and carried her into the house. Janine slowly followed him, still tingling from his touch.

While he was upstairs, she found the coffee and made a pot. She didn't know about him, but she could definitely use a soothing beverage.

By the time he came downstairs she had poured them coffee and had carried it into the living room.

"A woman after my own heart," he said by way

of greeting. "Thank you. I had intended to offer you something as soon as I got Miss Trisha down for the night."

"Did she ever wake up?"

"Not even by a flutter of an eyelash. That gal is out for the count."

She smiled, remembering the evening. "She had such a good time. I've never seen her eyes so big."

"I know. I hadn't realized how much she misses when I leave her at the ranch. She thoroughly enjoyed the mariachi band."

"Not to mention the Dixieland jazz."

"She must have walked for miles with us."

"I know. My legs were giving out before she began to wilt."

"But when she crashed, she crashed. One moment she was chattering like a magpie, the next minute she was asleep."

"I know. She has two speeds—flat-out and sound asleep."

They laughed softly and sipped their coffee. When they finished, Cameron took her cup and placed it on the coffee table next to his, then he applied a steady pressure on her hands to coax her to move closer to him. By the time he released her hands, they were side by side. That was when she realized that he had only released her so that he could place his arms around her.

"Thank you," he whispered, kissing her lightly on the mouth.

When she could think again, she said, "For what?"

"For bringing her to me. I would never have thought of it. I suppose I have a single-track mind. I knew I needed to work this weekend. It didn't occur to me that I could take a few hours and enjoy myself, as well."

"I'm glad you did. Enjoy yourself, I mean. It was good to see you laughing and relaxed."

"I'm only happy and relaxed around you, it seems."

She shook her head. "Not me. It's having Trisha here."

He took a lock of her hair and curled it around his finger. "It's true that I'm enjoying Trisha, but that's also because of you. As much as I love her, I have felt the obligation and responsibility of being her only parent more than I've been able to just relax and enjoy her as a child with her own personality and preferences. You've helped me get to know her better, and hopefully she's getting to know me better, as well."

"I'm glad. I think you'll both benefit from this."

He brushed her cheek with his forefinger. "Were you and your father close?"

Janine forced herself not to stiffen at his unwelcome question. After all, his curiosity was understandable. She just wished that she could give him a more positive answer.

"I never knew my father," she said in a low voice.

"Oh, I'm sorry. Was he killed in the service?"

She shook her head. "According to my mother, he was very upset when I was born and turned out to be a girl. There were some complications at the time of my birth. Both Mother and I almost died. When she finally recovered, the doctors told them she wouldn't be able to have any more children. So my dad left."

"Left? You mean he walked out?"

"According to my mother, he said he didn't want half a woman. He wanted a family. He had counted on having several boys. I don't know if he ever got them. Neither one of us ever heard from him again."

"Why that bast—"

She placed her fingers over his mouth. "No. There are many people out there who feel a family is extremely important."

"Well, of course family is important. But he had a family. How could he just walk away like that? I don't understand."

"Mother never fully recovered. As far back as I can remember she was always fragile. Perhaps it was just as well that he left. He didn't sound like the kind of person who had patience with anyone who did not have perfect health."

He hugged her. "That wasn't much of a life for you, if you had to look after your mother."

"I didn't know any other way to live so it seemed normal to me."

"Weren't you lonely?"

"Of course. But I learned to entertain myself."

"At least I had my parents until I was fifteen. They were there for me. And I had Cole and Cody. I can't imagine being on my own the way you were."

She touched his jaw, tracing a line from his ear to the corner of his mouth. "Thank you for caring. I really don't like to talk about my childhood."

"No, I can certainly see why. No wonder you teach kids. You're getting to enjoy what you never had growing up."

She shifted, always uncomfortable whenever her early life was the topic of discussion. "It's late. We both need our rest."

"I know, but I hate to let you go. Janine, you're becoming very important in my life, as well as Trisha's life."

She froze, hearing the husky intimacy of his voice. "Don't, Cam. Don't try to make something out of this. We're friends. Let's leave it like that."

"Friends, huh?" He nuzzled her ear, then bit the lobe. When she flinched he kissed it to make it better.

"Do you have any idea how much I want you in my bed?"

"Cam..." she began in a shaky voice.

"I know, I know. I'm still your host and you're

still my guest and I'm not going to take advantage of you. But if my mama hadn't raised me to be such a gentleman, I'd sure as hell give it a try!''

She began to laugh, then hastily covered her mouth. ''Well, in the interests of keeping your mama proud of her little boy, I'm going to bed and relieve you of some of your temptations.''

''Thanks a lot.''

''Don't mention it.''

''So when will I see you again?'' Cameron asked.

''When do you want to see me again?''

''As soon as possible,'' he admitted.

''I don't have much free time during the week.''

''Neither do I.'' He was quiet for several minutes. ''Maybe next weekend we could fly up to Arlington and spend the day at Six Flags.''

''Fly?''

''Sure. Pete will fly us up. We'll get a car at the airport, spend the day, then fly home.''

''Who's Pete?''

''Our pilot. He gets Cole and I around—to wherever we need to be in this state. It's too damned big to drive everywhere.''

''You have your own private plane?''

''The company does. Actually I think there's two, plus a helicopter.''

''When I'm with you and Trisha, I forget that you're part of the Callaways, and then when you say something like, 'Let's fly to Six Flags,' I'm jerked back into reality.''

"Why? Is there something wrong with flying to Six Flags?"

"Not to you. You've always lived like that. I guess I find it difficult to understand why you work so hard when you obviously don't need the money."

"I work because it's my responsibility to help Cole keep everything going."

"But Cody doesn't feel the same obligation?"

"No. He's never been interested in any of it. Oh, he loves the ranch as we all do. But he goes his own way."

"Does he work at all?"

"Yeah, he does, but don't ask me what he does, because I don't know exactly. I know he's got contacts in high places. He's been helping me try to get to the bottom of some of the incidents in a few of our companies."

"But being a Callaway doesn't particularly impress you, does it?"

"Not particularly. Is it supposed to?"

She just shook her head, feeling helpless to explain.

"Does it bother *you?*" he finally asked.

"I'm not certain," she said, trying to be honest. "Your life-style is nothing like I'm used to."

"Do you think you could get used to it?"

She didn't like the seriousness in his voice. "I

suppose I can be a friend to a Callaway." She grinned. "See, I'm not prejudiced!"

He grabbed her, pulling her onto his lap. "You deserve this and you know it," he growled and covered her mouth with his.

Once again, she felt almost as if she were melting. How had she allowed this man past her defenses? She didn't know when it had happened, or how it had happened. She just knew that she found him impossible to resist.

Six

Janine let herself into the kitchen of the small house she lived in, finally admitting that the Texas heat in August was too much for her. She had been working out in the postage-stamp-size backyard, encouraging her annuals to continue blooming by carefully watering them and removing the weeds.

Now she felt as limp as an overcooked noodle. She pulled off her gardening gloves and her sun hat, reached into the refrigerator and grabbed a large pitcher of iced tea. That in itself was a sure sign she was becoming an honest-to-God Texan. No self-respecting Texan would be caught in the summertime without plenty of iced tea.

She walked through the cool house and wandered out onto her front porch, which was shaded from the direct sunlight by an overgrown lilac bush. Even with the heat, there was generally a breeze. Today was no exception.

She sat on the porch swing, looking down at her shorts and sleeveless shirt in disgust. She looked like Pigpen, in the Charlie Brown comic strip. She would go shower and change as soon as she finished her glass of iced tea. For now, however, she intended to sit and rock, to take pleasure in her gardening accomplishments and dream of Cameron Callaway.

She had spent most of her idle time this summer dreaming of that man. School had been out for almost two months now, so she had more free time. She wasn't certain how it had come about, but most of her time had been taken up with Cameron and Trisha.

After their highly successful trip to Six Flags, they had made many outings around the state. Sometimes they visited places nearby, such as Breckenridge Park in San Antonio, or the zoo where Trisha got to ride an elephant. One time they took her to see Fort Sam Houston, where the inner section of the restored quadrangle had been turned into a wildlife preserve, almost a petting zoo.

Sometimes they went farther afield. One weekend they visited the Schlitterbahn Waterpark in New Braunsfels. Another time they drove to San Marcus to enjoy the Aquarena Springs water show.

Cameron had gotten tickets for the touring production of Cats in Dallas, and they had flown up to see it.

Trisha had loved it all, but she begged to return to see the dolphins at Sea World after a visit there.

The summer had been an obvious success in many ways. Trisha had discovered how much she enjoyed being with her father. As for Janine...she had fallen in love.

For more than three months the trio had spent almost every weekend together. When Cameron's schedule was unusually hectic, they would stay at his home in San Antonio or go to the ranch.

He had left Trisha at the ranch during the summer but he was making plans to move her permanently to San Antonio in September so that she could start kindergarten there. He had suggested that Janine might help him interview a combination housekeeper/companion for Trisha. Only the most qualified women were interviewed and she had found two with promise, but for one reason or another, Cameron decided against each one.

Janine sipped her tea and smiled. Wouldn't she enjoy being the one who was there for Trisha every day? Of course the idea was more impossible now than ever. How could she possibly see Cameron as her boss?

There had been a couple of times during their association when she had stopped fighting herself and enjoyed the moment, much like that first dinner they'd had together last April at the ranch. She would have needed very little, if any, encouragement to have made love with him now, but he had never taken advantage of her momentary weaknesses.

Quite honestly, she was frightened to allow their relationship to change. What they were sharing was very precious to her. Cameron had become the brother she had never had—teasing and tormenting her, hugging and nurturing her, always there when she needed him. Other times he was the father she had always wanted—intelligent, filled with wisdom and sound advice, understanding, undemanding, fully accepting her.

He had coaxed her out of the shell she had lived in all her life, making her believe that she had something of value to offer another person. He appeared to be happier when he was around her, and more relaxed. He laughed more easily.

So did she.

Since their relationship could never culminate into more than friendship, Janine didn't want to risk what they had by allowing them to become lovers. At the moment she could handle not only loving him, but being in love with him. But if she allowed their relationship to become more intimate, she stood a good chance of losing everything.

She wasn't willing to take the risk.

Thus far, Cameron had seemed to accept the limits she had set. She couldn't ask for more from a friend. What had been haunting her in recent weeks was the fact that *she* wanted more. How could that be? She had been shy around men all her life. It was as though they were alien beings whose actions were incomprehensible to her. By the time she reached high school she had spent most of her spare time studying at the library and reading fiction.

Until she met Bobby. He had pursued her with a single-mindedness that the sixteen-year-old girl she had been could neither ignore nor resist.

She took another sip of her tea and sighed. How strange. Today was the first time she had been able to think of Bobby with a sense of detachment. What had happened had not been his fault. A driver who had lost control of his car had veered into their lane and hit them. Bobby had done everything he could to avoid the oncoming car. She later heard that the police had commended him on his quick reflexes, which had kept them from going off the road and down the steep gully nearby.

They had been such kids back then. It was time for her to let go of the emotions that surrounded her memories of Bobby. He had chosen to break up their relationship after the accident, based on who he was and what he wanted from life. She could understand much better now that his decision had been the best thing for both of them.

She smiled to herself. Cameron had brought real healing into her life. Someday maybe she could explain to him what had happened to her during that traumatic time in her life and how severely her life had been changed. Never before had she believed she could look back with such a sense of acceptance of her situation. Having Cameron in her life had made such a wonderful difference.

A car pulled up in front of her house, and she idly glanced toward the street. She rarely received company—not unless they called first—so she knew that whoever had stopped was either lost and looking for directions or was visiting one of her neighbors.

Her eyes widened and she groaned, remembering how she looked. It was Cameron! He was already on his way up the sidewalk. When he saw her looking his way he waved. Darn. She didn't have time to slip inside and get cleaned up. Slowly she came to her feet.

"Hello, pretty lady," he said with a grin. "How've ya been?"

She glanced down ruefully at her dirt-smudged shorts and top and her bare feet. "As you can see, I've been gardening. You'll be pleased to know that I left some of the dirt for the flowers." She looked out at the car and saw that it was empty. "What brings you this far south in the middle of the week?"

He sank down on the swing and tugged her to join him. "I realized at about eleven o'clock this morning that I've been working too hard."

She grinned. "And what bolt of lightning managed to get your attention?"

He leaned against the chain holding the swing, closed his eyes and sighed. "I dunno, exactly. I woke up this morning with a god-awful headache after another restless night. I had trouble concentrating on my work all morning. Finally I told my secretary I was going to take a few days off for a little R and R."

"So you're going to the ranch, I take it?"

He opened his eyes and looked at her, his gaze seeming to burn into her. "No. I came to see you."

His timing couldn't have been worse. She was already in a very vulnerable position because she had finally consciously admitted to herself that she loved him.

"So how's your headache now?"

He closed his eyes once more. "It feels like a dozen buzz saws working at high speed," he admitted wearily.

"Would you like some iced tea and aspirin?"

"Sounds good," he murmured. "It just feels good to sit here with you and rest for a few minutes."

She went into the house and found the necessary pain relievers, then poured him a glass of tea. She was more worried than she let on. In all the time she had known him, Cameron had never taken off in the middle of the day like this. Beneath his deep tan, he looked pale.

When she returned to the porch she discovered he hadn't moved. "Cameron?"

"Mmm?"

"Why don't you take these and lie down for a while, give them a chance to work."

He seemed to open his eyes with difficulty. "Sure," he mumbled. "Whatever you say." He got to his feet and swayed. She handed him the tablets and drink and watched as he swallowed them. He had obviously gone home and changed before heading south. He no longer wore what he laughingly called his lawyer uniform—a suit. Instead he was in faded jeans, a lightweight cotton shirt and moccasins.

Impulsively she took his hand. As soon as she touched him, she blurted out, "Cam, you're burning up!"

"No wonder," he muttered, following her into the house, "It's hot as hell out there." He paused in the front room of her small house. "Now this is more like it, darlin'. Much better."

She led him into her bedroom and hastily removed the bedspread. "There you go. See if you can relax and rest."

Like a child, Cameron docilely sat on the side of the bed and slipped off his shoes, then wearily lay back on the pillow. "Mmm. Your pillow smells like you—like flowers and fresh air and sunshine."

She turned away, too touched by his comment to respond. She closed the blinds on both the windows so that the room lay in shadow, then pulled the chain of the large paddle fan in the center of the ceiling.

When she looked at Cameron again, he already seemed to be asleep. She leaned over and touched his forehead. He felt very hot and dry. Something was wrong, but she didn't know what more she could do. Maybe he would feel better after a nap.

In the meantime she would take a shower and change, then make them something cool to eat for supper.

Two hours later Janine was in the kitchen when she heard the bathroom door close. She realized that Cameron was finally awake. She waited for several minutes, and when he didn't come out she became worried. Walking into the hall she said, "Cam? Are you all right?"

She heard a muffled sound.

"Cam?" When she heard him groan she opened the door. He was sitting on the side of the tub, his head in his hands. "Do you still have your headache?" she asked sympathetically.

He stared at her in surprise and confusion. "Janine? What are you doing here?"

She thought he was teasing her. "I didn't mean to barge in on you, but I heard you groan and thought you might need something."

He glanced around the small room in bewilderment. "Where am I?"

Janine became truly alarmed. "Why don't you

lie down again, Cam? Will you do that for me?''
She walked over and coaxed him to stand, then slid
her arms around his waist.

He was so weak he could scarcely walk. By the
time she got him back to the side of her bed, her
muscles were trembling from the exertion.

''Damn, it's hot,'' he muttered, and before she
could stop him he'd stripped off his pants and shirt.
He stretched out on the bed with a sigh and closed
his eyes.

Janine's eyes were drawn to the only part of his
body that remained covered—by a pair of navy
briefs that gave new meaning to the word ''brief.''

It wasn't as though she had never seen him un-
clothed before. The three of them had spent a great
deal of time this summer in his pool. But this was
different somehow. More personal.

She turned away and went to her linen closet,
found another sheet and draped it across his body.
He didn't stir. Then she went to the phone and
called the ranch. When Rosie answered, Janine
asked to speak to Letty. After a few moments,
Letty picked up the phone and asked, ''Yes? Who
is it?''

Janine smiled. Letty had always reminded her of
the woman who lived next door to her when she
was growing up. The woman had been a cantan-
kerous old bat, yelling at all the neighborhood children if they encroached on her property even an
inch. But when Janine's mother had gotten so much

worse, it had been her neighbor who had come to care for her while Janine was in school each day.

"Letty, this is Janine. I need your advice."

"What about?"

"Do you have a family doctor?"

"What's the matter? You sick?"

"No, I'm not. But Cameron stopped by earlier today on his way to the ranch. He wasn't feeling well, so I gave him some aspirin and suggested he rest. When he woke up a few minutes ago, he couldn't seem to remember coming here at all. He's very hot to the touch. I think we need to get a doctor to him."

"Humph. You won't find any of those new doctors botherin' with house calls, I'll tell you that. Fred Whitney's been retired for more than five years, but he's still as sharp as they come. I'll get hold of him and tell him to go check on Cameron. Give me your address."

Janine felt relief shoot through her. Letty was going to help. She quickly gave her the address and hung up, then returned to check on Cameron. He hadn't moved.

She went to the kitchen and dished up some of the chicken salad she had made for their supper, knowing she had to eat something. Then she paced between the kitchen and the living room, ending each loop at the front door, staring out at the street. When a well-kept older sedan slid to a stop in front of the house, she gave a sigh of relief and opened the door.

The man getting out of the car must have been a commanding figure at one time. He was tall, but spare, with a shock of white hair and the keenest blue eyes she had ever seen.

"You must be Janine Talbot," he said when he stepped up onto her porch carrying a bag.

"Yes, sir, I am. And you're Dr. Whitney."

"Well, yes, that's what my diploma says, but folks around here have been callin' me Dr. Fred for more years than I care to remember."

She smiled. "Dr. Fred it is, then."

"So where is that young 'un, anyway? I haven't seen Cam in a coon's age. I was always having to patch him up for one thing or another when he was growing up. Did he ever tell you 'bout the time he fell out of the hayloft in the barn and broke his arm?"

She was ahead of him in the hallway. She stopped when she came to the bedroom door and nodded toward the bed. "No, I'm afraid he's never mentioned it."

"Not surprising. Got his backside tanned good for that one, broken arm or no. That loft was off-limits to those kids." He walked over to a straight-back chair and pulled it toward the bed. He sat down and took Cam's wrist between his fingers. Then he removed his stethoscope from his bag, slipped the ear plugs into his ears with the ease of long practice and held the other end to Cameron's chest.

Janine stood at the end of the bed and watched helplessly. The doctor continued to move the shiny disk around on Cameron's chest and listen…move and listen…until she thought she would scream with impatience.

Finally he removed the stethoscope. "Cameron? Wake up, son, and talk to me."

She watched with fascination as Cameron first frowned, then slowly opened his eyes. He stared at the doctor in confusion. "Dr. Fred?" he whispered through dry lips. "What are you doin' here?"

The doctor smiled. "Checkin' up on you, son. This young lady thought you might need some help."

Cameron's eyes wandered from the doctor to Janine. He gave her a lazy smile but didn't say anything.

"Cameron, how long have you been feeling poorly?"

"A long time," he said, closing his eyes.

The doctor grinned at Janine before turning back to Cameron. "Does that mean years, days or hours? I need you to be more specific if you can."

"I don't know, doc. A couple of days, maybe. Haven't had much energy. My throat's been bothering me."

"Let me see," he said, pulling out a small instrument with a light.

Cameron obligingly opened his mouth.

"Uh-huh."

Cameron shut his mouth and his eyes. Janine couldn't be quite so relaxed about the procedure.

"Do you know what's wrong?" she finally asked.

"Well, I suppose I could order up a bunch of tests, get some cultures, take blood samples, or I could tell you what I suspect based on years of experience."

"What do you think?"

"First of all, this boy's been pushing himself too hard for too long. Now you can't expect a body to receive that kinda treatment without it decidin' sooner or later to rebel. I suspect that Cam's body just decided to present him with its bill. Because he's run-down, it's my guess that he picked up the current virus that's all the rage in the medical journals and running around in all the doctors' offices. He's got all the symptoms."

"What can we do?"

He smiled at her use of the plural pronoun, making her aware of how possessive she sounded toward Cameron.

"Well, I could give him some antibiotics to take, and something for the pain and fever. But the absolute, most important thing he needs is rest, and I doubt he's going to want to do that much, knowing Cam the way I do. The minute he starts feeling a mite stronger, he's goin' to be pushing to get back to work.''

"And if he does?"

Fred shrugged. "No predictin', of course. But this is a hardy li'l old virus. People who get up too soon are relapsing, usually much sicker than the first go round. Those are the ones they're puttin' in the hospitals.''

"How long would you recommend he stay in bed?"

"Absolute minimum...a week. Ten days would be even better."

"How contagious is this virus?"

"No more than most. Why? You afraid to catch it?"

She smiled. "Not me. But I thought about having his daughter, Trisha, visit a little later when he's feeling better."

He shook his head. "Not until his fever's down. Little ones are cute and all that, but they drain a person right fast. Give him a chance to get his strength back first."

She nodded. "All right."

The doctor stood and stared down at Cameron. "The man's exhausted. Just look at him. I know the fever and infection didn't help, but part of this is just plain neglect." He shook his head. "People nowadays trash their bodies, then wonder why they quit working on 'em. Darndest thing I've ever seen. Then they want a bunch of pills to swallow and expect that to fix 'em up all right and tight, ready to keep running. It just don't work that way."

"I know." She started for the door. "Would you like something to drink before you leave?"

"Don't mind if I do, thank you. Oh, and if you'll show me where you keep your phone, I'll call in some prescriptions and have Oliver down at the drugstore deliver them."

Her eyes widened. "They'll do that?"

The old man grinned. "For certain people they will."

By the time he hung up the phone, Janine had poured his tea. "I made chicken salad to feed Cam before I realized how sick he was. Could I tempt you into eating some?"

Fred glanced at her in surprise, then smiled. "Now, how did you know I do most of my own cookin' these days?"

"I didn't."

"Well, then you made a darned brilliant guess. I never bother with stuff I have to chop and slice, not if I can help it. Your salad looks mighty appetizing."

"Then have a seat and I'll fix us each a plate."

She also brought out the fresh vegetable salad she had placed in the refrigerator earlier. They sat down and began to get better acquainted.

Fred Whitney had known the Callaways for years and had delivered the youngest two boys. He was filled with tales about the family, the land and some of the history of the area. Janine found him fascinating.

More than two hours passed before he reluctantly took his leave. He gave her instructions about what to feed Cameron, what not to feed him and how to deal with a grouchy patient. She felt warmed and accepted by the kindly old man. He started down the steps. "Oh, I almost forgot. Letty told me to be sure to let her know what was wrong with Cameron. I'd just as soon not have to talk to the old bat myself if you'd like to call." Since he'd already told her of several battles the two extremely opinionated and self-willed people had had, she wasn't surprised at his comment.

"I'd be glad to, Dr. Fred."

"I'll be around sometime tomorrow to check on our fella in there. If you need me before then, just give me a call at that number I gave you."

Because the doctor had been there when the medicine arrived, he had showed her how to give Cameron the necessary dosage. Speaking clearly and firmly, he had had Cameron sit up and take the tablets, then swallow them with water. She hoped she could be as firm.

She went back in and called Letty. As soon as the woman recognized her voice, she said, "What in tarnation is goin' on? Did you have to hospitalize him? It's been hours since you called."

"Uh, no. Dr. Fred said he was all right here, so

long as I make sure he takes his medication on time. He thinks he's contracted a flu virus.''

"I'm not surprised. Everybody I know seems to be coming down with something these days.''

"Yes. The doctor thinks that Cameron's is a little more severe because he's run-down.''

"Of course he's run-down. He skips meals, smokes too much, seldom sleeps more than four hours a night. What does he expect?''

"Well, he seems to be resting okay for the moment.''

"If you want, I could send some of the hands into town and bring him out here. It won't be the first time he's had to convalesce at the ranch.''

"I don't think moving him would be a good idea. Besides, I'm home all day now. I don't mind looking after him.''

"You sure?''

"Positive.''

"Well, okay, then. But if it gets to be too much for you, you just holler, you hear?''

Janine smiled at Letty's tone and choice of words. "I hear.''

"I'll let Cole know what's going on. He and Cam work closely together.''

"Oh! I'd forgotten all about his work. Yes, thank you. I'm sure Cameron will be relieved to know his brother knows where he is.''

"Tell him I'll be in one of these days to check

on him. That'll get him out of bed in a hurry,'' Letty said.

"I'll do that. Thanks for everything, Letty. You've been a big help."

"That's what family's for, young lady."

Janine hung up the phone and went in to check on Cameron. Since she had never had a family other than her mother, she didn't know what a family was for. She had never missed what she had never had. However, it felt good to know that there was someone to call when she needed help.

She didn't feel alone anymore.

Seven

There were flames shooting up all around him. He fought his way through the smoke and haze, trying to get away from the searing blast of heat that engulfed him. He had to find relief. He had to escape before—

There. There was the voice, calling to him. He recognized the sound of that voice—it offered coolness and a refreshing balm. If only he could find it. He continued to struggle on, a sense of desperation forcing him to fight until the smoke and the haze lightened and he saw her standing beside the gurgling stream, beckoning to him. He broke into a lumbering uneven gait, exhausted from his struggles. He stumbled toward her, knowing that if he could just reach her he would be all right.

"Raise your head, Cam, and drink this."

He felt a glass at his lips, then felt the cool water trickle over their parched surface.

"Here. Swallow these. They'll help."

His throat ached from smoke inhalation, but he forced himself to swallow. He was rewarded with more water. The flames began to die down, their heat lessening.

Then she placed him in the cooling stream and bathed him with the comforting water. Her hands soothed his body, stroking the heat away, leaving him relaxed and at ease. He drifted off, sinking deeper and deeper into the healing water.

Cam jerked awake, his eyes flying open. He was in a bedroom, but an unfamiliar one. It seemed small, from the little he could see in the dim light from a lamp beside the bed.

Blinds covered the two windows.

Where the hell was he?

He couldn't remember a damned thing. He raised himself on his elbow and a pain shot through his head. He groaned, certain his head was going to topple off his shoulders.

"Cam? Are you all right?"

He moved his head carefully toward the door where the familiar voice came from and squinted. "Janine?"

She floated toward him, wearing something long and flowing. "Is your head still hurting?"

An understatement. "Yeah."

She poured more water from a pitcher on the bedside table into a glass. She opened a vial and took out a tablet. "Here. Maybe this will help." She handed him the medicine. As soon as he placed it on his tongue she handed him the glass, then wrapped her fingers around his to guide it to his mouth.

The water was cool and refreshing. He drained the glass, then allowed himself to sink back into the bed again. "What am I doing here?" he mumbled, surprised at how disagreeable he sounded.

She smiled at him. "At the moment, you're fighting a virus."

"How long have I been here?"

She glanced at her wristwatch. "About twelve hours."

Why couldn't he remember? He last recalled being at the office. The whole thing was too complicated to work out. He closed his eyes, then suddenly realized that he hadn't thanked her for taking care of him. "Thank you," he said gruffly.

He could hear amusement in her voice when she replied, "You're welcome."

Cameron was sweltering. He pushed off the covers but someone kept replacing them. "It's too damned hot. Get those blasted things off me!"

"You'll become chilled without them. Lie still, please. I'll get you something to drink."

"I don't want anything to drink. I want to get rid of the covers!"

The hands moved away. "Go ahead, then. Have it your way."

He felt exceedingly proud of himself. He had won the battle with the sweet-voiced witch. He shoved them away, feeling the cool breeze touch his body, moving across him...touching, tingling, chilling him until he began to shake.

The covers suddenly appeared from somewhere, falling softly around him, protecting him, nurturing him, caring for him. He smiled to himself in pleased satisfaction and allowed himself to drift off again.

The next time he opened his eyes, the room was still coolly shaded from the bright light on the other side of the window blinds. The lamp beside the bed was off. He tossed the covers aside and lowered his legs to the floor. They were made of lead. He could scarcely move.

New determination caused him to reach for the bedpost at the end of the bed and haul himself upright. Only by hanging on to furniture and bracing himself against walls did he make it to the bathroom door. After relieving himself, he stared into the mirror over the sink in dismay. What the hell? He looked as though he'd been on a five-day drunk. He needed a shave, his hair stood on end and his eyes were bloodshot. There was a steady pounding in his head.

He grasped the doorknob and jerked it open, only to find his way barred.

"What are you doing out of bed?"

He stared at Janine in bewilderment. He hadn't seen her this angry since the first day he had met her. Her eyes were shooting sparks.

"Hi." He gave her his most endearing smile. It had no effect on her whatsoever.

"Dr. Fred said that you were not to get up for any reason. So get back in bed. Now."

"I had to go to the bathroom."

"Oh."

Ha! That shut her up. Her cheeks pinkened, which made her eyes look greener. He could feel his knees slowly buckling. Unless he wanted to collapse at her feet, he knew he was going to have to follow her orders.

Only then did he become aware that he was nude.

"What the hell! Where are my clothes?" He lurched toward the bedroom and made his way to the bed.

"You took off most of them when you went to bed," she said, following him into the room. She leaned against the doorway and crossed her arms. "I took off your briefs last night when I was sponging you off, trying to bring your fever down. Letty is supposed to have someone drop off some more clothes for you in a day or so."

He had climbed under the sheet and had it

bunched in his lap during her casual explanation. "A day or so! I need my clothes now!"

Her smile was consoling but firm. "No. You're far from over this. You have four more days of heavy-duty antibiotics."

"I don't have to stay in bed to take them, for God's sake."

"Oh, yes. These particular kind plainly state that you must stay in bed or they won't work."

He studied her suspiciously, but she didn't crack a smile. "I never heard of such a thing."

She shrugged. "It's a new kind of medication. However, you can eat something if you like. Are you hungry?"

He thought about that for a few moments, allowing himself to slowly sink back onto the bed. "Not really," he said.

"I've made some chicken broth for you. Why don't you try a cup?"

He nodded, then watched her disappear from the doorway. Damn, he couldn't remember a time when he had felt at such a disadvantage. He felt like something that had been dragged behind a horse for a few days, then left out in the sun. Meanwhile, she looked as cool as an ice queen, standing there in her shorts and matching blouse, her hair high on her head in some sort of topknot.

She returned with a tray holding a cup and a glass of iced tea. She placed the cup beside the bed, took the tea and sat down in a rocker he hadn't noticed before.

"I feel like a fool," he muttered, reaching for the cup of broth.

"Why?"

"I shouldn't be here, making you wait on me like this. I can't imagine why I came here if I was feeling so rotten."

"You don't remember." She made the comment as a statement, not a question.

He shook his head, carefully sipping on the broth.

"You said you were having trouble concentrating because of a bad headache, so decided to leave work. You stopped by here on the way to the ranch."

"Why didn't you send me on?"

"It never occurred to me. I'm sorry if you're uncomfortable being here. Letty offered to send someone to pick you up, but I talked her out of it."

He eyed her across the top of his cup. "You mean you *wanted* to look after me?"

Her grin caught him off guard. "Amazing, isn't it? I must enjoy being called a series of unprintable names."

"I did that?"

She nodded.

"I'm sorry."

"Don't worry. I don't intend to hold it against

you. You've been pretty sick, Cam. And you're not out of the woods yet.''

"Nonsense. I'm feeling much better. Just a little weak, maybe. As soon as I have some clothes I'll—''

"You'll stay in bed and rest.''

"But—''

"No arguments. Why don't you take some more of your medication so I don't have to disturb you with it in another half hour or so?''

Where had she gotten such an air of command? He'd almost found himself saluting her. When she handed him the tablets, he immediately swallowed them.

"Well, maybe I'll rest for a few minutes. Then I'll call Letty and…'' He closed his eyes and was hardly aware of the empty cup slipping out of his hand. She took it from him, and he smiled as he sank deeper into the pillow. Just a few minutes' more rest. That was all he needed.

When Dr. Fred arrived, Janine met him at the front door before he had a chance to knock. "How's our patient today?'' he asked with a smile.

"Anything *but* patient, I'm afraid. He's already demanding his clothes.''

Fred guffawed. "Then he really must be sick, if all he can think about around a beautiful gal like you is getting his clothes *on!*''

"He got out of bed this morning while I was in

the kitchen. When I found him he was so weak he could barely stand but that didn't stop him from giving me a hard time.''

"What was he doing out of bed?''

"Answering nature's call.''

"Ah. Well, it's too much to hope for that he'd allow you to attend to everything. So I suppose I'll relent and allow him bathroom privileges. But that's all. Is he awake now?''

"You can check, but I don't think so. He fell asleep in the middle of a sentence.''

Fred chuckled. "Good, good. Just what he needs. I'll admit the pain reliever I prescribed is strong enough to knock him out.'' He patted her on the shoulder. "I'll just take a peek, anyway.''

She watched from the doorway as Dr. Fred found his chair, sat down and took Cameron's wrist. Cameron didn't flinch. Then the doctor listened to his chest, checked his eyes and throat without awakening him. When he was finished, he patted Cameron's head gently.

Dr. Fred's eyes were twinkling when he came out of the bedroom. "He's already improved tremendously, thanks to you. His color is much better. He's still running a fever, but it's down considerably from yesterday. All and all, I'd say he's mending nicely.''

"I gave him some homemade chicken broth. He didn't seem very hungry.''

"That's all right. Just continue to keep the food

light. His body will know when it's ready to take on more nourishment. If we listened to our bodies more, we'd stay a lot healthier. You're doing a fine job looking after him, by the way.''

"Thank you.''

"He's a very fortunate young man, you know. Not too many of us get lucky twice in this life.''

Janine didn't understand what he was talking about and her confusion must have shown on her face. "My wife, Trudy, died almost fifteen years ago. I never found anyone that came close to taking her place. I'm glad that young Cameron found you. He's too young to spend the rest of his life alone.''

"Oh, but, Dr. Fred, we're just friends.''

He smiled and let himself out the front door. "Of course you are. That's the very best kind.'' She watched him walk out to his car and get in, then carefully drive away.

The bright lights suddenly flashed in front of him. He swerved, trying to miss them, fighting not to lose control. He heard a scream as the lights filled the windshield, and then he began to spin and spin, the lights flashing, the scream going on and on and on...

"Cam! Cam, honey. Wake up. You're dreaming, Cam. It's all right. It's just a dream.''

He fought his way out of the noise and confusion, forcing his way up out of the nightmare. He could feel cool hands soothing his face and shoulders. He clutched at them, feeling their solidness, relief rushing over him when he discovered she was real. She was there beside him, holding him, loving him.

"Janine?" When he opened his eyes he realized that she hadn't turned on a light.

"Yes, Cam, it's me. I'm sorry to awaken you. I heard you groaning and muttering and knew you must have been dreaming."

She was on the side of the bed. He had his arms around her. He gave a tug so that she toppled against him. He shifted, pulling her down beside him. "What are you doing?" she said with a muffled laugh.

"I knew it was you," he said slowly, still coming to grips with the knowledge.

"Well, yes. There's no one else here."

"No. I mean, even in the midst of the nightmare I recognized your voice immediately and knew that if I fought to get to you, I'd be all right." He held her to him, smoothing his hand over the back of her head. When she didn't say anything, he asked, "Where are you sleeping?"

"On the couch." Her voice was very quiet.

"Then I'm in your bed, aren't I?"

"I don't mind."

"Aren't there two bedrooms?"

"I use the other bedroom for storage and hobbies and things. I never bothered to furnish it with a bed. I didn't need one."

"I'm sorry you had to give yours up."

"I'm not." He could hear the sound of her smile in her voice. "Are you hungry?" she asked after a moment.

"A little."

"Let me get you something. You'll probably sleep better." She waited, but he didn't let go of her. She felt too good to him, held close in his arms like that. Then she pressed her palm against his chest in an effort to pull away, and he reluctantly let go of her.

She left the room without turning on the light. He was content, lying in the dark, waiting for her. When she returned she flicked on the small light beside the bed and handed him a cup of something steaming and fragrant.

"I didn't wake you to take your next dose of medicine. You were sleeping so peacefully I didn't have the heart. But you can take it now." She gave him the tablets, then slipped out of the room.

When he finished the broth he decided that she might not intend to come back into the room. He started to get up, then remembered his lack of clothes. Frustrated, he draped the sheet around himself and stood.

Irritated by his lack of strength, he made his way into the bathroom. He knew a shower would help him, so he threw off the sheet and climbed into the tub. Standing beneath the soothing spray helped to ease the aches that invaded his body. By the time he finished, he felt better, but knew that he wouldn't be able to run any races any time soon. He was already yearning for bed again.

When he walked back into the bedroom, this time with a large bath towel around his waist, he discovered that Janine had returned. Not only had she retrieved his dishes, she had also changed the sheets and made the bed. However, she was nowhere in sight.

Already feeling the trembling setting into his muscles, he turned off the light, tossed the towel aside and crawled thankfully into bed. Within moments he was asleep.

Janine lay awake on the couch for a long time, thinking. Perhaps she had been foolish to insist he stay there with her. Given the attraction they had for each other, wasn't she asking for trouble? At first he had been too ill for it to matter, but she could see that he was rapidly improving. Perhaps tomorrow she would suggest that he get a ride out to the ranch. Or, she could take him there if he wished.

Yes. That would be the best thing—for both of them—regardless of what her heart was telling her.

She was still awake when she heard him moan, and she guessed that his nightmare was back. Without hesitation she ran into the other room to bring him out of the mind-numbing terror that seemed to lurk in his dreams.

"Cam? It's okay, Cam. It's just a dream." She leaned over him, touching his brow.

With no warning, his hands grabbed her wrists and he jerked her forward, pulling her off balance. With a squeak of dismay, she tried to fall away from him, not wanting to startle him awake with her sudden weight on top of him. She twisted and rolled so that she landed on the bed beside him. Only then did she become aware that he had kicked off his sheet and was lying there nude beside her.

Before she could pull away he placed one of his muscular thighs across her hips, pinning her to the bed.

"Cam? It's me, Janine. Wake up, Cam, please." She spoke the words in a low voice, still hoping not to jar him awake.

"Janine," he mumbled.

"Yes, wake up now."

He released her wrists, but she still couldn't move. She placed her palm on his chest. He was too warm, obviously still running a fever. He stroked his hand across her body, then paused, fingering the cotton nightgown she wore.

"Wha' are you doin' in this?" he muttered, slurring his words. He reached down and grabbed the hem, then lifted the gown up over her head. It was still caught on the shoulder closest to him. "Hmm, that's better," he murmured. Once again he ran his hand over her body, from the top of her thighs to her throat, then back again. The second time he circled her breast, teased the crest with his fingers, then leaned over and placed his mouth over the aroused tip.

She stiffened at the unfamiliar sensation, then shuddered as a multitude of new feelings ran through her, turning her body to molten metal.

He shifted, nudged her legs apart with his thigh, and with a sigh she relaxed into the pleasure of feeling him pressed so intimately against her. His thigh was rhythmically moving against her. When he shifted his attention to her other breast she moaned and squirmed slightly, feeling an ache she had never known before.

He seemed to understand her bewilderment, because he finally touched her where the ache was centered, softly rubbing the tips of his fingers across the exact spot.

She arched with his hand, relishing in the delightful sensation. When he raised his head and kissed her, she thought there must be steam coming from both of them. She held him tightly, afraid to let go. Her hands slowly moved up and down his back, down to his muscled buttocks, then returned to the slight indentation of his spine. Then Cameron tugged her gown from her arm and shoulder and tossed it out of the way.

She reveled in each new explosion of feeling he provoked. His restless hands moved over her body, tantalizing her until she thought she would explode.

By the time he hovered over her, she wanted to leap on him and hold him fast against her heat.

There was no embarrassment, no fear. This was Cameron, the man she loved, the man who could drive her to distraction with just one look... Cameron...Cam...

Yes, just there. That was where the ache had first appeared and grown more intense. She caught herself holding her breath, wanting him so desperately, as he slowly pushed against her, creating more and more pressure until she was filled with the need, with him, with—

A sharp pain brought her partway out of the sensory place of wonder. She stiffened, but before she could protest, his mouth found hers once more and she realized that he was pressed firmly against her and fully inside. He leaned on his forearms on each side of her head and bathed her face in soft kisses, soothing her, calming her. In the deep shadows of the room, she couldn't see his face. But she could feel him as he lay against her so intimately.

He nibbled on her bottom lip, sucked on it slightly, then stroked it with his tongue. She touched her tongue to his lips, a movement that seemed to encourage him. His mouth came down on hers with a new intensity while he slowly lifted his hips from hers.

She panicked, not wanting him to leave her. Instinctively she drew her knees up and locked her ankles behind his thighs. He jerked his mouth away from hers and groaned. What had she done? She hadn't wanted to hurt him. She'd only wanted him to— Yes! Like that! She wanted him to stay with her. Oh, and he was. He was... She began to match his rhythm, lifting to meet him, straining to hold him.

He stepped up his pace, moving faster and faster so that she couldn't breathe, couldn't think, could only hold on, tighter and tighter, faster and faster until suddenly... Something seemed to explode inside of her, causing her body to convulse in seismic rippling movements.

Once again Cameron groaned. Then he, too, seemed to lose control, his movements no longer measured as he made one final lunge, burying himself deep within her, holding her as though he never intended to let her go, his face pressed against her neck.

They lay that way for an unmeasurable length of time, his weight pressing her into the bed.

She couldn't remember a time when she had felt so whole and complete. She loved feeling him relaxed in her arms, his breathing harsh in her ear. Lazily she stroked his buttocks and trailed her fingers up to his waist. His skin rippled everywhere she touched, but no other part of him moved.

After a while she lifted her hips tentatively and felt his movement inside. She smiled, then kissed him on his cheek. His hot cheek. His fevered cheek.

Oh, dear Lord. He was sick! How could she have

forgotten? How could she have... She struggled to move but it was no use. He was dead weight.

"Cam?" she whispered.

No answer.

Now what? She took a deep breath. He was heavy but not so heavy that she couldn't breathe. She wondered if she could shift him enough to get his medicine. No doubt he was due for more by now. She wriggled until she was able to shift his weight, rolling him onto his back where he stayed without moving.

For a long moment she leaned over him. His pulse had slowed and now had a reassuringly strong rhythm. She felt so limp she could scarcely move. With the last of her energy she filled a glass with water and took one of the tablets out of the bottle.

She raised his head. "Cam? You need to swallow this. Please?" She slipped the tablet between his lips and placed the glass there. He obligingly swallowed the tablet and the water. After she put the glass back on the table she knew she needed to get up, but for the moment all she wanted to do was lie there beside him.

He turned toward her, placing his arm and one of his legs over her, effectively pinning her to his side.

Since there was no place she would rather be, she sighed and closed her eyes. She would stay there just for a few minutes, then she would get up and return to her place on the couch....

Eight

Janine knew she needed to wake up. There were so many things to do. She had to check on Cam to be sure that— Cam! Her eyes snapped open and she found that she was staring into Cameron's eyes from only a few inches away. They were sharing a pillow.

That wasn't all they were sharing, she realized as she discovered she was pressed intimately against him and that he was running his hands over her body, her nude body. Before she could speak, he said, "Please don't ask me to apologize. I couldn't, not and show any sincerity at all, love. Do you have any idea how long I've wanted to make love to you?"

His words were husky and resonated through her body.

"When I first woke up this morning, I thought I must have dreamed again about making love to you. Since I've been running this damned fever my dreams have gotten even more erotic. This time I could remember so clearly how you felt when I..." He paused and kissed her. "But then I knew it was much better than anything I had ever dreamed. That's when I realized you were still here in bed with me." He grinned. "I have to admit that you were just what the doctor ordered. I haven't felt this good in a lo-o-ong time."

She could feel herself blushing—all over her body.

"Aw, honey, don't be embarrassed, I was only kidding. Are you upset with me? I don't recall quite how we got started last night. I just remember bits and pieces, but what I do remember was—"

"You were having another nightmare and I tried to wake you up."

"Oh." His expression was uncertain. "Did I force you?"

She had to be honest with him. "Not exactly. You grabbed my wrists and pulled me down and I, uh, I..."

He lifted her wrist and looked at it. "I didn't hurt you, did I? I'm sorry, honey. I wouldn't hurt you for the world."

"You didn't hurt me. I guess the truth is that

I've fantasized about you, too. What it would be like if we… Well, anyway, it's over and done with and I—''

He leaned up on his elbow and stared at her with disbelief. ''Over and done with? What are you talking about? You make it sound like a smallpox vaccination or something. Is that how you feel? Now that you've experienced your fantasy, it's all over?''

''No, of course not. I just don't exactly know what to say at this point, that's all.''

He was quiet for a moment, obviously thinking. When his eyes focused on her once more, he said, ''Yes, now I'm beginning to remember more. You were a virgin, weren't you?'' When she didn't answer, he repeated, ''Weren't you?''

''That doesn't really matter.''

''Of course it matters! I was more than half-asleep, still running that damned fever, and I took advantage of you. Otherwise you would never have—''

''No. I could have stopped you. I know I could have. The point is I didn't try because I didn't want to. I enjoyed making love with you. Very much,'' she admitted.

He smiled. ''That's good. So I didn't turn you off the idea.''

''Well, no.''

He slid his hand over her hips and tugged her

close. "That's good," he murmured, dipping his head toward hers and kissing her.

She couldn't think when he kissed her like this. She pulled away and tried to get her breath. "I don't think—" she began.

"Good idea," he murmured, placing a string of kisses along the base of her throat. "It's much better just to feel. This is even better than before. I can see you now and I'm fully awake."

"But, Cam, you've been sick and—"

"And obviously I'm on the mend, wouldn't you say?" He leaned down and pressed his mouth against the tip of her breast. "Mmm," he sighed with obvious pleasure, moving his hand along her thigh.

Her body understood what her mind was attempting to deny. She wanted him even more now that she knew what making love to Cam entailed.

When he raised his head again he looked at her and smiled. "You're shy, aren't you?"

She nodded, unable to find words to explain.

"This is a little more premeditated than last night, isn't it?"

Once again she nodded.

"Will you let me show you what it can be like?" His eyes had lost their teasing glint.

Janine knew that if she said no that he would let her go. Last night had been a spontaneous happening. Now that she had time to think about what they were doing she was afraid. She had never allowed a relationship to go this far, knowing full well that once a man knew the truth about her, he would not consider a serious relationship with her. She hadn't wanted to be hurt, so she had kept herself aloof for years.

This was different. Cam was different. What they shared was very special. Neither of them wanted more than this wonderful friendship. He had made it clear months ago that he never intended to marry again.

Spontaneous or not, they had moved their relationship into intimacy. She had made her choice last night. She wouldn't regret that choice. Not now.

"Show me," she finally whispered, a catch in her voice. Her remaining barriers had come tumbling down.

"What a darling you are," he said, swooping down and giving her a kiss that drove every thought from her mind.

He treated her as though she were a newly discovered treasure to be explored and revered. Each kiss, each caress, elicited a sigh that encouraged him to continue his loving explorations.

Only now she was aware of how sensitive her body was as he caressed her skin with his fingertips and his mouth. Wanting him to experience the same wonderful sensations he was creating within her, she timidly mimicked his movements, eliciting an immediate response that encouraged her to continue with her own explorations.

How wonderfully different a man's body was—the hard muscles covered by satiny smooth skin. She felt so daring, so unlike herself, as she boldly touched him and felt his skin ripple in an instant response.

"I want you so much," he muttered, almost as though he found the admission painful.

She shifted slightly, silently inviting him to take the next step. When he joined them she gave a quick sigh of pleasure, no longer concerned about anything but holding him, following him into new realms of sensuous delight.

She found the slow, very deliberate pace he set increasingly frustrating as her body built up tension. She began to meet his rhythmic movement with thrusts of her own, causing him to falter for a moment before grasping her more tightly and accelerating his movements until she could feel the tension spiraling up and up and—

She cried out when the release hit her, holding him to her as hard as she could, feeling his own body respond to the tremors deep within her. She clutched him to her, reluctant to let go. He rolled onto his side, still holding her against him, and they fell asleep in each other's arms.

Later that morning she was in the kitchen preparing breakfast when he came up behind her and nibbled on the nape of her neck.

"You're supposed to be in bed," she said sternly, although she didn't put much vehemence behind her words.

"But I'm hungry," he complained with a chuckle.

"I'll have your eggs ready for you as soon as the bacon is done."

He slipped his arms around her waist. "That isn't what I'm hungry for." He continued his nibbling.

"Well, that's all you're going to get."

He raised his head. "Really?"

"Really."

"Hmm."

"I'll bring this in to you shortly," she said without looking around.

After a brief silence, he said, "Why can't I eat in here?"

She turned and discovered that he was seated at the table, wearing his freshly laundered jeans and shirt. She sighed, knowing she was going to have some trouble with him. "You're supposed to be resting."

"Can't I rest sitting up?"

She removed the cooked bacon from the skillet, cracked the eggs, and dropped them into the skillet. "I'm sure you can. The question is, will you?"

"Yes. I promise."

He watched as she buttered the toast, placed the eggs on the plate, added the toast and bacon and set the meal in front of him. Then she quickly made a plate for herself and sat down across from him.

"You're a good cook, did you know that?" he asked when they were finished eating.

"Thank you."

"You're awfully quiet."

"Yes."

"You've been thinking."

"Yes."

"Too much."

"Maybe."

"I realized while I was shaving that I didn't use any protection last night or this morning. It's a little late to apologize but I figured that—"

"Don't worry about it."

"Well, actually, I'm not. Because if you should be—"

She put her fork down and looked at him. "You needn't concern yourself. I won't get pregnant."

"You're sure?"

"Yes."

He looked disappointed.

"I forgot to tell you that Trisha wants to see you," Janine said. "She sent that message through Letty when she called yesterday to see how you're doing. If you'd like, I could drive you out to the ranch today. Then if you want to stay—"

"Janine, what's wrong?"

"Nothing's wrong. I just thought—"

"You haven't looked at me since I walked into this kitchen. You haven't looked at me since you got out of bed this morning. I want to know what's wrong."

"What we did was stupid and irresponsible, and I don't wish to discuss it."

He grinned. "Ah. So now you're back to being your prim and proper schoolmarm self."

She took a bite of her toast, chewed several times, then washed it down with a sip of coffee, determined not to allow him to provoke her into saying anything more.

Her silence didn't seem to faze him. In a cheerful voice he said, "You know what I'd really like to do?"

"What?"

"Spend a few days in San Antonio with you. We've spent the past few months doing everything with Trisha. I'd like some time alone with you."

"You've spent the past few days alone with me."

He waved his hand. "That doesn't count. I was out of my head most of the time. I want to spend some time with you when I'm not about to pass out." She tried not to look at him but found it impossible. Slowly her eyes met his. She had seldom seen him so serious. "Please," he said. His eyes were pleading.

Didn't he understand how much she wanted to

be with him? She glanced down at her cup. "All right, but only if you promise to get your rest." She knew she was making a mistake, but she couldn't turn down the opportunity to be with him. She loved him.

His smile shattered her with its sweetness. "I promise." He looked at the kitchen clock. "I'll phone Trisha, and I'll tell Letty where I'll be, while you get ready."

It took only minutes to clean up the kitchen. Cameron was still on the phone when she went into the bathroom to shower and get dressed. She didn't intend to think of anything more than the moment. Cameron needed to rest and to relax. At least if she stayed with him, he wouldn't go back to work. She knew she was only kidding herself that she was doing it for him, but it helped to know that she was looking after him, as well as collecting memories for herself.

The shrill ringing of his phone shattered the deep night silence, and Cameron groaned, feeling as though he had just fallen asleep. He groped for the lamp switch, turned it on and glanced at the clock. It was almost two o'clock in the morning. Hell, they probably hadn't been asleep more than half an hour.

Janine hadn't moved. He couldn't help but smile, remembering her earlier remark when they had first come to bed and he made it clear that he wasn't the least bit sleepy. In her most prim tone she suggested that the only way he was going to get his needed rest was to stay *out* of bed.

The phone rang again and he grabbed it before the noise awakened her. It was true he had spent a great deal of time these past three days in bed, very few hours of which were spent in sleep. Janine was probably exhausted. He, on the other hand, had never felt better.

"Yes?" he spoke into the receiver.

"Cam? This is Cole."

Cameron sat up. "What's wrong? What's happened?"

Cole gave one of his deep chuckles and said, "Nary a thing, bro. I know I could have waited until morning, but the need to tell you that the twins just arrived into the world safe and sound was too good to keep."

"They're here? But isn't it too soon?"

"Only about three weeks. The doctor was pleased they decided to push up the schedule a little. Clint weighed in at five pounds five ounces, Cade weighed five two. The doctor seemed relieved. He said Allison didn't need them to be any bigger."

"Boys," Cameron breathed. "You weren't sure."

"Nope. The way they were situated in there we couldn't get a clear shot to tell, which is just as well. So now I've got me three boys and a girl. You'd better hurry or you'll never catch up!''

Cameron laughed and glanced around at Janine, who had turned over and was now looking at him with sleep-swollen eyes. "I'm working on it," he said into the phone, grinning.

"Well, what do you know? So Letty was right!" Cole said.

"About what?"

"We're talking about the lady who borrowed Allison's clothes last spring, correct?"

"As much as I hate to admit that Letty's right about anything, in this case, she's right on target."

"So when's the big date?"

"Uh-uh-uh. None of that, now. I've got me a skittish one who's prone to bolt at the least hint of permanence. I've got to handle this one with my customary subtle negotiating and elegant style."

"You mean you haven't asked her?"

"I'm working up to it."

"Well, hell. How much working up do you need?"

"All the time it takes. Tell me where Allison and the babies are, and we'll come see you later on today, after we get some sleep."

"Oh! Sorry. I didn't mean to interrupt anything."

"Just my sleep. I'm trying to get over the flu."

"Yeah, I heard about that. Letty's been keeping us informed about your health."

"She would," he muttered.

Cole told him the name of the hospital in Austin, gave him directions from the interstate, promised him a couple of cigars and hung up.

"I take it Allison had her babies?" Janine asked him when he turned out the light.

He pulled her over until her head was resting on his shoulder. "Yeah. They named them Clint and Cade, another generation of Callaways. Mom and babies are doing fine. I thought we might go see them later today."

When she didn't answer him, he added, "If you want."

"I'd like that," she said softly, after another long pause. "I'd like to thank Allison in person for lending me her clothes last spring."

"And I'd like them to meet you. This will work out just fine." He turned her so that his body was cupped around hers, holding and protecting her. He went to sleep with his hand resting on her breast.

How could she possibly sleep now that she knew she would be meeting more of Cameron's family in a few hours? She lay there, trying to understand what had happened to her during the previous months.

She had been content with her life. She had found a small house that she was seriously considering buying. She enjoyed her job and liked her coworkers. She adored her preschoolers. Before she had met Cameron, she had had everything she wanted in life. Or at least she had everything she had known she could have, given her circumstances.

How had everything changed in such a short while? When she had made her decision to go to the Callaway ranch, she'd had no intention of doing more than speaking with her pupil's father. The last thing she had wanted was to fall in love with him.

And yet…and yet what had occurred between them these past several months had evolved so naturally. They had become friends, sharing their time, their thoughts and eventually their feelings with each other. They had entertained Trisha and, in doing so, had themselves learned how to play again.

And then they had become lovers. How could she possibly regret learning how to fully express her love for this man?

The past few days had been a revelation in so many ways. She had thought she had known Cameron as well as any one person could know another, but she had never seen the playful, very physical, oh so sensual man who had spent hours with her, teaching her so much about herself.

He had teased her about his being the tutor while she was the student, and he had found such interesting ways to praise her for her aptitude and new skills.

Surely they could continue their relationship as it was. Of course they would have Trisha with them, but there would be time for them to have some privacy, as well. He seemed content to spend his spare time with her. Wouldn't that be enough?

When she thought about Cole and Allison and their family, a chill of unease skittered across the surface of her skin. Only time would give her any answers. For now she must rest.

Feeling Cameron's warmth pressed closely to her back helped her to relax. She lifted his hand and placed a kiss in the palm, then allowed it to rest against her breast once more.

What a wonderful way to wake up, she decided with a sleepy smile the next morning as she felt him expertly touching and teasing her. Cameron had learned so much about her these past few days. He had discovered all her pleasure points and explored them with great concentration and intensity whenever given the slightest opportunity. He had obviously found another opportunity.

She opened her eyes, still smiling. "I thought we were going to Austin," she murmured to the man who stared down at her from only a few inches away.

"We are," he responded agreeably, but in no way distracted.

"Then we should probably be getting showered and dressed, don't you think?"

"Excellent idea," he said, but he made no effort to move and since he had very effectively pinned her between him and the bed she could only shake her head and chuckle. "I'll scrub your back," he offered in a helpful tone.

Before she could respond, his mouth found hers and she forgot about everything but Cam—the scent of him, the taste of him, the sound of him, the wonderful sight of him, and most especially the feel of him as he captured her full attention.

She arched into him, taking his fullness, and joined him in a harmony of motion that they had discovered together. She loved this man so much...so very much. How could she possibly give him up, and yet, loving him as she did, how could she possibly hang on to him when she knew the sacrifice he would have to make for them to stay together permanently? She loved him too much to do that to him. She loved him enough to let him go.

But not now, dear God. Please, not now.

They had been on the road for several miles when Cam reached over and took her hand, placing it on his knee. "You've been very quiet this morning. Is something bothering you?"

She smiled. "Not really. I was just thinking about things, that's all."

"What sort of things?"

"Oh...you, your family. I guess I may be a little nervous about meeting them."

"Hey, they're going to love you, I'll guarantee you."

She was quiet for a few more miles before she said, "Tell me something about Cole and Allison. You said they grew up on the ranch together, didn't you?"

"That's right."

"I remember your saying that they have a boy and a girl besides the twins, but I don't recall their ages."

"Tony turned eighteen this summer and is ready for his first year of college. Cole wanted to send him back East to his old alma mater, but Tony wouldn't hear of it. A very independent young man is Tony. He's going to Texas A&M University." He drove for a while before adding, "Katie the terror will be three in September. She was named after Allison's mother, Katherine, and she's a real pistol. Cole adores her."

"That's a considerable gap in ages!"

"Not through Cole's choice, let me tell you. There's quite a story behind that relationship."

"Oh?"

"Not that they would care if you knew about it, of course. You see, a lot of crazy things happened back when our folks were killed. Life for the Callaways was confused and disastrous. Allison and her dad moved away. Cole continued his schooling back East and Cody and I muddled through the best we could with Letty. Four years ago last spring Cole discovered he had a son. Tony."

"Four years ago! You mean all that time he didn't—"

"Yeah. He didn't know that Allison had gotten pregnant. It's all past history now. They managed to get in touch with each other, worked out their problems and got married. Katie arrived stompin', chompin' and rarin' to go a bare nine months after the ceremony, which I thought was downright circumspect of brother Cole, given the circumstances."

"Oh, my!"

"If that wasn't enough, he comes up with twins this time. Guess he wanted to make up for lost time."

"Allison is going to have her hands full," she said faintly, "trying to care for newborn twins and a rowdy three-year-old."

"Oh, Cole's been planning everything. They bought a place on the outskirts of Austin, with plenty of room for growing kids and a studio for Allison. Plus he's hired enough help to keep everything under control and give Allison some time to work."

"I think I'm going to like Allison," she said quietly.

"I have no doubt about that. You're both as independent as hell."

She looked startled. "I don't see myself that way at all. You're always telling me how prim and proper I am."

"Well, I've been chipping away at that prim and proper facade these past few days, and what do I find beneath all that primness? A streak of strong independence."

"Why, Cam, you almost sound insulted."

"It certainly wasn't what I thought I'd have to contend with." He gave her a ferocious scowl.

She reached up and stroked his jaw with her finger in commiseration. He grabbed her hand, pulling her finger to his mouth and nibbling on it. "Mmmmmm. You do bring on a powerful hunger in me whenever you're around."

"Cam! Behave!"

"Yes, ma'am." He winked, and she could feel any resistance she might have against this man melt. Independent? Not likely. Not where he was concerned.

She waited at the information desk of the hospital while Cameron parked the car, then they rode the elevator to the maternity floor. They had no more than stepped out of the elevator when Cameron caught her hand and tugged her down the hallway—at almost a sprint—to where a tall slender young man peered into a nursery window.

"So what do you say, Tony?" Cameron asked, clapping him on the shoulder. "Do you think you were ever that small?"

The boy turned around and flashed a smile that was pure Callaway. Although his eyes were dark, his hair was as blond as Cody's. His expressive eyes were glistening with moisture, and Janine realized that he had been touched by the sight of his tiny brothers.

"Hi, Uncle Cam. For your information, I was never that small. Mom said I weighed over eight pounds!" He looked back at the babies. "Aren't they something?"

"Janine, in case you hadn't guessed, this is Tony Alvarez Callaway, my oldest nephew. Tony, this is a friend of mine, Janine Talbot."

The boy ducked his head in a shy nod. "Howdy, ma'am." Then his gaze looked back at the babies. Janine couldn't resist looking, too. The nurses had placed the twins directly in front of the window.

One was on his back, kicking, his face red and his mouth open. The other was on his stomach, his rump in the air, seemingly undisturbed by the ruckus.

"Isn't anybody going to come see what's wrong?" Tony demanded indignantly.

"They aren't going to neglect them, son," a deep voice said from behind them. Janine turned around in time to see Cameron hug the man who had just joined them.

She felt a lump in her throat, seeing the two big men so obviously glad to see each other. Some back pounding ensued, and a couple of cigars were offered and accepted. There was no doubting the love that existed between the three Callaways standing there in the hallway. She looked back at the babies, wondering if they had any idea how lucky they were to be born into such a loving environment.

She was watching one of the nurses pick up the crying baby and take him over to a table where she began to change him when Cameron took her hand and said, "Janine, this is Cole—" he raised their clasped hands "—and Cole, Janine."

"I'm very pleased to meet you, ma'am," Cole drawled, his hand reaching for her other one and squeezing. "I've heard a lot about you. I've been real impatient wondering when I'd get a chance to say hello."

"You've heard about me?" She looked at Cameron uncertainly.

He raised his hand and said, "I swear it wasn't from me, honey. Letty likes to keep everyone current on family business."

Cole tugged her hand slightly and said, "C'mon. I want you to meet Allison." He glowed just saying his wife's name, and once again Janine felt a lump form in her throat. She was aware how little she knew about men, but she was taken aback by these three and their lack of inhibition about showing their feelings. She allowed Cole to lead her down the hallway while Cameron and Tony followed closely behind, talking about school and rodeo events and livestock.

Cole paused just outside the door and tapped, then gently pushed it open. When he saw that Allison was awake, he grinned. "I brought you some company, honey." He released Janine's hand and kept on walking toward the bed where the most beautiful woman Janine had seen in a long while was resting. Her black hair and eyes were a sharp contrast to her fair skin. The look Cole and Allison exchanged was so personal Janine almost blushed.

Cole did the introductions. "This is Janine, honey."

Allison held out her hand and smiled. "At last we meet. Oh, I would have loved to have seen you in my clothes. You must have looked gorgeous in the blues and greens."

Cameron spoke up from somewhere behind Janine. "You got that right. I fell like a downed calf in a roping event, in less than eight seconds flat."

They all laughed, even Janine, although she knew she had turned a fiery hue at his teasing.

Later she didn't remember much about the visit. They didn't stay long, of course, but they were there long enough for her to see that she was learning new meanings for the word family. She was very touched. She was reminded of her childhood when, before Christmas one year, she had stared at the fairy wonderland in a toy shop's front window, imagining herself small enough to live in the tiny village with all the happy people, singing in the group with a mama, papa and the three children. She would stop each afternoon after school and press her face against the window, absorbed in her dreams.

Once again she was that child, wishing, fantasizing, her face pressed against the glass while she watched the Callaways. But she knew sooner or later she would have to go home and be alone.

Nine

"**W**hat did you think of Cole's family?" Cameron asked as they headed south toward San Antonio.

"They're enough to take a person's breath away. I never saw so much energy in one group of people. And you're saying that Katie is just as active."

"At least. Actually, Allison is fairly quiet as a rule, but she's really excited about having the twins here and everything being all right. She wasn't looking forward to those last few weeks of carrying them."

"I can imagine."

They rode along in companionable silence for several miles before Cameron said, "Janine?"

"Mmm?"

"I really appreciate your coming up here with me today."

"I enjoyed it. I really did."

"I've needed this time off. I'm sorry I had to get sick to realize that I've been pushing myself too hard. I don't know what I would have done without you."

"You would have gone to the ranch and Letty would have taken care of you."

"No, I mean it."

She glanced at his frowning profile and said quietly, "So do I. You've got a wonderful family, Cameron. I almost envy what you have, because you aren't even aware of how special it is to have people you can turn to and know that they'll be there for you no matter what."

He reached over and took her hand, placing it on his thigh. "You didn't have that while growing up, did you?"

"No."

"But things are different now, honey. Now you have me."

She tried to tug her hand back, but he wouldn't let her.

"I mean it. You aren't alone anymore."

She gazed at her other hand, lying loosely in her lap. "I know."

"There's so much I want to say to you, but dammit, I'm afraid."

She looked at him in surprise. "You? Cameron, you're not afraid of anything."

"I am where you're concerned. I'm afraid of losing you."

"I'm right here."

"You know what I mean."

"No, I don't. We're friends, Cam. That's very precious to me, something I've never had before, a friendship with a man. You've made it very special for me."

"But I want so much more!" he burst out.

She tugged her hand away and clasped her hands together in her lap. "Yes, I know."

"Seeing them today made me remember how happy I was when Trisha was born."

"Were you sorry she was a girl?"

"Of course not! I wanted whatever the baby turned out to be, but I wanted more. Andrea and I had planned to have several children and..." He shook his head in irritation. "But things happened and..."

"Yes, things happen, and life doesn't always work out the way we plan."

"I never dreamed I could love anyone else, and yet when I met you I felt like a schoolboy all over again, with a gigantic crush."

She smiled at his description and his wry tone of voice. "You certainly didn't act like a schoolboy. Those were some very experienced moves you were putting on me, mister."

"Don't you see, honey? We're so good together. You've made me laugh again and love again and want again. The world is mine again. I want it all—and I want it with you."

She didn't say anything. She couldn't, not after such a declaration. She knew exactly how he felt, because she felt the same way. The only difference was that she knew the world wasn't hers. She knew she couldn't have it all.

He deserved to have everything he wanted.

"How are you feeling?" she said, and he looked at her as though she had just lost her mind. What kind of question was that to ask at a time like this? she knew he must be thinking.

"I'm fine. Why?"

"Are you tired?"

"Not particularly."

"Are you up to driving me home? I've been away for several days and I need to get back."

"I don't want to, no. But if you feel you need to go home, of course I'll take you."

"Thank you," she whispered, her throat clogging with emotion.

They stopped in San Antonio long enough for her to pack the few things she had brought with her, then continued south, saying very little.

When they drove up in front of her house, she turned to him and said, "You're welcome to stay here, if you'd like."

He shook his head. "No. I want to check on

Trisha. It's time I talked to her about moving to San Antonio. I've been putting it off, hoping that I could tell her that…'' He shook his head. "Hell, I don't know. I guess I've been fantasizing too much lately, hoping things would change. Hoping that…'' He ran his hand through his hair in disgust.

"Let me be your friend, Cam. Please? It's very important that I don't lose you from my life.''

His head jerked up and he looked at her with new alertness. "It is?''

"Of course.''

"I thought that you were letting me know I was taking up too much of your time.''

"On the contrary. I'm taking up too much of yours. It's obvious that you want a wife and family. I can't give you that. You need to find someone who can.''

"Just because you never had a family doesn't mean you can't learn to become a part of one. Why, you, Trisha and I are already a family, if you could only understand. It isn't something you have to learn to do. It's just something you become. It's part of being.''

She leaned over and kissed him, then slowly pulled away. "Give Trisha my love. I'm sorry she won't be attending our school in the fall, but I think you're doing the best thing for both of you.'' She slipped out of the car and picked up her bag. "Take care now. Don't work so hard. Maybe we can get together some weekend once you have Trisha settled in.''

She turned away, proud of herself for sounding so light, pleased that she hadn't broken down. She unlocked the front door and stepped inside the empty little house, then closed the door and waited for the sound of his car to drive away. Only then did she allow herself to give vent to the grief and pain she had locked away these past few hours. Dry sobs began to tear from her tight throat while she slowly sank to the floor, her back against the door, sobbing for something she could never have, no matter how much she wanted it.

"Daddy, Daddy, did you know that Auntie Allison had her twin babies and their names are Clint and Cade and they're little bitty, only about this big—'' she demonstrated with her hands "—and Auntie Allison said that when they get some bigger she'll bring them to see me and let me hold them. And when they get big I can help 'em walk and—''

"Whoa, hold it! Hold it! Don't plot out their whole lives right at the moment, sugar. Let's let them be little babies for a while, okay?''

"Okay." She hugged him tightly around the knees. "I love you, Daddy. I wish we could have twins, then I could have someone to play with all the time and I wouldn't have to wait so long for 'em to come see me.''

Picking her up, Cameron went down the hallway, looking for his aunt. "Well, it would be a little difficult for you and me to have twins on our own, punkin," he said absently. "Letty?" he called.

"She's resting in her room," Trisha said obligingly. "Maybe Missy Talbot would like to have some twins for us. Could we ask her, Daddy?"

Cameron felt a pang shoot through him in the region of his heart. "I don't think so, baby. Ms. Talbot already has a full-time job."

"But lots of mommies work. And 'member that lady who bringed us our food that one time and she called me Missy Talbot's little girl?"

"Yes, darling. I remember quite well. Ms. Talbot was embarrassed by the waitress's mistake, wasn't she? Her cheeks got all pink."

Trisha giggled. "But she liked it, too. I could tell. Couldn't you?"

"I thought so at the time," he murmured. Attempting to change the subject, he asked, "Has your uncle Cody been here since the twins were born?"

"Uh-uh. Aunt Letty said she didn't know what she was gonna do 'bout him, 'cause she never knew where to find him when she needed him."

"Yeah, well. He'll show up one of these days. I know he'll be glad to know everyone's all right."

He walked into the family room and sank onto the couch with Trisha on his knee. "So tell me what you've been up to, young lady," he said, knowing that if he could just concentrate on his daughter, he could lessen the pain around his heart.

Three days had gone by since Cameron had dropped Janine off at her house. Three days since she had heard from him. It seemed like three years.

She had grown accustomed to being with him day and night since his illness. She'd had a heck of a time trying to fall asleep last night. Why hadn't anyone told her that once she had gotten used to sleeping with someone else she would have difficulty sleeping alone?

There was so much she didn't know.

Now she industriously worked in her yard each morning before the temperature soared. She found it soothing to be a part of the earth, as though it connected her somehow with the world. She was having trouble trying to reestablish her old routine, the one she had had before Cameron had become such a major force in her life.

She had always managed to keep herself busy, so why did there seem to be so much extra time in her day now? She would be glad when school started again.

She paused, listening. Was that the phone? With the house shut up because of the air-conditioning, she didn't ordinarily hear the phone. She scrambled to her feet and dashed to the house. As she tore open the back screen door, then the wooden one, she heard the phone ring once again. She raced to grab it.

"Hello?..hello?"

There was nothing but a dial tone.

Nothing in this world was more frustrating than a ringing phone that stopped ringing just before a person answered it! She slammed down the phone.

Whoever it was would call back if it was important. It probably wasn't important. It was probably one of her friends calling about lunch, or possibly a movie, or maybe...

Who was she kidding? She wanted it to be Cameron. She didn't know where he was. He might have gone back to San Antonio. He might be at work. He might have gone back to Austin, or even Dallas, or Fort Worth, or Houston. He might be anywhere.

Or he might still be at the ranch, only a half hour's drive away.

The only way to find out was to call.

Did she have the courage? After all, they were friends, weren't they? So what was wrong with a friend calling another friend? Just because he was a male didn't make him off-limits. They were used to talking to each other every day. It had been three days.

She would consider calling him.

But first, she would finish her yard work. Then she would take a shower, get cleaned up a little, put on some makeup...

To make a phone call?

Okay, so maybe she was going a little overboard. She needed to lighten up a little, see the humor in the situation. There was no reason to see it as a major tragedy. Just because she wasn't going to marry him didn't mean they couldn't continue their relationship—their wonderfully intimate, excitingly erotic relationship.

Besides, he had never *asked* her to marry him, so it wasn't as though she had turned him down or anything. He certainly wasn't an unrequited lover.

Who was she kidding? Why should he ask when she had already made her feelings on the subject abundantly clear? Unless a person was really into feeling the pangs of rejection, he wouldn't see a need to pose the question, would he?

Well?

So maybe he was feeling a little rejected at the moment. Who could blame him? Maybe he would like to hear from her. Maybe she would invite him and Trisha to dinner, if he was still at the ranch. Why not?

By the time she reached this decision, she had finished the yard, taken her shower, put on a clean pair of shorts and matching top, arranged her hair and was finishing applying the last touches of makeup.

She smiled at her reflection. That was the most cheerful she had looked in three days.

She marched to the phone and dialed the ranch's number. It was answered on the third ring.

"Hello," she said in her most professional voice. "This is Janine Talbot, and I was wondering if you could tell me where I might find Cameron Callaway."

"Oh, hi, Ms. Talbot, this is Rosie. I don't know where he is at the moment, exactly. Everyone's been outside most of the morning trying to find Trisha. He came in for a little while, but he's gone out again."

"Trisha? Trying to find her? She's lost?"

"We're not sure. Either lost or hiding somewhere. It's anybody's guess. Cameron said they'd had words this morning, and she'd run out of the room crying. He said he decided to give them both some time before he went looking for her. When he did, he couldn't find her anywhere."

"You've looked through the house?"

"Oh, yes, ma'am. About six of us looked everywhere we could think a five-year-old might hide. At first, Cameron was angry, but now I think he's more scared than anything. If she left the surrounding ranch buildings, she'll be next to impossible to find."

"Oh, no! This is awful. Should I come out?"

"I'm sure Cameron would like to know you're concerned, but you do whatever you think is best."

"I'll be right here," she said. Within minutes, she was in the car and pulling out of her driveway.

At the Big House she hurried to the door and knocked. Cameron was the one who answered it. When he saw her, he grabbed her and held on as though afraid to let go.

"This is all my fault. I was in a bad mood and I took it out on her. I was so stupid. I wasn't thinking about how she would react and I just—"

"It's okay, love," she murmured, holding him tightly. "She's okay. I'm sure of it. She's a smart little girl. She wouldn't put herself in any danger."

"But we've looked everywhere around here. And we've called and called. Alejandro has been rounding up his men. They're going to start riding out, looking for her."

"Surely she wouldn't have left the immediate area."

He shook his head, still buried in her hair. "Who knows? My biggest fear is that somehow one of our family enemies has found her. Up until now we've only received property damage, nothing that threatened a person's life, but then I think about the wrecks. If they were intentional, then we have a deadly killer somewhere out there, waiting. What if they came to the ranch? What if they saw her? I've been going out of my mind thinking about all the possibilities."

They stood there in silence for the longest while. Janine knew he was drawing strength from her being there. Thank heaven she had decided to call him.

"Ah, you're here!" Letty said behind them. "Good thing. This man's about driven us all crazy for the past three days. I hope this means that whatever you two quarreled about has been made up, because I never want to be around him in this mood again!"

Janine took Cameron's hand and opened the door. "C'mon. We can talk later. Right now we're going to find a missing five-year-old."

In the end, it was Janine who found her—for the simple reason that she didn't go into the hunt with any preconceived notions. Everyone else knew that there were definite areas where Trisha was forbidden to go. They knew it; she knew it. And Trisha had never defied those orders before.

Somehow Janine knew that today was different. Something had happened between father and daughter that had caused a rift between them, something that had never happened before.

She also knew Trisha, after having spent the past several months in her company. She was a very self-possessed, strong-willed and, yes, stubborn young lady.

So Janine stood in the ranch yard and looked all around her, studying the scene. If she were a five-year-old in a tantrum, where would she be most likely to go? After standing there absorbing her surroundings for several minutes, she started toward the barn.

"She wouldn't be in the barn. She knows better," Cameron said, following her. "It's too dangerous. We keep the horses in there, plus a bunch of our equipment. There's hay and—" Janine wasn't stopping, so he added, "Besides, we looked in there.'

"Yes, but you really didn't expect to find her, did you?"

"Not really, no. Like I just said—"

"It's amazing how you can overlook something when you don't expect to see it there."

She paused just inside the large doorway, letting her eyes adjust to the dimness of the inside. She heard a sound to the left of the doorway and looked over. One of the barn cats wandered out to see if the stranger was there to feed her. Although skinny, the cat was obviously nursing.

Kittens. Uh-huh. And where would a cat hide her kittens?

She walked over to the storage area where the cat had come from and looked around. There were no hiding places for a litter of kittens. Then she saw the ladder going up into the loft above. She immediately crossed to it and started climbing.

"My God! She wouldn't have tried something like that! Why, she could break her neck!" Cameron exclaimed. But Janine ignored him. She was following her instincts. She couldn't explain to him what she was thinking and feeling. She just had to go with it.

As soon as she reached the top, she crawled onto the hay and looked around. The loft was enormous. They could be anywhere.

She didn't bother to call Trisha's name. If the girl was here she would have heard them calling earlier; she had refused to answer then, so she wouldn't answer now. Janine stood, dusting her hands and knees, and began to explore.

By the time she found the corner where the three tiny kittens were curled up asleep, Cameron had joined the hunt, working the opposite side of the loft.

"Over here, Cam," she said softly. He immediately turned and hurried to where she stood.

Trisha had fallen asleep not far from the kittens. Her face was smudged with dust and tears, her blouse torn, and her hair was filled with bits of hay. Still, she looked quite unharmed.

Cameron knelt beside her. "Trisha?" he said, touching her lightly on her cheek. She stirred sluggishly. Her eyes looked puffy from crying. When she finally opened them, they seemed almost too heavy to keep open and they fell back shut.

"Trisha, honey, what are you doing up here?"

The child shifted and stretched out her legs. She again opened her eyes, this time focusing on her father. "Daddy?"

"Yes, darling. I'm right here."

Janine could hear the huskiness in his voice and experienced a similar choking sensation.

"Daddy? Did you know we have kittens? I saw the mama cat and she ran up the ladder like a fireman and I followed her to see where she went. Then she feeded her babies and she let me watch and then...and then..." She shrugged. "I guess I fell asleep."

"I guess you did. Didn't you hear me calling you?"

She shook her head.

"Are you sure?"

She looked surprised that he asked. "Uh-huh." Obviously it had never occurred to her to lie about anything.

"Well, it's past lunchtime and you've had everybody worried out of their minds. I think we should go tell them you're okay, don't you?"

She nodded solemnly and came to her feet. Only when she turned to go to the ladder did she see Janine, who had retreated to the exit of the loft when Cameron first started speaking to his daughter.

"Missy Talbot! You came to see us. Daddy said you prob'ly wouldn't come but you did!" She staggered through the hay and hugged Janine.

"Yes. I was sorry you weren't at the house when I got here," she said, stroking the little girl's curls.

"Yeah," Trisha agreed.

Cameron joined them and one by one they climbed down the ladder, Cameron going first, followed by Trisha, so that he could make sure she didn't slip.

Janine stayed quiet as Cameron sent out word that Trisha had been found. Then he took his daughter into the house and upstairs to clean her up and, as he put it, to give her the talking to of her life for scaring them all to death.

Letty suggested she and Janine go ahead with lunch, since she had a hunch he would be a while.

While they ate, Letty asked questions about the twins and if she had had a chance to meet Katie and what she had thought about the visit. Janine realized later that she had been so caught up in answering all the questions that she didn't have an opportunity to get nervous about talking to Cameron.

When Cameron came down later he waved off the idea of food and just had some iced tea.

"I had to set some strict punishment for this one. I told her she couldn't come downstairs for the rest of the day. She was crushed. She's been wanting to see you," he said to Janine. "She also solemnly promised me that she will not go anywhere on the ranch that has been set off-limits again."

"And you believed her," Janine said with a grin.

He looked surprised. "Of course!"

Janine laughed. "Ah, the joys of parenthood. Hope springs eternal, and all that stuff."

"Do you think she lied?"

"Of course not. I think she is an inquisitive little

girl. She will remember for a while. Then, as she gets older, and more and more alluring things are just beyond the rules..."

"I guess you know kids pretty well," he said glumly.

"She should," Letty said, pushing back her chair. "She's looked after enough of 'em. Now, if you two will excuse me, I've had about as much excitement as my ole bones can handle for one day. I'm goin' upstairs to rest for a while. I'll see you two later." She paused and peered over her glasses. "You *are* staying for dinner now, aren't you, Ms. Talbot? I'm not sure I'll want to be around Cameron tonight if you don't."

Janine grinned. "Thank you, Letty. I'd like to stay."

"Then I'll come back down later," she said tartly. "Otherwise I might have had 'em send me something to eat in my room." She left without a backward glance.

Cameron looked at Janine and said, "Let's go into the other room. We need to talk."

He led the way into the study. When she walked through the doorway, he closed and locked the door. "So we won't be disturbed," he said, waving her to have a seat. The room was lined with bookshelves. There was a large desk and chair at one end of the room, a comfortable-looking sofa and a grouping of chairs at the other. She sank onto the sofa and looked at him.

He sat at the other end, facing her.

"I don't understand. I just don't."

She could see he was hurting. The pain had etched lines in his face that hadn't been there just a few days earlier. She owed him an explanation, no matter how painful it was for her to talk about.

"You are a natural at mothering, Janine. You understand children so well. It's an innate gift, an extra sense that seems to tune you into them. And yet you keep insisting you don't want to marry and have a family. Is it just me? I mean, are you looking for someone who could be a perfect parent so that—"

"No, it's not that at all, Cam." She moved closer so that she could touch him. "Please. It isn't you at all. It's me. Don't you see? I'm the one who's defective."

"Defective! What the hell are you talking about? There's not a damned thing wrong with you!"

She took his hand and held it up to her cheek, rubbing her head against his hand much like a cat wanting to be stroked.

When she began to talk, her words were choppy. "I've never talked about this. Not with anyone. I never intended to say anything. Not ever. But you deserve to know, Cam. I love you too much not to tell you."

"You love me?" His eyes suddenly seemed to fill with light.

"Oh, yes. How could you possibly doubt it?"

"Well, for a while I thought it was possible. But then...when you said...and I thought..." He shrugged helplessly.

"Make no mistake about it, Cameron Callaway. I love you absolutely."

"Then for God's sake marry me! Put me out of my misery!"

"Marrying me would only add to your misery. I love you too much to subject you to a future with me. Please try to understand."

He shook his head. "I'm trying, believe me. But you aren't making any sense."

"When I was sixteen, I was in an automobile accident with the boy I was dating at the time. It was a wonder we both weren't killed. The other driver was, and there was some doubt that I would recover."

"You! But you're in perfect health. You're—"

"Most of the injuries were internal. You may have thought I was overly modest when we've been together, but I'm still self-conscious about the scars on my abdomen."

"I've never noticed them."

She smiled. "Good."

"So you are saying that because of your scars you don't want to marry me? They don't matter. You should know me better than that."

"Cameron, my internal injuries were very extensive. I was hemorrhaging severely. The doctors on duty did whatever they could to save my life. If they had had more time perhaps they might have attempted to repair some of the damage. But they were more concerned with stopping the bleeding.''

''I had no idea you'd gone through so much. Thank God you managed to live through it.''

''Yes. I'm very thankful. But when they first told me what they had done, I wished at first that I *had* died.''

''Janine!''

''I know. That's very selfish of me, particularly when you lost your wife and I was so filled with self-pity that I could wish away my life.'' This was much, much harder to tell than she had imagined. She had hoped that he would have guessed, but he showed no sign of understanding. ''I can't have children, Cameron. That's what I've been trying to tell you. They had to remove everything. I was given no choice. It was done before I even regained consciousness. At the time they weren't sure that I would regain consciousness. It's a fact I've had to live with ever since.''

His face drained of all color. She knew what a shock her news must be to him. But now that she had finally told him, she felt better. She had finally, at long last, shared the knowledge with another person. Somehow in the sharing, she had halved her pain. Unfortunately she had given it to him, something she had hoped never to have to do.

''Oh, God, love. I had no idea. Not even when you spoke of the surgery. I don't know what awful secret I thought you were trying to share with me. I just didn't consider it was that.''

''I know.''

''You love children so much.''

''Yes. Yes, I do. That's why I decided to work with them. It's been a wonderful way to have children in my life.''

He pulled her into his arms and held her close.

She knew that now he had received the shock of her news, he would recover more quickly and get on with his life. She hoped they would continue to be friends and knew that one day he would meet someone who would make the perfect mother for the children he wanted to have.

At the moment, though, she couldn't face the thought of seeing him with another woman. Perhaps that would change in time. Perhaps her love for him could continue to grow enough to encompass even that possibility.

He pulled away and she saw the tears in his eyes. ''I was such a fool, carrying on about wanting a larger family. No wonder you— I'm sorry, love. So sorry.''

''Please don't be. How could you know? I just thought you needed to understand why I'll never marry anyone.''

He grew still and stared at her so intently that she began to feel uncomfortable. ''What did you just say?''

''That you needed to—''

"No. That last part."

"You mean that I'll never marry?"

"Yes. Would you kindly explain how your not being able to have children has anything at all to do with your getting married?"

Now she was having trouble understanding him. What sort of silly question was that?

"Well, really, Cam, I think the answer is obvious, don't you?"

"No. Suppose you explain it to me."

She shrugged, trying to hide her irritation. "Every man who marries expects to have a family—it goes without saying."

"Does it?"

"When Bobby found out what had happened to me, he was terribly sorry. He even blamed himself for the accident, which was silly. He probably saved my life. He explained that everything had changed for us after the accident. He was very uncomfortable. So was I. He didn't have to tell me how he felt. We had talked about getting married some day. We'd even picked out names for our children...."

Cameron muttered an unprintable word, which caused her to jump. "So on the basis of one person's reaction, you decided that absolutely no man would want to marry you if you couldn't have children."

She clasped her hands and looked down at them

in her lap. "My father left when my mother couldn't have more children."

"God help us," he muttered. She wasn't certain if he was praying or cursing.

"Janine, would you look at me? Please?"

She glanced up and was relieved to see that his face had color once again.

"I am sorrier than I can say that the men in your life felt the need to father children so strongly that they would base major decisions on such an issue. However, I do not happen to share that particular philosophy. Besides, I've already fathered a child, a beautiful little girl who gives me a great deal of pleasure—except when she falls asleep in a hayloft and scares the living daylights out of me." He shifted, his arm going around her while he tilted her face up to his.

"Now listen to me very, very carefully. I am only going to say this once, and then I never want to discuss the subject again. Do you hear me?"

She nodded. How could she not hear him? He was only a few inches away from her.

"I love you, Janine Talbot. You brought me back to life again. I had buried myself away from everything that was good and happy and funny and alive. Then one rainy morning you came marching into my life and gave me hell, turning my life upside down and sideways. It's never been the same since. And that's just fine with me."

He stroked a wisp of hair from her cheek. "Now

then. Words can't begin to describe the devastation I feel where you are concerned, to know that you have suffered so many years thinking that no one would want to marry you because of your situation. You are wrong, Janine Talbot. Very, very wrong.''

She heard the words all right, but their meaning was slow to sink in. When it did, Janine felt a flush envelop her and her heart started pounding in her chest.

''Not only do I love you to distraction,'' he went on, ''but I fully intend to marry you. I will not take no for an answer, do you hear me?

''Yes, it's a shock to discover that you aren't going to be able to have my children. I've spent months fantasizing about how to act if I *accidentally* got you pregnant. I guess I hoped that if you did get pregnant, I wouldn't have to figure out a subtle way to let you know how desperately I wanted to marry you.

''The fact is, I'm shy as hell when it comes to saying things like 'I love you' and 'I want to marry you.' '' He paused for a moment, then grinned. ''Actually, that didn't hurt at all. Maybe I'll get more comfortable with practice. The thing is, we are already a family, don't you know that? You, me and Trisha have become a family. You just must have missed it, or maybe it's because you didn't know what a real family was. Well, I'm telling you. You're already a part of one. You're a

Callaway in everything but the name, and I intend to fix that as soon as I can.''

He stroked her cheek with his thumb, wiping away the tears streaming from her eyes. ''Oh, baby, I wish I'd known. We could have saved ourselves so much grief if only you'd told me sooner.''

''But, Cam,'' she said, brokenly, ''you wanted more children.'' She gave a slight hiccup, then buried her head in his shoulder.

''There are so many children who need a home, honey. You know that. We can have as many children as we want. We can plan for them. We can adopt an infant, or an older child. There's so much we can do. There's so much love to share. Let's don't waste any of it, okay?''

When she didn't answer, he leaned back and looked at her face. ''Why are you still crying?''

''B-because I—I'm s-so-o-o-o haappy.''

''Good. Then I'll take that to mean yes, you'll marry me. Is that right?''

She nodded vigorously into his shoulder.

''Immediately?''

She pulled away. ''Immediately?'' she squeaked, wiping at her eyes.

''Well, yes. You see—'' he actually looked sheepish ''—I, uh, thought that, to convince Trisha she should move to San Antonio and live with me full-time, I could tell her you would be there, too. Remember I tried to get you to come last spring as a housekeeper-nanny, and you said no? So I have

hired a housekeeper—who will look after Trisha
when you have to be at school—so maybe you'll
come as my wife and Trisha's mother. Would you
consider that?''

"Oh Cam," she said in a wavering voice.

"Please don't start crying again, okay? Anyway,
since school starts in a couple of weeks, I thought
if we got married right away, that would give us
some time for a honeymoon. Not that I haven't
enjoyed our recent rehearsals or any—ouch—thing,
but, oh, Janine, honey, I love you so much.''

She no longer felt like waiting for him to kiss
her, so she kissed him. She put all the expertise she
had learned from him into it, taking her time and
making certain that he understood just how much
she *had* learned.

She also began to unsnap his shirt, running her
hands across his chest and down to his belt buckle.
She felt him suck in his breath, inadvertently leaving enough room for her fingers to slide beneath
the belt and touch him. "I'm ready whenever you
are, darlin'," he whispered, nipping her ear.
"You'll never have to doubt that.''

With a sudden sense of reckless freedom, Janine
reached down and unfastened her shorts. "Let the
honeymoon begin," she said with a chuckle.

"Yes, ma'am!"

* * * * *

If you've enjoyed meeting
Cole and Cameron, the first heroes
of Annette Broadrick's exciting
Callaway family series,
more good things are in store!

Look for Cody's and Tony's stories in

SONS OF TEXAS:
COWBOYS AND WEDDING BELLS,

available from our Reader Service.

And as a special treat,
we're giving you a sneak peek at
another highly requested story
by Annette Broadrick.

Mystery Lover

will be available this October
in the BY REQUEST collection
DESTINED FOR LOVE.

Now,
see what the mystery
is all about....

One

Jennifer Chisholm opened her eyes in surprise and glanced around her living room. She must have fallen asleep while watching television. She couldn't decide what it was that had awakened her. Sam, her fourteen-pound tiger-striped cat, had made himself comfortable by draping himself across her as she lay on the couch. One outstretched paw rested softly against her cheek, the rest of him covered her to her knees. No wonder she'd slept so comfortably. She'd been sleeping under a fur coat—a living fur coat.

What time was it?

The rhythmic ticking of her clock was the only other sound in the room. She glanced to where it hung over her rolltop desk in the corner. The hands faithfully pointed out to her that it was ten minutes past two o'clock in the morning.

"I'm sorry, Sunshine. I'm afraid I miscalculated this one."

That was what had awakened her. Chad was contacting her. Jennifer's eyes widened. Her surprise wasn't due to the fact that she was suddenly hearing something when there was no one there—she was used to that. What had caught her off guard was that she hadn't heard from Chad since she'd told him off several months ago. There was only one person who referred to her as Sunshine—one person who didn't have to communicate with her by phone or in person.

When she was a small child she had referred to him as her invisible friend. The adults around her had been amused and a little sorry for her. An only child was often a lonely one. No doubt making up an invisible friend made life a little easier to handle.

Jennifer had never been able to convince anyone that she wasn't making him up. In time, she had stopped trying.

"Chad! What's wrong?" Her voice sounded loud in the room, but she hardly noticed. She could feel his agitation and pain, something she'd never felt with him before. Something was wrong— drastically wrong.

She tried to sit up, but Sam's weight on her chest

seemed to hold her pressed against the sofa and cushions.

"Nothing that you can do anything about, I'm sorry to say. I just wanted you to know how very special you've been to me all these years."

Jennifer had never heard him pay her a compliment before. She had once told him that he only came into her life to bully and irritate her, and he'd never denied the accusation. Now he sounded so full of regret...as though he were telling her goodbye.

Once again she tried to sit up. Pushing against the sleeping cat, she said impatiently, "Would you get off me, darn it? You must weigh close to a ton!"

Jennifer felt a jolt as her remark reached Chad just before he said, *"I apologize for disturbing you at this hour. I should have realized...."* He seemed to fade away.

"Don't leave, Chad!" she said rapidly. "I was talking to Sam,"

"Huh?"

"My cat. Don't you remember? I've had him for several years."

"I had forgotten the name."

"Please tell me what's wrong. You seem different, somehow." She stood up, concentrating on the voice in her head.

"That's not important. I just wanted to let you

know, Sunshine, that I love you very much... I always have.''

Chad loved her? The irritating, teasing, invisible friend of her youth actually loved her? Jennifer couldn't believe what she was hearing.

"No, you're not dreaming."

That was a perfect example of why she found him so irritating. She found it most uncomfortable to have someone who could monitor—and offer unasked-for comments on—her thoughts. But Jennifer had to admit that the past few months had been very lonely without him.

He'd been such an integral part of her life for so long that she hadn't realized how much she would miss his presence. If she'd known, she would never have yelled at him, ordered him to get out of her life and to leave her alone.

He had done just that.

Now he was back and she knew something was seriously wrong.

"What is it?"

"I didn't mean to upset you. I just needed to—"

"I'm going to be much more than just upset if you don't tell me what's wrong."

"I walked into a trap, I'm afraid. Well laid, I might add. They knew me well enough to know my curiosity would keep me following them until they had me."

"Will you kindly tell me what you're talking about?"

"It's too late to get into it. It's never been important for you to know what I do for a living. It's not important now. I just wanted to tell you I love you and hope life showers you with the blessings you deserve."

"Chad, please tell me what's wrong." She waited for a moment but got no response. "Chad?" There was no answer.

Frustrated beyond belief, Jennifer sank down beside Sam once more and stared unseeingly at the television.

How could he do this to her: check in to say goodbye and then leave again?

If she could just once get her hands on him she'd—

But that was the trouble. She had never laid eyes on him.

Dropping her hand wearily on the back of the sofa, Jennifer tried to clear her mind. Chad had a way of getting her emotions stirred up. He was good at that. He always had been....

Jennifer couldn't remember exactly how old she was when Chad had first made his presence known, but she knew it was some time after the automobile accident that had changed her life. Her mother, upon being questioned, had said Jennifer was just past five years of age when the accident had occurred. Jennifer remembered very little about it and often wondered if what she knew was what she had remembered or what others had told her later.

After several days in the hospital following the accident, her father had died, leaving her mother to find a way to support herself and Jennifer.

No one was to blame for the fact that Jennifer had trouble making friends. She was shy and often stood on the sidelines and waited for someone to include her in their games.

As she grew older, and her mother allowed her to go home alone after school, she returned to an empty apartment where she waited for her mother to get off work.

Jennifer had grown increasingly despondent in the months following the accident. Until Chad spoke to her one day.

Jennifer had stood looking out the window of their Oceanside, California apartment, yearning for the days when her mother had been home and would take her to the beach. Jennifer loved to play on the beach and to watch the waves as they came rolling in to touch the shoreline.

Now her mother had so little time for her. Jennifer had no one anymore.

"You have me, Sunshine."

Jennifer glanced around the room. There was no one there. She glanced at the television but it wasn't on.

"Who said that?" she finally asked softly.

"I did."

"Who are you?"

There was a brief pause before she heard, *"Chad."*

Jennifer started walking through the apartment, looking behind the doors, vaguely aware that although she was hearing someone, the messages seemed to come from inside her head.

"They are," he confirmed. *"I'm sending you thought messages."*

"Do I know you?" she finally asked, puzzled.

"It's enough that I know you, Sunshine. I just wanted you to know that I'm here. You don't have to feel lonely."

"Are you real?"

"Real enough."

"I mean, you aren't my guardian angel, are you?"

She could feel his amusement. *"Something like that, maybe. But I'm very much a human being."*

"How old are you?"

"Oh, I'm very old. Almost ancient."

Jennifer didn't doubt that at all. How many people could talk to you in your head? She'd never known of anyone who did that before.

She asked her mother about Chad when she got home. Unfortunately her mother had too much on her mind to really tune in to Jennifer's questions and absently replied that she supposed everyone had a guardian angel, and she was pleased to know that Jennifer's angel went by the name of Chad.

Of course her schoolmates made fun of her.

Jennifer discovered that she didn't care. They were probably so busy they didn't even hear their angels talking to them.

She could always hear Chad.

But by the time Jennifer reached her teenage years, she discovered that Chad was far from being an angel.

"Why are you mooning over that picture of a movie star?" he asked one day.

Jennifer glanced around, embarrassed to be caught gazing with longing at her idol's photograph. Then she realized she hadn't been caught. It was Chad.

"I'm not mooning."

"Of course you are. Why do you think someone like him would never notice you? You have a very nice figure."

"I'm skinny."

"No, you're not. And stop worrying about the size of your breasts. They're just fine."

"Chad!"

"Did I say something wrong?"

"I just wish I could see you as clearly as you seem to see me."

"You probably could, if you concentrated. All it takes is practice."

She had taken him at his word. Jennifer never managed to pick up anything to do with his appearance, but she had learned to contact him whenever she wished, which proved to be a little unsettling for him on one occasion.

"Chad! Mother said I can't go with Sue and Janey to the show tonight. You know that isn't fair. What can I tell her to convince her I won't get into any trouble if she'd just let me go?"

She waited for a few moments, but didn't get an answer.

"Chad?"

"Not now, Jennifer. I'm busy."

He'd never been too busy for her before. They'd been conversing for years now. He'd helped her with her homework, explained algebra to her so that she finally understood it. Why, Chad had always been there for her.

"Busy? Doing what?"

What she received then was something akin to a groan. *"Thanks a lot, Sunshine. You just blew that one for me!"*

"What did I do?"

"My dear, sweet, innocent child. There are times when my mind is on other things and I don't need the distraction."

"Are you with a girl?" she asked suspiciously.

"I was. I'm afraid my lack of concentration at a crucial moment offended her."

"Oh, Chad. I'm sorry."

"Believe me. No sorrier than I am."

She didn't know what to say. Jennifer had forgotten why she had flounced into her room. The idea that Chad had a life totally unrelated to hers had never occurred to her before. She had always taken him so much for granted.

Several days passed before she attempted to contact him again.

"Chad?"

"*Yes?*"

"Are you busy?"

"*What's up, Sunshine?*"

"Oh, nothing much. I was just wondering about something...."

"*Uh-oh. Now you're curious. I was afraid of that.*"

"Would it be possible for us to meet sometime?"

"*Possible, but not practical.*"

"Why not?"

"*Because I don't live in Oceanside.*"

"Oh!" She had never given his residence any thought either. "Where do you live?"

"*Why do you ask?*"

"Because I'd like to get to know you better."

"*What do you want to know?*" Before she could say anything she felt his laughter. "*Whoa, whoa. Wait a minute. Some of those questions are indecent. And no. I don't look anything like your favorite television hero.*"

"How old are you?"

"*Much too old for a little girl like you.*"

"Are you married?"

"No."

"Do you intend to get married?"

"Maybe."

"When?"

"Maybe I'm waiting for you to grow up."

"What good will that do, if I don't know who you are?"

"Ah, but I know who you are and that's what counts."

"You mean you've actually seen me?"

"Of course."

"When?"

"Whenever I come to Oceanside."

"Where are you now?"

There was a hesitation. *"I travel around considerably. Part of my job."*

"What's your job?"

"If I thought you needed to know, Sunshine, I'd tell you."

"You can be so irritating. Did you know that?"

"Now that you mention it, you aren't the first person who's pointed out that trait to me. Perhaps I should work on it."

"Perhaps, nothing." Jennifer was walking home from school and realized that more than one person passing her had given her a strange look. She supposed she did look a little peculiar, walking down the street arguing with someone who obviously wasn't there. "Are you serious about waiting for me to grow up?"

There was a long pause and she thought he wasn't going to answer her. *"No, I'm not serious, Sunshine. I guess I was trying to be irritating, as usual. My life-style isn't conducive to a marriage arrangement, I'm afraid."*

"Oh." Jennifer could feel the depression settling through her.

"But I'll always be here for you, no matter what. Don't forget that."

"How will I ever explain you to my husband?" she said, attempting to convey a lightness she didn't feel.

"You won't have to. I would never intrude when you didn't need me. Once you're married, things will be different."

"I don't want to lose you, Chad."

Jennifer could still hear herself repeating those words. Even when she'd gotten so angry at him, she hadn't really meant for him to take her so literally and to drop out of her life.

Chad was special. They had a very special relationship.

Now he was in some sort of trouble. If only she could figure out something she could do to help him. She'd do anything.

"Anything?"

"Chad! You're still there! Yes. Tell me what to do."

"I've been thinking...."

"Yes?"

"You are my only contact with the world right now. My abductors figured all the angles but that one."

"Your abductors! You mean you've been kidnapped?"

"More or less. They aren't holding me for ransom, though. They just don't intend for me to show up again."

"Could I call the police or something?"

"I'm working on that. Why don't you get some sleep while I think through my plan a little more thoroughly. Let me know when you wake up. Surely there's some way we can utilize our special communication."

She laughed. "I'd love to. You've done so much for me. Now it's my turn."

"We aren't playing games here, Sunshine. These people mean business. I really walked into a hornet's nest with this one. Now, go get some sleep."

Jennifer checked the door to be sure the chain was on and the lock secure, turned off the television and snapped off the lights. He was right. She would have to get some rest. If Chad felt he could wait until morning, then she'd try to get a few more hours of sleep.

She had a hard time quieting down her mind once she crawled into bed with Sam curled up behind her drawn-up knees. After all these years, she now had the chance to meet Chad in person.

Two

By nine o'clock the next morning Jennifer was driving her five-year-old Toyota toward Las Vegas.

For the past five years Jennifer had been living and working in the Los Angeles area. She was pleased with her job, her apartment and her lifestyle. To be more precise she was content to stay in the shallow of her life, never tempted to seek out the depths and excitement that others seemed to crave. Chad had a lot to do with her way of thinking. He had spent many hours talking to her about some of the trouble young women could get into if they weren't careful, especially if they were trying to prove something, to either themselves or other people.

Jennifer realized she didn't have such a need. She was content to be who she was and live her own rather unexciting life.

Therefore, this would be her first visit to Las Vegas.

Jennifer wasn't particularly looking forward to arriving there. Her attitude could be traced back to the fact that Chad had been less than forthcoming about what he wanted her to do.

Following his instructions, she had immediately hopped into the shower as soon as she awakened, quickly donned her clothes, then contacted him.

He immediately responded.

"How are you?" she asked, more out of concern than politeness.

"I feel a little groggy, but that's to be expected," was the reply.

"Have you been drinking?" she asked, surprised.

"No. But I got a fairly hard clout to my head last night."

"Oh."

"They've made it clear that I have offended their sensibilities by being so nosy. They have a very physical way of showing their displeasure."

"Who are 'they'?"

"I can't give you a positive ID at the moment, Sunshine. Are you still willing to help me?"

"Oh, of course. What do you want me to do?"

"Go to Las Vegas."

"Las Vegas? What are you doing there?"

"I'm not in Las Vegas. I want you to contact a man there for me. You'll have to see him in person and he's tough to reach. I would say almost impossible, as a matter of fact. But you've got to try. He's the only one who might have an idea how to find me."

"Who is he?"

"His name is Tony Carillo. He owns the Lucky Lady Casino."

Jennifer could feel her heart leap in her chest. "You want me to go find a gambler?"

"I'm not concerned with his personal habits at the moment, Sunshine. He's the one who can help me."

"What do you want me to tell him?"

"Wait until you get to Vegas and I'll tell you."

"Chad! Must you be so mysterious?"

"At this point, yes. You don't have to do this if you don't want to."

"I didn't say that. Of course I'll go."

Jennifer found a small bag and gathered a few of her clothes and cosmetics. No doubt she'd be gone the entire weekend.

The day was going to be another hot one, Jennifer decided soon after she left the apartment. But then, what could you expect in August? If she'd ever thought about going to Las Vegas, which she hadn't, she was sure she would have picked a cooler time of the year.

Jennifer could not get rid of the right knot of excitement that seemed to have formed in her chest. At long last she was going to find out more about Chad.

He had reluctantly told her that Tony was an old friend of his and if anyone could get him out of his present precarious situation, Tony could.

What Jennifer also realized was that Tony could tell her a great deal about Chad that she had always wanted to know.

Jennifer faced the fact that rushing to Las Vegas to help Chad was the most exciting thing that had ever happened to her—which certainly seemed to make a statement about her life.

Actually having Chad in her life was the only exciting thing that had ever happened to her. After a very careful poll among her classmates while she was growing up, Jennifer had discovered that she seemed to be the only person blessed with an invisible friend.

She had quickly learned not to discuss him with anyone, and what else, after all, did she have to talk about? Jennifer hadn't been interested in dating because she never knew what to say. She didn't care anything about cars and that was what most of the boys talked about.

So she had spent many hours talking to Chad about things she was interested in, things she could read about in books, or magazines. She had known he was much older than she was and had a great deal more experience with life. Yet he had always been very patient with her, willing to discuss any subject she brought up.

Jennifer smiled to herself, remembering how he had dealt with her questions about sex. Now that she thought about it, those questions should have been asked of her mother, but whenever she broached the subject, her mother had seemed embarrassed and Jennifer had allowed her curiosity about the subject to drop.

Chad had been much more matter-of-fact. She had been lying there in bed one night, thinking about some of the stories she was hearing at school, when Chad had spoken up.

"Don't believe everything you hear, Sunshine. It could get you into trouble."

"If you think that I would do something like that—" she started to say indignantly, when he interrupted.

"Of course you will...at the right time and with the right person. But sex isn't something to be experimented with, like a toy. The act of love is all tied up with our emotions. When it's used only as a tool to convince people around us that we're adults, we can get hurt and hurt many others as well."

They had talked long into the night, and by the time Jennifer fell asleep she felt as though she had graduated from childhood.

His lessons had stuck with her through the years.

Although she had dated once she moved to Los Angeles and began working, she had never been tempted to prove anything with anyone. Nor had she met anyone with whom she wished to share such intimacy.

Perhaps she wasn't the type to marry. She certainly didn't draw second looks in a crowd. Jennifer had always been disgusted that she'd stopped growing when she was only a couple of inches over five feet. Although she had often been told that her eyes were her most striking feature, whenever she looked into the mirror all she could see were wide blue eyes staring back. Even her hair wasn't a real color. She wasn't quite a blonde, nor was her hair dark enough to be considered brown. Jennifer thought of herself as an almost person. Almost average height, but not quite, almost a blonde, but not quite, almost attractive…but not quite.

Not that it mattered to her, she reminded herself firmly. She was content with her life. And now, she was doing something for Chad that would help to repay all the wonderful things he had done for her through the years. She smiled at the thought.

Eventually she thought about her job, and for the first time, she felt a little uneasy. Jennifer hadn't given a thought to whether she would be back home in time to go to work on Monday. If not, she wondered what she would do.

Jennifer had taken a secretarial course as soon as she completed high school. It had been important to her that she be independent as soon as possible. Her mother's health had never been good and Jennifer wanted to relieve her of the burden.

She could have stayed in Oceanside but preferred to get away, to make new friends, to experience new things. Her new life would have been very lonely if she hadn't had Chad.

Surprisingly enough, Jennifer made many friends at the school, and when one of them mentioned that the Cameron Investigation Service was looking for stenographers, she and two of the other graduates had applied.

Jennifer had been surprised at the size of the place. She wasn't sure what she had expected, but certainly nothing on the scale that met her eyes. The receptionist sent her to the personnel director, who tested her and had her fill out the necessary applications. The director explained that Mr. Cameron managed to keep several stenographers busy transcribing the reports he dictated.

C. W. Cameron had built quite a reputation, so Jennifer was told, as an insurance investigator. Although he was out in the field quite often, he kept in touch with the office and oftentimes called in and dictated on the machines that were set up to take telephone transcriptions.

Jennifer had been working there for almost five years and she thoroughly enjoyed her job. She had been Mr. Cameron's administrative assistant for several years now, handling as much as possible for him when he was out of the office, doing the preliminary investigations of cases—the tedious, time-consuming research that went with the sort of investigation—then turning them over to him to follow up the leads she uncovered.

They worked well together and he paid her quite well. Jennifer felt it was unfortunate that Mr. Cameron was such a cold, unfeeling individual. Perhaps it came with the job, or something.

After all the years she had worked for him, he still insisted on calling her Ms. Chisholm. In this day and age of immediate first names and instant friendships, C. W. Cameron was a throwback to another era.

He wasn't all that old, either. Jennifer had gotten a glimpse of his insurance file once, which stated his age at thirty-seven. He didn't look that old, until you gazed into his eyes. His eyes seemed to have too much knowledge about people and their behavior.

Some of the women in the office teased her about working for him, since he was single and more than a little handsome, with his tawny-colored hair and sherry-colored eyes. Jennifer shivered a little. He might be attractive, but he was too cold a person to ever attract her.

Jerry was more her type. She had been dating him occasionally for almost a year now. She really enjoyed Jerry. He was relaxed, easygoing, fun-loving, and did not pressure her to deepen their relationship. Too bad she couldn't combine the personality of the one man with the brilliant and incisive intellect of the other one. What a combination that would be.

Jennifer suddenly remembered that she had a date that night with Jerry, and she had totally forgotten about it. He would be over to pick her up and she wouldn't be there. How could she have been so absentminded? When Chad had contacted her, everything else had flown out the window.

She would have to call him and explain as soon as she got to Vegas. Explain what? Jennifer had never been able to find the words to tell Jerry about Chad. At first, it hadn't been important. They had been casual friends, neighbors until Jerry had moved to be closer to his new job. Occasionally he would have her over to eat popcorn and watch television. Once in a while she would prepare a meal for them and they'd go see a movie. After he moved, they spent less time together, but still called to see how she was doing and to talk about his job.

Jennifer had never stood him up before. Surely he would understand that something unexpected had come up that changed her plans.

By the time she reached the outskirts of Las Vegas, Jennifer was tired and hungry. She hadn't wanted to stop and eat, which was a good thing. Crossing the desert hadn't given her much opportunity.

First things first. She would find a restaurant, eat and call Jerry.

He answered on the fourth ring.

"Am I interrupting anything?" she asked.

"Oh, hi, Jennie. I must have fallen asleep. Couldn't figure out what was happening at first."

"Things must be tough on the job these days, huh?"

He laughed. "No. Just resting up for our big date tonight."

"That's why I called, Jerry. I'm afraid I'm going to have to cancel."

"Is there something wrong?" She heard the concern in his voice.

"Not really. A friend needed some help this weekend and I volunteered."

"Where are you? I keep getting all kinds of background noises."

"I'm in a restaurant."

"Oh. Well I'm sorry I won't see you tonight. I've been saving all kinds of things to tell you."

"Look, why don't I call you next week? We can check our schedules and pick another time, okay?"

"Sure. No problem. Well, you take care. I'll talk to you later."

Jennifer hung up and walked out to her car. The desert heat caused her to wish she'd worn something besides her jeans and shirt. One of her halter tops and a pair of shorts would have been more appropriate.

"Not in a casino, Sunshine."

"Oh! There you are. You pop up at the most unexpected times."

"I told you I'd contact you once you got to Vegas, didn't I?"

She shrugged and realized that that wasn't much of an answer. "Okay. I'm here now. What next?"

"I want you to go into the Lucky Lady Casino, go all the way to the back. You'll see a sign that says Manager's Office. Whoever is there, tell them that you need to see Tony Carillo. That you have a message from Tiger and that you have to see him personally to deliver it."

"Tiger?"

"That's right."

"And he'll know what I mean?"

"Sunshine, this isn't going to work if you're going to question and analyze everything I tell you to do. Are you with me or not?"

"Of course I'm with you. I wouldn't be here if I wasn't."

"No need to get testy. All right. The Lucky Lady is on the Strip. You shouldn't have any trouble finding it."

She didn't.

Now that the time had come for her to do something, Jennifer felt her heart begin to race in her chest. She had never before realized what a coward she was. There seemed to be no adventure in her soul. No doubt there were many people who would enjoy the mystery and intrigue of what she was now doing. But not her.

"You can back out anytime."

"Oh, shut up," she muttered. A couple coming out of the casino glared at her as they passed. "I'm sorry, I wasn't talking to you," she tried to explain. They pointedly looked around the area. No one else was around. Jennifer knew her smile was a little weak as she shrugged and hurried on in.

"I thought I taught you better manners, Sunshine."

She kept her head down and tried not to move her lips. "This is not the time to go into my behavior, Chad. I'm doing the best I can at the moment. I'm just not used to this sort of thing."

"That's what I've been trying to tell you. You've limited yourself too much all these years. You need to reach out and stretch your potential to its maximum."

"Right now all I want to do is find Tony Carillo."

"May I help you?" The beautiful young woman sitting at the desk in the manager's office asked Jennifer a few moments later.

"Yes, I'd like to see Mr. Carillo."

"Do you have any appointment, Ms.—"

"Chisholm. Jennifer Chisholm. Uh, no. I'm afraid not. Would you tell him that I have a message for him from—uh, er—Tiger?"

"Tiger?"

Jennifer could feel the heat in her cheeks as she determinedly kept her gaze on the woman in front of her. "That's correct. I'm supposed to deliver it in person."

The woman picked up the phone on the desk and dialed. Then she spoke quietly into the receiver. She waited, obviously listening to something, then responded and hung up the phone.

Her gaze was filled with speculation when she glanced back at Jennifer. "There's an elevator across the lobby. Push the top button. Someone will meet you to show you to his office."

"Good work, Sunshine. You passed the first hurdle."

"What do I do next?"

"Wait until you meet Tony, then I'll tell you."

"What's the matter, don't you trust me?"

"Yes, I just want to make sure they aren't giving you the runaround."

Jennifer stepped off the elevator onto plush carpeting. A young man about her age stood there waiting. He grinned. "You're here to see Tony, right?"

She nodded her head.

"This way."

She followed the man down the hallway and into a well-decorated office. A secretarial desk was on one side, and what looked like a wood processing unit was carefully covered. There was nobody in the office.

The young man tapped on another door, then opened it. Motioning for her to enter first, he waited until she passed him, then quietly closed the door behind her. She was now alone with the man Chad called Tony Carillo.

His office appeared to be the size of Jennifer's entire apartment. She looked at the ornate wall hangings and furnishings with awe before her eyes turned to the man who had gotten up from behind a massive desk and started toward her.

He looked to be in his mid-thirties, and was of medium height, with dark hair and eyes. He held out his hand to her as she approached.

"I'm afraid I wasn't told your name, young lady," he said with the hint of a smile. "The only information I got was that you have a message from Tiger."

"Jennifer. Jennifer Chisholm. I was told to—"

"Ahh. So you are Chad's Jennifer." He took her hand and held it between both of his. "Yes. He has chosen well."

"Chosen?"

"What I mean to say was that I've heard many things about you and am delighted to meet you at last."

"You know Chad well?"

He laughed. "Extremely well. We grew up together in California."

"Oh."

"So what can I do for you? You said you had a message from him."

"From Tiger."

"Right."

"You mean Chad and Tiger are the same person?"

"Yeah. It was a joke because we always hung around together. You know...Tony—the Tiger." His smile widened. "That was probably before your time."

"He's in trouble."

Tony's smile disappeared. He led her to a sofa and they sat down. "What sort of trouble?" he asked with a frown.

"I'm not sure. He said he walked into a trap."

Tony gazed out the window and she could tell that he was thinking. Finally, he turned back to her. "Where is he?"

"He didn't say."

"When was the last time you talked with him?"

"Well, you see—"

"Tell him late last night."

"Late last night," she managed to parrot.

"Uh-oh. Then something must have turned sour at the last minute. He thought he had them for sure."

"You talked to him recently?"

"Yes. He's working on something for me."

Jennifer gave a quick sigh of relief. "Oh, good. Then you can help him."

"Not if I don't know where he is. I know who he was dealing with, though. Max can play rough."

Jennifer wished she knew what more to say. Never had she felt more helpless.

"Tell him that I'm somewhere in southern Utah, in the mountains. I'm in some sort of shack. I haven't seen anyone since they dumped me here last night. I have a hunch no one is going to bother to see if I'm eating. There's nothing here."

Jennifer repeated Chad's words. When she finished, Tony started at her in confusion. "I thought you just said you didn't know where he was."

"Well, I didn't. I still don't. That isn't enough information to find him, is it?"

"It's a hell of a start, let me tell you. Max, the man I've been hoping to get enough evidence on to take to court, owns property in southern Utah. Before we had this falling out, he took me up there hunting a couple of times. I think I know exactly where that shack is."

"That's a relief, Sunshine. Looks like you've managed to get me some help."

"May I go with you to find him?" she asked.

"No!" Chad replied quickly.

"I can't see any reason why not. I'm sure you're anxious about him."

If he only knew. After all this time she was finally going to meet Chad face-to-face.

MEN at WORK

All work and no play? Not these men!

July 1998

MACKENZIE'S LADY by Dallas Schulze

Undercover agent Mackenzie Donahue's lazy smile and deep blue eyes were his best weapons. But after rescuing—and kissing!—damsel in distress Holly Reynolds, how could he betray her by spying on her brother?

August 1998

MISS LIZ'S PASSION by Sherryl Woods

Todd Lewis could put up a building with ease, but quailed at the sight of a classroom! Still, Liz Gentry, his son's teacher, was no battle-ax, and soon Todd started planning some extracurricular activities of his own....

September 1998

A CLASSIC ENCOUNTER by Emilie Richards

Doctor Chris Matthews was intelligent, sexy and *very* good with his hands—which made him all the more dangerous to single mom Lizette St. Hilaire. So how long could she resist Chris's special brand of TLC?

Available at your favorite retail outlet!

MEN AT WORK™

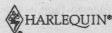 HARLEQUIN®   Silhouette®

Look us up on-line at: http://www.romance.net   PMAW2

Take 2 bestselling love stories FREE

Plus get a FREE surprise gift!

Special Limited-Time Offer

Mail to Harlequin Reader Service®

3010 Walden Avenue
P.O. Box 1867
Buffalo, N.Y. 14240-1867

YES! Please send me 2 free Harlequin Superromance® novels and my free surprise gift. Then send me 4 brand-new novels every month, which I will receive before they appear in bookstores. Bill me at the low price of $3.57 each plus 25¢ delivery and applicable sales tax, if any.* That's the complete price, and a saving of over 10% off the cover prices—quite a bargain! I understand that accepting the books and gift places me under no obligation ever to buy any books. I can always return a shipment and cancel at any time. Even if I never buy another book from Harlequin, the 2 free books and the surprise gift are mine to keep forever.

134 HEN CH7C

Name	(PLEASE PRINT)	
Address	Apt. No.	
City	State	Zip

This offer is limited to one order per household and not valid to present Harlequin Superromance® subscribers. *Terms and prices are subject to change without notice. Sales tax applicable in N.Y.

USUP-98   ©1990 Harlequin Enterprises Limited

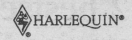 HARLEQUIN®

Not The Same Old Story!

 HARLEQUIN PRESENTS®

Exciting, glamorous romance stories that take readers around the world.

 Harlequin Romance®

Sparkling, fresh and tender love stories that bring you pure romance.

 HARLEQUIN® Temptation

Bold and adventurous— Temptation is strong women, bad boys, great sex!

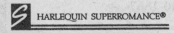 HARLEQUIN SUPERROMANCE®

Provocative and realistic stories that celebrate life and love.

 HARLEQUIN® AMERICAN ROMANCE®

Contemporary fairy tales—where anything is possible and where dreams come true.

HARLEQUIN® INTRIGUE®

Heart-stopping, suspenseful adventures that combine the best of romance and mystery.

 Love & Laughter™

Humorous and romantic stories that capture the lighter side of love.

Look us up on-line at: http://www.romance.net   HGENERIC

International bestselling author

JOAN JOHNSTON

continues her wildly popular Hawk's Way
miniseries with an all-new, longer-length novel

THE SUBSTITUTE GROOM

HAWK'S WAY

August 1998

Jennifer Wright's hopes and dreams had rested on her summer wedding—until a single moment changed everything. Including the *groom*. Suddenly Jennifer agreed to marry her fiancé's best friend, a darkly handsome Texan she needed—and desperately wanted—almost against her will. But U.S. Air Force Major Colt Whitelaw had sacrificed too much to settle for a marriage of convenience, and that made hiding her passion all the more difficult. And hiding her biggest secret downright impossible...

"Joan Johnston does contemporary Westerns to perfection." —*Publishers Weekly*

Available in August 1998
wherever Silhouette books are sold.

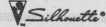

Look us up on-line at: http://www.romance.net   PSHWKWAY

MATERNITY LEAVE

Coming September 1998

Three delightful stories about the blessings
and surprises of "Labor" Day.

TABLOID BABY by Candace Camp

She was whisked to the hospital in the nick of time....

THE NINE-MONTH KNIGHT
by Cait London

A down-on-her-luck secretary is experiencing
odd little midnight cravings....

THE PATERNITY TEST by Sherryl Woods

The stick turned blue before her
biological clock struck twelve....

*These three special women are very pregnant...and very
single, although they won't be either for too much longer,
because baby—and Daddy—are on their way!*

Available at your favorite retail outlet.

Look us up on-line at: http://www.romance.net   PSMATLEV

**Available September 1998
from Silhouette Books...**

World's Most
Eligible Bachelors

THE CATCH
OF CONARD COUNTY
by Rachel Lee

Rancher Jeff Cumberland: long, lean, sexy as sin. He's eluded every marriage-minded female in the county. Until a mysterious woman breezes into town and brings her fierce passion to his bed. Will this steamy Conard County courtship take September's hottest bachelor off of the singles market?

**Each month, Silhouette Books brings you
an irresistible bachelor in these all-new,
original stories. Find out how the sexiest,
most sought-after men are finally caught...**

Available at your favorite retail outlet.

Silhouette®

Look us up on-line at: http://www.romance.net   PSWMEB1

Glamorous, hot, seductive...

THE AUSTRALIANS

Stories of romance Australian-style guaranteed to
fulfill that sense of adventure!

September 1998, look for
Playboy Lover
by Lindsay Armstrong

When Rory and Dominique met at a party the attraction was
magnetic, but all Dominique's instincts told her to resist him.
Not easy as they'd be working together in the steamy tropics
of Australia's Gold Coast. When they were thrown together in
a wild and reckless experience, obsessive passion flared—but
had she found her Mr. Right, or had she fallen for yet another
playboy?

*The Wonder from Down Under: where spirited women win
the hearts of Australia's most independent men!*

Available September 1998 at your favorite retail outlet.

HARLEQUIN®
Makes any time special ™

Look us up on-line at: http://www.romance.net   PHAUS3